LOVE IS
A
DURABLE FIRE

LOVE IS
A
DURABLE FIRE

Brian Burland

W · W · NORTON & COMPANY · NEW YORK · LONDON

Published simultaneously in Canada by Penguin Books Canada Ltd,
   2801 John Street, Markham, Ontario L3R 1B4
Printed in the United States of America.

First American Edition, 1986

Library of Congress Cataloging in Publication Data
Burland, Brian.
   Love is a durable fire.
   1. World War, 1939–1945—Fiction.   I. Title.
PR9680.B43B865   1985   823'.914   85–4855

ISBN 0-393-02218-8

W. W. Norton & Company, Inc., 500 Fifth Avenue, New York, N.Y. 10110
W. W. Norton & Company Ltd., 37 Great Russell Street, London WC1B 3NU

1 2 3 4 5 6 7 8 9 0

'... love is a durable fire
In the mind ever burning;
Never sick, never old, never dead,
From itself never turning.'

Walter Raleigh, 1552 – 1618

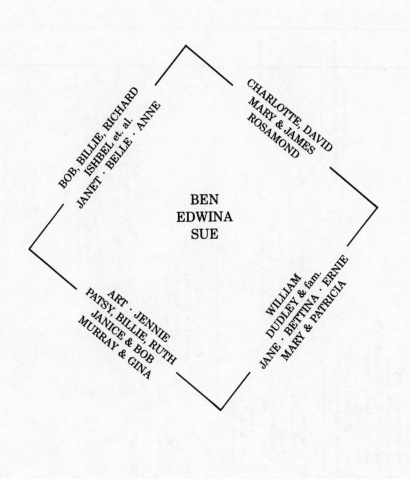

BEN
EDWINA
SUE

CHARLOTTE, DAVID
MARY & JAMES
ROSAMOND

BOB, BILLIE, RICHARD
ISHBEL et. al.
JANET · BELLE · ANNE

WILLIAM
DUDLEY & fam.
JANE · BETTINA · ERNIE
MARY & PATRICIA

ART · JENNIE
PATSY, BILLIE, RUTH
JANICE & BOB
MURRAY & GINA

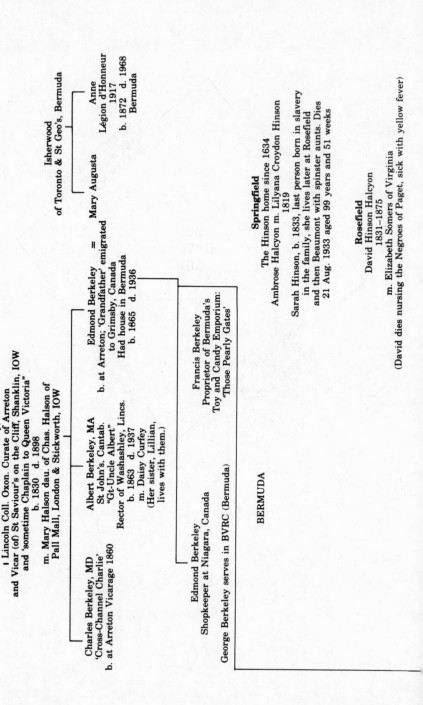

ENGLAND

Edmond Portman Berkeley, MA
Lincoln Coll. Oxon. Curate of Arreton
and Vicar (of) St Saviour's on the Cliff, Shanklin, IOW
and 'sometime Chaplain to Queen Victoria"
b. 1830 d. 1898
m. Mary Halson dau. of Chas. Halson of
Pall Mall, London & Stickworth, IOW

Charles Berkeley, MD
'Cross-Channel Charlie'
b. at Arreton Vicarage 1860

Albert Berkeley, MA
St John's, Cantab.
"Gt-Uncle Albert"
Rector of Washashley, Lincs.
b. 1863 d. 1937
m. Daisy Curfey
(Her sister, Lillian,
lives with them.)

Edmond Berkeley, 'Grandfather' emigrated
b. at Arreton   to Grimsby, Canada
                       Had house in Bermuda
                       b. 1865 d. 1936

Isherwood
of Toronto & St Geo's, Bermuda

Mary Augusta =

Anne
Légion d'Honneur
1917
b. 1872 d. 1968
Bermuda

Francis Berkeley
Proprietor of Bermuda's
Toy and Candy Emporium:
'Those Pearly Gates'

Edmond Berkeley
Shopkeeper at Niagara, Canada

George Berkeley serves in BVRC (Bermuda)

BERMUDA

Springfield
The Hinson home since 1634
Ambrose Halcyon m. Lilyana Croydon Hinson
1819
Sarah Hinson, b. 1833, last person born in slavery
in the family, she lives later at Rosefield
and then Beaumont with spinster aunts. Dies
21 Aug. 1933 aged 99 years and 51 weeks

Rosefield
David Hinson Halcyon
1831–1875
m. Elizabeth Somers of Virginia
(David dies nursing the Negroes of Paget, sick with yellow fever)

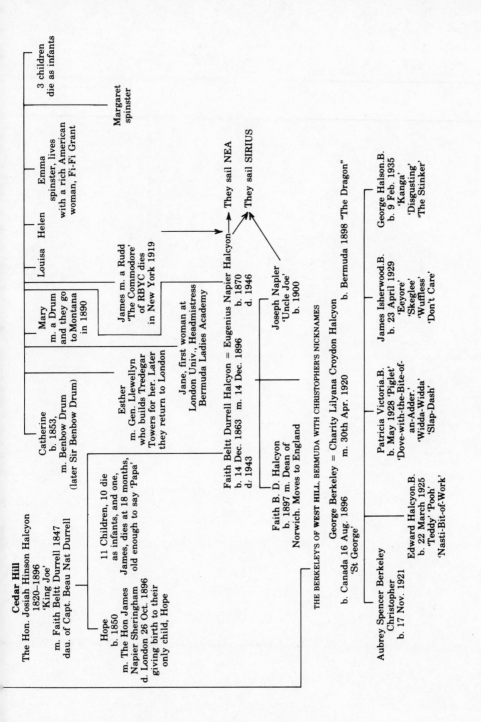

Cedar Hill

The Hon. Josiah Hinson Halcyon
1820–1896
'King Joe'
m. Faith Beltt Durrell 1847
dau. of Capt. Beau Nat Durrell

3 children die as infants

Margaret
spinster

Emma
spinster, lives
with a rich American
woman, Fi-Fi Grant

Helen

Louisa

Mary
m. a Drum
and they go
to Montana
in 1890

Catherine
b. 1853,
m. Benbow Drum
(later Sir Benbow Drum)

James m. a Rudd
'The Commodore'
of RBYC dies
in New York 1919

Esther
m. Gen. Llewellyn
who builds Tredegar
Towers for her. Later
they return to London

Hope
b. 1850
m. The Hon James
Napier Sheringham
d. London 26 Oct. 1896
giving birth to their
only child, Hope

11 Children, 10 die
as infants, and one,
James, dies at 18 months,
old enough to say 'Papa'

Jane, first woman at
London Univ., Headmistress
Bermuda Ladies Academy

Faith Beltt Durrell Halcyon = Eugenius Napier Halcyon ⟶ They sail NEA
b. 14 Dec. 1863 m. 14 Dec. 1896   b. 1870   They sail SIRIUS
d: 1943   d: 1946

Joseph Napier
'Uncle Joe'
b. 1900

Faith B. D. Halcyon
b. 1897 m. Dean of
Norwich. Moves to England

THE BERKELEY'S OF **WEST HILL**, BERMUDA WITH CHRISTOPHER'S NICKNAMES

George Berkeley = Charity Lilyana Croydon Halcyon
b. Canada 16 Aug. 1896   m. 30th Apr. 1920
'St George'   b. Bermuda 1898 "The Dragon"

Aubrey Spencer Berkeley
Christopher
b. 17 Nov. 1921

Edward Halcyon.B.
b. 22 March 1925
'Teddy', 'Pooh'
'Nasti-Bit-of-Work'

Patricia Victoria.B.
b. May 1928 'Piglet'
'Dove-with-the-Bite-of-
an-Adder',
'Widda-Widda'
'Slap-Dash'

James Isherwood.B.
b. 23 April 1929
'Eeyore'
'Skeglee'
'Wuffles'
'Don't Care'

George Halson.B.
b. 9 Feb. 1935
'Kanga'
'Disgusting'
'The Stinker'

A Fall from Aloft ends with:

Words Left Over After Writing About War

The year before my voice
broke
our convoy left Halifax
with over forty ships
and reached Greenock with
nineteen.
No heroics
just grey
white-flecked
ocean
and sky
and sometimes the spray was frozen when it
hit the deck.
There were bumps in the night
and I seemed to live in the latrines
and once, on a bright day,
I leaned over the rail
and watched our ship
plough through
and down
the bobbing heads
of the seamen
torpedoed on station in front of us.

One head, in memory,
seems to rise higher
than the others:
it has bruised and blackened
eyes
and shouts in anger, fury,
beating the waves
like a turtle,
"Save ME!"

The voice is still my own.

LOVE IS
A
DURABLE FIRE

Book One

I

England, James decided, was the dirtiest fucking place on earth – but he knew he'd have to cut out the Merchant Navy language or he'd get into trouble where he was going.

He was really going, he knew, to three places and the prospect of all three frightened him. First he was going to London to his father's agent – that was why he was on this filthy, blacked-out train – and then he was going to Lincoln to his great-aunts' and then he was going to school – to boarding school. First a prep school – which was bad enough because, as his elder brothers had told him, colonials were treated like dirt and you could get a beating at the drop of a lousy Latin verb – and then to public school, Fotheringham, where the first thing the big boys did to new boys was stand them up on the dining table and tell them to sing and every time you paused, even for breath, they threw bread soaked in tea at you. The way his brothers had told it, a British public school was worse than Alcatraz – and he had no reason to doubt their word.

Life was tough, he decided, there was no doubt about that. You were scared three or ten ways all the time and you had to keep up a good front however you felt inside. Keep smiling but be ready to put your dukes up.

Thirteen was a stink of an age to be – and he wouldn't really be thirteen until April, two months away – especially when he'd just crossed the Atlantic 'by himself' and the year was 1942.

1

'By himself' was his mother's phrase and he didn't think he'd ever find a truer one if he lived to be seventeen or even twenty-one, like Teddy and Chris, his brothers, and he was sure he'd never live to be that old anyway.

Of course, he hadn't come by himself, he'd come in a bloody great stinking Ersatz Yankee-built liberty ship in a small convoy from Bermuda and a gynormous one from Halifax and when they got to Halifax all the other ships from Bermuda were sunk (except the escort vessel, HMS *Charybdis*, which had simply disappeared) and when they left Halifax there were over forty ships and when they got inside the bar of the Clyde, in Scotland, they were alone again and for all he knew all the others had been torpedoed. But he knew that was an exaggeration: you couldn't tell because the whole convoy had been scattered by a North Atlantic storm – clappers of hell.

It had been stinking tough, too, serving as a 'peggy' on the ship – because a 'peggy' was a galley slave and pot scourer (and a slinger of life jackets into lifeboats during alarms). That's what he'd been, the lowest of the whole crew.

And it didn't help much to know then or now that he'd served as a peggy because he had to: travel was illegal for civilians and he had to serve as something because he had to get to England because, as his father and mother were always saying, no one was anyone unless they were a public school man first. (That was The Great Unwritten Law of the British Empire, you had to be a public school man – and, in his family, no one had missed out on this except his father . . .) And most of the men hadn't liked him because he was 'a bleeding snot' and they nicknamed him 'Lord Fauntleroy' and they called him that when they didn't call him a 'Lord's bastard' and the other peggies loathed his guts, but the peggy who loathed him the most was named McIntyre and he'd died of an appendicitis just before they made port. Which was sad but, as his friend Harry, an AB had said, at least they hadn't buried him in the sea which was 'a 'orrible way to go, mate – 'orrible'.

He dearly wished he had Harry with him now because Harry had sort of taken care of him. But Harry was back on the *Empire United* and had probably forgotten him already – entirely.

The train's wheels kept on going clickety-click, clickety-clock, clickety-cluk and it sounded to him like 'lost-at-sea, lost-at-sea . . . no more of him, no more of him, no more . . .' And the train seemed to roll like a ship and the water still seemed to pour over everything and he felt sick and tired and he was glad to be on land at last but he still felt scared, as if he was still at sea surrounded by waves, white caps hiding conning towers, torpedoes, mines . . . the ocean, the great oh-shun, the sea, the pitiless sea . . .

It was all a 'far cry', as Grandfather would say, from the sunshine and coral sails of their life in Bermuda.

Silence save for wind and the cries of long-tails and kingfishers: silence save for the bubbling little laughing from the *Sirius*'s bow when, with his hooded weather-eye, Grandfather looked (with humour, as well, at it all: what could be so silly as sailing boats in or out of races – what could be so comical as Man when he thought himself something more . . . what was it, more than a joke?) and touched the curved cedar tiller with his magic helmsman's hand . . .

The eyes looking for rippled water: and the whisper: 'Lord, give me a breeze – ah, that's it.'

Grandfather's gift: the Bermudian helmsman's – there was none better than him (though Uncle Josiah,

3

his son, as gifted in light air only . . .) in all Bermuda:
not even a Durrell cousin, but, perhaps, the
Sheringhams (two brothers) were his equal . . .

His gift of handling a boat as if it was – a woman,
perhaps . . .

And Grandfather's humour did not leave out
children the way most grown-ups did.

'Get aboard, dear boy,' Eugenius Halcyon had said,
his white flannel trousers bridging the six-metre and
the RBYC steps, when he, James, was about nine, 'if
you don't get aboard get a plank.'

Now, in England, he had even these memories
almost in ashes.

He'd seen ships torpedoed at sea; some that just lay
there and sank in the ooze like dead hippos and some
that broke in half like toys and some that blew up and
belched black smoke. He'd seen men scampering
about the decks of stricken ships like frenzied ants;
he'd seen men in the water, black faced, grey life-
preservers bobbing, yelling for help. He'd heard their
cries, 'Help . . . Save . . . Save me . . .' and he'd seen
their ship, their ship, plough through them, plough
them down and the appalling knowledge came to him
that those who ran the War – the vague all-powerful
inaccessible people – didn't give a damn for the sailors
in the sea, didn't hear their cries – he himself could
easily be one of them and no one would care – and
then he'd been glad that they didn't stop – because
that way you were a sitting-duck target, even a lousy
imitation peggy like him knew that – and then it
seemed that the only thing that really reached him
was that he didn't want himself ever to be in their
place. 'Not me, not me, anybody but me,' (which
proved he was a physical coward) and he knew that
was a really stinking way to feel because some of the
seamen really did feel sorry for the men in the water

4

and had tried to cut a life-raft free for them . . .

He had wanted to prove that he was brave, that he could take it. He had wanted to be a war-hero like his father in the First War and his brother in this one and he had found out that he was an absolute, abject, stinking coward – a physical coward which was, he knew, the worst thing you could be.

The trip was supposed to take about twelve days but they had been chased everywhere by wolf-packs of U-boats and then blown every which way by a fucking great North Atlantic storm and it took nineteen – or was it twenty-nine?

And he had run like a rabbit to the Captain, deserted his post, and if only he'd stuck it out one more day it would have been all right – because then they were 'home' as the men said.

'We'll be in Euston in a bit,' a soldier said. 'Close the window,' said his mate, 'you're getting soot all over us.'

He smiled at them but they didn't look at him and he felt certain that England would never be his home. His home was Bermuda where the sun was bright and the water still, and greeny-blue, and you could see the white coral bottom clear through twenty or thirty feet and there were angelfish every colour of bright, and tiny seahorses (his favourite creatures) . . . And the houses were pink and blue and green and clean and the people were clean – even most of the coloured people – and all the lavatories were clean not vile, stinking, putrid like the head on the ship – 'shit-'ouse' they called it – and the men's room of the pub in Glasgow where Harry took him and the gentlemen's room on this train where he'd just been where there was no water in the tap, no soap, no towels, no toilet paper, pee on the floor and excreta on the black seatback . . . Rule Britannia . . . and all he'd managed

5

was a leak holding his nose against the smell . . . Rule
Britannia . . .

And they'd soon be in London as the soldier said
and he would have to get his trunk from the goods
wagon at the back of the train. Would they want more
money? He'd already paid in Glasgow but someone
might demand more. Perhaps the trunk wouldn't be
there? Stolen already, quite likely.

And then he'd have to get a taxi – how much would
it cost? He felt under his coat and found the outline of
the chamois leather pouch under his shirt. Thank God
it was still there. He'd had ten pounds in it when he
left Bermuda – strange Bank of England notes and
his parents had tied the pouch with tapes around his
skin – and there were five left and he had one pound
in his wallet. He patted his hip-pocket – yes, it was
still there and his suitcase was up on the rack, yes,
and the stupid embarrassing bunch of green bananas
that he'd lugged all the way from Bermuda, a present
from his father to Mr Somers, the agent . . .

Ta-tum, homesickness again. It came and went in
spasms – mostly came, he thought. It was a funny
feeling, like falling in a dream but the trouble was, in
life, you never woke up and you never hit the
bottom – ta-tum.

But he should count his blessings, he really should.
He was on dry land and he wasn't dead and
everything was scary as hell but there was, now, a
chance that he would see Christopher soon.

Christopher might get a leave from the RAF
soon – even if it was just for a weekend. The thought
of Christopher's face, the crazy family blobberly nose
and the crazy yellow hair hanging over one side of his
forehead all the time, made his stupid eyes water
again so he blew his nose loudly as if he was dying of
tuberculosis or double-pneumonia.

6

Christopher's hair flopped on his forehead like Hitler's – only Hitler had ugly black hair and was a beast and Christopher's hair was sort of like the gold curtains in Granny's drawing-room, only paler, and Christopher was probably the best guy on earth . . .

Christopher had Grandfather's gift of steering a sailing boat – he hadn't had his gift develop as much yet, but he had applied it to flying.

He looked like a comic-book hero really – or rather he would do so if he didn't have that embarrassing, positively excruciating habit of calling you 'my dear' all the time, sounding like some spinster aunt at a tea party on the vicarage lawn.

He didn't mind being called 'my dear' when no one was around but Chris did it anywhere. Well, that was three years ago and maybe the RAF had knocked that shit out of him, as Harry would say – 'and Nipper, you've got to cut out that fucking bad language. . .' and he almost laughed and then he remembered, again, that he was a coward. He had quit, given in, and what was he going to tell Christopher?

Lie, that's all. You couldn't tell Christopher you were scared witless, shitless, as the men said, and no that was not literally true: you, James Berkeley were scared of going to the bathroom, scared of being seen. But no decent person could have stood that place – six toilet bowls in a row and no partitions even (never mind doors) and STINK.

War might be heroes and dogfights and the Battle of Britain and the wild blue yonder to some people but all he'd known of it was being seasick, homesick and scared sick and if that was war it was a dirty gyp and to hell with it, they could 'shove it up their pipe. . .'

But he was a coward, no doubt about that, and he had quit, deserted his post and people got shot for that in war and he supposed it was right. 'You oughta be

7

shot, my dear – sorry but you oughta be shot.' So he'd have to lie, that was all.

He was always lying, it was the worst part of his lousy character – but he couldn't seem to stop. Trouble with lying was that it got so complicated. There was the lie and then the cover-lie and then the cover-cover-lie. Then too there were so many people he lied to and you had to keep all the stories straight in your mind. It was an exhausting mess of entanglements: it was like living in a different story-book for every friend, relative and acquaintance you had. Scary too because one lived in peril, mortal peril, every minute, of being found out . . .

Fortunately, he'd left a lot of the mess behind in Bermuda (God almighty, such crazy things as the US Marine sergeant he met in Hamilton most Saturday afternoons – they went to the band concerts in the park together – and the sergeant believed he was an orphan who lived with his great-uncle who was a hunchback . . . Oh, God) and a lot behind on the *Empire United* and that was one good thing.

Then he was aware that the train was coming to a halt like a great iron-footed dragon and that all around them were strange echoing sounds – whistles, giant hissing machinery and shouts.

They were in the great cathedral of Euston and an incredible female voice was saying over the loud speakers, 'The tray-een in number ee-leff-ffen plataform is for – Sen-all-buns, Loot-un, Bad-Ford and gl-gla-glugh . . .'

His watch said eight o'clock and it was a grey and gloomy day and he knew he must move but he didn't want to move because even this packed compartment of the train had become, somehow, home. It was a sensation with which he'd become, recently, very familiar.

8

Then he found himself out on the platform with his cap and overcoat on and the suitcase and bananas in his hands. He thought he would wait until most of the bigger people had hurried away but suddenly he was confronted by a square-built porter in black.

'Wha-da-ya want, mate?'

'A taxi please.' He realized, with a shock, that the porter was a woman and tried to protest as she grabbed up his things but she was obviously having no truck from him. 'But I've a trunk at the back.'

'All roight, duckie, follow me,' she said and James knew instinctively – he thought – that she was kind – which was one advantage of having been in the Merchant Navy: working-class English people weren't all that strange and he could, he hoped, now tell a regular person from a sod.

She got the trunk (handling it as light and easy as if it were empty) and found him a taxi and then he didn't want to leave her either, she was home too but suddenly she was gone, or he was, he didn't really understand which and then he realized it was both. He had gone and she had gone.

He had given the address to the taxi-driver and the man hadn't spoken or turned, only nodded, and now they were moving.

He felt appallingly bereft. Nothing seemed to last in the world any more. It reminded him of that place in the Bible that he had heard in Sunday School: 'the dove found no resting place for its foot.'

When he had heard it in the cedar-beamed and whitewashed church, with the bright sun shining outside and the birds singing with colonial freedom, only the sound had appealed to him; now, surrounded by the cold, the grey-dark bustling, the seemingly felonious gloom of the enormity that was London, the words made him feel sick in the pit of his heart.

9

Had the driver heard the address right, 12 Bishopsgate? If the driver were to know about the money in the chamois pouch he would probably knock him over the head with a black-jack (no, black-jack was American, a billie then) and rob him. Because this driver might be that kind of a sod of a whore's pelt . . .

The lower classes, his mother said, were like Negroes and not to be trusted. At other times she said they were like children – so lovable.

Well, he found out that it was more complicated than that – maybe he was wrong but some of the seamen who he'd thought at first were so lovable turned out to be breams and some of the ones he'd thought were not to be trusted had turned out to be brave men and very kind to him when the chips were down – when the alarm bell had gone, which was bleeding often enough.

Perhaps, he thought, they were all OK – at any rate better than you ever imagined – when you just treated them like humans. He'd treated them like humans all right – he'd done it in the hope that they'd treat him as one, and as one of them.

And they almost had but not quite. He'd tried. He even tried talking like them, imitating them . . .

Poop! Poop! went the taxi-driver squeezing the black-bulb of the horn and the taxi weaved in and out of impossibly narrow places as if it was a wind-up toy – Poop! Poop!

. . . and sometimes they laughed at what he said but even if they hadn't really accepted him, he'd often felt as if he was a merchant seaman.

They stopped at a red light and alongside them was a big, handsome carthorse. A Clydesdale he would guess and there were other horses and carts around but different from Bermuda ones and masses of

10

bicycles – funny things with low handlebars so that the riders' bottoms stuck up in the air.

He realized, vaguely, that he could remember those bicycles and bottoms from his last trip to England when he was very little (four or five, wasn't it?) and he and his sister had gone to that awful boarding school in Bognor because his mother had to go to a nursing home ... It was just a boarding school for little kids, a nursery school really, and not a real boarding school like the one he was bound for now; it had been bad enough – but at least he and his sister had each other and now he didn't even have her...

Ta-tum. Homesickness again. Mummy, oh God, Mummy... he blew his nose.

He felt seasick, he thought, and then realized it was hunger because he could feel his stomach rumbling and then he realized that he hadn't eaten since Harry gave him the chips and pop in Glasgow and that was about three the afternoon before.

The taxi seemed to roll like the ship and it was funny the way the water still seemed to be everywhere and he felt as if he could still hear the humming of the ship's engines, generators and vents ...

It was strange that there were so many gaps in the buildings. Then he realized it was bombs, the Blitz, and he wondered how they could get everything so neat and tidy-looking so soon.

He pulled the label out of his pocket. 'Deliver to: John Somers Esq, Somers and Company, 12 Bishopsgate, London.' His father had said he was to pin it on the lapel of his overcoat after the ship docked so that he didn't get lost. Well, he just couldn't do it – he'd look like a baby, a sissy and be damned if he was going to look like a poofter, as Harry would say.

The taxi stopped at a vacant lot and the driver got

out and walked to the kerb. Maybe it was a trick? His father had said that taxi-drivers drove strangers around in circles just to put more money on the meter and his mother said, 'Yes, I always rap on the window with my umbrella and then they think you know London like a native.'

The driver stood on the kerb looking about, pushing his cap up at the back and scratching his head.

'Come on out 'ere and 'ave a look, sir,' the man called.

James hesitated then heard his own voice pipe, 'I'm not getting out until you take me where I have to go.'

'All right, mate,' the driver said peering in the window. 'But are you sure it's number twelve you want?'

James pulled out the label. 'Number twelve, yes. Somers and Company.'

'Twelve Bishopsgate. Well, it ain't 'ere. It's scapaed.'

' _ '

' 'Ave you ever seen it – before loik?'

A trick, perhaps, best not to answer.

'Musta been bombed. Look, there's nointeen over there and ten over 'ere but twelve – well, 'itler's done-it-in, chum.'

James felt as if he was going to throw up. If Mr Somers had been bombed where could he go? To Christopher? But where was Christopher? To his aunts in Lincoln – Washashley Hall – but how do you get there? What train? How much would it cost?

The driver climbed back in the driver's seat and then, turning, opened the sliding window. James looked down at the neat coconut mat on the floor, surrounded by a shining brass edge. 'Please take me to the police.'

'Aw right, little guv-ner. Tell you what. We'll 'ave a decko up the street and if it ain't there we'll go to the coppers.'

Could he trust the man? He sounded right – open and friendly. But he seemed a little too friendly.

It began to rain. The thought of sunny Bermuda . . . ta-tum – now he had one of those stupid stinking lumps in his throat.

Pull yourself together.

He asked himself, as he had so many times since he began this nightmare trip, why, how had he allowed himself to be forced into going? But they hadn't forced him, not Mummy and Dad, that was ridiculous. He had to do his duty, that was all, and his duty was to become a public school man.

It seemed as if his whole being was crying out, Mother! Mother! But it was not her, the woman, only, that he felt bereft of. It was his younger brother and sister, his father, the dogs, the house, the garden – all that was familiar, home . . .

Pull yourself together.

There were good things. Right now there were good things. Funny the way there were good things even in the midst of nightmares. He liked the taxi, the look of it and the feel of it manoeuvring in and out. He even liked the feel of the soft leather of the hard seat. He liked the smell of it too and the coconut mat and everything so neat and clean and the handle for you to hold on to.

Now the taxi was creeping up Bishopsgate, the driver peering from left to right searching the brass nameplates.

Again he felt hunger but not rumbling this time, rather it felt as if his stomach was filled with heavy chilled air.

He couldn't eat one of the bananas, not after protecting them all the way from Bermuda. You couldn't eat someone else's present – they were pretty green and hard anyway. He looked at the suitcase. Perhaps, when the driver wasn't looking, he could chew on that – after all, leather was made from animals and animals were food. There must, he thought, be some nutrition left in it. Then he shuddered, remembering Harry's remark about the lifeboat. 'And my mate, old 'Oley Wells turns around and 'ere's this stoker chewing on the bosun's arm – and 'im only dead a coupla *minutes.*'

His hands on his knees were grey with dirt and they looked so cold and dead that he began to think they were not part of him at all. The grey flannel trousers, his first pair of longs – he could vaguely remember being very proud of them when he left Bermuda – were dirty and streaked with oil stains from the ship. His eyes were smarting – from the soot of the train, he told himself – and he was afraid it might look as if he'd been crying when he hadn't . . .

But the awful truth was, he knew, that recently he'd sort of lost control. He was a physical coward. One minute he was OK and the next he was crying – not making a noise, just water pouring down his face and he had no control over it. It was horrible. It had started on the ship – when was it? Just before he went to the captain? No. It was when the tanker blew up and he was loading blankets, as usual, into the lifeboat – his No. 3 boat on the port side – and the awful void below and below that the ocean . . .

And then the storm came and he could hide the weeping then because everybody and everything was wet all the time and no one noticed. But afterwards he couldn't hide it . . .

Then he saw the sign, a bright polished brass one curved round the entrance of the building, BERMUDA AGENTS. Before the spasm of joy at the

14

sight of the word 'Bermuda' had registered in his mind he'd called to the driver.

'You're proper sharp-eyed, you are,' he said laughing but James had to be sure.

He jumped out and went up to the door. It was locked but written on the glass were the gold-lettered words, 'John Somers and Co'.

He ran back to the cab. 'It's locked.'

'But it's the place, ain't it? Roight. Cheer up then, mate. They've moved, that's all. 'appens all the time. Goering shuffles us around like a deck of cards. Cheer up. It's only eight-thirty and none of these posh blokes work afore noin.' He gave James a wink.

James remembered that his mother said that winking was vulgar. For an instant he had an insight that he was not going to agree with his mother for ever. He ought to agree with her, he *had* to agree with her. But sometimes she said such crazy, insane things. No, no, don't think that – that's evil, anti-God.

The driver climbed down. 'I'd wait 'ere with you, mate. But I got a regular at Liverpool Street in five minutes.' He started hauling James's trunk off the luggage rack. 'You can sit on this 'ere as pretty as you please and in 'alf an 'our your party will be 'ere.'

He carried the trunk up and placed it inside the vestibule. 'Not Wanted on Voyage' the labels said.

'You an American?'

'No,' James said.

'Funny. You look like an American.'

'I hate Americans.'

'Come-off-it, chum. They can't 'elp it. After all, they're just people.'

The meter said four-and-six. James wondered how much he should tip him – it would be awful to give too little and have the man be angry with him, think him a dumb kid or something. He gave the driver the

15

pound note. The driver gave him his change.

Blushing James extended a half-crown.

The driver smiled. 'You don't 'ave to do that, sir. A bob's enough. I already took out for the trunk, it's extra, see. Tell you what, give us a banana. I got grandchildren at 'ome never seen a banana.'

'I can't. You see, they aren't mine.'

'Skip it, then,' the driver said and, leaving James with the two-and-six still in his hand, jumped in his cab and drove off.

'Thank you,' James called, but the taxi had gone leaving only a little trail of smoke from its purring and popping exhaust.

He sat down on the trunk wishing he'd given the man all the damned bananas – then he realized that it was Saturday and that Mr Somers probably didn't work on Saturdays.

He bit his lip.

A woman went by with a bucket and a mop. She looked at his face and then looked down. James realized that he was holding himself as a child does when it wants to go to the bathroom. He blushed again. The woman made a clucking sound in her throat, opened the door with a key and closed it after her.

He'd just have to wait, that was all.

II

'When John Somers walks in the Bank of England,' his father had said to his cronies at the yacht club bar, while James listened sitting quietly in the corner as he was told – each son got taken to the RBYC for lunch, as a special treat, just before sailing, but Chris and Teddy were older and he was only just going-on thirteen and so he shouldn't really have been there – 'everybody bows and scrapes. Somers took me in there once. You can't just walk in the Bank of England like any other bank, you know – you can't even open an account without fantastic references *and* five thousand pounds. But Somers, who's so mean he has his penny stamps perforated with his initials so that his staff won't steal 'em, Somers raps on the gate with his umbrella – brass gates all polished and as tall as a house – and all hell breaks loose. Well, to look at him you'd think he was Scrooge's clerk but I bet he could write his cheque for a million pounds and they wouldn't bat an eye.

'But he's as honest and as loyal as the day is long. No sense of humour at all – I bet you, Spark Plug,' his father had turned to him. 'Spark Plug, I bet you the first thing John Somers will say to you is, "Did you pay the taxi?"'

Sitting on his trunk, James looked at his watch. 8:40. Then he saw a tall man in a black coat and a black homburg strutting diagonally across the street.

He stood up. The man walked right up to him and gestured towards him with his umbrella so that the handle almost, but not quite, touched his shoulder.

'I say, what have we here?

James smiled up at the stooped head with its long nose and brown eyes (behind pince-nez glasses – not like Dad's but with gold rims and a crazy chain) and nervously watched for the first gesture towards a handshake which was, he thought, a long time coming.

'Well now,' the glove came off. 'How very *nice* to see you, my boy. I hope you had a safe trip?'

'Yes, sir. Thank you, sir. I'm James, sir. My father told me to come straight to you.'

'You didn't have to tell me – you're the image of

your father. Well, we're very glad to see you – and how is your father?'

'He's very well thank you, sir. He sent you these bananas – but I'm afraid they're not very good . . .'

'How simply marvellous. Haven't seen a banana for years. My wife will be pleased.'

But a look of dismay, bewilderment, perhaps irritation crossed the man's face.

'The crew of the ship kept trying to steal the bananas – I had to keep fighting them off.' Would he swallow that? Never can tell with these old guys. Be careful – what do these Englishmen like? Deference certainly. Treat him like Grampy – or better, like a vicar. Hell, a bishop . . .

'How brave of you. I'm very glad you were so successful. I dare say you've had a tough time of it and you've obviously stood up to it like a man. Well, come along in now. I've a nice gas fire and we'll soon have you warm and get a cup of tea.'

'I was up all night, sir, on the train – in the corridor, standing up, no seats,' lied James, feeling himself being shepherded towards the door.

'How frightful – I must say you do look a bit . . . well, tired.'

'My trunk, sir?'

'Don't worry about it. We'll send someone out.'

Mr Somers's office was a mass of mahogany panelling, very grand, but the ceilings were so high it felt something like a church.

'I'm afraid we're rather cramped here,' Somers said, leading the way around a counter and through a highly polished gate. 'We were bombed out of Number Twelve you know, last year.'

'How awful, sir.' You're bloody right and don't I know – me getting delivered to a hole in the ground.

'Fortunately it was at night so no one was here but

18

we lost a great deal, of course – but so have a lot of other people.'

He led the way up a long thin corridor which smelled heavily of wax. 'Hardest thing was getting adjusted – you can't teach an old dog new tricks, you know, and we'd been there since 1812.'

'Yes, I know sir.' And then you must be – well, one hundred and thirty plus, say, twenty, equals one hundred and fifty . . . 'Course he knew Mr Somers meant the Bermuda Agents but what would he do if he said, 'It's OK by me, mate, you're the Wizard of Oz and one hundred and fifty years old'?

The inner office was enormous. It had a fireplace; raised-panel mahogany walls – even more elaborate than the others – with paintings of Bermudian sailing ships, complete with picture lights; two large walnut desks at opposing ends with carved high-backed chairs that looked like thrones, and, in the middle of the room, on a Turkish carpet, was an enormous fat-legged table piled with Bermuda newspapers – thousands of them.

The cleaning woman was just finishing up.

'I wonder, Mrs Barnes, if you would be so kind as to get this lad a cup of tea? I wouldn't ask except that he's come a long way – all the way from Bermuda in fact.'

'Oh, no sir,' she said. 'It's not my job to get tea. I've quite enough of that at 'ome. You 'ave to ask Mr H'Ashton for tea, sir.'

The narky bitch.

'Very well,' Somers said, looking over his glasses. 'And now if you'll be so kind as to leave us . . .'

James took another look at his father's agent. That down-turned, slightly opened mouth and the narrowed eyes from which, at that moment, an invisible ray seemed to be turned upon Mrs Barnes –

19

he was not a bloke to be mucked about with, as Harry would say.

'So tiresome,' Mr Somers said when she'd closed the door. 'The war has made most people more agreeable – but we're all tired –'

Silence.

'How old *are* you, my boy?'

'I'll be thirteen on the 23rd of April, sir.' He was surprised to see the man write the date down.

'Yes. Yes. Well, I'm rather tired myself. Fire-watching, you know.'

'Fire-watching, sir?'

'Yes. I've the rather dubious honour of being the head of the ARP for our parish – at home in Middlesex.'

Middlesex must be halfway between sex and no-sex – or halfway between man and woman – a poofter. Funny, funny – but he felt his eyes watering again and was relieved to see that Mr Somers had turned away.

The old man crossed the room and, bending stiffly in his dark-blue pinstriped suit, lit the gas fire. James saw the warm yellow glow reflected for a moment on the glossy surface of his winged stiff collar.

'We don't often light a fire, you know. Gas is very short.'

There was a discreet knock on the door which opened immediately revealing a small stooped man in a black coat and striped trousers.

'Oh, there you are, Ashton.' Somers took out his pocket watch.

'Yes, sir. Good morning, sir,' the man bowed, once, twice, holding his hands clasped in front of his chest. His collar was exactly like Mr Somers's, the tie tied in the same little knot.

'This is young Mr Berkeley from Bermuda.' Somers turned to James. 'This is Ashton. Ashton has been with us for twenty-seven years.'

James stood up feeling awkward. 'How do you do, Mr Ashton.'

'I'm very well, sir. Thank you, sir. I well remember your father, sir. And your uncle and both your grandfathers.'

'Yes. Yes. Well, Ashton, will you get Mr Berkeley a cup of tea?'

'Yes sir, right away, sir.'

'And bring me the Berkeley file.'

Ashton went out silently. Somers turned to James with a pained expression.

'Goodness sake don't call Ashton mister, my boy. It'll confuse him, you know. He's a good man, Ashton, but he's easily confused.'

James looked at Mr Somers's severe, austere and very British expression. He was not, he thought, a sympathetic person – which was a shame because James felt dearly in need of some sympathy. Most Limeys weren't sympathetic – at least, not the ones that counted, the gentlemen. It was very confusing.

'Ashton's a strange chap. Let me explain.' Somers took off his glasses and rubbed his nose with a finger and thumb, wrinkling his forehead and letting out a sigh. 'He was here for years. Always on time, hardworking and completely honest. Then, suddenly, just before the war, he went to pieces. Quite barmy. One day he just didn't show up. Vanished. It turned out that he'd left his wife and run off to the South of France with some – well – woman. Imagine, he was forty-five and he acted like that. 'Course he was back in three months. All his savings gone.' Somers methodically packed a curved pipe.

James noticed a small, oak-framed sepia photograph behind his head. It showed a woman in a high lace collar sitting very erect in an ornate wooden chair. His mother, obviously – a cold-looking old biddy too.

'We took him back which was, perhaps, more than he deserved. But, there you are – just call him Ashton.' A small smile played across Mr Somers' eyes.

James smiled back but inwardly shuddered at the thought of Ashton being caught in the South of France now. The Germans, with their boots and swastikas, would catch him and torture him. Probably pull his toenails out. Cut his balls off . . .

Ashton came in with the tea. James made the mistake of asking for sugar.

Somers laughed. ' 'Fraid it's rationed, my boy. We never have it at the office.'

Ashton went out and returned almost immediately with a file. James watched his back, bowed, waiting for Somers's instructions. Then he noticed that Ashton's palm, extended behind his back, towards him, James, contained two old and stained lumps of sugar.

The palm waggled.

Silently, James, hidden from Somers by Ashton's body, took one lump.

The palm waggled again.

James took the other lump.

Ashton's shoulders heaved as if relieved of the burden of an immense deceit. 'Will there be anything else, sir?'

'Yes. See if you can get Mrs Berkeley of Washashley Hall, Lincoln, on the phone. The number is Washashley 17 – no. We'd better not. Mustn't tie up the lines. Bring me a telegram form.'

'Yessir.'

'And Ashton – put some paper and ink in the waiting-room for Mr Berkeley – he may have some letters to write before we go to lunch. Come back for him in fifteen minutes.'

When Ashton had left, Somers said, 'He'll show you where to wash and everything. Now, tell me all about yourself.'

'I don't want to be a nuisance, sir, but my father said you'd put me on the train to Lincoln – I have five pounds.'

'Grand. Yes.'

'Is there a train today, sir?'

'Well, yes. But I think you'd better stay with us in Southall tonight. Tomorrow we can put you on the train. You could use a good sleep and a bath – couldn't you?'

'Yes. Is it very far to Lincoln?'

'No. Not really but it will take the best part of a day. You have to change, I think, at Grantham. Ashton will find out for us.'

'Is there any chance that my brother will be in Lincoln?'

'Christopher?'

'Yes, sir – or Teddy.'

'No. I don't think so. Teddy's at his crammer's in Camberley – doing very well, I trust – and Christopher's somewhere in Scotland. So you won't see him until he has leave.'

'I don't suppose you know when that will be, do you, sir?'

'Hard to say – but perhaps you'll see him before you leave for school.'

Silence.

'Did you dock at Southampton?'

'No, sir. We anchored at Greenock – near Glasgow. Dad said he thought Liverpool or Southampton but it was Glasgow.'

'Gracious. What a trip you've had. We'd better send your parents a cable to let them know you are safe.'

'I did it, sir, in Glasgow. I sent "Happy Birthday" so that it would get through the censors.'

23

'How very clever of you.'

James smiled broadly feeling first proud of himself and then ashamed: his father had drilled the Happy Birthday message into him.

'Did your father say what school he had in mind for you?' Somers was saying.

'Yes, sir. I think he thought the school where Teddy went in Bognor – or Chris's prep school at Little-hampton.'

'Well, we'll see.' Somers looked over his glasses. 'It isn't exactly very wise to be smack on the south coast right now – indeed, most of the schools have been evacuated. But don't worry, I'll take it up with your aunt.'

When Mr Somers took James to lunch, James discovered a road through the old man's seemingly complicated exterior and into his sympathy.

'Some days,' James said, 'there were so many attacks that the alarm bell went every twenty minutes.'

That worked.

'Terrible. Terrible.' Somers stopped in the street and looked down at him. 'Didn't your convoy have an escort?'

'Yes. But not enough and not all the time. At one point they were mostly Canadians. They weren't much good – one of them even rammed a tanker and it blew up right in front of us.' Careful. He might not swallow it.

'Actually, just the side of us.' You clever sod, that worked. 'You see, sir, the Commodore used to blow its whistle about every fifteen minutes – that meant that the whole convoy was to turn. Zig-zagging to escape the submarines.' Well, he ought to swallow that, it's the truth. 'This Canadian didn't turn – it was awful.'

Somers's face, turned again to James, crinkled as if he was in physical pain.

James felt better than he had for a long time – almost happy even.

They went into a tobacconist's. Mr Somers had a few bananas, that he had cut from the bunch, in his hand. He plopped them on the counter. 'What do you think those are?' he asked the proprietor.

'Don't rightly know sir. Never seen the likes of 'em. Muvva, come out 'ere.'

The place was a mass of glass-doored shelves, every one of which was empty except for cardboard advertisements. 'Craven-A.' Dad's cigarette. 'For Your Throat's Sake.' Ta-tum.

The bananas were admired. 'This brave lad brought them clean across the Atlantic,' Somers kept saying. First to the tobacconist (who finally brought some tobacco up from beneath the counter, as if it were a package of diamonds, and handed it to Mr Somers), then to the policeman on the street (while James watched and heard the strange scene around him as if it were a movie set: the bicycles and bottoms again, the strange lorries and their three-wheeled fronts, the taxis – all with their black-hooded headlights. The whole panorama busy and neat, independent, untouchable, not connected with him the way every stick and stone of home was) and then to the waitress.

'Isn't he a *one*,' she said. 'And so small too. The steak and kidney's off, Mr Somers, dear, but I've saved you some shepherd's pie.'

Despite his tiredness, shock and confusion, James did not fail to notice the beamed Tudor building they were in – it seemed to make happy and ancient vibrations within him: it was called Pyms and outside it was white with black beams and it was many storeys high and each storey stuck further and further out into the street, until, about five storeys up, it was hung over half the street entirely. Inside it was incredibly twisting and bent and old and comfortable with oak beams and small oak doors and purple carpets everywhere, and brass shining too – and smoke and people laughing and all manner of rattling crockery and hustle and bustle.

'When the tanker went up – blew up,' James said, 'some sailors were blown into the water. We had just changed course because of the Commodore's signal and we ploughed right through them.'

'I suppose you couldn't stop.'

'Oh no, sir. We'd be a sitting-duck target – anyway, we weren't allowed to. I wished like anything that we could save them – it was awful. All the water on fire. You could hear them shouting, crying out. Two of our crew cut a raft loose and let it fall into the water. The captain was so angry he had them locked in the chain locker – you see we didn't have enough life-rafts for ourselves after that.'

'Terrible. Terrible.'

James kept watching Mr Somers's eyes carefully. He had the man's full attention and that was what he wanted. He now no longer gave much thought to what was fact and what was fiction; he was involved in his own performance as a storyteller.

'My job was to throw blankets from lockers into the lifeboats every time the alarm bell went. I had to throw twenty blankets into each lifeboat on the port side. The ship rolled terribly and all the time the water was right beneath me. The ship didn't have any railing on the boat deck – just a little ridge about an inch and a half high and the boats were hung sort of out over the water and with every throw I thought I'd slip and fall into the sea and be sucked away.

'Then when the alarm was over I had to climb in

the boats and throw them all back – it was so cold.'

'How dreadful. You shouldn't have had to do anything like that.' Somers's face became increasingly creased with concern.

The sympathy seemed to flood over James; it seemed somehow connected with the ocean, the sea that still soaked him.

He was afraid that his words must sound like the frenzied rappings of a wound-up monkey on a tin drum – but he went on because this man, although an Englishman and thus a stranger, was of his world – a gentleman – and he'd forgotten how comfortable it was just to be with a gentleman.

'Do eat your soup, my boy.'

'We were just a small convoy when we left St Georges but then we steamed up to Halifax – two other ships and an escort. The escort disappeared one night and then the tanker was sunk and then our sister ship – the day after.

'At Halifax we got in with this big convoy. Fifty ships – maybe a hundred, I couldn't count them all. I think it was Halifax – the men said so but we weren't allowed to land.

'After that we were attacked again and again. By wolf-packs of submarines. We went south for days. Only the officers knew where we were but there was the spare wheel and binnacle in the stern – and of course, the log over the side – and one of the men plotted our course.

'We were always getting attacked. We went right down past Bermuda again. We went so far south that it got very hot and then we turned.'

Somers pointed to the soup. James ate some, being careful of his table manners for the first time since he'd left home. Somers ate his soup out of the side of his spoon the way they did – it made James feel good just to look at him.

'One day we saw the Azores – just great mountains sticking out of the sea. The men said it was a mistake to pass so close because of German agents. Of course, I don't know about the agents but I do know the day after we were attacked by a German bomber.'

'Frightful. How perfectly frightful.'

'I came up on deck and there was a great fat man – the cookie – standing against the railing and looking up.' Cookie, James thought, skinny as a rail and not quite all there – but no one would believe that . . . 'and you'd better make this yarn about the bomber good, nipper . . .'

'Cookie was looking up and way, way up in the sky, right over us, was this great black bomber. It just stayed there and stayed there.

'A woman came out on deck – she was a passenger – and asked what it was. Cookie just said, "A Jerry," and she ran back inside: she was terribly frightened. You know, sir, the men just thought it was funny – I mean, her being frightened.'

'I didn't know German bombers could go out that far.'

'Oh, yes, sir. But we were pretty well over by the Bay of Biscay by then, I think.'

That seemed to work.

'Didn't anyone shoot at this plane?'

'No, sir. They said it was out of range.'

'What about the escort vessels?'

'They had all gone by then. The men said the Yanks and the Canadians were to take us halfway and then the Royal Navy would escort us. But they had gone and the Royal Navy hadn't arrived yet.'

'Dreadful. Dreadful. Your father had no business to send you – I mean, that is, he couldn't have known what you were going to run into . . .'

'No, sir. He couldn't or he certainly wouldn't have sent me. This big bomber – it looked like a Dornier DO7 – just hung up there in the sky and then suddenly it let go this big red bomb. The bomb seemed to hover in the sky – they said it was radio-controlled and maybe it was because it did seem to change course.' Careful. Careful. You had to be careful with adults – the ocean one sailed was mined with the facts that living a long time had given them.

'But it did seem to change course away from us – and then, only then, did the alarm bell go and I did the blankets and when it was over the Commodore ship had gone. The men said she was hit and fell behind.'

James ate some of the shepherd's pie.

'It was awful where we lived. The screw to the propeller ran by and the ship was so badly made that every time the screw turned it made an awful screeching sound. That, and the alarm bell, made it very hard to sleep and nobody ever changed their clothes –'

'I can see that –'

'– we even slept with our shoes on.'

'Well, you were very brave to get through it all, James.'

'I did my best – one of the other peggies – and he was older too – cracked up and had to be taken to the sick bay. But that was after everything – I mean, you couldn't blame him because we got in so close to France that we had a dive-bomber attack – Stukas.'

'Is the pie all right?'

'Oh, yes, sir. It's delicious.' James wondered if he'd be able to remember all the details if he was asked to tell it again to Mrs Somers or somebody. The Stukas he could embellish a lot. Then there was the very real storm, but you couldn't explain how frightening a

29

storm was – it was like the waiting. No one would believe or understand that it was the *waiting* that tore you apart. Enduring terror for second after second, minute after minute and hour after hour and nothing to do but wait. Of course, probably, no one but him, a physical coward, would have been scared of nothing – just waiting.

In the late afternoon Mr Somers took him out to Southall. First they travelled on the Underground. Now it was Mr Somers talking, trying to tell him how the trains worked and explain where they were going on the little map above the handstraps of the opposing seats, but all James really noticed were the crowds already filling the double-deck bunks that lined the platforms of every station – men, women and children, pale, tired, gaunt ('green-looking' his mother would say) preparing to spend the night down in the foul air where the rattling red trains passed only a few feet from their bodies – and the fine netting glued to the train windows as protection against the blast of bombs.

The grim stoicism of these people frightened him. He knew he wouldn't be able to take living like that, not night after night. He'd rather, he thought, be up in the fresh air – bombs or no bombs – than huddled down here hundreds of feet below with all these people.

Later they came up above ground and took a bus for a long way and then they walked.

Finally, they turned and passed through two little brick gateposts. Mr Somers sighed with apparent relief.

'We had an iron gate but it went last year – for scrap, you know. Everybody has given their gates and things.'

For a rich man, James thought, the house was very small. In the hall two tin helmets hung from the coat rack, but the house smelled like a home and when he heard Mrs Somers's voice call out, feminine and warm, over a little rattle of dishes, 'Is that you, dear?' he wished that he could lie right down on the carpet and let it swallow him up so that he could stay in this house for ever.

He did not go to Lincoln on the next day, Sunday, as planned. Indeed, he fell asleep on Saturday, at about six o'clock, in the Somerses' living-room dropping the cup of tea that was in his hand.

He slept until five o'clock the next afternoon. 'It's lucky it's Sunday,' Mrs Somers said, 'or we'd have had to wake you.' Then she cooked him some powdered eggs – they tasted much better than the ones at sea.

'You can have a nice bath and go right back to bed – would you like that?'

'Yes, I guess I would – thank you,' James said.

'You look as if you haven't had a bath for weeks.'

'I haven't – but I did have two showers on the ship.'

'Well, they couldn't have been very good ones.'

Mrs Somers was taking down the blackout curtains. 'Jim, you've a train to catch and Mr Somers leaves in forty-five minutes.'

She had washed and ironed him a shirt (he put it on after he'd carefully retied the chamois pouch around his middle under his vest) and when he came downstairs she made him clean his shoes. For breakfast she gave him bacon on toast. He noticed that they had only fried bread but thought that it must be what they preferred. He wondered if English people ever had orange juice, cornflakes, real eggs and milk the way they did at home – or waffles on

31

Sundays with lots of maple syrup – and then he remembered the rationing and, embarrassed, could hardly finish what little was on his plate.

III

There was something refreshing about being in a new place. There was something refreshing about London – of course, he knew it was partly because he had Mr Somers's protection – and there was something refreshing about England, the country. There was a kindness and a no-nonsense quality about the people they encountered. It seemed almost as if there was goodness, human nobility all about and he felt it despite his fear and loneliness.

Liverpool Street Station was another cathedral of soot and smoke reverberating with the hiss and clank of trains.

The porter, again a square-shaped woman, trundled along beside them, pushing his trunk, a cigarette dangling from the corner of her mouth.

Somers walked along briskly. James had trouble keeping up with him.

'That all used to be glass before the war,' Somers pointed up at the vast framework of the station's ceiling – through which one could see the grey sky. 'It all went way back in 1940. Liverpool Street always gets it. In the First War it was a Zeppelin. I was in France then but Mrs Somers was an intern just around the corner.'

'My father was in France, too.'

They reached the goods wagon and the porter started to load the trunk. James moved to help her. 'Watch it,' she said simply and turned her back to him

32

swinging the trunk in one hand.

'Be sure that your trunk is transferred at Grantham, Jim. It wouldn't do to let it go on to Edinburgh.'

The train was not very crowded and Mr Somers found him a corner seat.

'Afraid I must go now. Do you want to pay me for your ticket or shall I put it on your father's account?'

'I can pay you, sir,' James said blushing, and reached to unbutton his shirt.

Booming echo of loudspeakers '. . . Burned-Toe-k, 'Are-low, Saw-bridge-uth ah-yund Bish-shops-stork-ffud . . . ornk . . .'

'Don't trouble. I thought you wanted to – we can put it on tick.' Somers held out his hand. 'Drop me a line so that I know you've arrived. And when you come to London *always* come and see me – all the boys do, all the Bermuda boys.'

Then he was gone. Ta-tum. 'All the Bermuda boys.'

James sat down. Opposite him was a white-haired parson. His presence made James feel safe – man of God, father, gentle Jesus meek and mild . . . James smiled. The man sniffed and put up his paper. 'The *Daily Mail*,' James read, 'Haw-Haw sinks Ark Royal again.' In another corner was a woman whose hair stood out from her head like fuzzy aeroplane wings. She had on a strange uniform. 'Woman's Land Army,' James read. What did this woman do? Do they fight the land, wrestle it, or fight for it?

Here he was alone again and going into the unknown . . . the train seemed to pitch and roll like the ship, the ocean still poured over everything . . .

He looked out of the window and stayed that way watching the ghastly slums give way to a picture-book countryside where all the distant hillocks and trees were tinted with a soft purple-blue – until he

33

read a sign, Grantham.

The local from Grantham to Lincoln was an old train without a corridor. (It was way past lunch-time and he was very hungry. He'd seen a place on the platform where they were selling buns and sandwiches and tea – but he was too scared to go in; he couldn't see any children in there and it might be for adults only.) James got in an empty compartment and sat, again, by the window. After a while a woman got in and sat opposite him.

She took out a magazine and opened it on her lap. You couldn't really tell how old she was – a grown-up anyway, somewhere between seventeen and thirty. By her clothes he guessed she was a shop-girl or a secretary. She certainly wasn't a lady but she wasn't a servant either. She might be one of those women but he doubted it.

She had on high heels and silk stockings and as the train clicked and clacked along she kept time by tapping her heels and toes. James thought she might be a dancer. Anyway she seemed very contented and completely unaware of his existence. Every now and again she would look up from her magazine, her eyes focusing on nothing, a sigh escaping her partially opened mouth.

The tapping continued without interruption. James thought that perhaps she had, the night before, been to a dance and that, in a way, her partner was still in her arms.

Her coat was open and her green wool dress was swelled by her breasts . . . James wished he was older. Wished he was rid of the burden of childhood, of being small.

The skirt of her dress did not reach her knees and as she tapped he caught a glimpse of flesh above her stockings.

34

Since there was no corridor he wondered if he should throw himself on her. But he knew that was ridiculous. But say he just did it, what would happen . . . ?

His mind dwelled on what must have happened in corridorless trains over the years. What had this compartment seen? He wished he'd seen as much – at least all the exciting parts: imagine actually, literally, seeing people make love . . . and then the young woman got out at a country station.

The train moved on towards Lincoln. James realized, with some horror, that he had an erection. He was afraid that it wouldn't go down and how could he get out at Lincoln and meet his great-aunts in this state?

The trouble was, he thought, that one had no control over erections. He always worried about getting one in front of a doctor during an examination – but, mercifully, it had never happened.

And then the tears were pouring down his cheeks again. He pulled out his handkerchief, blew his nose and kicked the seat opposite him. It was maddening not to have any control over it – and no warning. He sat down and a spasm of seasickness came over him. Ting, ting; ting, ting . . . ship's bells, where did the noise come from?

When the train stopped a moment of terror grabbed him: his aunts, Daisy and Lillie, might not be there; might not, if they were, recognize him.

He was sure he wouldn't be able to remember them because he was six when he last saw them. He couldn't even picture the house – but he could remember the car, the Rolls and a black Scottie dog that had bitten him . . . And the shadowy presence of Uncle Albert, huge and unapproachable – and now long dead.

He had no sooner stepped from the train, amid the

35

squeaking of brakes, when a little old lady with white hair under a bright country hat said excitedly, 'James? – yes, James.'

'Yes, ma'am,' he said and looked into her blue eyes. She put out a pink English cheek and he kissed it. Her hands, in big fur gloves, were on his shoulders. Her coat was a tweed, lavender-coloured, and she smelled of lavender as well. She was certainly small: her eyes were level with his.

'And this is your Aunt Lillie.'

They were very alike yet easy to tell apart – Daisy had buck teeth and was pretty and Lillie had straight teeth and was plain.

He moved forward to kiss Lillie.

'Och,' she said, waving her hand, 'don't bother kissing me. I know you boys just hate it, especially in public.'

Her smile was shy and quick and he realized two things at once – that he remembered them and that Aunt Lillie was his favourite. He fought back tears.

'Oh, you're so like your dear father,' said Lillie, wiping her eyes with a little lace handkerchief, '– and aren't I a FOOL.'

James, vaguely registering that no one at home in Bermuda called his father dear and that it sounded good, was suddenly embraced by the relief-giving knowledge that these people were family – his family. The stupid tears ran down his face.

'Such a Berkeley look – my, my, my.'

Daisy was weeping too and he loved their tears but hated his own.

'Well, come along,' said Lillie, 'let's get home – the whole silly lot of us.'

'Where's Fenders? FENDERS.'

'Don't fret so, Daisy – he'll be here in a minute.'

'FENDERS.'

36

A stocky man appeared wearing a blue serge double-breasted suit and a peaked cap and carrying James's trunk on his shoulder.

'Oh, there you are, Fenders. We can never find you when we want you.'

'Yes, madam. I was getting the young gentleman's trunk, madam.'

'This is Mr James, Fenders,' said Lillie.

'I can see that, madam.' Fenders saluted him, touching his hand to his cap.

'Do you remember Fenders, James? Don't know what we'd do without him.'

Fenders held out his hand which James knew wasn't right but he shook it.

'Just like your father if I may say so, sir. A fine-looking young gentleman. Welcome to Lincoln –'

Aunt Lillie was blushing.

'– it's grand to have a Berkeley back at Washashley – although you'll find us a mere shadow of our former selves, sir.'

Both aunts were exchanging glances and then Lillie said, 'Come along. Take the trunk to the car, Fenders, do.'

Fenders smiled at James, took the suitcase as well and marched off. His Aunt Daisy took his arm. 'Don't pay any attention to his blarney – I've so little control over him since Dearest died.'

Dearest?

Aunt Lillie walked on his other side. 'Oh, Fenders is all right,' she said, 'I'll tell you all about it later, dear – are you hungry?'

'No, thank you, I'm fine.'

' 'Course you're hungry – all boys are always hungry. We've a lovely tea all waiting and Mrs Pickle has even graced us with a cake.'

Outside the station, the sun came out briefly.

Fenders was strapping the suitcase to the back of an old taxi – a crumby Austin.

'Where's the Rolls?' James asked, remembering that Fenders had been Uncle Albert's chauffeur-cum-valet.

'Oh, we've no petrol at all now, you know, dear.'

'Yes,' said Daisy. 'Frightful, isn't it – they used to let us have a little but now only doctors and people have any ration at all.'

Fenders was holding the door and touching his cap again, his eyes twinkling.

If there was one thing about Washashley Hall, James thought, it was that it was goddamn spooky, so spooky you didn't dare say goddamn for fear it be heard by the innumerable ghosts and you be punished.

When he first caught sight of the house, as the taxi drove up the hill, he recognized it at once. It was enormous yet squat-looking; forbiddingly impressive yet airy and bright. The front façade was a mass of large multi-paned windows, three to each bay upstairs and down, centred by a porticoed door. The roof, of mossy slates and lead, and the many chimneys, looked as if they had been for ever and would be for ever. The huge house sat heavy on the ground with comfortable, ancient proprietorship. The first impression was that it was Georgian but most of it dated, he knew, back to the thirteenth century. Ivy covered part of the uneven stone walls like a beard on a craggy face and this exposure, the west, was, he remembered, where the house looked most friendly – especially with the sun making tall shadows across the front lawn.

'Yes. He doesn't really work for us any more – except sometimes doing windows and things,' said Aunt Lillie. 'He just came especially today to meet you.'

Fenders, sitting next to the driver, was only separated from them by the glass partition.

'He went into the Army when the war broke out but he was invalided out last year.'

'I'm sorry,' said James. 'How does he live?'

'Don't you worry about *him*,' said Aunt Daisy. 'He gets his cottage free and he gets all manner of things from the vegetable garden and the home farm – he's terribly spoiled.'

'He's all right, dear. And remember they have the cottage in exchange for the work Mrs Fenders does – so it isn't free at all.' She touched James's hand. 'She does the floors, you know – and very well too.'

'And just look at that suit. It's not his, you know, it's ours. Dearest gave it to him – he's a rascal.'

'Now, now, dear. He just wanted to be dressed up for James.'

'It's very kind of him.' James thought that he'd probably like Fenders; he always got on with the people the family called rascals.

They turned in the driveway and James noticed that the tall gates were still there – maybe just people with little gates gave them for scrap? They passed the oak trees and then the windy part of the drive where it was bordered on both sides by a wall of trimmed green shrubbery – over twenty feet high, he thought – that looked like Bermuda cedar.

The car swung around the turn and stopped at the steps of the front door which wasn't, James remembered, called the front door in this house but the 'south door' because the front door was really the porticoed one that people only used to go out to the front lawn and garden and that was really called the 'west door' – or 'Dearest's door' – and beneath the lamp (that looked like a streetlamp in a Sherlock Holmes movie) stood O'Neill, as worried-looking as ever, holding his hands clasped in front of his apron – a mattress cover? It looked like one.

It would be nice if O'Neill said, 'Welcome home, Mr James,' but all he said was, 'Yes, madam, yes, madam – the door to the Master's study is stuck, madam,' and smiled a little but would not look James in the eye.

His aunts went ahead in a flurry. Fenders was at his side; he took off his cap and showed James the insignia on it which looked like a little black pineapple.

'My armorial bearings, Mr James,' he heaved out his chest with a great breath. 'I don't often wear 'em now – but I got them out special. Before the War we'd not have met you like this, I can tell you, sir. No, we'd have the Rolls and a footman besides – do you remember?'

'Not very well.'

'Well, sir. When the War's over –'

'Fenders,' called Aunt Lillie from the top of the steps, 'please take the trunk around – James, come this way, it's time for tea, dear.'

James looked about the front hall remembering some things, not remembering others and then remembering some of them – it was like a voyage of discovery, rediscovery. Although the building seemed smaller, the ceilings seemed higher.

'– and if you hadn't reminded him he'd have brought the trunk in here tracking mud all over the –'

The whole place was much more sumptuous than he'd ever noticed before. The hall had black-and-white marble floors and he recognized the gold tables and the mahogany chairs with their crests painted so small. There was a silver salver to receive cards and on it was one card with the name: Prince Hermann de Saxe Weimar.

'– getting impossible. Last Christmas he came to help with the decorations and I found him smoking in the study – *Dearest*'s study.'

– but what had happened to the suits of armour?

'No,' laughed Aunt Lillie, 'we've never had any suits of armour – Wherever did you get that idea?'

Movies, thought James, disappointed.

'But there's lot of swords and guns and things that boys like – but you mustn't touch them of course – in the billiard room.'

'Oh, yes,' Aunt Daisy said, tittering with a lispy girlish noise through her buck teeth. 'I remember once how Dearest caught those naughty boys, Christopher and Teddy, sword-fighting on the – BILLIARD TABLE. Oh, he was cross– '

Of course, 'Dearest' was his Great-uncle Albert – he wished she'd stop calling him that, it was embarrassing.

'– but he never had need to thrash anyone, you know, because everyone – all the boys – were afraid of him.'

'And do you know,' said Lillie, 'your dear father, George – and yes – dear Francis had done the same thing years ago – before the First War. Such naughty boys – but not as naughty as Christopher and Teddy, of course. *On* the billiard table – if they'd torn the cover I don't know what we should have done.'

'Aunt Lillie, do you know when Chris will come – on leave, I mean?'

The hall had now turned into a T-shape, like a church, and here the ceiling was even higher – two storeys.

'Oh, dearie me, you've just missed him – he had ten days leave but he left last Tuesday.'

'Do you know where he is?'

'He never tells us anything,' said Daisy. 'As if we were spies. Last year he had his arm in a sling and he said it was "a nasty. . ." What was it, Lillie?'

41

High on the ceiling ducks were painted in flight –
the background was a pale-blue sky with fluffy clouds,
almost like Bermuda.

'A nasty sting from a cab horse.'

'As if we didn't know enough to know there aren't
cab horses any more.'

'But Mr Somers said he was in Scotland.'

'Perhaps – you'll have to ask him. He'll come again
in a few months. Such a good boy, he always comes
home – although heaven knows two old ladies must
bore him to pieces.'

Halfway down the wall was a wrought-iron gallery
with the initials, AB, in polished brass – perhaps it
was even gold.

'Oh, he shoots on the Fens and things. He looks so
handsome in his uniform – everybody stares at him. But
he won't wear it. Takes it off and puts on those awful
corduroys. I said he'd have to wear his uniform to
church – well, this leave he didn't even come to church.'

'Daisy, dear, if Christopher doesn't want to go to
church I'm sure that's his business. He's a man, now,
after all.'

'Dearest would not have allowed it.'

'I do wish he'd find a nice young gal – Edmund
always finds girls– '

'Lillie, *please* . . .'

'Oh, yes – I forgot – that last one really was The End.
Teddy can be so silly sometimes. . .'

The Aunts went to take off their hats – chattering up
the stairs, their footsteps inaudible on the carpet. Then
they were out of sight only to appear again walking
across the gallery above him. Aunt Lillie waved.

O'Neill was beckoning to him. He followed the bent
old man. He was ushered through a door and then the
door closed after him with a little click. A small room;

42

mirror, washbasin with marble top, coloured balls of soap in a bonbon dish; two brushes, silver, AB, again – a door beyond. Thank God, a lavatory. He remembered it. It looked like a plain mahogany bench until you lifted the top and there it was: Church, it said in blue on the white bowl – which seemed appropriate since Uncle Albert was a parson – but that was when they were little. If you pulled the chain too hard a splash of water came down on your head.

'Dearest' indeed, he thought, having a leak, the old guy's been dead since 1937 – five whole years, practically for ever. Then he looked up at the tall ceiling: it seemed quite possible that the ghost of his uncle might be hovering up there listening.

Brrrrr.

And he washed his hands, carefully not using the coloured balls of soap which were obviously for guests. Then he thought he'd better not use the mono-grammed towels either. Dad always said to use the bathmat and not spoil people's towels – but there wasn't one. He found a cloth hanging under the basin and used that.

That spooky O'Neill, never says anything. He remembered he'd once been what they call a chauffeur-cum-valet (Fenders's job) but then he'd got too old. And there was a story about him – a secret, but he couldn't remember what it was. Something about somebody being killed. Brrrr.

Oh, yes. His father had said: 'Poor O'Neill was the perfect Gentleman's Gentleman – then there was an accident on the Great North Road–ʼ Someone had run out. It wasn't anyone's fault. But O'Neill had been driving. 'He just went to pieces afterwards – he couldn't even be trusted to drive.'

Another time, James remembered, his father had said: 'Of course, Uncle Albert was naughty: he was

43

always jumping in the car and saying: "To Town, O'Neill, and don't spare the horses." '

James stood in the east wing of the hall beneath the ducks and looked out of the window. Garden below, herringbone brick paths. Tall trees with bare branches and large blackbirds making a tremendous cawing – the sound made him feel good, he didn't know why.

He heard a different sound and turned. A tiny old woman in black; apron white, silver hair. She looked even older than his aunts but her cheeks were as red and apple-like as Dopey's in The Seven Dwarfs. She was pushing the tea-tray. She stopped, looked at him fleetingly then turned her head down and half away – shyness, he thought – and then, with her head in the same position, her eyes looked up and found his again, she smiled a little smile and then silently whisked away.

He was looking at the walls; pictures, oil paintings, he thought he'd never seen as many paintings in one house as were in this corner of the hall. They each had little labels under them – black on gold. De Hondecouta. Anthony Van der Velde. The Hondecouta, even bigger than a movie poster, was a scene with a peacock, ducks, pigs and chickens – even the chicken manure was painted in. Who on earth would want a picture of a lousy farmyard? There was a nice one with lots of sky and greeny water and sand all glassy with the wet – J.M.W. Turner, it said.

His aunts came down. He noticed that they both wore little woollen gloves that left their fingers bare. Against the cold, he guessed. Coal fires glowed in every grate he'd seen but the place was bitterly cold – especially this two-storeyed part of the hall.

Soon the old woman with the red cheeks came back

44

with a silver kettle.

'Oh, thank you so much, Mrs Pickle,' said Lillie. 'James, do you remember our Mrs Pickle? She's brought the tea up herself – isn't that kind?'

Mrs Pickle curtseyed. Her waist was so slender and cinched-in that she looked in imminent danger of breaking in two. 'How-do-do, Master James,' she said in a heavy north-country accent.

'How do you do?' He should not shake hands nor stand if he was sitting but he was already standing so he gave her a little bow.

'For a moment I thought it was your father.' She gave her turned-away smile again, this time holding the tip of her finger to her mouth as if she were trying to hide behind it, and again slipped away. Old as she was there was something about her that looked like a coy girl.

'You see, Lillie. You see that? No cap – it's all going to pieces.'

'Now, now, dear, don't let it upset you – we can hardly expect Mrs Pickle to be cook, maid, bottle-washer and laundress and then expect her to dress as the lowest– '

'She doesn't do any laundry.'

'But she waits at table and goodness knows what else – at her age too.'

'She'd sit down right here if you gave her half a chance.'

'Well, we aren't going to – sit down, Jamie dear – they have their pride too, you know,' to Daisy. Then to James: 'She was our head cook, you know. In charge of the entire kitchen for years and years.'

'She looks like Little Red Riding Hood,' James smiled at Lillie.

'Isn't that funny – why, I always say that too – isn't that *interesting* – isn't that interesting, Daisy dear?'

45

But Daisy was looking hurt and didn't answer.

His bedroom, just as he had feared, turned out to be the one overlooking the graveyard. Spooky. It had a double-spooky four-poster bed which had a treble-spooky canopy which had a quadruple-spooky sag in it in the shape of a dead body. The fire in the small grate seemed to give out more smoke than heat.

This was the room, he'd heard his father say, that his Uncle Edmond, 'The Colonel' (who now lived at Niagara, Canada), called the Crow-Piss Room – because he said, 'The damn church bells sound every Sunday morning – when a decent fella wants to sleep – and wake up the crows which wake you up if you aren't already awake and who the hell wants to be waked up at the first crow piss of dawn?'

It was funny, the way some of the colonial members of the family made rather dirty jokes about the English-proper-Berkeleys. Funny for them anyway; they were grown-up. Graveyards really scared him and this one wasn't bright and whitewashed like Bermuda graveyards – it was really old, mossy, dark and haunted.

The church, Aunt Daisy said with pride, was once the chapel of the Hall and attached to the house – then, about two hundred years ago, the chapel had been given to the Diocese and the wall built between them.

The wall separating the Hall from the church was Lincoln stone and some twelve feet high and three feet thick – but to James's mind it was totally inadequate. Besides, there was a creepy squeaky gate in the wall and although it was always locked anyone knew that ghosts could walk through locked gates . . . they could float over walls if they wanted.

Funny about Uncle Edmond, he was a nice kind

man but everyone knew he wasn't a real colonel but a lieutenant colonel and the English relatives looked down on him because he was such a 'raw colonial'. Which was true, he supposed, because in England a crow was a rook and if you said piss at Washashley a picture was liable to fall off the wall.

James inspected the rest of the room. There was a gigantic wardrobe of bright mahogany – empty – and a chest-o-drawers with a bow front, also empty. The carpet was plain and wine-coloured and in the corner was a funny-looking box made of carved dark wood. He opened it: a white bowl with some toilet paper inside it: a commode.

Was he supposed to use it – surely not? He remembered only that his father had said that there was only one bathroom upstairs and that gentlemen were not to use it after eight in the morning – it was then the ladies had their baths. He decided he'd better always use the men's lavatory downstairs . . .

A knock on the door. 'I thought I'd do some of your unpacking now – before supper, dear. O'Neill should do it but he'd only get it all wrong.'

'Where does Christopher sleep, Aunt Lillie?'

'Next door – he and Teddy both, when they're here.'

'Can I go and see it?'

'Of course – but come back in a few minutes in case I need you.'

The upstairs hall was gloomy despite the many white-painted doors each with its brass knocker, brass knob and flowered china push-plate. Chris's door had an ugly knocker – a Lincoln Imp.

Their room was much bigger than his, looked out on the back garden and the stableyard, and they had ordinary twin beds, the lucky sods. It seemed very empty and he could see nothing that belonged to his brother except a matchbox in an ashtray.

47

In the drawer under the little mirror he found some buttons and a black case which contained a silver medal: 'A.S. Berkeley. Middle-weight. 1934. The Lion School.' It always seemed peculiar that Christopher's real name was Aubrey Spencer. He held it in his palm for a moment and then up against his cheek – then embarrassed, he put it away.

The chest-o-drawers was full of their clothes. In the very back of the top drawer he found several tiny envelopes. French Letters – he'd seen one once at school in Bermuda. He was filled with excitement. He took one out. It was rolled but the feel of the infinitely thin rubber – how can they possibly make it so thin? – aroused his groin. He put it back feeling guilty and ashamed. Not Christopher, he thought, he wouldn't – but Teddy might.

Wow, certainly one of his brothers was actually *doing it* to a girl – and before marriage. It was the kind of sin for which you weren't forgiven – ugh. Well, he couldn't do that yet but he thought he'd like to try one on some time when it was safe. Dare he?

He shivered and closed the drawer.

'We'll have to buy you your whole school uniform, James dear. As soon as we know what school we'll go up to Daniel Neal's and buy it – 'course we'll have to get your ration books first. Maybe we'll do that tomorrow.

'Well, you're all unpacked. Everything's here. Here's your sponge bag – you won't mind running down the hall to clean your teeth and wash, will you? We don't use those any more – no servants.' She pointed to the washstand which had a large china basin with a matching jug sitting in it and a matching soapdish and a round mirror on a thing like a broomstick.

Soon after supper – when James again lied that he never took sugar in his tea – they retired for bed.

To his immense relief there was a nightlight for each of them in a little alcove at the top of the stairs.

'You first in the b-r, James.' No sooner was he in bed, with the nightlight making spooky patterns on the canopy, than Aunt Daisy came in. She looked quite different, prettier and younger, with her fine silver hair falling on to the shoulders of her flowered dressing-gown and cascading way down to below her waist. She tiptoed over and kissed his forehead.

'Night, Aunt Daisy.'

'Night, night – sleep tight.' She patted his shoulder.

'Thank you – you too.'

She tiptoed out and he was left with her lavender-feminine smell. He was surprised that she was affectionate – after all, she was a childless woman. Lillie was only a spinster, but you knew right away that she was affectionate.

'Got everything, dear?' Lillie.

'Yes, thank you.'

'You sure?'

He wanted to ask her to leave his door open.

'Well,' she said brusquely, 'I'm sure you don't need it but here it is.' And she leaned over and kissed him smack on the mouth. One of her pigtails banged against his cheek. 'Breakfast is at nine but you don't have to get up for it – Teddy always sleeps until noon and Christopher sometimes sleeps all day. He didn't used to – I think it's the War, poor darling.'

'What do I do if there's an air raid?'

'I'll wake you – we don't often have them but when we do we all go down in the wine-cellar. It isn't the Savoy but it's safe – very democratic too. Mrs Pickle without her teeth, O'Neill snoring like a steamroller

49

and me reading the psalms. Well, God bless you.' She gave him a single pat that was more like a punch.

As soon as she had left he was overtaken with a spasm of homesickness more powerful than he had known before – even on the *Empire United*. The little nightlight cast eerie shadows and the fire gave out only a small orange glow in the blackness. He could hear a spooky ticking in the distance. It was all so strange, so unlike home.

He buried his head in his pillow to stifle the sobs and pulled the covers over his head.

His brain seemed to throb and whirr with confused and tormenting thoughts. It seemed, at first, as if it was simply an unbearable longing for his mother and father – for home, real home – but then he thought of the ship and how at least there there were bright electric lights on all night and men all around. Then he thought of home again and strange phantom-like doubts plagued him.

He didn't like this place, he didn't even like his spooky old aunts. The only people he really wanted were his mother and father.

'Oh Angels, help women!' she was always yelling. Was she crazy? No, of course not – it was just the heat – she hated Bermuda's heat. But they were always fighting – he guessed she hated his father. That was it. She didn't really hate him – James.

Perhaps it was all his fault. Perhaps it was his fault that they fought – there was a time when he'd fanned the heat of their fights. Why had he done it.

The only reason he could imagine was that he was basically evil. Why? Why? It was an awful thing to do. Possessed by devils – perhaps he was possessed by devils the way he'd heard his mother say he was. But then again, at other times she hugged him and kissed him and said she loved him.

And his Aunt Daisy, the Bermuda Aunt Daisy, Lady Sheringham, had told his mother that it was insane, murder, to send him across the Atlantic in war-time – he'd heard her. And his mother had got angry, livid, and said she'd rather 'have a *dead* son than a spoiled American-Bermudian juvenile-delinquent!'.

And what was so wrong with American boys anyway? – except that they had more things than he did and the things he wanted – like an airgun and a model plane with a real motor.

But why a dead son? What did she mean? She meant, of course, that she'd prefer him dead to the way he was. She was really saying she didn't love him because he was the way he was. He guessed she was right. He really was a juvenile delinquent – she said so and she only knew the half of it. Heck, a quarter. Say she knew about all the things he imagined when he was doing goo-goos – oh God, don't think of it. It's too awful, sinful and wicked.

But why had they let him cross the Atlantic? They couldn't have known what it was going to be like. They couldn't have. If they had, they wouldn't have let him.

Of course they didn't. Dad thought I'd probably have a stateroom – that's what the ticket said – and the paper that said I was a deckhand was just supposed to be a cover-up because travel is illegal.

And Aunt Daisy Sheringham was right – it was *insane* – they were hardly out of sight of Bermuda when all hell broke loose . . .

But he had to do it. It was his duty to become a public school man. He couldn't blame them. He remembered clearly: it was, at the very beginning, his idea. He'd begged to go over to England to school – but what was peculiar was that she agreed. Right away, she agreed.

It had never occurred to him that she would agree. He thought she'd beg him to stay – say it was ridiculous and that they couldn't take any chance with his life, not his.

It was no good making excuses for himself. They were right – after all Chris had come over and he'd been really in the War since '39. If they could take a chance on Chris's life of course they could take a chance on his – Chris was the eldest, after all.

But Chris and Teddy were grown-ups – he wasn't. He'd be thirteen in almost exactly two months – the 23rd of April, St George's Day. He hoped he'd feel different when he was thirteen, but he didn't believe he would . . .

He woke up. It was terribly dark. No light – they must be torpedoed – engine room hit. No, Washashley. Still night-time, not day. The little nightlight was still on. He had an awful pain in his stomach – terrible. Low down. Maybe it was an appendicitis. 'The worst thing, mate, at sea, is to get an h'appendicitis.' 'McIntyre died – 'is 'eart, they said – don't you believe it – h'appendicitis.'

But he was at Washashley and he had to get to a bathroom – quick.

Once out of bed he knew he couldn't make it – couldn't hold it – the commode.

There, shivering, he doubled over with pain. 'H'appendicitis – then you're a gonna.' 'When will they put doctors on ships?' 'Never, mate, not for the likes of you and me.' 'I 'ad mine out in Auckland. Yeah, for free. Wonderful place New Zealand – all the 'ospitals and doctors is free.'

Even though he was on land he probably wouldn't get to hospital on time – he'd die. He thought that he'd rather die than go to hospital and be cut up by doctors ... he could remember hospital, just vaguely, horrible.

He looked up and saw both his aunts standing there in the half-darkness and only then did he realize that he had been groaning with pain. He burst into tears.

'You go back to bed, Daisy.' Lillie came a little closer. He looked away. 'There, there, dear.' He realized that she was looking away too. 'Just a minute and I'll get a thermometer.'

As soon as she had gone he wiped himself quickly, closed the commode and jumped back into bed.

He didn't have a temperature, she said. What do I do about the commode – the mess, he wanted to ask .. ?

The next morning he woke up and his watch said 11:30. He got dressed quickly. I'll sneak it out and down the back to the downstairs lavatory, he thought, and then wash it out. No, it wouldn't fit in the basin – to wash it out.

He'd have to sneak it to the upstairs bathroom.

He opened his door carefully and looked out into the hall. No one. But it was a helluva long way to the bathroom – clear down the hall and half down the main stairs.

He ducked back for the commode. It was pretty awful-looking. He piled toilet paper on top until it was hidden, hauled the bowl out and went to the door.

He looked and listened. No one. Only, in the distance, the sound of a high-flying aircraft.

He got down the hall and then down the stairs and right to the door – locked. He tried again. Definitely locked.

He hurried back to his bedroom and put the bowl back. Phee-oo-ee. What could he do? Wait and listen.

53

He went towards the door again intending to watch the bathroom until whoever was in there came out – but he heard someone outside.

'James, dear, are you up?'

Aunt Lillie. Dammit.

She opened the door. 'Oh there you are. Come on down. You must be famished. Mrs Pickle always gets cross with us for being late – but she won't be cross with you because you're a man. Men have all the luck in this world, I always say. Come on.'

'Aunt Lillie . . ?'

'We can have a nice chat, can't we? You can tell me all about your trip – would you like that?'

'Yes, thank you.'

'Yes. Tell me all about yourself – hours and hours of it.' She started back down the hall. 'And then I can tell you all about myself – it'll take about two-and-a-half minutes. Heh-heh. Aren't old ladies silly?'

He followed her, saying a little prayer that the commode be taken up to heaven – taken up to heaven as in the dreadful Day of Judgment, taken up to heaven in all its glory.

She didn't leave him and he ate the porridge and the toast and the marmalade and drank the bitter tea. He wanted to go to the bathroom to have a leak but he was too shy to ask – besides it might invoke memories of his groaning performance the night before.

He began to tell her a watered-down version of the story he had told Mr Somers but he got no further than Halifax.

'Oh, Jamie – don't tell me any more – I really can't bear it. You're safe now. Try not to think about it.' She flapped her hands. 'Oh dear, oh dear. When your father got home in 1919 – he didn't look much older than you do now, isn't that funny? *But the same look in the eyes* – you poor boy. If it hadn't been for Daisy I

54

don't think he could have regained his sanity . . .' She
stopped, looked at him and then shook her head.
'Well, you'll just have to forget it. Long walks. That's
it, long walks. That's what your Uncle Albert said:
walk it right out of your system. That's what he told
George – your father.'

'Excuse me, Aunt Lillie.' He got up.

'What? What? Don't say excuse me, Jamie dear –
it's so middle-class.'

'I know. I'm sorry.'

'Just get up and go where you have to go. You can
always give a little bow – but then go. You can say, I
beg your pardon – but never excuse me, sounds like
nouveau riche people, factory owners. Run along,
then.'

He'd nip up the backstairs to his room, he thought,
but first he must have a leak.

IV

James opened the door from the downstairs lavatory –
cloakroom, they called it – only about six inches
before he stopped and drew back. Voices. Mrs Pickle
and O'Neill. In O'Neill's hands he'd seen the
unmistakable white cylindrical bowl of the commode.

'You take it, Mrs Pickle – it's woman's work.'

'I've had enough humiliations heaped on my head,
Mr O'Neill – thank you very much.'

'I'm not an upstairs skivvy, I'm the butler – I won't
do it.'

'It's disgusting – but Miss Lillie said you was to do
it. I'm head cook – I'm not cleaning up upstairs
messes.'

'Well, I wouldn't do it for anyone but 'er – I could

strangle Mr James, the little –'

'Let's hope it doesn't happen every day, Mr O'Neill.'

'I'll pack my bags – just once more, Mrs P, and I'll pack my bags.'

Would they come in? Surely they would to empty it. He knew that he should go out and apologize and take it – that was the manly thing to do. But he knew he wasn't going to do it.

'That girl Millie – she's got a toothache. I'll give her toothache when she gets back.'

Please God, don't let them come in here.

'No good nattering – take it out back.'

'Disgusting . . . horrible . . .' O'Neill.

Silence.

He peered around the door. Down the hall was another door covered with green baize – notices were stuck in the lattice tapes of it. That must be where they went.

God, he'd never be able to face them – and they'd tell Fenders as well, everybody.

He spent most of the first few days in his bedroom writing a long letter to his father on toilet paper – (English toilet paper made much better airmail bond, he soon found out, than it did toilet paper). He told his father that he was always cold and always hungry . . . he wanted to tell about his homesickness – but how do you tell a grown-up about homesickness? He covered the horrors of the convoy at great length – even a lot of made-up stuff about a submarine that surfaced and shelled them. He said that he didn't think that Chris was ever going to arrive and finally, he begged his father to, somehow, come over to England and help him because he was truly afraid he was going to die . . .

The letter grew longer and longer and when he

56

wasn't writing it he kept it hidden in Chris's room at the back of the drawer with the contraceptives. He didn't touch them now, he was too miserable.

He began to realize that he would never mail it. He'd have to ask Aunt Lillie for stamps and she might read the letter; well he could buy stamps himself if he found a post office – but it was hopeless, the letter would never get through the censors, not with all that convoy stuff.

He tried hard to avoid O'Neill and Mrs Pickle. When he did see them he tried to pretend he wasn't there – mercifully they didn't seem to acknowledge his existence either.

'He ought to have somebody his own age to play with,' Aunt Lillie kept saying.

'There isn't anybody suitable.'

'Well, he's got to play with somebody.'

'Well, Teddy should be back soon – shouldn't he?'

'Can I write to Teddy and Chris?' he asked one day.

His Aunt Daisy's desk was in the West Room – he could write there, she said. The West Room was, like all the downstairs, covered with pictures, big, small and middling: round frames, square frames, oblong frames. Some of the pictures were dark oils (mostly castles and streams and trees), some were water-colours and prints (a lot of soppy cherubs' heads). You could hardly see the walls for the pictures, clocks and mirrors and you could hardly see the floor for the bulky stuffed chairs and the little tables, loaded with china, you had to be careful not to bang into.

The desk was an incredibly elaborate thing entirely covered with inlaid wood of different colours – marquetry, Flemish, his aunt said – and shaped like an old spider's body.

He wrote standing up at it. The clocks ticked away, some high-pitched like ship's bells and higher, some

57

low – you couldn't be anywhere downstairs and not hear three or four crazy clocks. He wrote them identical letters. You could use a punch thing and it left the imprint, Washashley Hall, Lincolnshire. The paper was blue and smooth and rather beautiful.

He said he was lonely and not very happy and could they please come and see him as soon as possible. He signed himself, 'your everloving brother, James' which was the way Chris always signed his letters.

'Send them our love and kisses,' said Aunt Daisy.

'P.S. Aunts send love,' he wrote.

'Here's Christopher's address,' said Aunt Lillie. 'Be sure to get his number right – that's how the RAF knows where to find him.' Teddy was at his school – a crammer's – at London Road, Camberley, Surrey. Teddy was cramming to pass 'Special Entry' into the Royal Navy. He'd make it all right: Teddy was very bright and crazy about the Navy. Not me, thought James, I wouldn't go to sea again – not even if the war was over . . .

The stomach cramps continued to worry him: every time he went to the bathroom he had heavy vice-like pain in his lower abdomen. It must be an appendicitis, he thought, because he had one of the symptoms – diarrhoea. When he got up the pain continued – but less than before – and after walking about for a while, it went away entirely.

One day Fenders came in and, standing in front of the beige door, with his cap under his arm, invited him for a bicycle ride. Fenders's head was bald on top and very white-looking.

'I don't have a bicycle.'

'Don't worry about that, sir – come this way.'

'Thank you – I'll ask.'

He found his Aunt Lillie polishing silver with long

58

grey gloves on. The gloves came right up to her elbows. 'Look at me – I never stop – but I can't stand dirty silver and brass.' Yes, she said, he could go but be sure not to eat up the Fenderses' rations if he went to their cottage. 'You mustn't get beholden to them anyway, dear, so don't accept too much.'

He started to leave. 'Don't go through that way – downstairs is the servants' domain, you know – go round and meet Fenders at the kitchen gate.'

Fenders came around the drive pushing a handsome bicycle with one hand. 'Nice machine, isn't it, sir? Pity Mr Ted didn't leave his – a champion he has, five gears n'all. But you can borrow this one from time to time if you like, Mr James.'

'Oh, thank you. But I couldn't do that.'

'Certainly you can, sir. What's mine is yours. There's nothing I've got that any Berkeley isn't welcome to – that's what I always say.'

'What shall I ride today, Fenders?'

'You can sit on here, Mr James.' He patted the crossbar. 'And I'll show you about the village.'

'But doesn't Christopher have one? Maybe I could borrow his?'

'He took his with him years ago – an old Royal Enfield built in about '02, by the look of it. Isn't he a one, Mr Christopher – he don't need nothing fancy, he doesn't.' Fenders leaned towards him and said in a conspiratorial tone, 'We'll go out the front way – I'm not supposed to but it'll be all right with you with me.'

They walked down the drive.

'I thought everyone had to give their gates for scrap, Fenders. How come these haven't gone?'

'Scrap! Well, just look at them. They couldn't go for scrap. Why, your uncle, the Master – God rest his soul – brought them gates all the way from Italy. And a pretty penny they must have cost him too. Just look at 'em. Antiques, you know. Big, aren't they? It took four horses to haul them from Lincoln – but that was before my time of course. Scrap! I should say not – the Master would turn in his grave. Washashley is a showplace, you know. You can't muck about with a showplace as if it was just ordinary.

'Jump on, Mr James, and we'll be off.'

James got on. He'd been ridden this way many times in Bermuda – by his father, by his brothers – but now he felt very uncomfortable. He didn't like to be the cause of such effort, and he resented, somehow, the man's physical proximity. He didn't really know him after all . . .

James pointed to some iron railings that seemed to be set horizontally in front of every gate, as if to catch water. 'What are those?'

'Those are game keeps – to keep the deer herd from straying on to the public road. See look, over there – there's some of the deer. Beautiful, aren't they?'

'Lovely, and they are so delicate.'

'They are the best – the rarest – all the way from China. Grey-white, they are – you see, Mr James, 'tis said they were bred to match the walls of the Cathedral.'

They were west of the house and further west beyond them stretched the parkland, green slopes dotted with little woods and copses – of oak and elm and holly.

'That's all the Hall's land – see, right over to that ridge. Three odd miles. Beyond that is Heighington – Heighington Hall. Heighington's all right but not a showplace like us. It's said that in olden times there was an underground tunnel connecting the two houses.'

60

'No fooling. Really?'

'Yes. Really. No one can find it now – but it's there. It was to get away from the police, see, hundreds of years ago. Police raid one house and the family flees through the tunnel to t'other – see?'

'Gosh, I wish we could find it.'

'You'll have to ask your brothers – they've looked many times. In the wine cellar they look – it used to be a dungeon, once.'

The village stood on a hill and the hill was crowned by the Hall and the church. Beyond them, now, James's eye could take in a panoramic view of the valley of the Lee.

Fenders stopped his bicycle, and pointed off to the northwest. 'See, that's where the workers live – the factory workers of Lincoln, Ruston's mainly.' Across the river there were flatlands: row upon row of dark brick slums and ugly black factories.

But from where they were James's eye was drawn to the ancient city of Lincoln, on the hill beyond, a much larger hill than theirs and much more magnificently crowned – by the Cathedral with its three gigantic towers rising in misty majesty against the blue winter sky.

'They say there's a whole squadron of Spitfires – a whole squadron – just to protect the Cathedral. Something isn't it?

' 'Course I'm not Church meself – although I used to go to please the Master – everybody *had* to. The whole staff, you know. I don't think he even knew I was Presbyterian – or cared – but I didn't mind. He was a fine gentleman was the Reverend Mr Albert.'

'Yes, I don't remember him very well – except that he was big.'

'Big. I should say so. Six feet four. All of them was big – him and his two brothers. Why, it was said that

61

together they totalled over nineteen feet – the three of them. Nineteen feet, Mr James. They was quite a sight walking down Pall Mall, you know, arm in arm. They had a house on Pall Mall, Number 65 – Number 67 was the Master's club, and after that is no number, just St James's Palace.

'They were well known toffs – rakes, you know. But that was before my time – I was working for Solly Joell, then, you know. The Diamond King – from South Africa. Lad, did they have money – not real gentry of course – not aristocracy like you Berkeleys, mind – but, oh were they rich. I was just a lad then. A junior chauffeur like. We had eight Rollses. Mr Joell bought four new ones right off the stand from the Motor Show – every year, he did. Did you know I once drove the Prince of Wales? Yeah, what a lad he was. There's some stories I could tell you, sir, and no mistake.'

Fenders rode him all around the village. It seemed to be divided into two squares, one on the top of the hill, and the other on the slope from the graveyard down to the Lincoln Road. The lower square contained the shops, pubs and the homes of most of the villagers. They were, from the outside at least, a picturesque group of buildings all built of grey-yellow Lincoln stone and all roofed with thatch, curved red tiles or mossy slate.

'That there's where the chapel folk go.' Fenders pointed to an ugly little brick building across the Lincoln Road all by itself on marshy ground. 'Most of the village are Chapel, you know – not Church. But for goodness sake don't tell the Misses. Church has fallen off terrible since your uncle died too.

'Chapel's getting bigger and Church smaller but both are losing to the Socialists and Communists in Lincoln – meeting every Saturday night. In fact, Mr James, just betwixt the two of us, the only lot that stays constant are the oldest of them all – those who like their spirits straight from the bottle.'

The upper square contained the Hall and its twenty-seven dependent cottages. Separating the two squares was the Norman church and the village green with its Cross – yet the village green was also directly behind the Hall, just beyond the stables and out-buildings, just as the church was right beside it – so close, as James knew, that he could almost spit on it out of his window.

To the south, the walls around the Hall's grounds, separating it from the cottages, were not only as thick and high as the wall separating it from the church, but topped with jagged broken glass.

They stopped at the village green having walked the bicycle up the hill from the Lincoln Road. Fenders pointed over to the left.

'Don't it look big from here?'

From the front the Hall appeared only two storeys high – but from the back it was four.

'Bet you didn't know those rooms at the top existed, eh? For the staff – just windows at the back, see – that way the family don't never know they're there – privacy-like. There was seventeen staff when I first came in '29 – and there had been twenty-four or more before that.'

Some of the cottages in the upper square were ugly ('the Master built them after the First War – for renting, mostly') but most of them were as old as the Hall and looked very solid and cosy.

'These are the only two places don't belong to the estate – your auntie, the Madame, that is. That one's the New Rectory –'

'New? It looks hundreds of years old.'

'Can't help that – that's what it is. The vicar's in the Army, you know, and his old dad takes services

63

now – deaf as a post, can hardly walk and talks all wobbly – must be ninety if he's a day.

'And this place here,' he leaned over and spoke in his conspiratorial tone again, 'belongs to a joiner bloke. Red as a letter box, he is. Stony, he is – won't speak to no one. Can't think how he ever came by the house – as you can see it must've been part of the Hall once. But he's always owned it.'

The house was old, big and flush on the road so that its front door opened right on to it. James liked the look of it – the windows were big and each pane was sparkling clean – the door was heavy and handsome and possessed of a large glistening brass knocker.

'Dickens his name is. He has seven sons and all of 'em miserable, just like him. One about your age too – he's not so bad, really, the little one. Dicky Dickens. Pity, you could be chums with him – but they're just working folk so you couldn't – especially them being Communists and all.'

James wondered what a Communist was. He thought, vaguely, that Communists were Russians and the Russians were their allies. But he could remember a time when he hated the Russians because they had beaten and eaten up little Finland. Nowadays Russians were their friends and great guys – it was very confusing.

'I don't hold with Communists and Socialists – a bad lot, the lot of them. No respect for their betters. If they take over the world it'll be a sorry mess – they'd like to make themselves as good as me and me as good as you. Isn't that ridiculous? Respect for your betters – that's what Great Britain's built on.'

What's he really saying, James thought? He's trying to impress me with his loyalty. There was always something hidden – a secret – behind most things people said. He always wanted to find out what

64

it was – it was wicked of him, he knew, but he did. Perhaps Fenders envies this man, is jealous of his house.

'My cottage is right over there,' Fenders said, pointing to the nearest brick bungalow. 'One of the new ones – one of the best. You can come over any time you've a mind. My house is yours and my Missus knows it.'

'Thank you very much . . .'

'Mr Ted is over with us most of the time he's home – a rum lad is Mr Ted. And Mr Christopher's over a good deal himself. Come on, maybe the Missus can scare up some tea.'

'Thank you – what's that, there, Fenders?'

'That's one of the new village pumps. No one has running water you know – except at the Hall and Mr Barber, the lawyer – but at least we have pressure water now, we don't have to pump like we used to and there's four pumps instead of only one.'

The pump, at the side of the road, was painted silver at the top and straw was tied all around the sides – the whole thing looked like a big cock in a straw jacket.

Cut that out, James told himself. One of these days you'll go slightly nuts and start saying your thoughts right out loud – then you'll be for it.

They went in at a little wooden gate and walked round the back. James was glad the ride was over – his behind ached from the crossbar and when Fenders had leaned forward to make his conspiratorial remarks his breath was awful – stale smoke and greasy sausages.

They went through the back door into the little porch. Fenders wiped his feet elaborately, James did the same. A dog started barking. Fenders opened the next door. 'Mother, we're here – shut up, Flossy, you moth-eaten old bitch.' Fenders grabbed the dog, a dirty-white Pekinese, by the ears and wiggled them back and forth, roughly. 'Aren't you an awful old thing, then.' From his voice it was hard to tell whether he was being affectionate or cruel. Then the dog yipped in pain, growled and tried to bite him. 'Missed me again, Flossy,' he said, and banged her on the head with the heel of his fist and turned to James, laughing.

James smiled. 'She's a fine dog.'

'Yes. Pedigreed and all, you know.'

Mrs Fenders, a dark, gaunt woman, came in wearing a garish flowered frock – put on for his benefit, he guessed. He was afraid that he might have winced at the sight of the dress – and so he smiled again, to cover it, if he had. (He had a rubber face, his mother said, you could always tell what he was thinking. He had to be careful of that.)

She curtseyed. Her eyes, behind impossibly thick glasses, looked like small blue jellyfish.

He bowed. 'How do you do . . ?' He didn't know what he should call her. 'It's a lovely cottage you have.'

The furniture, packed in the little room, was a sort of modern medieval oak, glistening with wax. A little fire laughed in the grate of the immaculately blacked stove. Everything had obviously just been cleaned.

'Our little house is always open to you, Mr James,' Mrs Fenders said. 'Humble as it may be – it's always open to any Berkeley.'

'Mr James knows that – now come on, woman, get us a cup of tea.'

'Shan't be a moment –'

'Come on, sir, I'll show you around.'

'– kettle's on.'

There was a front parlour beyond – that looked as if no one ever used it – with stuffed furniture and a glass-fronted cabinet, prints of Highland scenes on the walls and china souvenirs everywhere: Skegness, Blackpool, Edinburgh ... a little china chamber pot with a picture of Hitler at the bottom. 'Drop your ashes on old Nasti – The Violator of Po-land.'

James admired it all, playing the role of the young master the way he believed Fenders wanted him to.

'Every stick of it's ours – there's not many in the village as well off as us, I don't mind saying. And we've the end bungalow and a bigger garden than anyone – I grow all our vegetables meself.

'Well, are you ready, woman?' Fenders shouted.

'It's really been ready for half an hour, Bob,' she said timidly from the next room.

The daughter came in. She was younger than James, about eleven he guessed, heavyset and dark – very like her father. She looked at James and tittered.

'Come here and give Mr James a curtsey,' Fenders said sternly. 'This is our Rosie, Mr James.'

Rosie tittered again.

Fenders went towards her with his hand raised as if to cuff her. Embarrassed, James realized that he wasn't fooling.

Rosie bobbed, holding her skirt – a pink party affair – out with each of her hands. 'Pleasta meetcha, I'm sure.'

'A fine way to talk,' Fenders said gruffly. 'Mind your manners, my girl, or you're for it. It's, "How do you do, Mr James". Say it.'

'How to do, *Mr* James.'

'That's better – but not much. Now go help your mother.'

To James: 'She never used to talk that terrible way – picked up that accent in school.'

Back in the kitchen James was given the best chair by the fire. Fenders sat opposite him in the only other armchair. Mrs Fenders had laid a white linen tablecloth and was busy setting out places with her best china.

'Mr James and me'll have ours here.'

'Oh, no Bob. I'm sure Mr James would like to sit at the table.'

'I don't mind really.'

'We'll sit here, woman.'

He suffered through a tea of bread, butter, jam, buns and heavy fruit-cake. He knew they could ill afford such luxuries in money or rations but he knew also that he must accept them. The tea was dark and bitter; the butter tasted peculiar and the fruit-cake was sickeningly sweet.

'Is everything all right then?' said Mrs Fenders.

'Oh, it's delicious,' James said smiling. 'Thank you most awfully.'

'Well, how do you like the Hall, Mr James?'

'Very much, thank you.'

'Very run down, sir, but you wait 'till after the War. We'll be back in shape – we'll show them what the Berkeleys are. Mind you, the Misses do their best – Miss Lillie especially –'

'Oh, Bob, Miss Daisy is always busy in the garden – pruning and such.'

'Yes, dear,' he put a derisive inflexion on the word. 'She's fragile, I know. Excuse me, sir, but if Miss Daisy did in a year what Miss Lillie does in a day – she'd have a heart-attack.'

'Bob!'

'Don't misunderstand me, Mr James, makes me proper sick to see either of 'em doing anything – they weren't born to it.'

'Even before the War you couldn't stop Miss Lillie – oh, the Master did depend on her so.'

'Well, the Hall just can't afford the staff right now – that's all. Half of them are in the forces

68

anyway – even the girls. If not they're on war work. But I keep in touch. Them that are still living here, they know that when the War's over their places will be ready again. They're waiting. Then I write to the others – I've a nucleus all ready. Just let the War be over and your father come over and give the word – and the Hall will be itself again.'

'I know he depends on you,' James said, thinking that that was what Fenders wanted to hear.

'Depend on Fenders, he can.'

Silence.

'How do you fancy *Mr* O'Neill and her ladyship Mrs P?'

'Oh, they seem very kind.'

'Coupla old busybodies – mark my words. Not a thing doesn't go on in the Hall but the whole village hears about it from those two – I bet the village folk know what day you change your drawers. If the Master was alive I'd have them out in no time – as it is, there's no sense worrying – couldn't replace them.

'Now – I'll get my keys. I've something to show you, Mr James.' Fenders stood up, gave his trousers an upward heave – he wore a belt as well as braces – and reached for his coat.

'It'll be the car, I bet,' Mrs Fenders said with coy pride.

'Never you mind what it is, woman.' Fenders went into the parlour and Mrs Fenders began to clear. You could only tell what she was looking at by the angle of her head, and she moved it about constantly with jerky movements like a frightened bird. When she looked at him, James wondered if she saw the world as blurred as the world saw her eyes.

'You'll have to meet sum of my girl friends,' Rosie said, tittering again. 'Most of them are mooch older than me.'

James blushed. Rosie had put a particular emphasis on 'older'. Hearing a sharp sound he turned to see Fenders standing in the door.

'I've told you before, my girl – if you don't mind your place,' his eyes flashed like Bella Lugosi's, 'I'm going to take my belt to you. Do you hear?'

Rosie busied herself with some plates.

'DO YOU HEAR?'

'Yes, Dod,' she said meekly.

'Have you forgotten what it feels like? – have you?'

'No, Dod.'

Outside Fenders said to James, as if he were an adult: 'These girls nowadays. I swear I don't know what the world's coming to. How I'll ever get her a position in a good house *I* don't know. She can't even speak properly. Talks like the regular local trash she runs around with. If she gets familiar with you again, sir, you let me know.'

'She seems to be a very nice girl.'

'You're too much of a gentleman to say anything else, Mr James. But no daughter of mine is going to hold any ideas above her station – not by a long chalk, she isn't.'

'Will Rosie work at the Hall after the War?'

'No, no, Mr James. I don't believe in whole families in the same job. It's enough me and the Missus working at the Hall – I didn't like that from the start, Missus knows too much. I like to keep home and job separate. After the War I won't let the Missus work at all – not if I can help it. And Rosie, well, I'd like to see her get into service with a titled family. She could do it too if she'd play her cards right. Very smart at school she is – she's just got a lot of silly ideas in her head. But she'll grow out of that, you mark my words.'

They walked down to the village green and turned left towards the back gates of the Hall. A man was

70

loitering by the wall.

'Hello, Bob.'

'Hello yourself.' Fenders gave a twitch of his lip as if he'd encountered an odious smell.

In the cobblestoned stableyard it had begun to get dark. Fenders walked with a proprietory swagger up to a heavy door and unlocked it. 'My workshop,' he said proudly. 'We still have something left, I can tell you.'

He led the way through an adjoining door to the next room. A dustsheet covered what James thought could easily be a fire-truck but was – he knew – the Rolls.

Fenders rolled the sheet back. 'Did you ever see the likes of her? 1925 20-25 with Barker limousine body.'

The monstrously large body glistened in the light of the single bulb. The windscreen, shaped like the bow of a ship, rose vertically, straight up without the slightest cant, about three feet. It opened in three horizontal louvres of glass.

'She's a grand old gal. Five hundred thousand miles and not even a decoke. Not a scratch on her – 'course nobody but me and O'Neill has ever touched the controls. Here, climb in, Mr James.' Fenders opened the front door, James sat on the high black leather seat – the place smelled of saddle soap and French polish. 'You can start her by merely flicking the Advance and Retard – not now because we don't have any petrol but when the War's over, and when your Dad gives the word, sir. Well, I'll just put in the petrol and reconnect the battery, check the points – then she'll go first time.'

There were three enormous levers that rose up from the floor on the right of the heavy steering column. James asked what the third one was.

'Dipper.' Fenders lowered the lever forward.

71

James watched, incredulously, as the headlights, which stood on long stems like sunflowers, physically dipped forward.

Showing him the back seat Fenders said casually, 'You can stand up in here – with a top hat on.'

The carpet was black bearskin and the back seat covered with a pale-coloured tapestry depicting ladies and gentlemen dancing in a formal garden.

'I drove the late Master in this to the Coronation. On the Great North Road coming back I hit eighty with himself sitting up in the back sipping his whisky and not even noticing we was moving hardly.

'After about ten minutes I heard through the telephone, "Fendis, Fendis, not so fast my good man – we must be doing fifty." "No sir," said I, "just forty-five sir." '

'It's beautiful. Can we go for a ride?'

'Not now, sir. No petrol. No licence. No insurance – nothing. But after the war . . .'

James was duly shown Fenders's trophies in his workshop. Pictures of cars and horses; rosettes of blue and red and yellow and many horses' hooves. Fenders fondled a pair of silvered hooves with both hands. 'A lot of horses are a lot better than a great many humans, you know.

'And here are my tools. I've had them since I took my course at the Rolls-Royce factory in Derby.'

'Fenders, when do you think Christopher will get leave?'

'Hard to say. One month, two, maybe three. Fighter pilots are very much needed, you know – 'course they get treated preferential – I mean it ain't like they was common soldiers or anything.'

'Is he a fighter pilot? I thought he just flew Lysanders.'

'That was years ago, lad. You'll have to ask him

72

yourself. He tells me a few things every now and again – on the QT. He don't tell anyone else, you know – I guess it's on account of me being a former sergeant and all.'

'Do you know when Teddy will come?'

'Mr Ted – he's a wry one. I dare say there's some girls around who wonder too – but don't tell the Misses. Well, I wouldn't snitch on him. He's just a lad. But it would make Miss Lillie so cross. She's a one, Miss Lillie.'

'Yes. I like her very much.'

'This place would fall apart without her. You should've seen Miss Daisy when the Master died. She went all to pieces. Did you know she locked the Master's bedroom after he died? Yeah, I had to break in – you know, when the undertakers came. Tom Watkins fixed the door next day and it's been locked since – no one's been in there for five years – *five years.*'

'Goodness – who has the key?' James wondered which room was his uncle's. He hoped it was one of the ones farthest away from his – he wished it wasn't there at all.

'I dunno. Miss Daisy I suppose. Did you know them two sleep together now? Yes, Miss Daisy moved in Miss Lillie's room the day he died. Been there ever since – the two of them in the one bed too.'

James felt affronted and guilty but tried not to look either. He knew he shouldn't let Fenders talk this way to him – it was disloyal. It was strange the way servants always gossiped to him: he supposed it was because they knew by instinct that he wouldn't stop them. It was the same way in Bermuda with coloured people – he hadn't stopped them either. It really did seem that English servants and coloured people were the same after all.

'She was potty about the Master – poor girl. He was more like a father to her – but twenty years is a long time too. Can't blame 'em. She was potty about the old man – used to sit on his lap, you know. Yes, right in the drawing-room she would – just like a little girl. I suppose they thought we didn't know – 'course I wouldn't tell no one but the family. I mean, the other servants didn't know – I wouldn't tell that lot. I mean, you get to be a man's valet for years and years and you know everything. He treated her like a daughter too – wouldn't let her do anything. And she was absolutely potty over him. Well, now she's potty about your father. Yes he's her favourite – didn't you know that? Yes, she never talks about anything else except "Dearest" and "Dear George". Of course, the Master was very very fond of your dad too – talked about him a lot. I was very close to the Master, you know – especially towards the end. Yes, he didn't have no secrets from his man Fenders, he didn't – yes, I was more like one of the family to him.'

'Well, I've got to get back for supper. Thanks very much for showing me everything – and for the tea.'

'Don't mention it. Any time you want my bike, just ask.'

'Thanks, Fenders. Goodbye.'

'. . . and Jamie,' Aunt Lillie said when he got back, 'don't you let Fenders get too familiar. He's too big for his own boots as it is. And watch out for that Rosie – she's a little terror.'

'Fenders needs a man to handle him. It's better when Christopher is here – but the only person who could really handle him was Dearest . . .'

He heard from both his brothers the same day. (He'd heard from Bermuda from his mother twice. The smell of her powder on the paper made him feel sick with excitement and longing – but all she ever said was that she hoped he was well and being a good boy and then a lot of stuff about the weather.) At breakfast, he sat and looked at the unopened envelopes on the silver salver for some time. Then he opened Teddy's.

Wed.

My dear James,

I start my exams next week. Been swatting like hell. When they're over we are all going up to London for a bit of a binge. After that I'll come up to Washashley – probably about the end of the month. Maybe we can have a binge too.

Best to Fenders and Tom – if you see him. Love and all that to the Aunts,

Yours aye,
Teddy

P.S. Welcome to England. I'm looking forward to hearing about all the ships you saw on your passage over.

Well, it would be nice to hear Teddy oohing and aahing over the ships in his usual enthusiastic way. Binge? He hoped Teddy meant the movies.

He took Christopher's letter into the billiard room and read it sitting on the red leather top of the brass bumper that surrounded the hearth.

10th March 1942

My dear Skeglee,

So glad to know you've arrived safely – at last. When you are lonely and unhappy it's best to keep busy. Walk, read – there's lots of old magazines in Uncle A's study. Some of them are fascinating:

75

*Illustrated London News*es that go right back to the
American Civil War. Also complete set of *Punch*.
There's also millions of books – of course you can skip
all the musty ones on Philosophy, Religion and
Church Architecture (and one I remember called
Hunting For Ferns in The Fens) but I think you're old
enough now for Dickens (try *David Copperfield* – no,
too sad, *don't* – try *A Tale of Two Cities*. Damn fine)
and there's a whole set of Alexander Dumas (try *The
Three Musketeers* first and *The Count of Monte
Cristo* – which is my favourite).

Then they're two books I liked at lot but I can't
remember who wrote them – isn't that awful and I
call myself a writer!? They're called *Beau Geste* and
Beau Ideal – you can find them easily because they're
right underneath that sword Sir John Berkeley used
at the Battle of Worcester Bridge (incidentally, don't
tell Aunt D or Aunt L but the Royalists lost that
battle and old Sir John wasn't in command anyway
and he wasn't killed, indeed I think he had enough
sense to run away) more later.

Later. I'll tell you more about Sir John when I see
your Mickey Mouse nose.

Keep busy, Skeglee. It's what I try to do here too
because there's so much waiting around, rather
nervously, for shows that invariably get scrubbed.

I can't get away until the first week in April and
then only for a weekend. However, if we wait until
about your birthday (the 23rd, hurrah) I could
probably wangle five days. I'll try that OK? OK.

Can't wait to hear all about Bermuda.

Don't let Aunt Lillie do too much – she's a bad heart
and pretends she doesn't. Try to get her to sit down
and do nothing once in a while. Last leave I sat her
down and gave her a cigarette – didn't work of course
but, Skeglee me lad, you haven't seen anything until

you've seen Aunt Lillie smoking. She held it as if it were a firecracker and kept saying, 'I feel like a fallen woman.' Give my love to them both. Tell Aunt Daisy that I dug up and separated the daffodil bulbs around the sundial (as if you could ever read it in this climate) and replanted same last September – she was worried.

Hugs
Your everloving bro
Christopher

P.S. Elevate chin, Skeglee, just because you're named after the east end of a westbound ship doesn't mean you have to act Dismal Desmond. OK? OK.

C

He read it over and over and every time he got to the 'hugs' he had to get out his handkerchief. Pull yourself together, you crybaby. Dismal Desmond was their favourite stuffed animal – a Dalmatian dog with droopy ears and sad/affectionate eyes. Dismal had been Chris's originally but everyone in the family had taken him to bed, until little George left him out on the tennis court and it had rained and somehow Dismal got riddled with worms. There was nothing else for it, their mother said, he'd have to be burned in the incinerator. Vicky and he had bawled their heads off, but Dismal Desmond had been burned anyway. They didn't stop bawling (whenever they talked of it) until Christopher, home from England for the summer holidays, offered to read the burial service over him.

'Yes,' Vicky said, 'but no skipping – the whole service – including hymns.'

Well, it was nice of Christopher to suggest the books and he would look at the *Illustrated London*

*News*es – but he didn't really like reading. It was such an effort and, compared to movies – or even comic books – not much ever happened.

It felt good to be called Skeglee again (the way Chris wrote a letter you could hear his voice) and remember that the skeg was the lowest and sternmost part of a boat and thus the most likely to be covered in weeds and barnacles. Chris had crazy names for them all: little George was sometimes The Stinker and sometimes Disgusting. Vicky was sometimes Widda-Widda (which was short for Dove-With-The-Bite-Of-An-Asp) and sometimes Slap-Dash (but Slap-Dash was coupled with Don't Care – Slap Dash 'n' Don't Care – and Don't Care was him, James). Teddy was always Nasti – for Nasty-Bit-Of-Work.

He went into the West Room right away and wrote to Chris. He thanked him but said that almost two months was an eternity of time and to please come sooner if he could. He said he really would rather have a shorter time soon rather than a longer one later – if Chris didn't mind. He was desperate, he said, and underlined it three times.

He wrote to Teddy too and told him that three weeks was a long time and to come sooner if he could and have the binge here and not have it in London.

Aunt Lillie found him crying. He mustn't do that, she said, Berkeleys don't cry. 'Think what would happen if the servants saw you. Think of Christopher – now what would happen if his men saw him crying? They'd never follow him into battle now, would they?

'Besides, dear, crying ruins your looks, they say. You're a fine-looking young man – don't you want to grow up to be as handsome as your father?'

'_'

'Yes, of course you do. Berkeleys are always

handsome – why, Uncle Albert and Uncle Charles and Uncle Edmond were the best-looking pages, it was said, that were ever at Court. Why they were the Queen's favourites.'

It was nice of her to say he was handsome especially when he knew he wasn't. His mother always said how good-looking they all were, describing each one in turn – except when she got to him she sort of stepped over it: 'Oh, yes, you look just fine, James – especially when you are very carefully dressed up.' Once she'd even said he was common-looking – and that, he knew, was the worst thing you could be.

'That's it. Blow your nose and get your coat and cap and you can come down to the village with me and post your letters. You can carry my baskets for me if you like – would you like that? Yes, come along then.'

Aunt Lillie shopped at the Co-operative Society. 'It's cheaper,' she whispered as they went out the back gate. 'And we have to watch our pennies. Daisy doesn't know I do it – so don't mention it. Of course I'm just learning about these things – we used to have everything sent out from Lincoln – the housekeeper telephoned for everything – terribly expensive.

'So now I go to the Co-op and sometimes I meet the gardener's wife there and sometimes Mrs Fenders and sometimes farm girls I don't even know. And we talk about how to manage with the rations and how to cook powdered eggs – we chat about the War and the weather and before I know it it's all over and I don't have to go in there for another four or five days.'

The sun came out suddenly and made the Village Cross stand out almost white against the dark clouds; beyond the Village roofs you could see the Fens with the sun striking a patch of yellow and green here and a patch there and the patches moving and then fading away and your eye picked up another.

79

'You know, Jamie dear, I used to be so embarrassed that I used to go in there and pretend I wasn't there at all. Not talk to anybody. Just hand in my list and my book. Well, after a while I just said to myself, "Lilian Curfey, you are a stupid old fool – people are just people," so now I talk to everyone. Of course most of them know enough to call me madam but if they don't I just pretend they did – why, the greengrocer's wife calls me "dearie" and if you think about it, why shouldn't she? It's rather sweet.'

They walked down the hill and cold air pricked at his cheeks and ears. There was something tingling about English air, he thought, it made you want to run and skip.

' 'Course, I don't tell Daisy about it – she wouldn't understand, poor dear – we have to protect her, you know.'

Aunt Lillie put her hand, in its big rabbit-fur glove, through his arm. 'Good morning, Mrs Colter.'

'Luveley day, madam, isn't it?'

'Yes, isn't it lovely.' She squeezed James's arm and whispered, 'Used to be a scullery maid. Poor dear – her husband is a prisoner-of-war and her boy has a terrible goitre – how nice it is to have a nice strong man's arm to lean on again. You feel better now, don't you dear?'

'Yes, I'm fine. Aunt Lillie, are the Curfeys and the Berkeleys related? I mean besides by marriage.'

'No, Aunt Daisy marrying your uncle is all. There're no more Curfeys at all after us – isn't that sad?'

'Yes.'

There was something fine, refreshing, about the village of Washashley. It seemed as if the ancientness of the houses, the very stones themselves gave off an aura, a sensual aura, that was recognized by his body, his being. Also the eternal, changeless quality of the people's lives there, comforted him.

'We had a brother, you know – David. He died in the Boer War. Daisy always says he was killed – but, speak-the-truth-and-shame-the-devil, he *died*. He got some wretched tropical disease. Awful, Englishmen should never go to the Tropics. Kills 'em off like flies, Albert always said.

'Your uncle was my father's curate – think of that – yes, years and years ago. Doesn't it seem strange? Then Father died and Albert became the rector – not here of course – down in Hertfordshire, at Waverley. But Father died and Albert took care of us. He and Daisy were married when she was sixteen – a lovely wedding, the blossoms were out. Was it '96? '86? Goodness me, I can't remember. Then we sold the house and Albert got the living here and we've been here ever since.'

The days went by with agonizing slowness. Fenders had got a job with the bus company that linked the village, and several others, to Lincoln. He said he'd take James for a ride one day – he was expecting to do a run to Waddington, a nearby RAF station, and they could see the planes – in the distance, at least. In the meantime James could use his bicycle.

James was pretty sure that Fenders loaned it to him with a motive – he was sucking-up, as they said in Bermuda – but he accepted. It was a fine machine with a three-speed gear and a dynamo light.

The black and smooth English roads seemed slick and speedy after Bermuda's white and bumpy ones. He rode the bike every day and took it back to the Fenderses' cottage just before dark.

Sometimes he explored, pretending he was a ship of discovery, and sometimes he pretended that he was

81

Chris in a Spitfire shooting down German planes. The light, with its black blackout hood, was his machine gun. Br-br-br . . . and he'd zoom from one side of the road to the other, banking the machine perilously. Once he banked too steeply and the front wheel snapped inwards and he was thrown to the road. The game was shattered and he sat there feeling a perfect fool. No one was around. He got on the bike and rode away and then, suddenly, his body was racked with shivers and he didn't know why except that he'd made a fool of himself and it was an awful thing to make a fool of yourself.

Sometimes he just rode and daydreamed. What was he going to be when he grew up? Lots of things. Maybe be a famous racing-car driver with Christopher – or better still, a pilot.

Those Hindu Holy Men had come to West Hill – travelling around the world, they were, telling people about their past and future. They were certainly spooky, all right, because they had told his father, he said, things about his past that he had never told anyone – and some he hadn't remembered until then. They asked his mother what her greatest wish was and she said. 'That the brotherhood of man become a reality.' 'For that, lady, we charge you nozzings.' They had wanted to tell the future but she said she didn't want to hear about the future – she trusted in God. Then they had said the big thing, the thing his mother was always talking about: three of her sons' names would circle the Earth.

Well, it would be him and Christopher for sure, he thought. The other one would be either Nasti or The Stinker – you couldn't tell yet. Maybe he and Christopher would be famous fliers – anyway they were certainly going to be famous.

When it rained he became gloomy and frightened.

The motion of the bike was like the ship again and wet roads like the awful Atlantic and he longed for the sun and warmth of Bermuda and felt certain he would never see his home again.

But soon he learned that when these gloomy times came, he could go and catch a glimpse of the Grey-White deer – the swiftness of their moving was refreshing, almost like wind on the water in Bermuda.

If you got close enough, even their skin flicked and rippled like water . . .

One day when he was walking past the wall of cedars along the front drive he remembered Bermuda, and how he and his cousin Willy Sheringham had been in their first sailboat race together.

There were almost forty boats in the race – all different sizes and shapes and handicaps . . .

Grandfather could easily be seen watching from the upper lookout of Cedar Hill – watching through Beau Nat Durrell's telescope.

Grandfather watched for a long time and they did the best they could in the race . . . Then suddenly, his cousin said: 'He's snapped the glass closed and gone in.' 'Angry with us. We've done something wrong.'

Hours later, when they were mooring the *Longtail* at Red Hole, Grandfather came by.

It took him a long time to speak – as if he was making good and sure he was listened to.

'How many boats were in that race?'

'Almost forty, Grampy.'

'Yes – and you fellas got into a hook – a tight hook – a race with one boat. You fellas got into a tacking match.

'Let me tell you something. What's the purpose of a boat race?'

83

'To sail.'

'Yes – that too. But the purpose of a race is to be the first boat over the finish line.

'Now let me tell you something: don't race one boat. Race all forty. Never mind about what one boat does. Race to be the first boat across the finish line.'

The more he thought of it, the more he liked it.

V

One day, when he rode the bicycle out to the railway bridge to watch the trains go by – hoping each train might bring one of his brothers (although he knew it was the wrong railway line) Rosie rode up on her bicycle and stopped right in front of him.

She had on a kilt and sweater and, without dismounting, propped herself up by putting her foot on the side of the bridge.

'Luvely day, i'n't it? What are you doing then?'

'Nothing.'

'My girl friend will be along directly.'

Sure enough a girl rode into view and stopped next to Rosie, adroitly jumped forward off her saddle and stood astride her bicycle and rang the bell, once, twice, three times.

She was older, all right, she was bigger than he was and her sweater was pushed out in the right places – not big but a handful on each side – and she swung her head and torso about so that her scarf unwound from her neck. Then she carefully arranged the scarf back over her shoulders again and looked at him. She was aware of what she had, he thought, and wanted him to be aware as well.

'Betty,' Rosie said. 'This is James – he's from

America.'

'No, I'm not. I'm from Bermuda.'

'What's the diff anyway?' said Rosie.

'Are you stopping in Washashley, then?' Betty asked.

'What – I beg your pardon?'

'Are you stopping?'

'Yes. We live here.'

'You do talk funny.' Rosie, tittering again.

'Whatever did you cum to Washashley for?' Betty.

'My aunts live here.'

'Seems funny reason to cum from America.'

'I'm to go to school here.'

'Where, at the grammar school in City?'

'No,' Rosie cut in, 'he'll go to one of those posh schools – you know, like in the silly books.'

'It's not decided yet,' James said.

'Shall ye cum to my house?' Betty asked. 'We can play the wireless.'

'I don't know – perhaps I should ask.'

'Don't tell me you 'ave to ask for a thing like that?'

James was uneasy at Betty's house – a two-storey 'modern' down on the Lincoln Road – not only because he knew he didn't belong there but because her parents were out.

They played the radio.

'Do ye dance?' Betty said.

Rosie giggled.

'No,' James said, 'it's stupid.'

'He's bashful,' Betty said. 'Let's draw the curtains – it's nearly blackout anyway.'

James turned to Rosie. 'Your father is a very kind man.'

'Why?'

'To lend me his bicycle.'

'He's daft. Him and his silly cars and horses.'

'You wouldn't think him so nice,' Betty put in, 'if you knew what he does to Rosie.'

'Oh, shud-up, Betty.'

'Tell him, Rosie. Tell him what he does.'

'Shan't. It's nun of your business.'

'He beats her. Yah –'

'Shud-up.'

'– he beats her on her bare bottom.' Betty ducked a cushion Rosie shied at her. 'He beats Rosie's muther too –'

'You bluddy bitch.'

Just then Betty's mother came in. 'What's all this, then?'

She was a large handsome but coarse-looking woman carrying a big leather shopping-bag. 'Muther. This is Rosie's new young man, James Berkeley.'

James blushed but got ready to shake hands.

The mother calmly put a cigarette in the side of her mouth and lit it. 'James who?' she said, turning away from him.

'Berkeley,' Betty said. 'You know. The H-A-L-L.'

'Berkeley?' the mother said through her cigarette. 'Never-heard-of-it.'

Silence.

'Well, I'd better be going,' James said. 'It's ... it's nearly tea-time.'

'Cum again,' the mother said flatly without turning.

He hurried out.

The Aunts heard about it.

'You can't go into those people's houses, James,' Aunt Daisy said with her usual lisp. 'And with that frightful little Rosie too. Your uncle would never have permitted such a thing.'

'He needs a young man of his own age – that's all.'

86

'But there aren't any.'

'There's the Dickens boy.'

'Lillie, really – the Dickens boy.'

'Well, he's got to play with somebody – the Dickens boy is the same age and he's a good boy.'

'The Dickens boy! What is the world coming to when my own sister suggests ... I suppose you'd invite the boy here?'

'No. Of course not – but it's not as if the boy was middle-class or something awful like that. He's a decent working-class boy. Much better. He wouldn't have any silly ideas – least I don't think so. Why, they could just play outdoors. Outdoors like two birds –'

'Let's not discuss it.'

When Aunt Daisy gave him his goodnight kiss she had softened. 'Please don't do that again, Jamie. It hurts us so.' She patted his cheek. Aunt Daisy had a sort of magnetic touch that gave off electricity – but soothed immediately.

Aunt Lillie gave him the usual smacker and punch. 'You're a bit of a devil – you look just like your father. He was a young devil too – I suppose that's why I've always loved him so much.' She punched him again. 'But no more girls of that sort – you're much too young. I'm going to go and see Edith Dickens tomorrow. She used to work here, you know – but they're fine and upstanding people. Just ordinary, but hard-working and honest.

'One of their boys is even an officer in the Army. When she told me I thought she said "with" an officer and I said, "Oh yes, a batman – how nice, it's much safer to be with an officer." But he *is* an officer. Isn't that extraordinary?' She pinched both his cheeks. 'But don't tell Daisy – I mean about the Dickens boy being an officer – she wouldn't understand.' She let go of him. 'Things are changing and we have to accept change. But there are some things that must not change, Jamie dear, and they are our standards of *decency* – and this house is not going to change, it's going to stand. It's going to stand as long as I have breath in my body. Well, God bless you. May St George and all the angels keep you strong.'

'St George's Day is my birthday.'

' 'Course it is – why do you think I said it? It's a fine thing to be born on St George's Day – so was Shakespeare. But I don't think Shakespeare was a very good churchman.'

Dicky was skinny, dark-haired and had a very pale complexion. He wore strange high-laced black boots, long socks (the 'wrong' kind, his aunts said, because they had a pattern at the top: 'A young gentleman never wears long socks with a pattern – they're for council school boys'), navy blue shorts and a grey jacket with all three buttons always done up.

James found it difficult to understand his accent and his strange ways. Dicky clearly found him strange too.

'Thou art daft,' Dicky often said. 'I can't cum and play now – I've me chores to do.'

Dicky didn't get home from school until 4:00. James would arrive and follow him while he did the chores. The chores involved the animals in the Dickens' small backyard: chickens, ducks and pigs.

The place smelled terrible but James tried to ignore it. He tried to help – even with the pigs' slops.

'Give over,' Dicky would say. 'You dorn't know what you're doing and we can't afford to waste any.'

'What do you keep the pigs for?'

'Are ye daft? For eating.'

'You kill them yourselves?'

' 'Course.'

'Do they have names?'

'Pigs dorn't have names – dorn't be so soft. Where'd ye get that silly cap?'

'Bermuda. My father gave it to me.'

'It's all floppy, i'n't-it? Where's Bermuda then?'

James told him and told him how beautiful it was there.

'Well, why did ye cum here then? If it's so luvely there, why'n't you stop there?'

'I came to go to school.'

'Dorn't they have schools in Berluta?'

'Yes. But not as good ones – besides, I have to go to Fotheringham where my brother went. I can't go to Harrow – where my eldest brother went – I'm not clever enough.'

'I've six brothers – cum on, I've to fetch laundry now.'

Mrs Dickens took in laundry. It had to be fetched and delivered from all over the village. James, Dicky said, was soft because he got tired carrying his end of the basket. (It did seem strange because Dicky was smaller and much thinner than he.) Fotheringham was soft too – they didn't hold with them schools. His elder brothers had all won scholarships to the grammar school – and that cost enough, which was 'class prejudice'. Them fancy schools would soon be 'dun away with'.

James tried his Donald Duck act – it had always come in handy during tight squeaks in Bermuda. He did a very good Donald Duck act.

'Up your ass,' he quacked.

'What ye say?'

'Go and fuck yourself.'

'Why do ye make that daft noise then? Art crazy?'

'It's Donald Duck. Don't you think it sounds like

89

him?'

'Never heard of it.'

'In the movies – the comics. You know, Donald Duck?'

'I dorn't. It's wicked to go to movies – besides, I dorn't 'ave time.'

Well, he guessed, it was like Vicky said in Bermuda – swinging her crazy pigtails and with her eyes hooded in her 'listen-to-me-you-poor-jerk' look – 'Jam-Jam, you think you can get away with anything – but I tell you you've got to have better than a good Donald Duck act to get by in this world.'

His uncle, James learned, was a wicked landowner who'd hidden behind his priest's robes and exploited the poor. His aunts were useless drones – although Dicky allowed that he'd heard 'ta ugly one does do summit-like around place'.

They agreed that both of their biggest brothers were officers fighting in the same war. 'My older brother is champion, he is.' James said that his was too – had Dicky ever met him?

'Don't be daft. Me go t'Hall?'

'Chris is nice. He wouldn't mind. You'd like him. He wouldn't mind you coming to the Hall – it's just my old aunts who mind – they're just old-fashioned.'

'My dad would mind – I can tell you that. My dad would flog me if I went t'Hall.'

'Does your mother hate the Hall too?'

'I dorn't know – probably.'

'But she used to work there, my aunt said.'

'All the more reason to hate it then, i'n't-it?'

'No. Some people like it – Fenders likes it.'

'He basks in t'others glory, does Fenders. He's a lackey. He'd grind the face of any worker just to keep in with owners. He's a traitor to his class.'

'He's been very kind to me – lends me his bike.'

'That's what I mean – I wouldn't lend my bike to anyone.'

'Not even a friend?'

'I might – to a friend.'

'I think I would to a friend. Do you have lots of friends, Dicky?'

'No. Don't 'ave time – I've too many chores and school is very hard.'

'I don't have any friends at all – not here. I used to have friends in Bermuda.'

'Give-over about this Bermuda place – you've your aunts and brothers.'

'They're old and my brothers aren't here – you have brothers here.'

'They dorn't like me. They treat me bad. I'm not good in school or anything. I'm much younger than all of them are – 'tis only my brother John that I like. He's champion.'

'I bet he is. When will he have leave?'

'Dorn't know. Not for ages. He's in Africa.'

'That's too bad.'

'Do you want to know a secret?' Dicky's brow furrowed over his dark eyes. He kicked the ground. 'Do ye?'

'Sure – of course.'

'Orh. I won't tell ya.'

'Go on, tell me.'

'You'd only laff.'

'No I wouldn't – honestly.'

'Sometimes I cry about my brother – just like a daft baby.'

'Well, I'll tell you a secret – I cry about my brother every night.'

'Do ye?'

'Yes.'

Silence.

'Do you think we could be friends, Dicky?'

'Aye – I don't mind.'

Dicky certainly held some strange views. James felt disloyal to his family for not defending them – but Dicky was a friend and the only one he had. Besides, he thought, what's the sense in arguing? Dicky obviously believed in what he said so intensely that he'd never change him.

James always smiled at Mrs Dickens when she answered his knock but you never knew quite what to expect from her. Most of the time he felt that she regarded him as spoiled and useless.

'Cum in,' she'd say – but then to Dicky: 'There's no time to play today – some of us that earn a livin' want tea early.'

At other times he and Dicky would be talking and she'd say: 'Shut up, Dicky, and let your brother study.' It was not unkind, it was simply final.

Only two of Dicky's brothers were at home. One, always in his grammar school uniform, never spoke but simply gathered up his books and went upstairs as soon as James appeared. The other, about sixteen, was big, barrel-chested and tough-looking and always greeted James by calling out to Dicky: 'Your posh mate is here.'

'Don't tell me that one's clever,' James said.

'He is. Won scholarship, he did.'

'I can tell that he's not as clever as you.'

'He is though – and watch it, he punches something terrible. And he's an arm-twister.'

Dicky said that his mother was 'Chapel' and very devout. They all had to go until they got jobs – after that they could decide for themselves.

'John is Chapel – least he goes when he's home to please Muther. T'uther two in forces are in Party.

92

Bully is in Party and Stephen and I are undecided.'

One day Dicky showed James into their front parlour. It was a big room with a high ornamental ceiling and a large handsome fireplace which was boarded over. James had the feeling the house had fallen on bad times – it might, even, have once belonged to a squire or a knight . . .

'This is our organ,' Dicky said with a strange cold haughtiness. ' 'Tis the very best. Even the one in Chapel is not as good.'

It was a complicated affair with an enormous bellows pump. 'Do you play it?'

'Don't be daft. I pump.'

'I wonder what this house was – I mean in olden times?'

'I know what it is now.'

'What?'

'Bluddy draughty.' He punched James on the arm and went into peals of laughter. He laughed so long it made James uncomfortable. Then he stopped suddenly. He did it quite often: he seemed to go through long periods of his natural gloom and then burst into this laughter. He seemed to want you to share it with him – but James couldn't quite do it.

Mr Dickens was frightening. He was a little man who seldom spoke, even to his wife, and never to James. As soon as he got home he took off his jacket and boots and buried himself behind a paper called *The Daily Worker*. Dicky would signal and James would quietly leave.

'On Sundays,' Dicky said, 'when Muther plays organ he goes to the pub.'

Sometimes they went for walks and talked and achieved moments of complete, uncomplicated understanding. Dicky always carried a spongy rubber ball in the pocket of his jacket – it made the jacket look

93

even more ill-fitting than it was.

They played catch from one side of the road to the other – often throwing the ball so that it just missed the backs of passing cyclists.

Dicky's hands were always either bright red or blue-looking. 'Oo, but I do hate the cold,' he'd say and flap his arms against himself like a penguin.

Sometimes they'd play catch clear around the village and end up exhausted at the top of the Hall's parkland and without a word take out their penises (Dicky just pulled up his trouser-leg but James undid the zipper that Dicky had before called a 'soft American thing – like a woman's dress') and pee together against a thick oak or beech.

Dicky's cock was small and undeveloped like his, which was a comfort after all the great floppy bananas he'd seen on the *Empire United*. Even the other peggies were developed and had cocks that seemed almost grotesque in comparison to their bodies – it made you feel stupid, inadequate and babyish. He had to keep hiding himself from them – but Dicky was the same as he was.

One day Dicky said, holding himself, 'Did ye know I was a mistake? Wasn't meant to be born at all.'

' 'Course you were.'

'Naw. I was mistake. I wasn't meant to be at-tall. My bruther told me. Dad got tight. It was May Day. Dad got tight. Muther was home from Hall. Dad comes home and just tells Muther to get upstairs. "No," she says, she doesn't want it. "Well," he says, "I want it *bad* – so get off clothes." That's what he said – my bruther told me. He said, "*Get-up-them-stairs*." That's how he talks sometimes – real common. But that's how I was born. I was mistake.'

'I think I was a mistake too –'

'Oh, shud-up.'

94

'No, honestly I do.'

'But you've a younger brother, 'aven't you?'

'Yes. I do have a younger brother.'

'Well, there's the difference, i'n't-it?'

'I don't know.'

'Yes. It's funny being a mistake – sometimes you feel as if you're not here really. Maybe that's why I'm so dumb – being a mistake 'n'all.'

'I've had that feeling of not being here at all – really I have – but I don't feel it now. And I don't think you're dumb. I think you're champion.'

'Do ye *really*?'

'I do.'

They shook on it.

At other times they had misunderstandings. Dicky had a dog, an ugly black mongrel with a tail that curled in a taut circle. Except when Dicky took the dog for a walk it spent its existence on a short chain in the backyard. It howled incessantly.

'Why do you tie him up.'

'You can't let a dog run wild. Are ye daft, he'd bite someone.'

'No, he wouldn't – he's suffering.'

'A lot you know, smarty. He's already bit Mr Watkins and the postman.'

'But he only bites because he's been tied.' James remembered it was the same with some of the dogs that Negroes and poor white people kept chained in Bermuda. 'Honestly, I know quite a bit about dogs – my grandfather has six and we have two – in Bermuda, we do. There's about twelve on the property and none of them ever bite.'

'Ooh, shud-up. Thou damn know-it-all – and leave me and my dog be.'

One day, when James had tired of leafing through *Illustrated London News*es (the real old ones only had drawings of battles and things and these he thought highly inferior to photographs; he liked the photographs of World War I and thought the trenches looked quite cosy – but then he'd come upon a picture of a ship at sea and he'd feel dizzy and close the book) he came out into the cross of the hall and was just stepping down the white marble steps (they looked wonderful and always reminded him of films about ancient Rome – 'Bring my chariot, Cissius') towards the south door when he saw a figure beyond it: pale green sports jacket and Old Fotheringhamian tie. It was Teddy.

He yelled and yipped and jumped down the steps – two feet together – and bounced up and down.

'Easy, man, easy,' said his brother, fending off his embraces and punches. 'How are you, anyway, old top?'

'Fine, why'n't you tell us you were coming, Teddy? I would –'

'Thought I'd surprise you. You've grown.'

'No, I haven't. But you have.'

'Yes, I'm nearly five foot ten now – hope to make six feet, you know. We're the ancestral ancient leaves of the jolly old family tree.'

'There you are, dear boy,' said Aunt Lillie coming down the steps with a half-cleaned silver tray under her arm. 'Why didn't you tell us? Did you bring your ration book? Certainly hope so – or we'll all starve. Are you well?'

'I'm grand, Aunt Lillie. How are you?'

'Did you pass your exams, Teddy?'

'Won't know for six weeks at least – but I think I did well in my interview. There were all these

96

admirals – a few captains but mostly admirals – and I think I got by all right –'

'Oh how marvellous – your father will be pleased.'

'It was the luckiest thing, Aunt Lillie – really peculiar really. You know, they put me through all that business of "Turn round" and then when you're turned round one asks "Do I have a beard?" I was prepared for that – there were two beards and one was the questioner. I even had memorized the decorations on each of 'em – Well, then they ask you to turn again and when you're facing them they ask you exactly what time it is: that's when you remember that there was a clock on the wall you *were* facing. Well, I snapped out the time to the minute – but then this peculiar thing happened. This admiral said he saw I was from Bermuda. I said, "Yes sir", and then he asked a lot more questions and I snapped out the answers – then he said, off-hand, "Do you know a family named Halcyon?"'

'Did he *really*, Teddy?' James asked.

' "Yes sir," I said. "Do you know a young lady by the name of Miss Charity Halcyon?" "Yessir," says I. "She's my mother, sir."'

'What a coincidence, dear boy.'

'Yes – and he blushed, Aunt Lillie. He blushed. I bet he must have been one of the midshipmen that used to dance with Mamma before the First War. I knew I was all right then – a bloody good break anyway – but I didn't, of course, even crack a hint of a smile.'

'Teddy – your language. Did you bring your ration book?'

'I had a simply wizard time in London,' Teddy said, as they walked down to get his trunk where the bus had dropped it by the old iron benches in front of the

Cross. 'Went to three flicks in one day. Tried to get in the Windmill – but they wanted too much – ten bob, or something. The Windmill's a place where the women dance with no clothes on – stripped, in case you don't know. We went to two pubs – but only Forbes-Smith, a pal of mine who is really eighteen, got any beer.'

'Where's your bike? Fenders said you had a super five-geared one.'

'Oh, that old thing – sold it some time ago. Some bounder pinched it and when the police got it back it was pretty bashed about – so I flogged it.'

He was so English he seemed almost a stranger.

They carried the trunk back. James, who had the back, kept bumping his knees on it.

'We have to go through the south door.'

'Like hell we do. Through the back – if they don't like it they can lump it.'

'Aunt Lillie said never to.'

'Haven't you caught on to the drill, old man? You just say "oh, I forgot" and that does until the next time.'

They went through the back door and into a hall with a vaulted stone ceiling – all the ceilings on the bottom floor turned out to be stone, like paving-stones, with ancient carved faces every few feet, staring at you. Brrr – spooky.

'It's like a church.'

'You mean like a bloody crypt.'

'What's a crypt, Teddy?'

'It's where they put dead people, you idiot.'

They went up some stone steps and into the Servants' Hall. It was an enormous room – more carved faces and lots of thin latticed windows. A fire was burning in the very small iron grate, set in the gigantic stone fireplace, and Mrs Pickle sat in a

98

rocker knitting with her feet on a tiny black mat.

'Hello, Mrs P. How's the rheumatism?'

'Same as always, Mr Ted. How be ye?' She just nodded to James and he smiled, but she didn't smile back so he looked away.

'Grand, grand. I expect to be in the Navy soon. Has your son made regimental sergeant major yet?'

'Nor, nor. He's still lance corporal.'

They went out the door and up more stairs – wooden now and seeming warm after the stone.

'You should see her son – Martin, his name is. Dumb as an ox. Has a head as flat as a pancake and his feet are as big as Thames barges. You should see him – he's so stupid you'd hardly believe he's human.'

O'Neill was in the pantry.

'I'll take that, sir,' he said rather feebly.

'Don't trouble, O'Neill. You'll put your back out again – and then Les Madames will be after me.'

'I could take an end, sir, if you like –'

'Just open the ruddy door.'

O'Neill's fingers, holding the door with both hands, shook as they passed. O'Neill looked down and to one side, but James couldn't tell if he still remembered the commode – O'Neill didn't ever seem to look at anyone.

In Teddy's honour they had lunch in the dining-room. James liked the room, it was big and baronial and had three sideboards and one of them was a very beautiful Sheraton one, small, with a bow front and lions' heads for drawer pulls. (He liked particularly the way the table was laid – the spoon and fork for the sweet crossed like swords over every place-setting.) The sideboards were cluttered with crested silver – urns, salvers, entrée dishes, wine coolers, and candlesticks with arms that looped the loop. Today he didn't look

99

at them at all: he watched Teddy's face and listened to his almost endless talk.

Teddy had brownish skin that always looked sun-tanned. He had brown curly hair and an aquiline nose and bright blue eyes and straight hooded eyebrows. He was the best-looking member of the family, everyone knew that. Teddy was Mother's favourite – she said he was an Adonis – whatever the hell that was.

O'Neill shuffled about in his black pumps – the buckle on one had gone rusty. Millie appeared and disappeared. Millie had awful long black hairs on her legs and her uniform smelled if you got too close.

(It was fun – and funny – the way each member of the family played games of amusing and winning a servant to his or her side. All these games were played in silence and seldom, if ever, mentioned. Clearly, Millie was attracted to Teddy and so Teddy played to her – like an actor on stage. Clearly, O'Neill watched over Aunt Daisy . . . and, very clearly, all the servants liked Aunt Lillie and so watched her play – though she made almost none. James wondered which servant would become his ally? Perhaps Fenders . . . ?)

'There's nothing we can do about it, dear,' Aunt Lillie had said. 'If you boiled it tonight, by tomorrow she'd have it that way again. Pretend it doesn't exist. And dear James – don't mention smells. It's all right to just me – but a gentleman never mentions smells to anyone, much less a lady – smells don't exist – and a very good thing too.'

James had answered the question about the first escort of his first convoy – the cruiser, HMS *Charybdis*.

'Couldn't be *Charybdis*, old boy. Must have been D

100

Class – you know, *Danae, Dauntless, Dragon* ...
Dunedin is sunk, of course. The *Delhi* –'

'I've been *on Dunedin*, Teddy.'

'Really?'

'Yes. We all did – Dad took us. In the dockyard.
They let me work a range-finder.'

'Well, she's sunk. Terrible loss of life too, I believe.'

Teddy still looked a little like a Bermudian but he
certainly didn't talk like one. He was talking of
sinking as if it was cricket or football. James thought
of the men in the water and the ship that lay there
like a dying animal and just silently slumped lower
and lower. Then he remembered the nice officer on the
Dunedin, the one with white flashes on his lapels.
He'd shown them all over – he and Vicky. The officer
had liked them – Vicky especially, he pulled her
pigtails – and given them ice-cream, ginger beer
which stung your throat. 'I'm not a sailor at all –'
White Flashes had said and blushed. '– Actually,
actually, I'm a poet.' Maybe the officer had drowned –
down, down. Maybe he'd been caught in the engine
room the way he, James, had always feared he would
be when he took the heavy pot of 'char' down ...

But Teddy ... He must say something to interest
Teddy.

'The *Ark Royal* is sunk.'

'What?'

'*Ark Royal* is sunk. I read it.'

'No, no. *The Royal Oak*, boy.'

James wanted to sleep in the same room as Teddy.
No, Aunt Lillie said, the bed was all made up for
Christopher.

'Besides, old boy, I don't go to bed until midnight.'

'Will you stay with me, Teddy, in my room until I'm
asleep?' James said when they were alone. 'You see,

101

as soon as I close my eyes I see ships and submarines and the Stukas spitting fire.' That seemed more impressive than ghosts and homesickness.

Teddy agreed to stay for a while.

'Please stay until I'm asleep – test me – after a while test me and if I don't answer you'll know I'm asleep.'

'We'll see. Depends how long it takes.'

'Please, Teddy – I get so scared.'

'Come on, old boy. Close your eyes – I'm here.'

Silence.

'Chris – do you get homesick, for Bermuda I mean?'

'I'm Teddy, actually. No. Not any more. I haven't for ages. Used to at prep school but I got over it by the time I went to Fotheringham. Come on, go to sleep.'

Silence.

'Teddy, are you going to be at Washashley now for good – I mean until I have to go to school?'

' 'Fraid not. Awfully sorry about that, old man – I have to go to Worcestershire to look at a school day after tomorrow.'

Ta-tum.

'Can I go with you?'

'No – sorry. I'm afraid that's impossible. You see, I have to get a job teaching. The RN can't take me for several months even if I do pass – so Mr Somers suggested this job and I have to go for an interview. Truth is, it's partly for your sake – your school is going to be either in Malvern or Hereford and that's the two places I'm to look for a job. So I'll be near you.'

'Please take me with you.'

'Absolutely impossible. Come on, go to sleep now, please. I said I'd wait a while – but now you're taking ages.'

'You could ask Aunt Lillie.'

'We can – but it won't work, old boy, I know it.'

'How long will you be gone?'

'I don't know. Depends how it works out – one or two weeks anyway. But I should be back before I start the job – unless they ask me to begin right away.'

'The day after tomorrow is awful – I've been waiting weeks and weeks . . .'

'Come on, don't cry. Tell you what, I'll take you to the flicks tomorrow – there's always a couple of double features in Lincoln on a Saturday. OK?'

'Yes – I guess so.'

'Well, close your eyes then.'

He did. He tried counting sheep. He heard a noise. He opened his eyes. Teddy's green coat was disappearing around the door.

'Teddy!'

'Oh, God, what now?'

'Just leave the door open, please.' Then Teddy was gone. He pulled the covers over his head as usual.

He was awakened by Aunt Lillie shaking him. It was still night-time and he felt very weak and heavy with sleep.

'An air raid, dear. Wake up. We'll all go to the wine cellar.' She gave him his dressing-gown. 'Better bring your nightlight.'

He could hear the distant wailing of the siren – it sounded like cop cars in American movies . . .

The wine cellar was down a flight of stone steps from the hall, beneath the pantry. You descended into a well of flagstones and then turned left and there was a thick wood door with iron straps and studs and an iron grating in the top. It certainly looked like a dungeon. The walls inside were honeycombed with recesses, from the floor to the ceiling, and in each recess lay a wine bottle cradled in sawdust. The floor was sprinkled with sawdust too.

There was no electric light, just candles and nightlights. There were five cots and several upright chairs and a card table.

O'Neill was sitting on a chair in an overcoat. His gas mask was slung over his shoulder and you could see the legs of his pajamas, rolled up at the bottom as if they were much too long for him, and then his slippers with his old toes sticking out.

Mrs Pickle, also in an overcoat, sat on a cot, with spectacles on, reading – or pretending to – a newspaper. She got up when they came in.

'Where's Millie?' said Aunt Lillie.

'Madam, I couldn't wake her – I shook and shook but she just snored on – the lazy thing.' She made chewing motions with her mouth and, without her teeth, her chin seemed almost to touch her nose.

O'Neill jumped up. 'Beg pardon, madam, didn't see you. I . . .'

'Sit down, O'Neill.'

'It's awful – simply awful,' lisped Aunt Daisy. 'What on earth do they want to bomb *us* for?'

'They're after Rustons, probably, madam,' said Mrs Pickle. 'They won't cum near here – but my Martin's Myrtle is down there – with the lad.'

'Everybody stop worrying. James dear, sit down there and wrap yourself in a blanket. Where's Teddy? – oh, there you are.'

'I went outside. Ruddy dark night. Can't see a thing – no searchlights and no sign of aircraft – theirs or ours.'

'Teddy. You are not to do that again.'

'No danger –'

'Well, I'll go and make some tea,' said Lillie. 'And Teddy, you'd better wake Millie – no, no, that won't do, will it? Mrs Pickle, you make the tea and I'll wake Millie.'

'I dorn't want to go up there, madam. I heard planes.'

'Well, I'll make the ruddy tea then,' said Teddy. 'I wish I'd stayed in bed. Nothing's going to happen.'

'Thou'rt not making tea in mar kitchen, Mr Ted, thou art not.'

'Sh-sh,' said Teddy and went back to the door.

There was a distant but distinct sound of aircraft.

'Jerries for sure,' he said, 'you can tell 'em easily – they have a harsher sound. Gr-gr-gr. Listen. Ours go Rr-rr-rr.'

'I'm going for Millie.' Aunt Lillie strode out carrying a square black English flashlight.

'Are they near, Teddy?' James asked.

The sound of aircraft engines was louder. James guessed that if they could hear them at all down in this cellar they must be very close.

There was a screaming noise, like tomcats fighting, from the door. It was Millie being led by Aunt Lillie. Millie simply held her mouth open and squealed. Aunt Lillie thrust her down on a cot. 'Oh-oh-help-Jeesus . . .' Millie seemed to be saying through her squeals.

'You'd better slap her,' said Mrs Pickle, getting up and wringing her tiny hands in front of her waist (which seemed no less thin for the overcoat). 'Madam, slap her.'

Aunt Lillie shook Millie. 'Shut up, girl. Do you hear? Shut up – or I shall have to slap you.'

Millie subsided into saying, in a weak voice, 'Gentle Jaysus, gentle Jaysus, gentle . . .'

There were distant thuds of bombs. The white kitchen cups on the table by James's cot rattled. Well, there's one thing, he thought, it's not as bad as being at sea. Just as Harry always said, 'Worse things happen at sea.' Then he realized it was a pretty brave remark – because, when Harry said it, with his deep laugh, they were at sea. Even if we're hit we won't have to be *in* the sea – to swim for our lives in the awful ocean. You can bomb a house but you can't sink it.

'Jamie, are you all right?'

'I'm fine, Aunt Lillie.'

'Teddy, get some brandy, please – Ted, where are you?'

'He slipped out, madam,' said O'Neill. 'I knew he would.'

There were louder thuds. Millie continued her calling to Jesus. A loud, sharp sound –

Pah-thow.

– James jumped up.

'Just a wine bottle, dear – a cork. O'Neill, have you remembered to turn the bottles?' said Aunt Lillie.

O'Neill's averted face looked blank.

'O'Neill?'

'Yes, madam. Every week, madam.'

'It must be that Burgundy again. It had a rough crossing, Albert said. Now I'll read us a nice psalm. Millie, shut up that racket – nothing is going to happen to us. It never has and it never will.

'The Lord is my shepherd, I shall not want –'

'Lor' is my shepherd, I shallot wan' –' echoed Millie.

James needed to pee.

Then he realized that his hands were wet. It was the damned tears again. He wiped his face on his dressing-gown sleeves – it was so stupid, this silent crying when he wasn't even scared. No one seemed to be looking – then he saw Mrs Pickle's eyes staring, across the room, right into his. Her pink cheeks crinkled in the candle light – she put her fingers to her mouth and blew him a kiss.

106

Aunt Lillie was on the 27th psalm when the All Clear sounded.

'Why did the two wars have to happen, that's what I'd like to know,' said Aunt Daisy. 'After all, we're all related – I mean, even the Royal Families were related.'

O'Neill said, unasked and with extraordinary clarity: 'The world was our Empire, wasn't it, and the Germans wanted it.'

'Wizard show,' said Teddy. 'Our chaps drove 'em off. Hurricanes, I think. You scared?'

'No, of course not – it was nothing.'

'Well, then, old boy, let's get to sleep – but hurry up, it's cold.'

Aunt Lillie was talking about the King's Christmas speech and his stutter: '. . . the poor lamb – such an agony for him – but I did think he was better than last year. A little better. Didn't you think he was better, Daisy?'

There were four cinemas in Lincoln, Teddy said. 'Let's take a decko at *The Echo*,' he kept saying. *The Echo* turned out to be a newspaper. 'Wizard – there's this wizard flick about a destroyer. I've seen it – but I'd see it ten times over. You'll love it.'

'It isn't going to be about the sea – I mean convoys and things, is it?'

'Well – it's really about fighting ships. Nothing frightening, old boy. The Royal Navy always pulls through and all that. You know. Come on, let's check the buses.'

They took the bus into Lincoln. Fenders wasn't driving and it was one of the new 'utility' war buses with slatted wooden seats – just like the seats on ships' tenders.

Outside the Odeon James saw photographs of the

film – men in the water with black oil on their faces.

'Teddy, I don't want to go in.'

'Come on, man, we have to get in the queue.'

'Look – I don't want to see it ... I've seen it already.'

'The flick – you've seen it? You couldn't have. Come on – there's a funny one after.'

'Please – can we go to the cowboy one at the Regal?'

'Cowboys and Indians! You must be crackers. Come to this one and then I'll take you on a binge afterwards.'

He remembered, it had always been this way with Teddy. He always got his way: arguing was useless, he didn't even seem to hear you.

The cinema really was pretty impressive. It was four times as big as any in Bermuda and it had very comfortable seats. They sat upstairs. Teddy had bought some cigarettes and lit one.

'Nothing like a good old fag,' he said, 'have you ever seen smoke blown out of the nose?' He did it.

'It really is a wizard flick.'

The lights went down. James braced himself by sucking in his stomach.

The picture had hardly started when they showed men in the sea with the black oil on them. He closed his eyes. After a while it wasn't too bad. It was one of those start-over-again films that took you back in time. There were scenes in homes and some of dockyards. Then when they showed the sea again he just closed his eyes. He did it for a long time. He'd close them and then open them for a while and if it frightened him he closed them again. Trouble was you could pretty much tell what was going on from the voices and noises – even just the music really.

The captain of the ship was a handsome man – Noel

Coward, the poster had said, the Great Star: well, he sure didn't act like a coward, but as brave as a rock – indeed James felt safer when he was on the screen. He knew what he was doing; he was even something like the captain on the *Empire United* – only bigger, not bald, and talked the same sort of way.

That's it, keep on saying – remembering – that it's only a movie. Trouble was, it didn't look a movie – it looked real. To make this film they must have had real ships and used the real sea and that was what was frightening.

He became increasingly aware that the *Jarvis*, which was the name of the ship, was going to be sunk. Of course, it was – that's how they got into the water in the beginning.

'Teddy – I have to go.'

'Sh-sh. It's the best part.'

'I have to go.'

'What, to the lav?'

James got up and climbed over Teddy and ran up the aisle.

He saw a green lighted sign that said Gentlemen and rushed towards it. No one was there. He pushed open the door of a cubicle and locked it behind him and just made it to the bowl and threw-up.

That bastard Teddy. That fucking fuck of a chancred-up whore's pelt. The stench of the man pee from the bowl came up at him – it was just like the ship. The room rolled and he heard the sound of ship's vents and generators. He threw up again.

The spasms stopped. He flushed the toilet and then sat on it.

All the men in the movie had acted like heroes – it only showed what a sissy he was. But all the men on the *Empire United* hadn't acted like heroes – or had they? It was very muddling.

109

After a long while he thought he could risk getting up and going to a basin and washing out his mouth – he thought he could risk being that far from the bowl.

His legs ached from the seat. They were asleep. He could hardly stand. Come on, pull yourself together – stamp the feet. Stamp. The water tasted strange. It might not be drinkable – OK, he wouldn't swallow any. Oh God damn Teddy and his bleeding Navy anyway. He'd go and find the Washashley bus – maybe even Fenders would be driving. He looked in the mirror. He seemed to look OK.

He checked his jacket, shirt and tie. No, there was no mess, he'd been careful of that . . . If there was one thing he knew something about, he thought, it was how to be sick without fouling up yourself or your clothes.

'Are you all right? Crikey, I clear forgot about you.'
'_'
'Come on. The flick's over – but they have the singing now. Damn soppy but after that there's the funny film. You'll like it, it's George Formby.'
'Is it really just a funny one?'
'Yes. I promise. You'll love it –'

There was a man playing an organ on the stage. His back was to the audience . . . coloured lights changed the organ and the man all different colours. The words flashed on the screen:
'We're going to hang our washing on the Siegfried Line . . .'
The organist got up and bowed. The colours kept changing. The organist sat down and played again and the organ sank slowly into the floor. You could see the man's hands pulling out stops and the sound went on after he and his organ had gone.

110

George Formby wasn't all that funny. He sang too much, too long and badly. He laughed at his own jokes. He talked broad north country and the audience loved it. People, James decided, liked to hear themselves on the screen – or something close to it. Compared to Bob Hope, James thought, Formby wasn't much; compared to Abbott and Costello he was even less. James remembered their zany patter: 'Who's On First?' He felt he'd give almost anything, perhaps even a finger, to hear those jokes – that would really take the War away. . .

Outside it was already almost dark. In Bermuda he often liked to live in the movie after he got out – to pretend he was a cowboy and his bicycle a horse . . .

On Sunday they had to go to church with the Aunts. They went through the little iron gate in the wall (squoin-oink, it squeaked just like a Boris Karloff movie). As usual Aunt Daisy put flowers on Dearest's grave. The grave was against the church wall, outside the chancel door, and marked with a tall cross carved with leaves and grapes.

The bells were pealing a cadence of descending notes, sounding sweet, ancient, holy and peaceful – every now and again one bell would hitch, pause a little too long and James liked that best of all . . . eternal and comforting, even in one's bones . . . All is well when peal the bells of Washashley, he thought.

Uncle Albert had been to both Oxford and Cambridge – 'very few people have,' said Aunt Daisy – and these facts, together with the dates of his birth and death were recorded on the cross. At the base of the cross, written so that you had to circumnavigate it to read it, was: 'Christ's Rector of the Parish/of Washashley and Heighington/1897-1937/ Beloved by All.'

Aunt Daisy stepped back and crossed herself.

Teddy drew him away. 'Drives me crackers,' he whispered. They waited in the vestibule outside the church door. Teddy took out a sixpence and dropped it in the poor box. 'The poor,' he scoffed. 'It's probably beer for Tom Watkins.' 'Who's Tom Watkins?' 'The head gardener's son. Used to be the handyman – but he was a poacher really. Stole Uncle Albert blind – but he's a good man at heart.' Then Aunt Lillie came smiling in with her flowered hat slightly askew.

There was no other person besides the organist in the church. They sat in the family pew and all four immediately kneeled to say their separate opening prayers. James never got further than 'Dear God . . .' although he tried – then he always waited until someone else moved first.

'Maybe we ought to spread ourselves around a bit,' whispered Teddy. 'So that it looks like a full house.' Aunt Lillie sh-shed him.

'Dearest donated that,' Aunt Daisy told James, indicating an elaborate bright painted carving of Christ and the two thieves on their crosses that traversed the arch between the pulpit and the lectern. She had told him this twice before. Uncle Albert had also donated the brass lectern and paid for new bells and the restoration of the Norman tower.

James liked the ancientness of the church. He also liked the graves in the church floor, the ones you had to be careful not to step on. Some were slate and some brass and they all had words and dates and some had the shapes of medieval men and women, their hands clasped in prayer, etched on their surface marking the bodies below. The bodies would be bones and dust, he knew, and he was not in the least afraid of ghosts because he could feel them all about and they were utterly benign and gentle, the ghosts in this sanctified

112

and hallowed place – besides, it was day-time.

The bells stopped and the bell-ringers came from behind their purple curtain and sat in the back pew.

There was a hurried patter of feet and Millie came in carrying a prayer book in a white gloved hand. In her Sunday best she looked even plainer than in her uniform. She genuflected – which was something he didn't expect her to do – slipped into a back pew and knelt down and buried her head in her hands like a little girl.

The organ stopped playing 'Jesu Joy' and started on a hymn.

520 the board said and James found it for Aunt Daisy and was about to find it for himself, but she whispered, 'Share with me, dear,' as she always did, and smiled at him as if he was someone else. You could feel it was the physical closeness she liked.

'Love divine, all loves excelling...' James had always liked the hymn. It was a good tune – but here at Washashley it was played like everything else, much too slowly. So slowly you could hardly balance on a note long enough. He sang very softly anyway. He wasn't a very good singer – as his mother always said, he sang slightly off-key. Besides, holding the prayer book with Aunt Daisy meant he was almost singing in her ear.

But it was a great hymn even slow. They got to his favourite lines:

'Jesu, Thou art all compassion,
Pure unbounded love Thou art:'

He didn't know quite what it was but there was a twist, a surprise, somewhere in the words and it made him tingle ... and the ragged, surpliced procession went past: the sexton carrying the cross (the butcher's

113

son, bald and with a prominent and very active Adam's apple), three choirboys, a choir woman, and the vicar. The vicar seemed to walk with a limp of both legs. His voice trembled but, to James's ear, he sang true. Holding his prayer book and still singing he gave a little bow of a smile as he passed the family.

The last hymn was announced.

'A wizard hymn,' Teddy whispered, 'it's for sailors.' Teddy sang it very loud and painfully off key. *Funny the way she thinks I'm off – why doesn't she pick on him?*

'. . . For those in peril on the sea . . .'

Well, that was certainly right. It gave him a lump in his throat. He had to bite his lip. *Think of something quick.*

Say the vicar farted right now?

'. . . Our brethren shield in danger's hour . . .'

A brethren shield, James thought, was the very best shield to have – he supposed Harry had been his brethren shield. *Harry, Harry. Where was Harry now?* Bucking the seas of the Denmark Strait or passing Gibraltar or sweating off Trinidad with the vents busted. 'Fucking 'orrible Yankee tub – no portholes.' Probably jumping into his shoes with the alarm bell clanging. 'Oh hear me when I cry to Thee' – 'That Greek's making smoke and will give us all away.' 'Cheer up, Faunty boy, worse things 'appen at sea.' Maybe he's swimming for his life or dead, floating face down in the water . . . *Oh fuck, fuck – the stupid tears again and Christ's house is no place to say . . .*

Mrs Pickle had made Teddy Yorkshire pudding for lunch because it was his favourite.

When O'Neill had shuffled out, James asked Aunt Lillie a question that had been bothering him for

114

some time.

'When do the servants eat?'

'Why, they're eating right now, I expect, dear.'

'But we have the food – and there doesn't seem to be enough – I mean, for us as well as them.'

'But they don't have the same as us, dear.'

'In Bermuda Dad always carves for the servants first – Grampy Halcyon does too.'

'Well, that's very nice. I've always thought that perhaps we ought to give them the same as us – but heaven knows what would happen if we did.'

'How could we?' Aunt Daisy said. 'How could we have roast beef for us and also for twenty odd people downstairs?'

'But there are only three.'

'Don't you worry about it, Jamie dear. It would spoil them – besides, they get the same amount as we do – the same amount as everybody in England does. It's all rationed, you know.'

James could hear his grandfather saying, 'Now let's see, Doris likes a drumstick – and Lavergne likes the Pope's nose – though heaven knows how anyone could.' It didn't seem possible that a person as nice as Aunt Lillie could be so selfish, so unjust.

They walked over to the Fenders to have tea. The Fenders made a bigger fuss and laid out an even more gross table than they had the first day for him alone.

Teddy told all about his exams and the interview again.

'Ah, sir. That's what comes from being well-connected, isn't it? It's your right, mind, Mr Ted, and you take it. And shan't I be proud with two of my gentlemen officers in His Majesty's service? Well, the first time you get a leave, Mr Ted, old Fenders will do your uniform for you. Why, Mr Christopher says I put such a crease in his trousers he cuts himself sitting down.'

'Oh, yes, Bob can do wonders with an iron.'

Rosie made a face of contempt. No one but James noticed it. ' 'Course I can, woman – a fine Gentleman's Gentleman I'd be if I couldn't – more cake, lads? Oh, yes, I knew you would, Mr Ted. I know my Mr Ted –'

Rosie made another face.

'– and Mr James? Come on, that's what it's for. When my Missus makes a cake it's a waste to us unless you're here. You can't be poisoned by that skinny Mrs P all the time, now, can you?'

James took the cake although he didn't want it. Perhaps Fenders did 'try to keep in with the owners' but you believed him, you couldn't refuse him.

'It'll be a proud day for me to see Mr George's face when he sees his two sons in uniform – and what about you, Mr James, sir? Shall you be in the Guards?'

On Monday morning Teddy went off with his suitcase. James went as far as Lincoln Station with him and bought a penny platform ticket and waited outside the door of the train's compartment. When the train started to move he walked along beside it. Then he ran and then the platform ended.

Teddy waved.

James tried to shout, 'Come back soon,' but his voice wouldn't work. Anyway, he'd already said it.

He walked round Lincoln for a while and didn't go back to the Washashley bus-stop until he was sure his eyes weren't bloodshot any more.

Fenders was there talking to two other drivers.

'Here he is, men, here's our James.' He was introduced to them. He shook hands with them –

116

Fenders seemed very pleased. Fenders seemed relieved that James immediately understood that certain rules of the Berkeley-to-servant relationship must be suspended.

'You're from the Big House then?' asked one of the men.

'Yes, I'm the smallest part of it.'

'Oh, he's a one, is our James.'

'Just you, then, and the two old ladies rolling about in that great place?'

'Yes.'

'How many rooms 'as it got?'

'Never you mind, Ted – it's got rooms, and many of 'em big enough to put your bus in.'

'Cor, the luck of some people.'

'It's just an accident of birth,' James smiled.

'He said it! – accident of birth. That's all it is. He said it.'

'Pity more aren't like you, lad. Well, the best of luck to ya, I say.'

The other drivers wandered off. 'Excuse me being familiar there, sir – but the likes of them wouldn't understand us. They know nothing about manners. Right?'

'Of course.' It occurred to him that Fenders was actually ashamed to call him 'Mr James' in front of his cronies – and now he seemed ashamed that he hadn't.

It was confusing: he wanted to be friends with Fenders and he knew that Fenders, deep down, wanted to be 'familiar' with him. Why couldn't a servant be a friend as well? It never worked, the family said – even the Bermuda family. 'Be friendly – never familiar.' Well, that wasn't friendly. He thought that when he grew up he'd have servants who were friends – real friends – or he wouldn't have any at all.

117

VI

The rooks were cawing in the tall trees behind the Hall when he got off the bus. The elms and oaks had pale green leaves now and some of the other trees just looked pinkish against the sky – 'shoots,' Aunt Daisy said, 'spring shoots.' England was strange after Bermuda's bright colours but England was beautiful too in a strange grey way.

He felt very lonely. It was past four o'clock – maybe he could go and make friends with Dicky again? Keep busy, Christopher had said . . .

If only Christopher would come – but it was now settled, he was coming at the end of April and that was a month away.

Mrs Dickens came to the door. 'Oh, it's you,' she said. 'Just a minute and I'll see.'

After a while Dicky came out. He closed the door after him.

'How are you, Dicky?'

'Champion, thanks.'

'Would you like to play catch?'

'I don't mind. Let's play football in Mrs Ryan's field.' They walked through the back gate in the huge brick wall of the Dickens' yard. Mrs Ryan was the tenant of one of the Hall's old cottages. 'I've me holidays now – you can cum over any time after dinner.'

'After dinner?'

'Aye. Any time after wunn. I hear your brother was here.'

'Yes – but not Christopher, Teddy. He isn't as nice. You wouldn't have liked him.'

'I didn't say I wanted to make his acquaintance.'

'I know you didn't.'

They played soccer with Dicky's old ball, putting down their jackets and sweaters for goalposts. It was difficult to adjust to such a small ball and Dicky's boots had a decided advantage. Often the boots hit James's shins – only accidentally but it hurt and James could not understand why Dicky thought it so funny. Every time it happened he'd go into one of his fits of laughter.

Later they sat down on the grass exhausted. 'I've a secret to tell you. Do ye want ta hear it?'

'Of course.'

'It's my bruther – he's Missing.'

'Not your eldest brother – John?'

'Aye, the same. War Office sent telegram to my muther. He's Missing – and they say that he's Presumed Killed. It was a battle in Africa. He was in infantry. He'd just been promoted too – to captain.'

'Oh but Dicky – that's awful. Your best brother . . .'

'Oor. I dorn't mind.' He was chewing a piece of grass.

'What do you mean?'

'I dorn't believe it. I dorn't believe he's dead. He can't be dead – not John. Besides, I can hear him talking – sometimes, I can. I can almost see him – I can *feel* him. So he must be alive.'

'Yes, I would think so.'

'Do ye? Do ye really?'

'Yes.'

'Really? You're not just saying it?'

'No. If you can hear him.'

'He can't be dead,' his voice was now a low squawk. 'I can hear him *calling* to me.' Dicky began to sob and James could see him struggling to hold himself in. The sobs came out in tortured gulps.

'Look, Dicky. The Army *have* to say "Presumed

119

Killed" – even if there's the slightest chance that it's so. They can't take the chance of being proved wrong.' He tried to think ahead of his own voice. 'Look, they couldn't say "Presumed Alive", now could they? They couldn't say that and then later have to come back and tell somebody's family they were wrong. No, they have to prepare people for the worst. If you can hear him he's all right.'

'Say that again, please.'

'What – that he's alive?'

'No, all of it about Army and what they have to say.'

In the days that followed they became, again, close friends. They walked the country lanes together sometimes arm in arm. James kept reassuring Dicky and listened to his endless recollections of John. He told Dicky all about Christopher too and kept adding that he was terrified lest Christopher got shot down.

'John is alive,' he said. '*I even can feel him myself.*' The lies seemed justified to comfort Dicky whose grief James did feel – indeed he felt as if he'd never felt another's grief before.

But he was strangely certain of one thing: that Dicky's brother John was as dead as a nail in the Washashley church carpet.

He couldn't tell Dicky that he simply longed, he couldn't wait, to see Christopher – because Christopher was coming – and he couldn't tell Dicky that he was afraid, terrified, of going to boarding school. Soft, daft, Dicky would say.

The worst thing, he thought, about going to the school was that he'd never been there and there was no way of imagining what it was going to be like – if only he knew what to expect.

Weeks passed. Fenders took him to Waddington

120

aerodrome. Fenders drove one of the utility buses this time and going out there was no one but them in the bus. James sat on the wood-slat seat next to Fenders. It was a nice place to sit, right in the front, and the bus had a windscreen something like a plane James had seen in a movie. Fenders drove quite fast and kept looking over at him and winking and laughing and they flashed by the countryside and hugged the corners so close that sometimes the bus's side brushed the hedges.

Fenders sang Scottish songs all the way and he showed James how to 'double-de-clutch'. A great rev of the engine, then the gear slammed up and then the engine roaring like a banshee. Fenders laughed again, his eyes twinkling, and maybe he did beat Rosie and his wife and maybe he was familiar but he was generous and fun to be with . . .

There was nothing to see at Waddington save a few bombers parked in the distance. They waited outside the gates for their passengers and when they came James searched the face above every blue uniform in the vain, he knew, hope that one could be Chris. Then he realized that none of the men were officers.

A man with a flash that said 'RAF Regiment' came and sat down beside him. He was now next to the window, separated from Fenders.

The man offered Fenders 'a fag' and Fenders said, 'Tar – would you mind changing places with the lad, he's with me, see?'

'Not at all, chum.'

And when they were on the last leg and the bus was empty again James told Fenders about Teddy looking for a job near where his school would be.

'Hereford, you say? I know the job he's got in Hereford. Oh, the bad lad – Hereford's where he worked in the lumber camp – last summer. He has a bit of skirt down there, he does.'

James didn't want to believe it but Teddy had been gone a long time . . .

And then one day O'Neill came into Uncle Albert's study and said, 'Pardon me, there's someone to see you, Mr James.'

Christopher! Christopher!

But it was Dicky standing in the Servants' Hall with his cap in his hand. 'Shall ye cum for walk?'

Outside, Dicky's black dog was tied to the railing. They had walked round the driveway and past the south door and past the curved green wall of cedars and past the oaks and out of the gate and were in the green parkland where the great beeches grew, when Dicky said:

'They sent back my brother's things. They sent back everything – even his shaving brewsh.' He just stood there holding the dog's rope, tears pouring down his grey cheeks and every so often his thin body gave a silent and wretched heave that seemed almost like a convulsion.

James thought hard. 'He's coming back, I tell you. You know, I had a dream the other night. I saw him walking in your gate – I did. A tall dark man in an Army greatcoat carrying a swagger stick.'

'No. He's had it. Besides, he's not tall – he's a little short bloke – Oh, God, he *isn't*. He was . . . Oor, they've gone and killed him – him as wouldn't hurt nobody . . .'

Silence.

'It makes me sick – at home, it does. They're all carrying on – even Dod. Muther's all right – she dorn't say much. But they didn't none of them *luv* him – not like I luved him. And now I've nobody. . .'

'I tell you what, Dicky. You know the Red Indians have a belief – about brothers. Anyone can be any-

122

one's brother – a blood brother.'

Dicky didn't seem impressed.

'We can be blood brothers. All we have to do is cut ourselves and then put the wounds together. Then your blood will be part mine and mine part yours. Would you like that?'

Dicky was silent.

'I would like to be your blood brother,' James said.

Dicky hesitated and then took out his pocket knife and opened it. He held it over his hand and then hesitated. 'It might get infected,' he said with dark suspicion.

'No. Not in a brotherhood ceremony. God wouldn't allow it. Give me the knife.'

James took the knife and cut himself across the inside of his index finger. It was harder than he thought and it took three tries before he drew blood.

Dicky took the knife and made a deep gash in his finger without hesitation.

They put the wounds together.

Suddenly something strange and embarrassing was happening. Dicky's dog had jumped on James's leg and, wrapping its front paws around it, was jigging against him as if he were a bitch.

The dog had done this several times during the weeks before – but never with such determination.

'Get him off,' he shouted and kicked himself free – but the mongrel jumped on him again. 'Get him off.'

'He's only playin',' Dicky said and went into one of his fits of laughter.

James kicked himself free again but the dog came back – he could see its erect, pink, animal cock – and clutched more desperately.

'Get him off, he's disgusting.' He kicked again and again and tried to run and fell.

123

The dog jumped on him. He seemed all over him. James managed to land a hearty kick in the dog's stomach. It yelped and bit him on the leg. Only then did Dicky do anything. He simply grabbed the dog's rope and pulled him away. But he continued his crazy laughter. He held the rope and bent double laughing.

James stood and fumed, then he turned and started to limp away.

'Are ye hurt bad?' Dicky called after him. 'He was only foolin'.'

But James, assaulted by a half-remembered yet very dark memory, heard himself shout: 'Go to hell!'

His voice was far more savage than he had expected. It sounded final. Dicky turned away.

James hurried off, and, gaining the shelter of a little copse, he leaned up against a beech tree – which seemed, at the moment, the epitome of strength and security – and putting his forehead against the rough bark, burst into tears.

Why me, he thought, why doesn't the dog molest him? It seemed all too likely that there was something wrong, peculiar, about him and that the dog sensed it.

It had seemed so innocent, then, in Bermuda, when they were about nine and ten – he and his cousin LeFroy Drum. It had seemed just an extension of the thrill of disobedience: like stealing watermelons or loquats or, in winter, breaking into their own summerhouse and lighting the fire and lounging on the couch with their feet up and smoking and pretending they were getting ready for a poker game.

At the Drums' house, when his aunt and uncle were away for the day and they were left with the coloured maid – who stayed in the kitchen and didn't care what they did as long as they left her alone – they would draw all the blinds in LeFroy's room and make the bright day dark and cosy. They would lock the door and then pretend to be a man and a woman, a husband and wife.

He didn't know who started it – probably himself. Certainly it had been he who had suggested that they go through the entire act: 'I'll be the man and come home and then we can start by kissing and then take off our clothes and get into bed' – because LeFroy had objected to the kissing. 'It's sissy,' he said.

But they had done it. In the locked and dark room they had entered into a different world. It was as if they became a movie. (The magic of the movie only stopped when they would disagree: '*I* want to be the man,' LeFroy said. 'No, *I'll* be the man.' Then they'd agreed to take turns.)

Dark and cosy in the room the movie began. LeFroy protesting at the kissing, but only a little, like a shy girl. Getting out of their clothes they seemed to tingle in every part, every inch of their skin – they became skin, skin and cocks, as erect as thickened asparagus tips.

They caressed and clutched at their almost identical sunburned bodies. They got on the bed and squirmed and kissed . . .

'Turn over, darling, I want to give it to you.'

'No.'

'Come on, it's your turn next.'

They tried it with LeFroy lying face down, bottom bare, on the bed. Impossible. They tried it with LeFroy kneeling. Impossible. Even when he held his cheeks apart exposing his brown-tinged ring, penetration was impossible.

But finally with the caressing and rubbing James reached the strange, utterly pleasurable, unreal ecstasy of the transcending spasms . . . Oh, oh, oh, oh

125

... What were they? From where did they come? What had happened, since nothing had happened except that his cock went limp again?

Then it was LeFroy's turn. They had agreed, it was only fair. Strange too, James became erect again – didn't he? – when LeFroy made his equally hopeless attempts to penetrate ... and then LeFroy would have his moments of ecstasy.

Sometimes they'd play like this for hours; sometimes all afternoon.

Once they'd tried it in the shower after swimming – lying, kneeling on the cement floor. It never worked the way they'd hoped. Just the spasms and being left feeling as if something was missing, something wrong.

Now at Washashley he worried: perhaps there was something wrong, sexy and evil about him – that even the mongrel sensed? For he had not left it alone there. He and LeFroy had fallen apart.

He became 'best friends' with another cousin – a more interesting one, who, like him, liked sailing in the summer, playing hockey on roller skates on a cement tennis court in the winter. (LeFroy was not much good at either.) And this cousin, again his age and blond and sunburned like himself, he, James, had introduced to the sins of 'skin'.

It must have been a year later because they had no truck with playing-acting, with being man and wife and kissing. They simply rubbed and touched and tried to stick it up each other's bottoms and gave up and then rubbed against each other until the spasms came.

It was a very evil thing to do, there was no doubt about that.

And then, worse still, he'd played about with

126

Charlie, the lower-class boy, 'the oik' as his parents called him. And Charlie's cock was developed – monstrous big. How, he had thought, could anything get that big?

It was as big as the cocks of the men on the *Empire United*. . .

But with Charlie it hadn't worked either and he hadn't even been able to have the spasms – it all began to seem too evil . . . but he had let Charlie try and perhaps he was peculiar and that was what the dog sensed . . . and with Charlie they hadn't been on a bed but down by the Paget marsh, an evil and haunted place and even if God, who saw everything, hadn't seen it, certainly ghosts and devils had. The marsh was haunted with the ghosts of slaves – their slaves – who'd died, sinking in the ooze, trying to build the path of gigantic London paving-stones to the church. The marsh was also haunted with the bones of the washed-away graves from the Paget graveyard in the downpour of '88. He'd heard about it all . . . the marsh filling up like a lake and the bodies being washed from their graves and then the lake going down like a bath with the stopper pulled and the water and the coffins and bones being sucked through the cave and into the harbour – whoo-oosh!

And the men on the *Empire United*. They were evil. 'Port-'ole Drill', they kept saying and he hadn't known quite what they meant but he was good and suspicious and then Cookie, who wasn't 'all there' really, had blabbed it out.

'Port-'ole Drill. Port-'ole Drill. When I first went to sea, Port-'ole Drill was Port-'ole Drill. Catch you looking out a port-'ole and they close the long clamps on ya 'ead and then down with your drawers and the 'ole fo'c'sle was up ya – one after t'other. Te-he-he-he.'

And Cookie was peculiar, sissy, a poofter really, the

127

men said – 'but 'armless, past it'.

And the two other peggies, the bigger ones, had once said, threatened, that they would 'fuck' him. And he had been terrified of them, what if they caught him alone?

They would fasten him in the port-hole – catch him in the galley or somewhere where there were port-holes on that evil-smelling, rolling, throbbing ship – and tear down his pants. And there would be nothing he could do ...

He'd feel the great thickness of the man-sex probing between his legs. Those things so big in comparison with his – what had his coloured nanny once called it? – his 'whistle'. And the man-sex might well succeed where the boy-sexes had failed. It would be monstrously impossible – you'd have to have a hole as big as a horse.

Oh God, he wanted no part of sex any more – and now even this stinking black curled-tail mongrel dog wouldn't leave him alone.

There was some dark memory – way back in childhood, even before playing House with his cousins in Bermuda, he couldn't remember it, yet it wouldn't leave him alone ...

Now, he was sitting on the soft grass by the great beech's trunk. It was so peaceful here. Trees, he thought, trees and grass and the sky were restful, beautiful things – they were no threat at all. They just existed green and still and kind.

If only he could talk to someone. But it was impossible. It was worse than the cowardice. Just imagine going up to Chris, saying, 'Christopher, I've been a bugger at least ten times – maybe twenty.'

God almighty, what would Christopher think of him? He certainly would never speak to him again – he might even arrange to have him sent to a reform school. Well, perhaps that was what he deserved.

But be damned if he'd let that happen: be damned if he'd tell anyone. He'd just have to live with it, live with it and keep it dark, that was all.

Besides, it was quite possible that the fantasies during goo-goos, that he did by himself, were the most evil things of all – the women he held captive in dungeons and whipped and tormented into submission ... he wouldn't think of it...

His hand smarted from the knife cut and his leg ached from the dog bite. He'd better go and soak them and have Aunt Lillie put iodine on –

Again he caught a glimpse of the fleet and lovely Grey-White deer – there – there – yes, he could just hear the tender munching of their mouths on the soft English grass.

Stay, stay, deer – come to me.

And then one day he woke up and heard the sound of the church bells pealing but he wasn't quite awake yet and he wondered why he was happy – he wasn't usually happy but there was some reason why he was today and what was it? Then he was awake and remembered: it was his birthday.

He jumped out of bed and pulled on all his clothes and then his eye saw something flapping outside the window. He rushed to it and pulled up the heavy sash – the old panes of glass always made everything outside look crooked and wobbly – and stuck his head and shoulders out. The sound of the pealing bells seemed to splash all over him, the air smelled of new-mown grass and from the church tower a gigantic white flag was billowing in the breeze. The flag had a red cross – the Cross of St George. It was the simplest, least cluttered and most majestic flag he'd ever seen. It was so beautiful it was almost painful – this

129

ancient flag of the Crusaders, fluttering from the Norman tower over the graves and the new-trimmed grass.

St George's Day and Christopher was coming. Christopher was coming at last.

At breakfast Millie curtseyed and wished him many happy returns and O'Neill even smiled. There were presents beside his plate. Aunt Daisy gave him a silver fountain pencil. 'We'll have the jeweller in Lincoln put your initials on.' (The pencil looked about a hundred years old – but he didn't mind.) Aunt Lillie gave him three shoebags of brown linen and she had embroidered an elaborate 'B' in red on them in old-fashioned script – like the top of the newspaper in Bermuda, *The Royal Gazette and Colonist Daily*. And he had an airmail letter from Bermuda with beautiful stamps on it – the King's head in the corner and then a picture of a longtail flying over water. How big and full of bright colours Bermuda stamps were – especially after the mean-looking and ugly little English stamps. It said, 'Do Not Open Until April 23rd', and inside it had a postal order for two pounds, twice what he used to get, and 'heaps and heaps of love from Mummy and Daddy and Vicky and George'.

Outside the lawns were all slippery with dew and moist and fresh and the daffodils were out and some other flowers that had heads like little white bells and some others like little trumpets and it was his birthday: he was thirteen and the sun was even shining.

He went into the drawing-room where the white marble Adam fireplace was (it was the room he liked best because it was brighter than the others and not quite so cluttered and, even he, he thought, raw colonial and former peggy, realized that the things in it were priceless and beautiful), and sat in the bay

130

window and watched the Lincoln Road. He watched and waited all morning.

In the afternoon he 'borrowed' Uncle Albert's binoculars and watched the road through them. He counted the buses as they passed, one to, one fro, each hour, ten past the hour. He waited until he felt as if he'd waited a week – he even began to feel ill with waiting – and then it was time for tea.

'You poor darling,' said Aunt Lillie. 'You look as if you've been out in the rain and it isn't even raining.'

'Well, a little waiting is good for the soul,' said Aunt Daisy. 'But I confess I've never liked it. When Dearest was away I didn't know what to do with myself.'

Aunt Lillie pulled the tea-cosy off the royal-blue and gold tea-pot. 'Christopher will be here. When Christopher says he's coming on the 23rd of April he's coming on the 23rd of April. And it's the 23rd of April until midnight.'

'Can I wait up for him, please?'

She hesitated.

'It's my birthday.'

'Of course you can, dear. Of course.'

There was a beeping of a strange car horn at just after six o'clock. James ran to the south door and flung it open and saw a blue-clad figure unfolding himself from a little low-slung MG. It was a strange man and the strange man was Christopher and he had shoulder flashes that said 'Bermuda' and the sight of the word was like an electric shock and made James feel dizzy.

He was hauling a briefcase from the back seat and saying, 'Come in and have a drink' and then he turned and dropped the briefcase smack on the gravel and shouted, 'Skeglee, old buddy. *Skeglee.*'

There are times, James discovered, when things happen to you, when events fly by so fast that you

131

have no idea what has happened until some time later when you can recall them slowly by yourself.

There were bear-hugs and Christopher's rough face (now as rough as Dad's) scratching his and Christopher kissed his neck and when he took his head away from Chris's shoulder a patch of the blue was black. 'Man, you even *smell* like Bermuda,' Chris kept saying. The other strange man's name was Squadron Leader Leatham and he kept saying, 'I say.'

'I say – this is a grand place.' 'I say, I really wouldn't mind, old boy. I really wouldn't.'

James had let go of Chris's arm and blown his nose and admired the car and grabbed the arm again and Chris had patted him on the shoulder as if he was a dog – he'd forgotten Chris's crazy pats – and the Aunts came out and everybody moved in a whirl and then they were in Uncle Albert's study and Chris gave the squadron leader a whisky from the J.R. decanter, ('It stands for James Rex – so do be careful, it was Dearest's favourite') and the Aunts didn't want any and Chris sent O'Neill for a lemon pop for him and helped himself to some whisky and without his cap his fine blond hair fell over his forehead as usual – over the funny eyebrows that went up in the middle like a gull's wing – and he said in his shy way, as if he wasn't really old enough to drink when of course he was, 'Happy days.'

'Bottoms up,' said the squadron leader and Aunt Daisy looked as if someone had slapped her and Aunt Lillie said, 'Are you a Leatham from Devon or from Norfolk, young man?'

'I'm from Chesterfield, actually.'

'Aunt Daisy was stroking the hair back off Chris's forehead. 'Dear boy. Dear, dear, dear boy.'

'Oh, I don't know of any Leathams from Lincolnshire.'

And the squadron leader couldn't stay for dinner, he had to go. He shook hands with Aunt Daisy and then Aunt Lillie followed them into the hall and Chris and he went ahead to open the door and turning he saw the squadron leader smiling a crinkled-up face (pain?) smile at Aunt Lillie and heard him whisper: 'Take good care of him, Miss Curfey.'

And there they were outside and he was holding on to Chris's arm again.

'Well, cheerie-bye, Bermuda.' The squadron leader opened the little door of his MG and slid one leg in gingerly. 'Sure I can't pick you up on the way back?'

'No, thank you. I have to take this young man to London and get his school uniform – I'll take the train from Waterloo.'

'Bungho.'

'Bye.'

Chris had another whisky and took it to the dining-room with him.'

'It's really not much of a dinner – just pork pie, I'm afraid.'

'I love pork pie, my dear, I haven't had it since my last leave.'

'Chris, what was that decoration the squadron leader had?'

'What?'

'The blue striped decoration.'

'DFC – he was in the Battle of Britain.'

'You were in the Battle of Britain – why didn't you get one?' Aunt Daisy moved her chair closer and put her hand on Chris's arm.

'I wasn't in the Battle of Britain.'

'I thought you were, dear.'

'I was flying, yes – but I've told you before. Look, it's like this: there's a lot of difference between playing cricket *in* England and playing cricket *for* England.'

133

'I don't understand cricket,' she said.

'Oh I do – used to play it when I was a gal – I was a bowler and a wicket-keeper.'

James sat across the table watching his brother. Chris looked very well considering he would be twenty-one in November. At seventeen and eighteen you were in your prime and nineteen was perhaps the best age because eighteen was a man and at nineteen you had a whole year's maturity . . .

'Funny, I don't recall any Lincolnshire Leathams.'

'Well, they're here, Aunt Lillie. His father is a solicitor.'

'Well, then – that explains it – we wouldn't know any solicitors.'

'We know Mr Scorer.' Chris smiled, first at him, wrinkling his nose, and then at Aunt Lillie.

'But of course we know Mr Scorer – he's *our* solicitor.'

Chris laughed and drank some whisky. 'I've a present for you, Skeglee, my dear – but it isn't much.'

Here he goes with those 'my dears'. 'What is it?'

'Wait and see.'

O'Neill put a silver tankard beside Chris's arm. 'Oh, thanks, O'Neill – I forgot to ask. How's your back?'

'Mustn't grumble, sir. Mustn't grumble. But bless you for asking.'

As O'Neill went by him, James smelled a distinct smell. A fart. A silent fart. What his father called 'a Butler's Revenge'. It was very hard not to laugh . . .

O'Neill went out.

'Christopher, dear, please don't speak to them at the table.'

'Sorry, Aunt Daisy. Lost-me-head. Service life, you know. Democracy and all that. But I thought it was all right with O'Neill – after all, he used to give me baths.'

134

'He never did such a thing ... Did he?'

'He did – he used to let me play boat with the soap and sometimes he blew bubbles out of his mouth.'

'Did he, Chris?'

'Yeah, with soap – it must've tasted horrible.'

'Don't say "yeah", dear.' Aunt Daisy stroked Chris's arm again. ' "Yes" is such a nice word.'

'Poor old O'Neill – he certainly was different before –'

'Is the beer all right, Chris, dear? I tried to get Jeffrey's but they didn't have it.'

'Delicious, thanks, Aunt Lillie.'

'Can I have some beer please?'

'I should say not.'

'Here, Skeglee – you can have a sip.' He pushed the tankard over.

The beer tasted bitter and the tankard was moist and beady cold on the outside. He had a second sip. Aunt Lillie looked cross.

'It's all right. Dad always gives him a sip – Skeglee's been on-the-beer since he was five.'

In his bedroom Christopher unpacked his valise. The present was a perfect replica of a Boulton Paul Defiant, about nine inches long, made out of some strange new black material. It was complete and exact even down to little bumps for rivets.

'It's to scale and everything. They're used for training – aircraft recognition. Don't tell anyone – but I swiped it for you.'

'You won't get into trouble will you?'

'No. As a matter of fact, Skeglee, and just between you and me and the German agent in the wall – they're as extinct as Pterodactyls now.'

'Did you fly one, Chris? Did you?'

'Very briefly. You see that turret there? Well, that

turret shook the Germans up, that did. They came at you from behind thinking you are just a Hurricane – and then they ran into that little item. Worked fine until they caught on.'

'Did you shoot down any Germans?'

'When I was flying Defiants I never saw any – and a damn good thing too. It had a few weaknesses did a Defiant, Skeglee, my dear.'

'I think it's the best plane ever – I've always liked the look of them. I saw them in my book in Bermuda.'

'Well, they did a good job over Dunkirk, I'm told.'

'Were you at Dunkirk?'

'No, no. When Dunkirk was on I was up in Yorkshire flying Ansons.'

'Avro Ansons – those old things?'

'Fine workhorse, Skeglee.'

'I think your uniform is wonderful – the wings and "Bermuda" and everything. How many Germans have you shot down, Chris?'

'Oh, at a conservative guess about elementy times a lemon.'

'Come on, how many?'

'A few. I'll tell you about it some time – not now. Often my job is to avoid them.'

'Oh. Can I sleep in your room tonight?'

'Well . . . look, I don't think so. You see, I snore.'

'I wouldn't mind – I get so scared by myself – I keep seeing the Stuka dive-bombers that attacked us.'

'Stukas?' the eyebrow went up even higher.

'Yes. We got chased everywhere, Chris. By wolf-packs of submarines and we were way over in the Bay of Biscay and these Stukas came. And after they'd dive-bombed us they came down low and machine-gunned us.'

'Terrible. Terrible.'

'It really was. I was on the top deck, Chris. I was in

136

a loading chain for an Oerlikon and this Stuka flew at us from the side – it came so low that it had to climb to get over the ship next to us – then it went low again right down on the water. And all I could see were these crooked-shaped wings spitting fire coming right for me.'

'Gull wings – yes. They do have gull wings.'

'And just as this Stuka was raking us with lead, Chris, the man came out of the funnel – you see the funnel was also the wireless place. And the wireless operator came out and he was hit by the machine-gun bullets and he lay there on the deck kicking and screaming . . .'

'How awful, Skeglee. Take it easy, now.'

'Yes – and do you know what, Chris?'

'What?'

'The blood ran clear across the deck and into this little thin gutter right where I was standing.'

'Well, that must have been pretty grim.'

'It sure was – I threw up.'

'But I bet you got a Stuka or two – didn't you?'

'No. Nothing. We had six Oerlikons on each side and we blazed and blazed at the Stukas and so did the other ships and I don't think the Stukas were hit even once.' And he'd made that up on the instant and Christopher, who looked a little disbelieving before, now looked painfully concerned. Oh, you sod, you must be the cleverest liar in Christendom.

'You've had a rough time – Mr Somers told me a lot about it. He is very concerned about you.'

'Mr Somers? Oh yes, he was a crazy old guy.'

'He's far from crazy, I can tell you.'

'I just meant he was strange – and he is nice. He sent me a postcard today – it just said "Happy Birthday" – but he's nice.'

'He thinks you are a very brave lad – and so do I.

137

Come on, let's go down and play Twenty-One.'

'What's Twenty-One?'

'Teddy didn't teach you? Surprises me – he's always after winning pennies from someone.'

'Chris. Teddy wouldn't play anything with me and he took me to an awful scary movie – and now he's down in Hereford with some girl, and he told me he'd gone there to look for a job so he could be near my school –'

'No, he's doing that all right. He's got it too – he's going to teach at a school very near yours.'

'Chris. I don't think I like Teddy very much, he's selfish.'

'Oh, Skeglee. You've got to understand him, that's all. Teddy's living in the wrong time – he's an Edwardian character really. Don't let him worry you. Come on, Twenty-One.'

They went down the upstairs hall. Chris had changed into an open shirt, a sports jacket and corduroys; James carried his plane. When Chris was changing, James had been surprised that his legs were hairy on one side – like a man – and sort of scrubbed smooth on the other. 'Uniform rubs 'em off,' Chris explained. James had never seen Chris's legs except when they were sunburned and all the hairs were yellow and gold from the Bermuda sun. Chris also had a scar on his shoulder. It was purple-looking. 'Gee, did you get wounded?' 'No, Skeglee, had one too many beers and rode into a barbed-wire fence on a motorcycle.'

'How many times have you been wounded?' 'Minus two times.' 'You've been wounded twice?' 'No, I haven't been wounded – twice.'

'What planes have you flown – besides this one?'

'Oh, Tiger Moths.'

'Come on – everyone's flown those old things.'

'Damn fine kite, I can tell you. That's really flying. I'd sooner fly them than anything – it's like sailing all by yourself in Bermuda.'

'Is it really?'

'Yes, only better. You fly by the seat of your pants – it's great fun. Don't even need to look at the instruments. What I fly now – well, there's not the same feel – and it's almost all instruments. No romance – no feel of wind and sky and air currents.'

'Gee, Chris, you must be a great pilot – I like to sail too but you were the best sailor – Grampy said so.'

'Well, I'll never be as good a helmsman as Grampy is, that's certain.'

'You fly Mustangs, don't you?'

'Yes. How'd you know? Teddy, I suppose.'

'Yes – and Fenders. What else have you flown?'

'Oh, Lysanders.'

'What else?'

'Spitfires.'

'Did you really? Why don't you fly one now?'

'Because, Skeglee, I just take orders. This fat Limey group captain looks at my shoulder flashes and says, "Burma, eh? That's near Indiah, isn't it?" "No, sir," I says. "It's 581 nautical miles due east of the coast of North Carolina." "North what?" he says. "America," I says. "Merica, eh?" he says. "Put the blighter on Mustangs." So here I am.'

'Do it again Chris.'

'Too tired. But you know, Skeglee, I figure that Limey started out thinking I was an East Indian, then thought I was a West Indian and finally settled on Red Indian.'

'Can I sleep in your room tonight?'

'Er – no, James, me dear. You can't. Tell you what though. I'll stay with you in your room until you are asleep.'

139

'Teddy said he would and then he ducked out and left me.'

'Why, that bastard. I used to do it for him – I'd like to have a penny for every time I did it for him.'

'I never thought Teddy was scared of anything.'

'Oh, he was – when Uncle Albert was dying –'

He grabbed Chris's arm. 'Please, don't, Chris. I can't bear to think about it.'

'Skeglee, my dear, the dead can't hurt you. The only kind of ghosts there are are good ones –'

'Don't –'

'It's true – you worry about the living, Jamie, they are the fellows who can hurt you.'

He clung to his brother and Chris ruffled his hair – he hated grown-ups who ruffled his hair but when Chris did it he didn't mind.

'Jamie, I'll tell you a funny story about Uncle Albert so that you'll know him and won't be afraid of his memory –'

'OK.'

'He was the epitome of a generation that's now gone. Let me explain: once when we were driving back from his club in Pall Mall – to home, to the Hall in the Rolls – it was a day-time drive and we ran into a bit of traffic – which was very unusual in those days.

' "Hurry along as quickly as you can, O'Neill, I've to marry a couple this afternoon."

'O'Neill said, "I'm going as fast as I can, Your Honour – it's these other cars, these little cars in the way."

'Uncle Albert's reply was incredible and, somehow, marvellous. He said: "The middle-classes have no right to have autocars – they've *no business having them*." '

'Really?' James started laughing.

140

'Truly. Amazing, eh?'

They walked down the wide stairs. 'Do you know what this is?' Chris patted the railing of the bannisters, below which were intricate carvings in black oak.

'Life of Francis Drake?'

'Oh thou Skeglee basket – it's the life of Walter Raleigh. See, here's his birth at the top and down, down, all his adventures and travels and at the bottom of the stairs – the stern of his ship. Oh, a much bigger man than Drake, Skeglee. Have you read what it says along the bottom?'

'No.'

'Oh thou unobservant, incurious ne'er-do-well. It says – come on, count it out – it's one beat for each step: "But love is a durable fire in the mind ever burning; never sick, never old, never dead, from itself never turning." Raleigh wrote that when he was in jail.'

'Why was he in jail?'

'Because he was a sailor – adventurer, a charmer, a poet, a lover – and a bum, a crook and a loafer. Know what King James did to him?'

'No. What?'

'Chopped his bloomin' head off.'

'Ugh – what for?'

'Jealousy, me dear. Sheer jealousy. That'll teach you, Skeglee. Never shine too too bright or you'll get chopped.'

'How did we get the staircase?'

'History doesn't relate. But "love is a durable fire . . ." how-about-that? And we remember Raleigh and nobody remembers the King at all. You know why? Because he never wrote *nothing*. Whee-ee-ee – come on.'

Christopher shuffled the cards like a card shark in a

141

movie. 'There's just one rule about this game – I have to win or I quit.'

'What are you doing now – in the war, Chris dear?'

'I'm flying recky – reconnaissance. Safe as houses, Aunt Lillie. I'm really just a flying photographer. Why don't you stop doing things and sit down – like a good girl?'

'I'll just polish these few things.' She had a whole tray of brass knick-knacks in her lap and another tray full of flat silver on the table beside her.

'You make me feel guilty.'

'I like to do it, Chris. I really do. What else is there for me to do?'

Aunt Daisy's knitting needles clicked away.

'Have you seen those little things, Skeglee? The little brass ornaments? – they were made in the trenches during the First War.'

'Yes.' James had seen them in Uncle Albert's study. A replica of an old-fashioned tank about two inches long with guns in its turrets that wobbled; a little rifle with fixed bayonet – all sorts of things.

'I like the boot best – such fine work,' Chris said. 'It's damn hard to work with brass – look. The brass came from shell cartridges. The bootlace is copper, I think – yes, copper. And look, you turn the boot over and it has a hole in it.'

'It's clever,' said Aunt Lillie.

'Sad – the poor blighters – that's what they had – holes in their boots.'

'Never mind – it's all over now.'

'I don't mind – I think it's beautiful. I mean – those fellas were in a living hell yet they made something out of it. Made this boot – I think it has something to say about the invincibleness of the human will to create.'

'My gracious,' said Aunt Lillie, 'whatever do you mean?'

142

'I mean – nothing. I suppose I mean I can't write anything any more and they could . . .'

'Dearest loved those little things so much. The men brought them back – you know, tenants and people – and gave them to him as a present. They were so grateful to him.'

'What for?' Chris asked good-naturedly.

'For keeping their jobs for them – things like that. Seeing that their families were all right and praying for them. He said a special prayer at every service, mentioning each boy from the village by name.'

'The tank,' said Chris, 'was invented in Lincoln – in the White Hart Inn. Imagine that.'

'Yes, it was our invention,' said Daisy. 'In the First War.'

'And then the Germans used it on us in this War – that's how they overran France. But it's the boot I love – so human, so moving.'

'They do that now in Bermuda, Chris. They say your name every Sunday, they do.'

'Oh-me-gawd, bringing Uncle Albert presents, it's primeval – they were keeping-in with the witch doctor – come on, Twenty-One.'

Chris staked him to six pennies and James knew he was trying not to win but then his mind seemed to wander into the game and he won all the pennies and then got up suddenly and paced about with his hands in his pockets.

'Aunt Lillie,' his voice was so sharp that everyone looked up. 'Can I have that boot? I mean, to take back with me. To have in my pocket.'

'You'll have to ask Aunt Daisy, dear.'

' 'Course you can have it.'

'Silly – but I'd like to.'

' 'Course you can. Albert would want you to have it.' She got up and put the knitting in her chair. 'Here.

143

Here. Take it now.'

'No, no. It's yours. Don't pay any attention to me.'

'Here,' she pushed it in his hand. 'It's yours.'

'Thanks,' he said and, bending over, kissed her cheek. 'Excuse me, I'm just going to get a drink.'

'Goodness sake don't say excuse me,' said Lillie, but Chris had gone.

'Drinks too much – poor darling.' Daisy.

'Well, Dearest – I mean, Albert – always had a drink after dinner.' Lillie.

'But that was brandy. Besides, he always said that a man didn't need strong drink until he was forty. Beer and wine were all alright – but no spirits until forty.'

'Now don't say anything, Daisy dear. Leave him alone. He may not be forty but he's fighting a war.'

'Yes – perhaps you're right. But I don't think whisky is right for him – brandy would be better. Mr Churchill has brandy – oh my goodness, we've missed the News.'

Chris came back. The whisky in his glass was dark and made funny little wavy patterns – as if it was oily.

'Did you hear the News today, dear?'

'Fortunately, no.'

'Why ever do you say that?'

'Well, my dears, I suppose it always sounds the same to me –'

'Oh, no – it's always exciting. Why remember that Sunday afternoon when you dear boys shot down all those Germans? Why, we didn't *leave* the wireless for a moment . . .'

The Aunts had kissed him goodnight (it was funny how he had relished their attention before; now he was glad when they had gone – because Chris was *real* family) and Christopher was sitting on the end of the bed. James told him about the stomach cramps he had every time he went to the bathroom – 'and I'm afraid I've got an appendicitis.'

'Why didn't you tell the Aunts?'

'I was embarrassed –'

'Well, we'll have to go to the doctor tomorrow.'

'I don't want to – he might say I have to have an operation.'

'Well, you jerk, you'll have to take that chance. You can't have something wrong and not go to a doctor – that's how people get really sick.'

'But I don't want an operation – I'd rather die.'

'Well, you won't die either way. Operation or no operation. What would Mummy say –? She'd pack you off to a doctor right away. So stop nattering. Tomorrow morning, mate – and damn you anyway, I wanted to sleep in. Now you go to sleep.'

'Chris, do you ever get homesick?'

'Yes. I'm always a little homesick for Bermuda – but if I keep busy I'm all right.'

'I'm always homesick – I mean except when you are here.'

'Well, Skeglee, you do get over it – I promise you that. I mean, you don't get over it – that's a lie – but it does get less. It gets so that you can manage. Now go to sleep.'

Silence.

'Chris – do you know what I found in Teddy's drawer? I was looking for some writing paper. Do you know what I found?'

'I think you're killing time. All right, what did you find?'

'Some French letters – no fooling, I can show you.'

'Get back in bed. I know they're there.'

'Are they yours then?'

'No. Teddy's. He bought them on a dare – I think.'

'You don't think he's actually . . ? I mean, done it to a woman?'

'No. I don't.'

'Have you ever, Christopher?'

'No.'

'Why?'

'You serious?'

'Sure.'

'Look – the way I figure it, Skeglee, is that someday I'm going to meet the girl I love. I'm looking, so I hope she's waiting. I'd like her to come to me pure – and I imagine she'd like the same from me – I want it that way.'

'I agree – but some men don't, do they?'

'No. Some don't. Some don't care. But to me, to commit that act without love is just about the worst sacrilege – I mean, just the same as to commit it with love is absolutely the best – the most beautiful.'

'Yes. It must be.'

'Go to sleep now, old buddy – it's really late.'

'Will you wait until I'm really asleep?'

'Yes.'

'You promise?'

'Have I ever lied to you?'

'Yes – once, in Bermuda –'

'OK, OK. Shut up now. I'm serious.'

The next thing he knew it was day again. He tried, after breakfast, to convince Christopher that his pain had gone – but only half-heartedly: he knew he must face the music. Life was certainly a lot of facing the music.

Dr Smith was quite young as doctors go and had a broad Scottish brogue and wheezed like a sick horse. He poked and prodded and asked James if he threw-up often and if it burned a lot. Yes. Did the pain only

146

come when he had a bowel-movement?

'Nearves – nearves, is all,' he said to Christopher.

'James did have a rather frightening Atlantic crossing – in a convoy.'

'Oh, aye,' the doctor looked at Chris and winked. 'James, is it? A fine name. Well, lad – stop worrying, eh? And don't sit on the lavatory too long – just do your business and get up. Right?'

'Yes, sir.'

'Well, pull your britches up then – you're as hearty as a young oak.'

Outside the brass sign said: James McG. Smith MD (Edin.). James walked along beside Chris feeling as if he was two inches off the ground.

Static Water Tank. 10,000 gallons.

'What's a Static Water Tank?'

'For air raids – in case the main's bust. They're everywhere. Are you happy now, you Skeglee basket?'

'Yes – thank you Chris. I was really scared.'

'I thought I'd have a look around now,' Chris said when they were back at the Hall.

'Oh, I'll come with you, dear,' said Aunt Lillie. 'I'm afraid I feel as if everything is slipping – slipping just a little each day.'

'Well, if you'd only put away about half of this silver and brass.'

'Couldn't possibly – the place would look naked. Besides, Daisy wouldn't be able to bear it.'

'Well, she certainly wouldn't be able to bear your getting sick from overwork, would she?'

'I have to keep Washashley up, Christopher. I just have to – it's my bounden duty.'

'Well, it's your life – and it's your property. I can't fight you.'

' 'Course not. And it's Daisy's property – not mine.

147

It's mostly Berkeley, so it is yours. I'm just the custodian.'

'Well, I wish you'd just custode half of it into the attic and forget it.'

They walked out the south door and into the walled garden – the gate was wrought iron and had the crest painted on a round medallion above it. It made you feel pretty important, James thought, to have your own crest on a garden gate – especially when you'd been a lousy peggy for so long. The walled garden was full of shady paths and then sudden open spaces with greenhouses, and then more shady paths beyond.

'Old Watkins can't do everything,' said Aunt Lillie. 'He only has two helpers now and they are just boys – and of course that Tom is no good at all.'

Aunt Daisy joined them. She was carrying a basket of daffodils and had some secateurs in her hand. She made a feint stab at James with the pruners. He smiled.

James thought the paths were beautiful – gravel on the mound in the middle, that made a lovely crunching sound when you walked, and moss on the side.

'I'll go down and visit the Fen farms on Sunday afternoon.'

'Oh, don't trouble,' said Lillie.

'Scorer told me that that fella Bailey is six months back on his rent –'

'I don't want to hear about it. I don't want money mentioned ever.' Daisy bent and pulled up a weed and dropped it on the path. 'Dearest never mentioned money to me once in his life.' She pulled another weed. 'Why, we don't have to worry, do we?'

'No, Aunt Daisy. There's nothing to worry about – you just have to be careful, that's all.'

'Oh, there's Watkins. WATKINS.' Aunt Daisy

148

walked away.

'Christopher, you mustn't worry about going to the Fens – if someone is behind, Scorer can take care of it. It's his job. You've a war to fight.'

'Oh, I'll just look in.'

'I wish you wouldn't.'

'You get the money all right from Bermuda, Aunt Lillie?'

'Yes. Every month. Your poor dear father – I do hope he can manage.'

'You're killing him, Miss Curfey. You're just a couple of old leeches –' (Aunt Lillie's face looked worried – as if she felt it was true) 'who steal him blind and have denied his sons a roof over their heads since – when was it? – 1930?'

'Oh, you are naughty.'

'Poor old Watkins – he looks older than ever.'

Watkins was hobbling along after Aunt Daisy. He was so bent it looked as if he was a hunchback.

'But he never stops – he never complains. I think he does more now than he did before the War.'

'Good old Watkins. How on earth does a man like him end up with a son like Tom? It doesn't seem fair, does it?'

'I don't think he minds – he cares about his flowers more than anything else.'

'If I had a son like Tom I'd be heartbroken.'

'Well, I hardly think you'll have a son like Tom, dear.'

'When I think of Uncle Albert's fowling pieces – it just makes me so livid I –'

'Well, maybe he didn't take them.'

'Oh, Aunt Lillie, who else would? O'Neill? – ridiculous. Fenders? – not on your life. Millie or Mrs Pickle? Millie hasn't got the imagination and Mrs Pickle wouldn't steal a bent pin.'

149

When they were alone James said to Chris: 'It could be Fenders who took the fowling pieces – I don't think all those silver trophies are his.'

'Well, they aren't ours – that's certain.'

'But real silver, Chris – inkwells made out of horses' hooves. They couldn't be his, could they?'

'They could. Don't worry. Fenders doesn't steal – I know. He's a braggart but he wouldn't steal. He wouldn't steal even if it was only because he knows which side his bread is buttered – and Fenders is better than that.'

'But he tells lies.'

'OK, Skeglee, forget it. But I'll tell you one thing – just to relieve your mind. Even if Fenders did steal – and he doesn't – Mrs Fenders would make him put it back.'

'Her eyes are really awful-looking.'

'Yes – but she's a damn good woman, Mrs Fenders.'

'What are fowling pieces?'

'Guns. For shooting birds. Matched guns. And these were magnificent – about a hundred years old. They must have been worth fifty quid each – I don't know, maybe five hundred. But I don't care about that. Those guns belonged to Uncle Albert's great-grandfather – our great-great grandfather. And that's what makes me so damn mad.'

'Are all these lands and stuff ours?'

'No, you dope. Aunt Daisy's –'

'But it's Berkeley land, isn't it?'

'Yes. I suppose she'll leave it to Dad and the Colonel and Uncle Francis. But some day I'll take you down and show you two places where the Berkeleys really come from.

'The Isle of Wight and Arreton Vicarage where grandfather and Uncle Albert and Uncle Charlie were all born. St Saviour's-on-the-Cliff.

'That's where great-grandfather was Chaplain Royal to Queen Victoria when she was at Osborne House – no matter, except that grandfather never adjusted to being the discarded childhood friend of royalty.'

'Grandfather of Grimsby, Canada?'

'Yes. You know those water-colour portraits in the drawing room – the boys on the beach on the Isle of Wight – the five portraits in circular gold frames –? Well, those are the three Berkeley boys and the two princes – one prince grew up to be King George V and the other they called Prince Eddy – he died.

'Grandfather never got over it – Uncle Charlie just laughed about it – and Uncle Albert, I guess, had to be rich and splendid – grand – although he was a church man.'

'Where is the other place?'

'Down in Somerset. Steyning Manor and the estates of Stoke de Courcy. It's really lovely. Steyning is a tiny old manor house and the land sweeps away down to the Severn estuary. You should see all these stone Berkeley knights, about four foot seven tall, lying on top of their graves next to their ladies.'

'Steyning Manor must be great. But we have our own knight and lady buried here at Washashley too – Sir Gwain Boere –'

'I suppose it's silly really – most people would think it silly – the family living in that one house for eight hundred years. I mean, *I* rather like the idea but most people would say that a family who live in one house for eight hundred years aren't a family, aren't people, they're a tree.'

'Will you take me to the Isle of Wight – and to Steyning too some time Chris?'

'Sure. When the war's over. We'll fill the old Flying Earth-closet up with petrol and barrel on down.'

'Flying Earth-closet?'

151

'Yes. That's what Dad calls the Rolls. Don't you think it looks like one?'

'Chris. Which family do you like best? I mean, the English or the Bermuda?'

'I like them both. But I guess I feel closer to all those seafaring Halcyons and Durrells and Beltts than anybody. All those people sailing all over the world in those tiny but superb ships – and, well, Bermuda is just so beautiful.'

'Yeah – and sunny and warm.'

'You know what I think about, Skeglee? Well, when I'm tired of England – tired of the war – I like to think about building a little wooden shack down overlooking the marsh –'

'The marsh? That's too spooky for me.'

'Yes, spooky and quiet. I'd just like a shack by myself. I'd like a wood stove and piles of books and hundreds of records. I'd like to stay there and have a little rest and peace – about seven years, I would say.'

'All by yourself? Couldn't I come and visit you?'

'What? – oh, sure – you and that skeglee mate of yours, Widda-Widda. You could both come – but I don't want anyone dropping their anchor. Well, no, you could drop anchor – I just don't want anyone putting down a mooring.'

'Why?'

'I want to think out all sorts of problems and riddles – like why is a person born six weeks premature – and what does it do to you?'

'You were born premature – sure – I forgot. But why do you want to be down in the marsh?'

'I want to be by myself, my dear. Don't you ever just want to be by yourself?'

'No – not really. I get too scared.'

'I don't want to go to a scary movie, Chris.'

152

'OK. What about a cowboy one?'

'Yes – I love cowboy movies – but I guess . . . I guess you don't.'

'Sure, I do. I've always loved 'em.'

'Really?'

'Yes. They're so relaxing.'

'Have you ever been scared in a movie, Chris?'

'Certainly. Frankenstein scared hell out of me. Saw it at the Colonial Opera House. When I got home it was dark and I threw my bike against a cedar tree and tore in the back door and up the stairs – why, I think I was still running when I got in bed.'

They decided on the double feature at the Regal. 'You call me an hour before the show starts, Skeglee. I'm going to have a rest.'

'Chris . . . Chris, will you wear your uniform?'

'No.'

'Why not?'

'I don't want to.'

'Please. I'd really like it.'

He begged. Chris remained adamant. 'Please, Chris – it makes me feel – well – safer. It's about the only way I've felt safe since I got off the ship – when you have on your uniform.'

'Oh, all right,' he sounded tired. 'Just this once.'

James jumped up and down – to be with Chris in his blue uniform and pilots's wings . . . To be a pilot was the best thing a man could be, and the RAF was saving the world – and everybody knew it, and he'd stick close to Chris so that everybody would know that Chris was his brother – they could tell, same hair, same blobberly nose . . .

And they were stared at a lot – on the bus and walking through the city and then in the cinema lobby. (Where Chris quickly took off his cap and put it

153

under his arm. 'So that I don't get saluted, dummy. No one has to salute anyone without a hat on.')

As they were waiting for the lights to go out Chris said a strange thing. He leaned over and whispered: 'Have you ever noticed, my dear, how ugly English people are in a crowd? I mean after Bermudians, all these people look as if they just crawled out from under a rock. I'd pay five quid just to sit among some nice sunburned people again – and some nice brown-coloured people. God, I never knew how I'd miss 'em – this lot are downright disgusting, my dear, disgusting.'

The cowboy film was really good, and, just like in Bermuda, James went right into the film and fought it out until the last bad guy had slumped over dead and then there was the kiss and he really went into that – but you had to pretend that you hated it: that it was sissy stuff. But how great it would be to have it, be just you and a beautiful soft girl all alone in a cosy log cabin in the tall-treed West – and you weren't small but strong and quick on a horse or a draw or a soft-sweet kiss on a mouth . . . and, my God, look at those things sticking that blouse out . .

Then the lights came up and an organ began to play.

'Oh God,' said Christopher and slumped down into his chair so that he couldn't see the words flashed on the screen.

Finally the organ played 'There'll Always Be An England' and the people sang very loud. '. . . if Ing-land means as much to you as Ing-land means to me . . .'

'Come on, Skeglee. I'm sorry. I've had it – I have to go.'

'Why?'

154

'You can stay – I'll meet you outside after the next film. You can stay if you like – but I have to go.'

'I'll come – I don't mind.'

Outside they walked along in silence. They walked over the iron bridge over the railway tracks. You could hear the sound of a shunting engine – fung, fung, fum-fum-fum-fum.

Chris pushed open a door that had coloured glass above – almost like a church – Saloon Bar. James pulled his cap down hoping he'd look older – or invisible.

'I beg your pardon,' Chris said to the young barmaid, taking off his cap again, 'but I don't suppose you have any whisky, do you?'

'Sorry, sir – we don't.' Her eyes roved around his uniform, the wings and then back to his eyes. 'I can try, sir. Half a mo.'

'It's all right – mild and bitter, a pint. And a lemon pop, please.'

She drew the beer, pulling two great china knobs – like erect cocks, James thought and shuddered – and she put the drinks down on the bar. Then she disappeared through another door.

The Saloon Bar was empty but you could hear talking and laughing from the Public Bar next door and see smoke rising over the partition.

The girl came back and put a small tumbler of whisky next to Chris's hand – the hand looked very beautiful too, with the veins standing up on the back, like Grampy Halcyon's, and the long fingers drumming. She leaned forward – much too closely, James thought, and said,' 'Drink it up quick, sir, it's more'n me job's worth – do you want water?'

'No water, thanks.'

Chris smiled his shy smile and then downed the whisky – one gulp, pause, a look about, another gulp

155

and it was gone. He put the glass down and she whisked it away. He had a big swig of beer and then put a pound note on the bar top.

She went for change.

James, seeing Chris down his beer rather quickly, gulped at his lemon pop. Prickly bubbles went up his nose.

Chris picked up the change and put it in his trouser pocket. Then, looking shy again, he folded up the ten shilling note and put it in the girl's hand.

'Oh, I couldn't, sir – not from *you*.'

' 'Course you can, m'dear,' he said.

She smiled – as if she had been kissed.

Outside they walked towards the bus-stop.

'Look, Jamie. I'm sorry about that – in the movie, I mean. That's why I don't like wearing this uniform unless I have to – I mean, all that "There'll always be an England." It makes me feel sick somehow – embarrassed. Can you understand?'

'Oh, yes, Chris – I guess I do.'

'It's all this hero-worship of the RAF – makes me sick. I don't know. It's hard to explain. It's something like when I went to a pantomime – when I was about your age too. Peter Pan it was and this damn man comes out on the stage and says "Clap your hands if you believe in fairies." And I wanted to crawl into the floor – and everybody claps like ninnies. I wanted to die. "Clap your hands if you believe in fairies" ... "There'll always be an –" It all makes me sick.'

'Don't you like flying – being in the RAF and everything?'

'Oh, the flying is fine. Forget it, Skeglee. I guess my liver's out of order, as Granny would say.'

Silence.

'Chris? Will we win the War?'

'What? – oh yes. We'll win.'

156

'Teddy says no one ever beats England ever.'

'Well, perhaps he's right.'

'When I was in the convoy I thought . . . you won't laugh, will you?'

'No. 'Course not.'

'Well, there were so many submarines – and we couldn't seem to do anything to them and I began to think that Hitler would win.'

'Well, he won't. It's the only thing that makes any sense, Skeglee – beating this bastard Hitler. He's the most evil man who ever lived – he's the worst monster of all time – and because of that he can't win. Don't worry about it – evil can't win.'

'I used to worry but I don't so much now I'm on land.'

'You're all right now, Skeglee, buddy.'

'Chris?'

'What?'

'I don't worry when you are around. No German could beat you, Chris.'

'Yeah. It's possible they couldn't . . . I mean, buddy, there are horrible people in the RAF. Why, there's a chaplain I hate as much as any German.'

'_'

'That's what I mean about people – hero-worship and crap. There are some people who just revel in other people dying. This chaplain likes nothing better than a burial service. He loves it. His eyes light up when he says the words – the bastard, all he does is sit on his bum – he doesn't have to go up there.'

'Is that why you don't go to church, Chris?'

'What?'

'Aunt Daisy says you don't go to church any more.'

'Oh, that. I do. Sometimes I just like to sleep in, that's all. I'm lazy.'

James took his arm. 'No, you aren't Chris. You're

157

wonderful. I wish it could stay like this for ever – just you and me together.'

'Come on, you jerk – here's our bus.'

'It's Fenders's bus too.'

Fenders jumped up.

'Good to see you, Fenders.'

'Oh, you do look a treat, Mr Chris. I'll say you do. Come on, I can ask these people to move back.'

'No, no. I wouldn't hear of it. How's Mrs F and Rosie?'

'Well, we was just wondering if you'd forgotten us – heard you got home two days ago.'

'Too tired to even think – and James has had me on the run too.'

'Yes. Isn't he a one? Been pining away for you, he has, sir – mind you, old Fenders has tried to do his best.'

'I'm sure you have. Very good of you, Fenders.'

'The Missus and I would be honoured if you'd take a spot of tea with us on Sunday, sir – like old times.'

'We'd be honoured too – but just tell Mrs F not to out-do herself. I told her last time – any more of her shenanigans and I'll . . . I don't know what I won't do to her.'

Fenders laughed. 'Oh, you're her favourite. You know that – nothing's too good for her Mr Christopher.'

Chris sat at the end of the bed. He looked much smaller in his civvies.

'I'm awfully scared of going to school, Chris. How many more days do I have?'

'Five. The second of May. But you don't have to worry. I'm taking you to London and I'll put you right on the school train – at Paddington. Teddy will meet you at the other end – I'll probably even know the

158

master at the train anyway. They'll take care of you.'

'But what's it like? What really happens?'

'It's just a school – you have schoolwork and games. It's like Saltus in Bermuda – only it's a better school and you sleep there.'

'I'm really scared.'

'Well, you'll soon make friends. It takes only a couple of weeks. They may tease you a bit at first – thing is, just not to rise to the bait. Don't fight back – just smile a little – but not too much. Come on, don't make a face – you can do it. It should help that I'm an old boy – you tell 'em that. God's sake, I had to go there cold – and I was nine and you're thirteen.'

'All right, Chris. I'll do my best.'

'Go out for the boxing team as soon as possible – that always gets you respect.'

'Are you sure?'

'It did in Bermuda, didn't it?'

'Yes.'

'Well, all right then – don't think about it, right now. Tell you a secret – just take peanut-butter in your tuck box and not jam.'

'Why?'

'They'll steal the jam. But, English boys have never heard of peanut-butter – I used to tell them it was a mixture of shark's oil and turtle shit. They'd never touch it.'

'Really, Chris?' James laughed and laughed.

'Tell you what, have you got a stamp collection?'

'No – only some in a shoebox.'

'Well, I'll give you mine. It's a damn fine collection too – three whole binders full.'

'Gee, thanks, Chris.'

'And we can go to London and I'll give you a quid and we can go to Stanley Gibbons and buy the newest Bermuda stamps that have come out.'

159

'Who's Stanley Gibbons?'

'It's the best stamp shop in the world. They have everything. It's in the Strand – now go to sleep.'

'Will you write me lots of letters – to The Lion School?'

'Sure.'

'I'll write you lots and lots.'

'By the way – when did you last write to Mummy and Dad?'

'About two or three weeks ago.'

'Well, I write every week. Have done for twelve years. Very important – and never miss if you are in sanitorium sick – it worries hell out of Mamma.'

'I wish I was home in Bermuda.'

'Cut it out. Then I couldn't give you the stamps or take you to London. Say, have you ever had a Frog aeroplane?'

'No.'

'Well, they're wizard. They fly too – and maybe we can find a Shuko car – well, I guess we won't be able to find one of them, they were made in Germany. Go to sleep now, old buddy. We can cut the grass tomorrow.'

'Chris – ?'

'I mean it. That's enough. If you don't try to sleep I'll leave.'

'I just wanted to ask you about making friends with English boys – it's hard, isn't it?'

'Well, it's different – they sort of hang back and wait for you to prove yourself. Just take your time – they're not as open as Bermuda boys – but then Bermuda boys like us aren't as open and friendly as coloured boys either.'

'How do you mean?'

'Well, I had a Negro friend – when I was little – who used to say that everyone was his friend until

160

they proved otherwise. He treated everyone like his best friend as soon as he met them – if they turned out not to be worth it, then he dropped 'em. I must say it sounded pretty good to me. But the English sort of say, everyone is my enemy until they prove themselves to be the same as me, then they may be my friend or they may not.'

'Sounds horrible.'

'It's just a different system, that's all. You just have to be yourself – don't be too aggressive but don't take any guff from 'em either. They used to tease me about being a colonial and sometimes I'd just kid them back. Other times I'd just smile. If they persist you can shrug and walk away – it usually works. Why, do you know I've even been snubbed for being a colonial in the RAF? – yes. But it passes away. There's an Australian in my outfit – he and I are friends. Now they call him "Colonial Aussi-Variety" with respect – 'course, he's a shit-hot pilot.'

'What do they call you?'

' "Bermuda" mostly – but I don't take any guff from them.'

'Teddy said it was better to *become* a Limey.'

'Well, that's his style. I suppose he said to himself, he couldn't lick 'em so he'd join 'em. But I've always preferred to remain a Bermudian – that's where I was born.'

'You mean Teddy was scared – a liar?'

'No, man, take it easy. He's just what he is – look, he's been in England now since he was nine. He's been in England as much as he's been in Bermuda.'

'But so have you.'

'Yes. I went one way, he went another. Besides he's young yet . . . Forget it.'

Just before they left Washashley, Christopher said in

161

answer to James' questions: 'Look, I'll show you, Skeglee – airplane combat, dog-fighting is relatively simple:

'All the aerobatics you learn are just to give you confidence in your training – to make you be able to say, I can do anything.

'In combat, it's much more simple: the fighter plane that can turn inside the other – look', he put his hands up like two saucers, 'wins – he can strafe the other.

'As to when someone gets on your tail – there are only two possible good avoidance manoeuvres: the half roll – and the controlled spin. The controlled spin has the advantage of looking to the enemy as if you are hit . . .

'All the rest has to do with altitude – height. It's invariably best to have a height advantage – for speed and manoeuvrability.

'But I have a strange trick – sometimes I like to get flat on the deck – down among the trees and birds – no one else will risk it, and they can't see you down there.'

VII

And now they were barrelling towards London in a beautiful express train that must be doing, Chris said, seventy miles an hour.

Chris had on his uniform again and their carriage said 1st Class – but the arm-rests on the seats had been sewn up into the back-rests. 'Before all officers had to ride First Class – but now it's first come first served and a damn good thing too. It was silly – you would have two or three people in a First Class compartment and Third Class jammed and people standing in the corridors.'

162

Again his trunk was in the goods wagon and he had two more days before he had to catch the school train and Chris kept saying, 'Live for now – enjoy the ride – look forward to London.'

'How lovely-looking he is,' Aunt Lillie had said – and he thought, at first, she meant Christopher. 'Such a smile – so like his dear father – such a mouth . . . well, go quickly, dear boys, don't look back.' Aunt Daisy had clung to Chris's arm until it was time to get on the bus.

'Poor Aunt Lillie,' Chris had said on the bus. 'It's all so impossible somehow.'

'What is, Chris?'

'Keeping up the Hall. Sometimes I can't think why Uncle Albert wanted all that stuff – why should a man of God care so much about things? One of the finest collections of china in England – Gad, beautiful though it is, what's to happen to it? And all that ruddy silver – more than two people can keep clean. Sometimes I just wonder what's going to happen . . .'

'But Dad is going to take over.'

'Yes, but can you really see Dad as a country squire? And how would Mummy get along with the Aunts? – only with a lot of friction, I would guess.'

'Mummy loves Aunt Lillie – I bet she does.'

'Well, it doesn't matter now. We have to take care of those old dears and I expect they'll live to be a hundred – Aunt Daisy will anyway.'

'How old are they?'

'God knows. They both lie about it – least Daisy won't let Lillie say how old she is for fear people will figure out how old *she* is. But Aunt Daisy has to be over seventy which means Aunt Lillie is over eighty.'

Now the train made exciting and very rapid clicking sounds and the telegraph poles flashed past and beyond them impossibly green fields and hedges.

163

The fields were dotted with cows and horses and then he saw some men in strange drab green uniforms with a simple circle of a paler colour in the middle of their backs.

'Who are they?' There were other people in the carriage but he wasn't shy or afraid of them with Chris there.

'Eyetie prisoners. Absolutely harmless. Most of the time they don't even have a guard. They are a funny gutless lot – but I understand they work very hard.'

'I'll say they do,' said a fat man in a baggy tweed suit. 'I've twenty of 'em on my place – near Doncaster – and they can work circles round local lads.'

'I don't doubt it,' Chris said and smiled and it was right, you could feel good if you just forgot about the future – trouble was he couldn't for very long.

'Before the War,' Chris said to him in a low voice, 'you used to be able to eat on this train – a restaurant car. And you could get beer too – which is what I'd go for right now.'

Places flashed by – they just crash-whizzed through other stations as if they didn't exist. Ely, James learned, was not in a county at all – all by itself in a place called the Isle of Ely . . .

'What king lost his jewels in the Wash?'

But James didn't know and the man from Doncaster interrupted to say that he admired 'all that you brave lads are doing' and 'I've a daughter in ATS – drives a big lorry and she's only a wee bit of a thing.'

They passed an ugly sign stuck in the middle of a field. 'News of the World. World's Largest Circulation.'

'World's filthiest paper,' Chris said, 'but when you see that you're close to London. Wonder whether we'll come in to King's Cross or Liverpool Street.'

'Oh, Chris,' James whispered, 'I just thought of

164

something awful – I left a letter of mine in Teddy's drawer – a very private letter.'

'The one to Dad?'

'Yes – oh, you didn't read it, did you?'

'I put it in your trunk – in your writing case.'

'Thank goodness – but you didn't read it, did you?'

'No. I was tempted but I just read who it was to and the date.'

'I should have burned it.'

'No, you mustn't burn anything you write. If you are going to be a writer you must learn to keep everything.'

'But some things are embarrassing as . . . hell.'

'No matter. Keep it all. You never know when it will come in useful – I have every letter I've ever received. It's all useful. Do you keep a diary?'

'No.'

'You ought to. I've kept one since 1931 – it's damn bad writing, I must say, but it has just enough in it to make me remember what it was like to be ten years old. Did you know Dad kept a diary right through the First War?'

'No – have you read it?'

'Certainly not. But I hope I will someday – it will be invaluable – priceless. He started it in 1911 – at the Coronation of the old King, think of that.'

They were now passing through slums and going much slower.

'Did you know Dad was going to be a writer once?'

'No – will he ever, do you think?'

'No. It's too late. He had to spend all his best years working to make money for us – so we'll have to be even better writers for him, won't we?'

'I hate that.'

'What's the matter, Skeglee?'

'I hate those.' James pointed out the seemingly

165

endless houses of dirty brick and the pathetic sooty clothes-lines and the dirty and often broken windows – in one, someone had a box for flowers painted a brave green but nothing grew in it.

'Yes,' Chris said and pulled his mouth to one side so that the end of his blobberly nose twisted and went red. 'Yes. Well, never you mind, buddy. That's what some of ourselves like to believe we're fighting a war for – no more slums, no more Depressions. A fair shake for everybody.'

The Doncaster man leaned over and rubbed his fat work-worn hands together between his knees. 'Orr – you'll never change it, lad. That lot like it where they are.'

'I'm sorry, sir, I don't agree with you.'

'Orr – you'll learn. Up home we put baths in new Council 'ouses just before War – and what do you think Council found?'

Chris didn't say anything.

'Pigs. Pigs in bath – the tenants kept pigs in bathtubs and went dirty themselves. Orr, you never change 'em. And them as didn't 'ave pigs poot coal in the bathtubs. Oh, aye, you'll learn.'

'Your reasoning is totally –' now Chris's whole face was red '– fallacious.'

'You an American?'

'Yes – partly.'

'Dorn't 'ave slums in America, I suppose?'

'I said I was part American – not part US citizen.' Chris pointed to his shoulder flashes.

'Never 'eard of it.'

Then they were walking along the platform. 'That bastard,' he fumed, 'to think we're fighting to save his bloody . . . bacon. Literally, bacon.'

They got the trunk, and then Chris had his RAF cap pushed back and on the side of his head and he let

166

out the piercing whistle that James had always envied.

People turned and stared but a taxi appeared from nowhere and stopped with a squeaking of brakes.

'Whatcha, Yank?'

'Christ no, not again.' Then suddenly he became very English. 'Do you know where Southampton Row is? Good, the Bonnington Hotel then – and it costs exactly one and thruppence.'

'And two-and-six for the trunk, sir.'

'I'm aware of that, driver.'

The Bonnington had an awning and looked something like New York – except there were sandbags outside, no doorman, no porter and the lift had been destroyed by incendiary bombs.

But they got a room with twin beds and James bounced on them. 'Just like home, Chris. Box springs – and our own bathroom!'

'I know. That's why I come here.'

The windows were all covered with black paper and you could only see out by raising a sash.

Chris sent a telegram to his squadron.

'Do they always have to know where you are?'

'Yes. You hardly ever get called back early these days – but we used to. Once I got called back and it was just a ruddy inspection – "Aussi-Variety" went over-the-hill and got busted back to sergeant pilot for it.'

'What school, sir?' the man at Daniel Neal asked.

'The Lion School, Littlehampton, please.'

'You mean Malvern Link, sir.'

'Yes – sorry. Forgot it was evacuated.'

'Right, this way.' The man gestured as if he was a church warden ushering them to a pew and walked as if he was on a tightrope.

167

The cap was bright yellow with a black lion in the front. The blazer was bright yellow too – and very handsome.

'Damn good stuff – pre-war too.'

'Yes, sir – it's about the last of it.'

Chris said he should wear the cap right now.

'No,' James whispered. 'I'll look silly. We might bump into some boy who goes there already.'

'In London? Very doubtful.'

'I don't want to.'

'All right – but you'll have to day after tomorrow.'

'Don't – please, Chris.'

Chris insisted that he have a tuck box and gave the man his name. 'The matron will have to sew your nametapes on –' Then the tuck box appeared – a handsome wooden chest with black metal straps and corners and James B. Berkeley painted in black letters across the top.

'How did they do it so fast, Chris?'

'Oh, practice. They've been doing it for some time.'

The salesman smiled.

They were able to get everything on the list except the long socks – including some real sissy, poofter things called 'house shoes' that had elastic where the laces should be.

By the time they had finished James felt ill. It was just hunger, he kept telling himself.

They had tea in a narrow little shop a few doors down from the Bonnington. 'The grub at the hotel is ghastly.'

The waitress smelled worse than Millie. They had toast and jam and there were three rock buns and Chris insisted that he didn't want any.

Chris bought two tickets at a place called Keith Prowse to a show called *Arsenic and Old Lace*. 'I'd like the best seats in the house, please.'

168

'Stalls, sir?' The man picked up the phone.

'Of course – in the middle and down front too, please. It's funny – I promise you, Skeglee. It's the funniest damn show ever – two old ladies who keep poisoning people and burying them in the cellar.'

James pulled at the bottom of the long RAF jacket. 'I don't like the sound of it, Chris. You're being like Teddy.'

'Trust me, buddy. It's all laughs – and the dialogue is slick as anything.'

And it was funny. The two old ladies were something like Aunt Lillie and Aunt Daisy – only a bit more like Bermudian spinster aunts because they were American. James had never imagined before that the subject of death could be funny – but it was.

At first the stage sets put him off – it didn't seem real like a movie and you couldn't enter into the thing, lose yourself. But then when the nutty guy, who thought he was Teddy Roosevelt, came on, James laughed so hard he had trouble catching his breath.

The air-raid sirens went halfway through the third act – nobody moved and the play went on. It just made everything more exciting and happy and James knew that no bombs would fall near them.

Chris was the nicest guy to see something with because he kept looking at you and sharing it all. His laugh was low and deep and often came through his nose and he wore his 'I-told-you-so – these-people-are-as-crazy-as-us' face.

Outside they walked the neat pavements and Chris kept slapping James's shoulder and going into peals of laughter. 'Charge!' he'd shout and lunge forward. 'I tell you, Skeglee, if Grampy saw that show he'd asphyxiate himself.'

James could hear his grandfather's voice: the best

thing, perhaps, about Grampy Halcyon was that he was always looking for the laugh that was in everything:

'I'll tell you fellas something about any race – if the wind is going to change, it's gotta favour somebody.' His eyes twinkling, touching your eyes like a compass needle. 'So I'll tell you something about any race: you can go to starboard or you can go to port – the fella who goes up the middle has lost the race.'

His eyes looking, asking the question, did you get it?

'Grampy – did you and the Sheringhams really beat *all* the Americans who ever challenged the *Nea*?'

'Well, I'll tell you what, son – we always gave 'em plenty of chance to read her name. So that they could spell it right when they got back home.'

'You beat them all, in a Bermudian boat?'

'It was only for seven or eight years. And the boat, the *Nea*, was the best part. I mean, with Halcyon, Sheringham and *Nea* as the three links – the boat was the best of the three.'

'And then you beat all the Americans in the *Sirius*?'

'Yes – your dad built her – and she was the best instrument in *that* trio. Fella named Aas – Ooos – a Norwegian – he designed *Sirius* – he should get most of the credit.'

'And you beat all the Americans?'

'No, some of 'em who came for us were British. A lotta credit, too, should go to professional pilots – black fellas. You take most Bermudian successes, and there's a secret weapon on board. In our case, Chummy Minors. But, in *Sirius*, we gave them all a reading lesson – for a while.'

'You mean you were beaten?'

'In the world of sailing, everyone gets beaten some time. Every boat gets beaten some time. Only boat I know who was never beaten was *Nea.*'

They stopped at a pub and people even made room at the crowded bar for them. Again Chris got a whisky, this time from a middle-aged Cockney woman with a cameo brooch, as big as a horse brass, fastening her blouse in the middle of her motherly-looking chest. 'There you are, ducks, it's supposed to be Regulars Only mind – here, lean over.'

Chris leaned over, putting his ear down to hear what she had to say, but she grabbed his cheeks and kissed him on the mouth. 'There love, and God bless you.'

Chris blushed and when he turned towards him James saw there were tears in his eyes.

'What's the matter, Chris?'

'Oh, nothing – she just knows, that's all.'

'Knows? Knows what?'

'Everything.'

He didn't quite understand it – but he had the feeling that it would be a scene that would come back to him.

Again he noticed the missing buildings – like pulled teeth – and the strange pock-marked façades of others. In some places, particularly behind the Bonnington, whole blocks just didn't exist – levelled – and nothing but the shapes of old cellars and weeds growing here and there.

In the second pub James was turned away. 'Just wait outside, Jamie. Won't be a moment.'

He lay there under the covers thinking of all the things he wanted to ask Christopher about school. Finally he said, 'When will I see you again, Chris?'

'Well, I'm afraid you are only allowed out of school for one Sunday afternoon a month – least that's what it was in my day. But I'll come down the first

171

opportunity I get.'

One Sunday afternoon a month. He found himself crying – (damn it, damn it, the same lack of control) – it seemed impossible that people could be so cruel, yet he knew it was true.

Chris looked over. 'Easy, Skeglee. Tell you what. If I ever fly near Malvern I'll come down as low as I can and waggle my wings and signal – with the engine. So you keep a lookout.'

He bit his lip.

'Sorry, old lad – but we all have to do it. You do want to go to Fotheringham, don't you.'

James nodded without looking at him.

'Elevate chin, Skeglee, tomorrow we'll go to Stanley Gibbons and find a Frog plane – maybe at Hamleys in Regent Street. Best toy shop in the world. And we can go to the Brasserie Universal and have a drink. They'll let you in there – it's also a restaurant. All the Bermuda boys always go there – that's where we all meet.'

'Really? Chris, really? Who?'

'Wait and see – now go to sleep or I'll slug you.'

He woke up and found himself being shoved under the bed. The light was on but it was fluttering low then high.

'Here. Wrap this blanket around you – it's nothing – but just to be safe. Here, now this one about your head.' There was the sound of thudding explosions – much louder, he thought, than any he had heard at sea, sharper in intensity anyway. 'Around your head – in case of flying glass – come on.'

Chris was in his clothes and shoes already and climbing under his bed. 'Gad,' he said, 'bloody Goering. He can't take a joke.'

Bam-bam-bam-bam-bam and then a further-away

172

interlocking sound, bam-bam-bam . . .

James could see nothing and then he made a hole in the blanket folds so that he could see Chris. Chris's eyes looked back at him and wrinkled in a smile.

'I heard the sirens quite a while back but I didn't think anything would come of it – so I let you sleep.'

You could hear the drone of planes overhead and the ringing of bells outside. Then there was a noise of continuous banging even sharper than the bombs – ack-ack, he guessed, and Christopher said, at the same instant: 'Ack-ack. In Bloomsbury Square, I expect.'

Things quieted down and the All Clear sounded and Chris said, 'I shouldn't have brought you – I thought the blasted Blitz was over years ago.'

'I don't mind, Chris. I'd rather be with you and die than be without you.'

His brother looked at him. 'Oh, you rotten Skeglee bastard, I believe you would.'

Chris went out after saying he'd be right back – and when he asked to go too Chris said, 'Shut up,' in a strange distant tone and was gone. He sat on the bed shaking and then he needed to pee and barely made it to the bathroom in time.

'Come on, get dressed. We're getting out of here.' The skin on Chris's face was taut-looking.

'Why?'

'Don't ask questions – just because I'm superstitious, that's all. I've phoned the Regent's Palace – we've got a room there. No bath, but a room. Maybe we can get a bath tomorrow.'

'Why don't we stay here?'

'Because I have a hunch – that's why. We're going to the Regent's Palace. My hunches are all too often right.' He slapped the wood of the bureau.

James's limbs felt weak and heavy. His watch said 4:20.

They stood on the pavement for a long time and couldn't get a taxi. Then Chris said he'd walk down to Holborn Circus and bring one back.

James sat on the trunk as he had done outside Mr Somers's office his first day in London.

Some men went by in helmets and overalls. 'Come on, Arthur, come on.' 'They got the kiddie's hospital again. Come on – we'll be digging all night for the poor things.' 'No, no. Couldn't be . . .'

There was a glow in the sky coming from behind the hotel – it seemed strange because behind the hotel was all bashed flat – he'd seen it.

And then a taxi was doing a U-turn in the street and before it stopped Chris had the door open. It was a surprise to see him and James realized that a part of him had accepted, already, that Chris would never come back. Indeed, he'd already debated whether he should phone Mr Somers or go to Liverpool Street and take the first train back to Lincoln instead of to The Lion School. But now Chris was here and he had a whole day and a half left.

The Regent's Palace was quite a way off – above Piccadilly Circus, Chris said. He pointed out a strange wooden pyramid-like thing in the middle of the Circus.

'A beautiful statue is under there. Eros. An Old Fotheringhamian designed it. Sir somebody Gilbert – probably a distant relative of ours. He went to Fotheringham back in the 1870s, I think.'

'It's a small world, ha-ha,' James said without humour. 'And please don't mention it – school, I mean.'

'Cheer up. You know why people are always saying it's a small world, Skeglee? It's because our ruddy class – the people who own parcels of the world – even small parcels – are so small a number. Think of it:

Aunt Lillie knows virtually every County family in England – of course, she's a professional – but still. Here we are.'

The Regent's Palace was bustling with people, mostly service men and women, even at this late hour.

Their room didn't seem much bigger than a pillbox but it had two beds, a bureau and a basin.

'Come on. Let's hit the hay.'

'Will there be more bombs?'

'No. This part of the West End never gets hit. Besides, even Goering's bombs have too much self-respect to land on this place.'

James was staggered to see Chris pee in the basin. His cock was different-looking – like Teddy, he was circumcised. James wasn't, and neither was little George. Roundheads and Cavaliers, Teddy called it. He thought it looked neater to be circumcised, certainly it looked more grown-up. 'You shouldn't do that – people have to *wash* there.'

'Sorry, old lad. Everyone does it. It's all right if you run the water at the same time – besides, it's only beer and a little whisky and whisky's a disinfectant.'

James had a pee himself. He stood on his tuck box to reach.

'Just think how far we've fallen – we are now two streets away from Uncle Albert's mother's house – Number 65 Pall Mall, two doors from St James's Palace, where grandfather Berkeley was a page.

'Don't forget to say your prayers.'

'Do you say your prayers?'

'Yes – always. Least I always manage the "God bless Mummy and Daddy" and all that. Funny, isn't it, the way we do just what we did when we were kids?'

'Do you, Chris? I would have thought you were too

old and would say something in Latin or something –
or nothing at all.'

'Oh, I say plenty of prayers, don't you worry.
Sometimes when I'm flying I even cross myself – just
as if I was a server again at St Paul's.'

'Do you? I said a lot of prayers on the *Empire
United*. I used to God bless the whole world –'

'Good. Go to sleep. Tomorrow I'll show you the
Brasserie Universal.'

James lay there thinking how incredible it was to
be big – grown-up. To be like Chris and be able to
cope with London. Whistle up taxis in the night and
know where to go and what to do when you get
there – but Mummy would be horrified at Chris
peeing in the basin, even Dad would.

In the morning they walked around Piccadilly Circus
and through Leicester Square. A great black cinema.
Odeon. 'That's the biggest movie-house in England.
Has leopardskin seats.'

'Real leopard's skin?'

'I don't know – it looks like it.'

'Must've taken an awful lot of leopards.'

'And there's the Café de Paris – it was . . . caught
fire early in the war.'

They walked into Trafalgar Square and there was
Nelson's Column looking just as it did in the movies.

They went into St Martin's-in-the-Fields. They
kneeled down in the very back pew. 'Dear God . . .
make The Lion School easy and let Chris come
soon . . .' He peeked at Chris. His head was bent over
very low and his back was very straight – he didn't
kneel keeping his bottom on the pew like most
irreverent grown-ups. Chris seemed to be praying
very hard.

'Come on, Skeg, I'll show you around. This church

has lots of connections with Bermuda – indeed, some of the original owners of the Bermuda Company, back in the sixteen hundreds, are buried here. In the crypt.'

'In the cellar? – I don't want to go down.'

'OK. Suit yourself. It isn't scary. Once I spent the night down there sleeping on a grave.'

'You didn't?'

'Sure.'

'Why?'

'Couldn't get into a hotel – it was either that or sleep in the Underground. I preferred here.'

'I wouldn't have done it. Were you alone?'

'No. No. Even I wouldn't sleep there alone – one of the Worthington boys was with me. Mike. He's out in Malta now. It was during the Blitz.

They walked towards the Strand.

'Chris – it's the unknown I'm scared of – I don't know what school is going to be like.'

'They can't kill you, Skeglee –' A soldier saluted Chris with a great long sweep of his hand up to his forehead. Chris just gave a chuck-away touch towards his cap. 'They can't kill you – that was my old motto – keep saying that to yourself. And live for the immediate, not the future – the future usually doesn't happen. I knew a chap at The Lion School who made himself sick over worrying about getting a caning. He was there four years and he never did get caned once. See, he worried for nothing.'

'Were you ever caned?'

'Of course – well, three times.'

'I hope I never am.'

'Don't worry about it – it hurts and then it's gone. Say, "They can't kill me" – it always works.'

Stanley Gibbons was small-looking from the outside. Chris took out a pound note. 'There you are, you can spend that.'

'Can you afford it?'

'Of course.'

'But I have the two pounds of my birthday money.'

'You'd better save that – you'll need it for your summer holidays.'

'But I don't want to take up too much of your money – will Dad pay you back?'

'Of course – or we can say I'm paying him back for the hundreds of pounds I've cost him – thousands really.'

'But it's *your* money.'

'James – if you were me and I was little George, The Stinker, would you buy him a few lousy stamps?'

'I guess so.'

'So shut up.'

It didn't really seem right: Chris was always spending his money. He'd seen him give Fenders a cheque for ten whole pounds. 'It's just a token,' he'd said afterwards. 'A sort of retainer. I give him a little when I can and he helps out at the Hall.' But he really would like to get some of the new Bermuda stamps – Chris's collection stopped with King George V.

It was an incredible place: you could ask for any stamp from anywhere in the world and they would have it.

He bought the new Bermuda set from $\frac{1}{2}^d$ to 1/- and then the '37 Coronation set. The pound was gone.

'How much is a Perot stamp worth now?' Chris asked the salesman.

'Oh, it varies, sir.'

'Say about 1848? How much is it worth – about?'

'As much as six or seven hundred guineas.'

'Don't trouble. I don't want to buy one – we have one.'

'Do we, Chris?'

'Yes. At least, Grampy does – it's the rarest of

Bermuda stamps. Practically the rarest of any stamp – don't you remember Grampy's? He keeps it in a cigarette tin in one of the pigeonholes of his desk – right beside a tin for fish-hooks and a bottle of distemper pills for the dogs. All of which is next to Beau Nat Durrell's spyglass and a calabash bailer. Come on, are you happy now?'

Outside James said: 'I shouldn't have taken your money.'

'Flying pays dough, Skeglee. I'm rolling in it.'

'Really?'

'Truly.'

They walked back to Piccadilly and went down the steps off the street into the Brasserie Universal. It was an enormous place with imitation oak beams and imitation old tavern chairs and tables. It was on two levels – the upper area seemed to be for younger people, and, below, most of the people had grey hair and civvies. The place was crowded: men, mostly servicemen, at the bar; couples or groups in the table areas.

'Hello, Harry. How are you?' Chris put his cap on the copper counter and a little fat man turned and held out his hand.

'Don't tell me, sir. Bermuda, of course . . . Flight Lieutenant . . . Flight Lieutenant Berkeley.'

'You never miss, Harry. This is my kid brother, James. James, this is Harry. He takes care of us all – holds letters and packages and gives messages.'

James shook Harry's hand – it felt fat and rather limp.

'Pleased-to-meet-ya, Mr Berkeley. You gonna join up too?'

James shook his head.

'Harry's the best man to know in London – he can get you anything from nylons to the crown jewels.

Any of the boys in town, Harry?'

'What's'isname – Boo – Booley.'

'John Bewley. Where is he?'

'Well, he was here this weekend. I think I 'eard 'im say he only had a weekend though, sir.'

'Damn – well, I'll have a look around.'

'Do you want any, sir?'

'Don't know – really.'

'Three nicker – the best though?'

'All right.' Chris paid him.

'No greatcoat? I could put it in your greatcoat.'

'Left it at the hotel.'

'Never mind. On your way out, sir. I'll wrap it in newspaper and put it in your 'at.'

'Right, Harry.'

Christ sat James at one of the tables and then went into the bar. He was soon back – no Bermudians.

'Sorry – and to think we just missed John Bewley – do you remember him?'

'Hardly at all – even his younger brother is older than I am.'

'He's been in the RAF since September '39 – a few classes ahead of me. We always met on the *Reina* coming over and going back – before the war I mean. Or on the banana boats.'

'I saw the *Reina* – she was in our convoy.'

'Really?'

'Yes. All painted grey – she looked like a great grey elephant compared to us.'

'I suppose she would – what do you want?'

'Lunch, please.'

'OK, Skeglee – lunch.'

A large man in a double-breasted suit and using crutches came towards them. He had one leg – the trouser-leg of the other was folded up neatly and fastened with a pin.

'Hey, don't I know you people? Yes – Onions – I can tell.' He moved with great agility and stopping in front of Chris transferred both crutches into one hand and held out the other. 'You remember me – Gibson's the name. Parker Gibson.'

'Christopher Berkeley – and my brother James.'

'Sure – I know your daddy – know your mother too. Francis's boys, eh?'

'No, sir, George is our father.'

'Oh, yes, oh yes – God's sake don't sir me – I ain't that old, you know.'

James knew the man and was afraid of him and wished he'd go away – but Chris offered him a drink. Jaysus, as Paddy on the ship would say, it was spooky: he'd been scared of this one-legged man in Bermuda – and that only seemed like yesterday – and now, thousands of miles away in London, suddenly here was the man again.

'Don't mind if I do. Gin please. A pink gin if we can get it.' Mr Gibson talked a staccato and rather exaggerated Bermudian. 'So you're with the Raf? Eh?' No wait for a reply. 'Yes, I know all your family – have for years. I was with the *Gazette*. Argued with 'em and went down to Trinidad on the *Chronicle*. Now I'm over here to be where the fighting is – restless lot we Gibsons, always have been.' Chris looked a little nervous. 'You know Mike Worthington?'

'Of course. Is he here? He can't be.'

'Sure – at my place in Baker Street. Him and his young bride – fact, I just left 'em. Thought they'd like a little privacy.' He winked once at Chris and then once again at James. 'Young folks, you know – and my flat is werry small, werry small.'

'I haven't seen Mike for years – no, almost fifteen months. Good old Mike. I heard his wife was over – Mr Somers told me – but I thought Mike was in

181

. . . the Near East.'

'Malta – the b'y's a hero now. He got a DFC.'

'Good – funny John Somers didn't tell me.'

'John Somers?'

'Yes – you know, the Bermuda Agents.'

'Oh, yes. I don't bother with them – too stuck-up for me. Ha-ha-ha.'

They got gins and then Mr Gibson went off to phone the Worthingtons.

'Chris – I know him. He's an awful man. He drinks and hits people with his crutches –'

'Well, he can't do it here – and you'd like to see Mike Worthington, wouldn't you?'

'Yes.'

'I've never met his wife.'

'Mr Gibson has stepsons in Bermuda. The Craig boys. Do you remember? They were really tough – Mr Gibson used to beat them with his crutches. And the biggest Craig boy once beat him up and burned the crutches. He's an awful man – I tell you, Chris, Mum and Dad wouldn't like us to have anything to do with him.'

'Easy, man, easy. He can't do us any harm – and he's a Bermudian, isn't he? Stop worrying.'

'Well, he gives me the creeps.'

'I guess I do remember him vaguely. Wonder how he lost his leg? – he's much too young for the First War.'

Mr Gibson came back and said the Worthingtons would be right down. Chris said they had better eat and Mr Gibson wanted another drink.

'You have one with me, now, lad.'

'No, no,' said Chris, 'we're so delighted to see someone from home.'

'It's my round,' said Mr Gibson but he let Chris pay and then Chris ordered two steak and kidney pies.

James found it hard to eat – Mr Gibson made him feel seasick. He kept asking Chris: 'How're you fixed – you know what I mean?' 'Fine, thank you.' 'Well, let me know – wouldn't want any onion to be in London and be lonely – for a little piece. No, the boy don't mind, does he? No, thought not.' He laughed and put a heavy hand on Chris's shoulder.

At last the Worthingtons came down the stairs. Mike was a pilot officer and James had never seen him before – but his little blonde wife, James swallowed and blushed, was the same girl who had been on the *Empire United*. The only woman passenger, the girl he had watched with such longing from a distance – his 'Virginia'. He'd fought men for her; fought dragons, and he had lain beside her naked in a bunk and kissed the tip of her nose and brought her iced tea, with mint leaves, all smoky from the sugar . . .

'Chris – b'y – good to see you.'

'Mike, you water rat.'

'This is my Julia – you remember Julia – used to be Julia Law?'

'Of course – I've admired you – from afar anyway – and this is my brother James.'

Everyone shook hands, the men slapped backs and everyone talked in such broad Bermudian accents they might have been fishermen – Negro fishermen at that. Even Chris sounded a little phony talking that way.

She was very beautiful, even more beautiful than before, and she had pale blue eyes that seemed to twinkle when she smiled. She didn't say much and James tried not to look at her – the blonde hair and the freckles (a Bermudian heritage that only they, the Berkeleys, seemed to have lost out on) and the small but full and pointed breasts that peeped around her cardigan pushing out the sweater beneath it, made his ears go hot.

Mike was telling about flying in the Mediterranean – off Malta.

'Oh, man, let me tell you about this gawdamn Macchi that raced my tail –'

'Let's get Julia a drink first.'

'Oh, just a ginger ale or something for me.' Then she met James's eyes. 'Don't I know you – haven't I seen you somewhere . . ?'

'No,' James said.

'Oh' she said. 'Probably just at home – isn't it strange the way you can recognize people – I mean as Bermudians?'

'Well, Julie, would you recognize this fella as a Bermudian?' Mike smiled at Chris and looked him up and down. You could tell he really liked Chris.

'Yes – I think so.'

'Well, he's a cool bird, this Limey-Bermudian. A cool bird. Nerves of steel. He and I met and we couldn't get a hotel room any place – heck, he shouldn't't've even been palling around with me, him being an officer and me just a lousy sergeant pilot then.'

'Oh, I forgot that,' Chris said.

'So he says to me he knows where we can sleep – in a church! In the bloody cellar too – with all the stiffs. I was too in awe of him to argue – him being Cranwell and Pukka and all that. Christ, he takes me down there and all we've got is a couple of little candles and he starts to tell me a lot of Bermuda history and then he lies down on the slab of a grave and the next thing I know he's snoring. I sit there with my teeth chattering – and he's asleep.'

'Well, there was nowhere else.'

'Without you, mate, I wouldn't have done it – I can

tell you.'

'What do you hear from home? How're your parents?'

Everyone's parents were well. Julia's father had won an MC in the First War. 'Now he won't give me such hell,' Mike said. 'That's all I care about – that bastard has to look me in the eye.' He laughed in a high peal.

'They'll all be proud,' said Chris, 'you must be the first DFC we've won – Bermuda, I mean.'

'Oh, you know – it comes with the rations. You wanta hear how I won mine? It's no military secret, that's for sure.' He laughed again. His laugh was very catching and he drew everyone in by looking from face to face. He was very suntanned and his teeth glistened as white as a boiled shirt-front. He was heavyset, much shorter than Chris, and reminded you somehow of a bird.

'We were flying Beauforts, see? Now you know what a Beaufort can do – both throttles wide, pushed right through the gate, and an old swordfish could go faster. Now we had torpedoes – well, you put a torpedo under a Beaufort and the seagulls overtake you. Well, we had to make a run on this Eyetie convoy – least we thought it was Eyetie. Turned out to be Germans. One wing went in – and bram-bram-bram – every one of 'em shot down miles short of the target. Another wing went in. Bram-bram-bram. Same thing. So we went in. I look over on the right – pow – he's gone. So I shouts to my bombadier, "Let that bloody thing go." He says, "We're still out of range." "Not out of their range," I says, "let the bugger go." Whoosh, away it goes. The kite feels like a young bird and I bank her over as sharp as hell and head for home hopping the waves.'

Silence.

'Is that all? How'd you get the medal, b'y?' said Mr Gibson.

'Sure. I was the only one left – they *had* to give me the bloody medal.'

Everyone laughed. Mike ordered drinks for everyone. He and Chris had pints of beer and Gibson a gin. Julia had a lager and James, despite kicking Chris under the table in the hope he'd get a small beer, got lemon pop.

'Tell us what you've been doing, Chris.' Mike turned to his wife. 'Old Berkeley's really the tops – a shi' – red-hot pilot.'

'No. I just like flying – sometimes I think what I like best is how great it is to be alone. I get fed up with people – service life, I mean, and it's so wonderful to be alone up there.'

The Worthingtons ordered food – they hadn't eaten all day, they said, and smiled into each other's eyes – then Mike turned to Chris and she was left smiling at the back of his head.

'I sure envy you fighter boys – I've always got a crew and a kite that handles like a truck. You're on Mustangs, I heard?'

'Yeah, Mike. Something like that.'

'And you fly alone? No squadron or anything?'

'Often – usually, actually.'

'You lucky bastard. Well, I can't complain. I've seen lots of action and I hope to see a lot more before it's over. I bet you do too, eh Chris?'

'Well – not exactly. It's just a job of work.'

'He's just modest.'

'No. I wish it would end tomorrow.'

'Not me, man – I'd like to go on flying for ever. Even if it did end, I'd get a job flying somewhere – it's in my blood.'

Chris just smiled.

186

Julia was looking at him. 'I wish it would all end too – but for Mike's sake –'

'Oh, Christ. All women are like that, honey – come off it. I don't intend to get hurt. Believe me, I'm too yellow to want to get hurt. I never do anything 'cept I figure the chances are on my side – isn't that what you do, Christopher?'

'Yes, I try.'

Silence.

'Now, let me buy you b'ys a drink – waiter!'

They had another round. Julia didn't want any.

Chris was looking at Julia. 'You're awfully – pretty.' He looked startled at himself.

'Why, thank you.' She blushed.

'Quit flirting with my wife, Berkeley. Just because you out-rank me.' He laughed with the high-pitched staccato sound again. 'Heh, let me tell you about this Macchi that jumped me off Malta. Ever seen a Macchi? Italian. Damn fine fighter – goes like the clappers of hell – and me in this Beaufort. I see this bird in my mirror as small as a bee. When I look again he's as large as life and right on me. Well, I can't do anything. If I bank to the right or left he'll rake me good. If I dive he'll get me – if I climb, see, even worse. So what can I do? Just sit there and wait.

'I kept looking in the mirror and I had the stick rigid in my hands and both feet poised over one pedal – the right pedal. I figured I'd wait till I saw the flash of his guns and then jump hard on the pedal and hold the stick rigid and skid over. Then I saw it – flashes coming from all over him. I jumped on the pedal and skidded across the sky like a tin tray across the floor – zoom, he went by, missing us, as if we were standing still.

'Well, the bastard made another pass. I saw him coming. I thought, "Shall I go to the right or the left?

187

Will he expect right again or left as a change?" Well, I waited this time until I could *hear* his bullets ripping into us – then I took both feet and gave a tickle on the left rudder and then I swung both feet over on the right again and stamped down hard – zoom, we went over, and zoom, he zipped by. Fooled him again. And around he came again. Christ what a beautiful bloody aircraft.

'This time I was really scared and I thought, "This time he'll think I'll go left so I better go right – no, he'll think of that so I'll go left – no, he'll think of that so I'll put my chips on right again."

'Well, damn if he doesn't make his run and there's no shooting – he goes right over the top of us and then buggers off. Were we lucky – I guess he was out of ammo or had a gun jam-up or something. But I tell you, I don't care to meet any Macchis again. Can you beat that?' The question seemed directed at himself.

'You b'ys are really doing a job – I wish I could be more help.'

Chris got up and said he'd be right back. He crossed the room and went into the phone booth next to Harry's cloakroom.

'He don't say much, does he?' said Mr Gibson as if James wasn't there.

'He won't say anything to anybody,' James heard himself say. 'But he was flying in '39 – he was even at Dunkirk. Flying over Dunkirk in a Boulton Paul Defiant – and he was wounded – very badly too – in the shoulder.' Oh boy, oh boy, here you go again – and what if they ask him themselves? 'But don't say anything. He hates to talk about it. He absolutely hates it.'

'You don't have to tell me anything about your brother, man,' said Mike. 'I know. His record makes mine look like a Sunday School outing – he and John

188

Bewley. Christ, those fellows have been in since the beginning.'

'Yes,' said Julia. 'You must be very proud of him – and he's so distinguished-looking too. But don't tell him I said so.' She laughed the same bubbling laugh he remembered hearing on the ship. 'At least not until after I've gone.' Her accent was very soft and Bermudian. James had the feeling that if he closed his eyes and willed it hard enough he would open them again and find himself home – perhaps even looking west up the harbour with the water rippling, making flashes of gold in the sunlight, or sitting on a beach at the south shore with the sand dazzling white and the girls going by with bottoms firm-bouncing in their tight bathing suits.

'Where's he gone – we gotta go soon?'

Chris came back. 'I forgot to check in – I did it last night but then we moved hotels and now I can't get through to the first one – but I don't suppose it matters. I can send a telegram later.'

Mike said: 'Tell Julia about the first Focke-Wulf that jumped you.'

Chris smiled: 'Gad – don't know about that – but I can tell you about the second one that did. I was in this Lysander at the time: fortunately this Luftwaffe fella hadn't seen me. I had the choice of either hitting the Focke-Wulf with my Very pistol or my thermos of coffee – I chose, rather wisely, I think, not to do either.'

Everyone roared with laughter.

The Worthingtons were leaving for Mike's navigator's place in Surrey. Mr Gibson had to go to work. Chris told them that he was going to school the next day – James tried to smile. Julia Worthington shook his hand and wished him luck. Then she wrote out an address for Chris. 'I'm sure we'll meet again. I'm just

189

certain of it.'

' 'Course we will, honey – why, they live in Paget.'

'Yes, it's just down-de-road,' she said, imitating a Negro accent and laughed again.

Chris wrote his number on a calling card and gave it to her.

'That's all we need?'

'Of course, honey. Same as me. If the Raf doesn't know where to find its own we're really in trouble.'

He and Chris crossed Picadilly through the Underground station and then walked up Regent Street towards Hamleys, the toy shop.

'Nice bloke, Mike,' said Chris, 'if a little uncouth – loves his wife though. She's a cut above him, didn't you think?'

'Very nice.' James was worried that Chris might meet her again and that she might mention the *Empire United*. His exaggerated stories – his lies – would be exposed. He blushed just thinking of it.

'Mike's a rough diamond – but probably a damn good soul.'

Two sailors saluted Chris.

'They're terrific, those Worthingtons – but Granny and Grampy wouldn't understand the humour – so you could hardly take Mike home to Cedar Hill – eh?'

'No – or to Washashley. I bet he'd swear in front of anybody.'

'All that cursing in front of his wife – I guess it's okay . . .'

'Yes – and she kept blushing. But he was funny, wasn't he, Chris?'

'Yes. But it might have been even funnier if it had been just men. And the poor girl is pregnant too.'

'How do you know?'

'Didn't you notice?'

James flushed with rage and didn't quite know why. They walked along in silence for a while and then he said, 'Was all that true about the way he won the DFC?'

The street, with its long curve of tall buildings, was excitingly handsome – it looked the way he had expected all of London would look – But that dirty skunk Mike violating *his* Virginia . . .

'No – of course not. He was just making a joke. Hell,' Chris held the newspaper-wrapped whisky bottle in his hand, 'I meant to leave this at the hotel – I look like a damn Yank wandering around town with a bottle under my arm. Should have brought my coat.'

'I'll carry it, Chris. I don't mind.'

'Bless you, Jamie – but that would be worse. It's all right.'

'I really didn't like that Gibson man. Chris – I hope I never see him again.'

'Well, you never know how life has treated him – maybe he's had a rough time. I think we're all terrible snobs. The Halcyons are bad enough but the Berkeleys are impossible. Anyway, I just realized something. Mike can't be more than eighteen and a half – or nineteen. He must have lied about his age to join up – and I was being snobbish about a few curses . . . Here we are. Here's Hamleys.'

The shop was very big but very bare.

Chris asked for Frog model planes and they were directed to the third floor.

An old man came over. 'Not since 1940, sir – weren't they wonderful?'

'Damn.'

'I'm awfully sorry – but if you remember them, sir, you'll remember they were made out of very thin metal. As you well know, that's what real planes use

191

today. Everything goes for the War. Why, do you remember how cigarettes used to come in tins? Yes, and have beautiful silver wrapping? Chocolate bars too – Cadburys had silver paper and then a blue wrapper with *real* gold letters. Lovely it was.'

'Do you have any model planes?'

They were shown fat unpainted toys such as toddlers push about the floor.

'No – how about balsawood – the kind that you wind up with an elastic and they fly?'

'Good gracious no, sir. No rubber, of course – and balsawood – well, "they" must use it for something because there isn't any.'

Life belts, James thought, that's what they use it for.

They walked back to the hotel. Suddenly, the way it does in a city, time had slipped and the afternoon was nearly spent ... The Lion School seemed to be looming awfully close – he kept thinking about it every few minutes and, ta-tum, his stomach heaved in that falling feeling.

'Sorry about the Frog.'

'It's OK. I have the Defiant.'

'Well, cheer up – we could go to the Odeon Leicester Square. Would you like that?'

'Sure – I'd love it.'

No, there wasn't a room with a bath for them, the desk said.

Chris phoned the Bonnington. He gave his name and rank. He was about to hang up when he said, 'What? – yes – yes – that's right – yes. Would you read it to me, please?' A long pause. 'Yes – what time was it sent? Yes, oh Christ – yes. Thank you, good-bye – no, tear it up.' He put the receiver down very slowly.

192

'Bad news, old buddy. I was due back at 1500 hours – three o'clock. God, what a break. I have to go – you'll have to get to the train by yourself –'

'Oh, no, Chris. No.'

'Sorry. Can't be helped. Never rains but it pours. Well, elevate chin. Look – Teddy's going to meet the train at Malvern. All you have to do is sleep here and tomorrow take a taxi to Paddington. Your train leaves at 2:15. The school pays – you just have to find the part of the train that says Lion School. It'll be on the windows. There'll be a master there and you just tell him who you are.'

'But tonight – ?'

'You sleep here. I'll pay the bill before I go – then tomorrow you just call for a porter and tell him to get you a taxi. At Paddington you tell the porter to take you to the school train to Worcester and Hereford. I'll write it all down for you.'

'_'

'Maybe I could call Mr Somers – trouble is, I don't like to bother him – but I can if you want.'

'No. It's OK. But when shall I eat – tonight, I mean? I sort of hate eating – alone. I mean I've never done it.'

'Oh God, OK. I'll fake it. We'll eat before I leave tonight – if there's a train. But, here's a tip, buddy, when you have to eat alone, just buy a newspaper and bury your nose in it.'

Chris's train left at 6:19. They went to the Lyon's Corner House. Chris carried his briefcase.

It was the first cafeteria James had ever been in. It was crowded and frightening. He followed behind Chris and took what he did. The place seemed to be just a noise of babbling talk and clattering plates and cutlery; smells of gravy and the sight of shuffling human bodies all rolled together. He had already decided that he would not eat at all the next day when Chris paid – 2/9 and 2/9.

They found a table but he had forgotten to get a knife and fork and spoon.

'Over there,' Chris pointed.

He could see the cutlery but the people wouldn't let him through the line. 'Excuse – excuse,' he kept saying but they just went by – body, body. 'Not 'alf.' 'Hold on, love.' 'Smashin', in't-it?'

Chris came up and simply put his hand out and stepped in between people and emerged successful.

When they got back, two more people were sitting at their table. Chris smiled and shrugged.

James hunched over the food. He didn't want to eat anything but he knew he must. He would soon be alone again – indeed the feeling, just as he had had on the train from Glasgow and so many times before, was already creeping over him – the world was a hole, a void, and you were falling . . .

'You know the Berkeley trick?'

'What trick?'

'No goodbyes – when I have to go I'll just jump in the taxi. I won't look back. It's easier that way – I know, believe me. I've always done it that way – originally it was Mummy's idea –'

'OK, Chris . . .'

'OK. Elevate chin, Skeglee –'

Out on the street Chris had his cap on the back of his head again – a crazy slant, very un-English. He even looked happy. It was an act but he looked happy. His Bermudian whistle rent the air.

Let no taxi come! But a taxi was already there. Chris swung open the royal-blue door.

'Good luck, m'dear.'

The door slammed. 'Waterloo,' voice muffled.

The taxi pulled away and started around the

194

Circus, and then was stopped at a red light only a few yards from him. He started towards it – then stopped. It stayed there a long time and then it started around the Circus again and then it was gone – it was as if it never had been.

Just a few seconds ago he was whole and now he was alone. Piccadilly Circus and hundreds of strangers and just a few hours before he'd been with four Bermudians and now they were gone. He thought he'd give anything to even have that man Gibson.

He walked about the streets for hours and when it began to get dark he went to the hotel and went up to the room and locked the door and peed in the sink and cried.

Then he began to lay his clothes out ready for the morning. White flannel shirt, school tie yellow knit, short trousers grey, long socks grey, blazer and cap yellow.

Life was tough, there was no doubt about that. You were scared three or ten ways all the time and you had to keep up a good front however you felt inside. Keep smiling but be ready to put your dukes up.

VIII

He woke up and looked over to see if Chris was awake. No Chris. His watch said 7:30. His stomach rumbled.

Ponk, ponk – taxis outside.

He had a pee and then drank a glass of water. Then he remembered how once in New York he'd heard his father call for a meal to be sent up. What did he ask for – ?

He picked up the phone. Nothing happened. He

waited a long time. Then he jaggled the receiver.

'Yes.'

'I'd like to get some food.'

'What's that?'

'Some breakfast – some breakfast sent up, please.'

'Oh, you want the dining-room.'

Click-clack.

'Main dining-room – Scott speaking.'

'I'd like to get some breakfast sent up – to my room, please.'

'Madam, I'm sorry. No Room Service. There's a war on.'

He got dressed very slowly. He had a lot of time to kill.

He looked out of the window but there was nothing to see except a shaft, from which came sounds of rattling dishes, and a small glimpse of a side street.

At 8:30 he tried the door to the lavatory down the hall. It was locked. At 9:00 he tried it again. Open. He was not going to be caught-short on the train the way he had been when he first got on the ship . . .

Back in the room, it was 9:20. Perhaps he should read? There was nothing to read but the school list – and the letter he'd written to his father. He didn't want to read either of them.

He sat on Chris's bed. Then he smelled Chris's pillow – but it smelled of nothing but hotel pillowcase.

At just after eleven there was a knock on the door and then it opened before he could get to it.

' 'Ello-'ello. You leaving today? Right – well you'll 'ave to go or they'll charge you for another night. Room's probably taken anyway.' She was a little woman with no teeth and a raspy sharp voice.

James rang for a porter. They said they'd send one right up. He waited and waited.

'I can't wait all day. I 'ave to 'ave you out.'

196

'I'll move my things into the hall.' He hauled the trunk and then his tuck box outside and put his overnight case and his blue raincoat on top.

At last, the porter came. He was very old and frail-looking.

'Oh blimey. I'll 'ave to make two trips – taking a taxi?'

'Yes, to Paddington.'

'You go down and I'll meet you at the front.'

James didn't like the sound of it. He picked up his raincoat and suitcase and, feeling he was abandoning the rest, walked to the lift.

The doorman wouldn't let him out the door. 'Receipt please.'

'My brother paid my bill last night.'

'Receipt please.'

Chris must have taken it. He went to the desk. No one waited on him – they took care of grown-ups who had just walked up when it was his turn. It happened again and again. His trunk might be out in the street – stolen already, for all he knew.

At last a gaunt-looking clerk listened to his story. 'We don't give two receipts – it's most irregular,' he said and went away. But he came back with one.

The doorman wasn't even there. Outside he found his things on the pavement. A taxi was sitting right there on the kerb.

'Could you take me to Paddington Station, please?'

'What are you doing – running away from home?'

The question was brusque, serious. This time he knew he was going to cry – but then the taxi-driver got out of his cab, laughing.

'Coo, you must be going for good.' He loaded the trunk, upended, on the platform beside the driver's seat. 'Coo, what you got in 'ere – buried treasure?' It was the tuck box – James didn't understand, and then

197

remembered it was quite empty.

'Yes sir, yes sir.' It was the porter, running up.

He felt in his pocket. No change. He took out ten shillings. 'Could you change this?'

'No, sir – too early.'

The taxi-driver changed it. 'Give the sod a sixpence.' But James gave him two-and-sixpence.

On the way the driver opened his glass partition and shouted back, 'You all on your own?'

'Yes. I just came all the way across the Atlantic on my own – but I know London like the back of my hand.'

'You do, eh? Where you come from?'

'Bermuda.'

'Coo, Ber – wha?'

'Bermuda.'

'Oh yes, I never been there I 'aven't – but I've been to Palestine. Yep, me and Lord Allenby, we've been to Palestine.'

James kept asking him questions.

'No – the bombing don't worry us, mate. Takes more'n bombs to worry a Londoner. You take the King – he's been bombed. Buckingham Palace's been bombed. Think the King would move – ? Not bleeding likely. There he was in the paper, a photo – lookin' at the rubble of his 'ouse with a little smile on 'is face.'

They stopped at a traffic light. A bus pulled up on the outside of them. His taxi-driver looked at the bus-driver and drummed his fingers on the wheel. 'Hello, gloomy,' he yelled.

The bus-driver slipped open his window. 'Wha?'

'Hello gloomy!'

'Everybody else is gloomy,' yelled the bus-driver. 'Why the hell should I be out of fashion?'

Off they went again.

'You take this 'Itler – they keep talking about

198

'anging 'im when the war's over. 'Anging is too good for 'im. What they want to do is strip 'im naked and let the women of London have 'im. They could take care of 'im – the women of London.'

It was past noon when they got to Paddington. Chris had said to give the driver a shilling tip. He gave him three shillings – and felt guilty. He did it just so the man would like him – he was always doing things like that and it wasn't even his money.

'Cor,' said the porter, 'the two-fifteen school train don't even pull into the platform 'til past one-thirty.'

'Just take me to the platform.'

'Well, I don't mind if you don't – Where's your father?'

'Dead.'

'Oh, dear – come on then.'

Paddington was cleaner than the other London stations he'd seen. He sat on his trunk again and waited. He kept looking for other yellow caps and was glad each time he couldn't see any. There was a counter behind him selling food and the smell of it made his stomach churn.

You could go there and get some tea and a bun. But you can't leave your things. Coward, you could take some of them and keep looking back.

Over past the platforms was a great big Static Water Tank. 50,000 Gallons, it said.

At 1:35 the train was pulled in by a little shunting engine. There were all sorts of names on the window – he could only read two. 'Pickford House' and 'The Elms' – small world again, The Elms was Teddy's school at Bognor. Probably not the same one and certainly it was no good to him anyway.

The train was all black with soot and dirt, but underneath it looked streamlined and you could see yellow and brown trying to struggle through . . . GWR

was written everywhere. Great Western Railway ...
There must be hundreds of schools out to the west,
and all their names were written on this train's
windows.

He kept pulling at his cap but it just wouldn't fit on
his head properly – it was too small. Daniel Neal
hadn't had a cap his size – 'You've a fat head,' said
Chris. James imagined his head looked, to other
people, like a great big egg – or sort of deformed like
the heads of Martians in Buck Rogers.

Schools, schools – he had a few ambitions for
himself that went beyond schools – maybe it was good
to think of them. He'd like, of course, to be a writer
and a poet like Christopher (and that young officer on
HMS *Dunedin* – funny how thoughts come to you – he
remembered now: the man's name was Thwaites,
Michael Thwaites. And he wasn't a midshipman but a
sub-lieutenant and he'd already written a famous
poem called *The Jervis Bay* – about a ship that drew
enemy fire upon itself to let a convoy of mostly
refugee children get away ... That was a mighty
brave thing to do. James now knew just how damned
brave it was.

(At sea, all he'd wanted to do was save himself. And
now, poor Michael Thwaites, who'd written the great
poem, was himself, probably, drowned in the torpedoe-
ing of HMS *Dunedin* – of course he was, his parents
had said so. 'Michael Thwaites went down on the
Dunedin.')

Well, he still wanted to be a writer – and, of course,
he'd like to be a flier too. But he'd also like to be a
racing-car driver – just like it was before the war, a
red car and plenty of petrol and chocolate bars
wrapped in silver paper and labelled with gold paint
... And just race cars for the fun and hell of it – roaring
around at 80-100 miles an hour, making a noise like

the clappers of hell.

And then, too, he'd like to be a good helmsman of a sailing vessel – like his Grandfather Halcyon and like so many of his Bermudian ancestors. (The best Bermudian helmsmen alive now were Grampy Halcyon, and his, James's, godfather, Willy Sheringham . . .) He'd like to win ocean yacht races . . . or just bum around the waters of home . . .

Or maybe he'd be a boatbuilder like his Dad, the best builder of wooden ocean-going vessels . . .

And suddenly it came to James, standing there in Paddington Station, on that May day in 1942, when a rare shaft of sunlight streaked through the glassless roof and touched him: most of all, he wanted to be a great lover, to love beautiful women – to love A REALLY INCREDIBLE BEAUTY . . . and to have her love him . . .

Maybe even Julia Law Worthington . . .

The shunting train had stopped grunting and was only wheezing now.

So, Charity, his mother, had said the Holy Man had said three of her sons' names would circle the globe, eh? Three. If there was only one thing certain in his mind, it was that one of them would be himself.

A whole bunch of girls in grey felt hats started arriving now and he felt sick – he knew what he had to do, and it was get something to eat quick – if a whole bunch of yellow caps like his showed up, he'd have to join them, and he might not eat for hours – a day.

He picked up his suitcase and left his trunk and tuck box and went off to the counter where the food smells came from.

He joined a queue and kept looking back and got some change out. At last a woman in white said:

'What would you like, matey?'

' _ '

' 'urry up, then.'

'Tea – and a sausage roll.'

'Sausage rolls are off.'

'A sandwich.'

'Cheese or tomato?'

'Both please.'

'One or the other.'

'Cheese then,' said James, wishing he'd asked for tomato.

There was no room to sit, so he went to the window and put down his suitcase and kept looking back to his trunk – which he couldn't see – so he gobbled the sandwich and drank the bitter tea and it tasted good.

Then he saw a whole hurry of yellow caps like his and, jaysus, as they would say on the *Empire United*, he needed to pee bad.

He knew what he should do – and that was join the group of yellow caps immediately. But he might then not be able to pee for some damned reason or other – and, first things first.

He finished his sandwich fast and took his suitcase and went outside into the bustling noise of the platform. GENTLEMEN a sign said, with a barber's pole under it.

He looked over at the group of yellow caps and there was a short fat man in a suit with an umbrella who seemed to be looking all about – then he seemed to see James and gesture towards him.

James nonchalantly went down the stairs under the Gentlemen's sign.

WASH'N'BRUSH-UP 3d

The place was as big as a cathedral with about fifty urinals, as big as baths with glistening brass supply pipes – all empty. He had a quiet pee and then carefully shook himself, buttoned up his fly, inspected

202

his trousers. They looked OK. He grabbed his suitcase and climbed the stairs.

Biting down the agony of shy hesitation to join the unknown group, he headed towards them with what he hoped was a firm tread.

Some of the yellow caps ogled as he approached, some seemed busy nattering with each other – James felt very left out.

One smaller boy was crying – his mother dabbing his face with her lace handkerchief, after she'd licked it. James felt sorry for the boy who looked lost and miserable – while the mother looked impatient and angry.

When he was almost up to the group the master turned and said, in a lispy foreign accent: 'Who are you?'

'Berkeley, sir. Berkeley.'

'Good – good.' The master, in his brown suit, checked a list and ticked his name off. He pulled out a gold watch.

'Is your twunk labelled – here – Collins – you and Berkeley put your twunks in the goods van together, will you?'

A large boy about his age with glasses – one lens was broken – came forward. 'Yes, sir.' He looked at James: 'Where're your things?'

James pointed.

'We'd better make two trips.'

They did.

'Where are you from?' James asked, as they walked back.

'Wimbledon.'

'I'm from Bermuda.'

'Is that so – thought you sounded like a Yank.'

'I'm not a Yank – although Bermuda's close to America.'

James wanted to talk more, but Collins was talking

203

to someone else with his back to him.

THE LION SCHOOL, the sign said over their section of the train.

'Come along – get aboard now,' the master said.

'Old Vegetable wants us on,' Collins said in a low voice – to his mate.

James got on board taking his suitcase – and was glad he ended up with a corner seat by the window. He knew it was a long way west – and, if there was one thing he liked to do, it was to look out at new countryside he'd never seen.

'Mr Vegetable, sir. Can I open the window?' someone asked.

'No, leave it please – thank you.'

In a little while, as the train filled with all manner of uniformed school boys and girls, Mr Vegetable said: 'Berkeley, have you eaten?'

'Yes, sir.'

Soon the train started forward and soon too it was going at a helluva clip – almost as fast as The Flying Scot on which he and Christopher had travelled to London.

The way west seemed very long indeed and James was soon hungry. It wasn't long before he discovered, by listening, that Mr Vegetable's real name was Von Tobel – a Kraut, the boys whispered.

He wondered what the school would be like and pictured a great big red barracks with ivy and iron gates and a swimming pool inside. He hoped his bed would be a corner one and with some privacy for undressing and enough blankets – and getting to a bathroom not too complicated.

Most of all, he wanted a friend. He knew no one but Collins and Collins was quite busy with his mates.

The journey seemed interminable, through strange

but beautiful farm and river land (the most enchant-
ing place he saw was Worcester, where the train
stopped for a while – he knew it was the capital of the
county his school was in – and the whole city looked
like a time-capsule taking you back to tranquil
medieval days: all the buildings ancient and of
beautiful yellow stone and a green cricket field on
which a game was being played and you could hear
the clout of cricket balls and the spire of the
Cathedral rose behind the game and he would have
liked to have stayed there for ever) and the station,
when they got there, quite unlike what he expected.

It was little and had a small brick building shaped
like a house.

He looked around for his brother, Teddy – but he
was nowhere to be seen. Chris had said Teddy would
meet him –

But James didn't like to ask anyone: 'Trouble with
The Lion School is that it's been sold since I was
there – has a different headmaster,' Chris had said.

They filed out and into a crocodile and James asked
about his trunk.

'Don't worry – old Bill gets them.'

Where was Ted? He couldn't have forgotten . . .

The school had small wooden gates, just big enough
to let a car through, with a modest latch – the
driveway was short and the building not like an
institution, but a large home – about 1920, James
guessed.

What was a lovely surprise were the Malvern
Hills – he'd never seen anything like them before.
They were like three giant elephants that towered
over the whole place – towered in a rotund and benign
way.

Bermuda had no hills this high; they were strange
and red and dark brown, as well as green.

(There had been a time back on the train when he had had to bite on his lip: he'd looked at his watch and it had said 4:00 and, at Washashley they'd be having tea and Aunt Lillie offering bread and butter and Aunt Daisy saying the water wasn't hot enough and that you couldn't do a thing with O'Neill now that 'Dearest' was gone – he wondered if they would think of him, or mention his name? Aunt Lillie would, he thought. And it would be even nicer to be at the Fenders' house where you didn't have to watch your manners and there was the sickly sweet cake and Fenders smiling and whistling and twisting the dog's tail.)

The next thing he knew of The Lion School was a bossy woman named Matron who everyone seemed to be kowtowing to. 'Every boy get your number and go upstairs and unpack immediately.'

He didn't, at first, always quite understand what the boys said – but this Matron had a voice that could cut the paint off walls, anyone could understand her – even Hitler, James thought.

The front hall was all blue- and wine-coloured tiles ... Yes, he thought, the place had been a house – not grand like Cedar Hill in Bermuda and not ancient and a 'showplace' like Washashley – but pretty impressive, nonetheless. It was superb relief to discover the school was like a house – and not the great brick institution he had imagined.

'Berkeley, you are in the V and VI Form room – you both play and have your classes here,' Mr Montrose, the headmaster said. James realized that the two Forms were lumped together.

Mr Montrose was pale and grey, but seemed to move with speed and grace – as if he were a dancer.

Collins said, 'Mr Montrose is a great mathe-

matician – and he was once a great rower – at Oxford.'
James had noticed the crossed oars in the front hall.

'Berkeley, you are in the senior dormitory,' said Mrs
Montrose – who James instantly recognised as a
motherly and sympathetic woman. 'Hosefield and
Llewellyn will be with you and they are super
chaps –'

James got the impression that Hosefield and
Llewellyn were a couple to be 'reckoned with.' Mrs
Montrose looked like Wallace Simpson – only with
soft brown English eyes.

It all happened in a whirl and very soon it was
bedtime, and they'd unpacked and eaten and gone to
bed.

As he went to sleep, James thought of Bermuda and
of his grandfather, and of the wallet, that he had now,
that Grampy had given him – he wished his grandfather would write. He didn't really dare hope that
anyone in Bermuda would be thinking of him now . . .

He began to cry, silently, as he tried to get to
sleep – you could hear many of the younger boys
crying – not so silently. . . .

Book Two

IX

James's extreme tiredness let him sleep, but when he woke up in the morning it was with this thought: 'Where in hell am I? Oh yes, The Lion School, Malvern, England. Ta-tum.'

He thought of Bermuda.

'Angels help women,' was his mother's most often repeated remark – three or eight times a day. 'Oh, God, help women.'

'Mae West help men,' his father would say, his eyes twinkling behind his pince-nez glasses, like Mr Roosevelt's.

Ta-tum. And Grandfather, the gifted and revered Eugenius, had had a stroke and that was why he hadn't written. And anyway Grampy 'only had eyes for Granny' and, after her, mostly only for Chris.

Later his first morning, James was in the Montroses' drawing-room (which was also Mr Montrose's study) where he saw an absolutely beautiful painting of an RAF plane. He no sooner saw it (he was being asked questions about his ration book) than he blurted out: 'That's a Mustang, isn't it – my brother Christopher flies one of those.'

'Our eldest, Geoffrey, flies one too – and one of our old boys – Cramer – he painted it and gave it to me,' said Mrs Montrose.

'How wizard,' said James – using Teddy's word that seemed to be common usage here too. It was clear that Geoffrey was adored by Mrs Montrose – and by Mr Montrose as well.

'Our Geoff is in a Ranger squadron – has been shot

down twice,' Mrs Montrose said: 'I certainly hope it hasn't happened to your brother?'

'No. Never. Thank you, ma'am.'

'But our Geoff escaped,' said Mr Montrose. 'Once he was shot down over France – but he gave the Jerries the slip and got home.'

'How fantastic,' said James. He was a little envious – but he was also made much more aware of just how dangerous Chris's flying was. 'Ranger' was a word that was spoken of here with awe . . .

Mr Montrose had fingers all split with chilblains but his handwriting was incredibly neat and handsome.

James quickly noticed that smiles worked on Mrs Montrose – and, to his surprise, on Mr Montrose too.

'He's an old miser – cares only for his turkeys and chickens and fruits. He's rich as the Catholic Church . . .' a boy had said.

'But he's not a bad bloke,' another had said.

'He can't half hit with a swagger stick,' Collins said.

'Oh, he's all right,' said Llewellyn.

Llewellyn had come in from Wales where his father was a parson.

'Hello, Holy,' Collins had said.

Llewellyn grabbed Collins's arm and twisted it – though Collins was a good bit larger than he. 'Take that back.'

'All right, Llewellyn, I'm sorry.'

James was amazed that the exact same phrase was used as had been used at school in Bermuda: 'Take that back.'

Llewellyn was king – he was also called Captain of the School and Captain of Cricket.

He looked at James: 'Are you any good at bowling?'

'Don't think so.'

'Oh damn – we need a bowler. Can you play cricket?'

'Yes.' James expected they would all be far better than he was.

'We'll try you out. Maybe you can bowl.' Llewellyn had a dark handsome complexion and very quick and intelligent eyes. He was full of vital energy and his brown hair bounced off the back of his head as he walked.

The centre of The Lion School was not Mr or Mrs Montrose, nor a combination of the two.

'They don't even like each other, I don't think,' said Llewellyn. 'It's Mr Healey who's the backbone of the place, Berkeley.'

'Oh yeah, why?'

'You really a Yank . . .'

'I'm not, I'm a Bermudian.'

'What the hell's that?'

'It's a beautiful island in the middle of the Atlantic – all blue and bright.'

'You're a liar,' said Collins.

'I'm not a liar,' James said, taking the instinctive step closer to the much larger boy.

He guessed Collins was tough but not as tough as Llewellyn by far – and not as tough as he, James was – at least, that was his instinctive guess.

'I'll clean your clock,' Collins said.

They were in the dormitory.

'More likely I'll clean yours.' He stepped up until his shoe was against Collins'. 'Take that back about me being a liar – right now.'

'Jesus, he means it,' Llewellyn said. 'Go on, hit him, Berkeley.'

'I will hit you, Collins – if you don't take it back. No one calls me a liar – *ever*.'

Collins drew back his fist and then looked in James's eyes – he backed down.

211

'You can't even take a joke, Bermuda,' he said.

'Take it back about me being a liar.'

'All right, then, I do.'

James was surprised at himself – for a while there he'd acted instinctively, as if back at school in Bermuda. He hoped he could keep it up, but he doubted it . . .

'Healey's an absolute peach. He's eighty-four years old. Older than God's grandfather – but he knows everything,' said Llewellyn.

'Everyone loves him,' said another boy. 'He's absolutely fair – like Solomon.'

'You only said that because you're Jewish, Joell.'

'Oh, shut up,' said Mogs Llewellyn. 'Healey *is* like Solomon. But he's rather frail.'

'Now here's the drill, Berkeley. If Healey hits you – you have to pretend to be hurt, see? He has this little stick he calls Tickle Toby. If he hits you with Toby, you pretend to be hurt, all right?'

'All right – sure.'

'He's a wizard old bloke – we all would do anything for him.'

Mr Healey was the V and VI Form Master. He was like an aristocratic ramrod – with a shock of white hair.

His nose was aquiline, his hands exceedingly handsome and well kept – though bent and twisted with age. His eyebrows bristled long and fierce – but when James looked into his eyes, he recognized there a tenderness and intelligence, an integrity that he hadn't seen since he'd last looked into his grandfather's eyes at Cedar Hill, Paget, Bermuda.

'Who are you, boy?'

'Berkeley, sir.'

212

'Oh, you are, are you. Where are you from?'

'–' James couldn't speak.

'We certainly hope you can bowl, boy.'

To his anger James realized that the uncontrollable tears had begun to run down his cheeks.

'I beg your pardon, sir,' he got out. 'May I leave the room?'

'What? What?' Mr Healey's brown eyes were so bright they seemed to give off sparks. 'Yes – yes – go at once then.'

James went to the bathroom and burst into tears. This uncontrollable crying was so embarrassing. He had no idea where it came from, or why, and so he could give himself no excuse.

This first time he was so long gone that Healey sent Llewellyn for him.

'You'd better come back or even Healey will get angry.'

'I'm coming.'

James knew everyone could see he'd been crying – he decided his only defence was to hold his head high.

(He had been given a desk and a place for his tuck box – the desk had a top that opened upwards. James was glad. It provided a place to hide – temporarily, when it was needed.)

'Define *amo*, boy,' Healey said.

James looked blank. Somewhere way back he knew the answer – but there was a convoy and a lot of water in between.

'Well, Berkeley. What does *amo* mean in English? And I don't mean in the war, or in the military sense at all. The Latin, *amo*.'

'–'

'Oh, dearie me, did you learn nothing at all in Bermuda?'

'Yes, sir.'

213

'How long were you in Bermuda, boy?'

'Always, sir. We've been there three hundred years.'

'I see. What's it mean then, Joell – tell him what *amo* means?'

'To love, sir.'

'Yes, Berkeley, boy. *Amo* is the Latin word for love. I think you'd better write it on the board.'

'Soppy old word – to love, who cares,' someone whispered.

James took the chalk and, as he did so, he noticed that Mr Healey's hand shook terribly – much worse than O'Neill's back at the Hall.

'Just write *Amo* means Love. Go on. And then you'll never forget it. You see, boy, love is the most important word – in Latin and in life anyway – if not here at The Lion School.'

James wrote it.

A little later Healey said: 'Well, Berkeley boy, can you say the French word for love?'

He was going to say 'Fuck' – and he was glad he didn't. That was not French, but the Merchant Navy's word.

He hid by lifting his desk-top.

'Put the top down, boy, and look at me.'

James couldn't move.

'Well, Llewellyn, give us a French sentence with love in it.'

James put down his desk-top – on which were carved and written at least fifty names and messages – and looked right into Mr Healey's now exceedingly severe gaze.

The eyes said: you don't know anything at all and you are going to be a great nuisance.

James felt his mind go blank and knew he couldn't think and was afraid that there was no hope of his

thinking in the foreseeable future ... He bit his
tongue to stop any tears.

After lunch (in the dining-hall James soon picked out
the coat-of-arms of Fotheringham: three beer barrels
and a chain-mail coat among all the other public
schools to which the boys at The Lion were destined)
they played cricket in the nets.

They played 'Bowls-Out-Goes-In' – a tough game
because it favoured the best. The best batters batted
the longest and the best bowlers got in to bat again
the quickest – all most boys cared about was batting,
of course.

Fortunately for James, that afternoon he was
concentrating on batting – and fortunately, too, he
didn't know he was being watched. For, if he had
known, he would not have done well.

After only a short while it was quite clear to him
that Llewellyn was a far better bat than he was – and
so was not only Collins but Joell, and Joell's younger
brother.

But James kept trying, and much to his surprise, he
kept getting 'in' quite often. To his annoyance he
never seemed to stay there half long enough – because
what he too wanted to do far the most was bat.

They played almost all afternoon.

It was a lot of fun, and James realized when he
stopped that this intense exercise – this game,
cricket – made him able to forget the *Empire United*.
When he was actually playing cricket, the water
stopped pouring and flowing over everything: it was
the only time it had happened (except for some of the
time with Christopher) since he left the ship on the
Clyde.

They were walking away ('It's tea-time,' Joell Major
said) when, suddenly, Mr Healey came out from

behind a hedge.

'Give me that ball, Berkeley. I want to show you something.'

James gave it him. Healey took it and rubbed one side only into the groin of his trousers. 'Just one side, you see, boy.'

Mr Healey rubbed and rubbed. 'Now you go and try and hit what I bowl at you.'

James took the bat and went into the net. Mr Healey moved and ran like a man made of wood and old ratchets – but he delivered a ball that James saw, carefully swung at, and missed entirely.

Then Healey said: 'Now, you rub it – just one side – and now you bowl it at Llewellyn. Just bowl easy – holding it like this. Your fingers down the seams – see, boy, simple. Bowl it.'

James did as he was told and, without thinking much about it, aimed roughly for Llewellyn's stumps.

James's ball curved as Healey's ball had – but Llewellyn hit it clear out of the field.

When James got it back, Healey said: 'Do it again – but rub it hard first.'

Despite careful preparation and aim, Llewellyn clouted the second ball about the same as the first.

Mr Healey put his finger to his mouth as if signalling James not to give in.

On the third ball Llewellyn missed the curve and it took down two of his stumps – the middle and the leg.

'There you are, Llewellyn,' Mr Healey shouted excitedly. 'He doesn't know anything about Latin – but he's our new bowler.'

In the changing room Mogs Llewellyn seemed very friendly.

'What did old Mr Healey mean?' James asked quietly.

216

'He means you will be our second bowler.'

'For the Second Eleven, you mean?'

'For the First Eleven, you damn ass, Berkeley – no one cares a damn about the Second Eleven at this school. You'll open the bowling with me this Saturday.'

'You're fooling?'

'I damn well am not, Berkeley. And you'd better not let us down – The Lion School and Mr Healey too.

Two days later James received a letter: it wasn't from Bermuda, or from Christopher – but it made him extraordinarily happy.

'Embossed stationery, I say, that's pretty posh,' said Mogs. 'Washashley Hall, Lincolnshire – we've two of those, I don't think.'

James read:

Thursday

Dearest Jamie,

O how we've all missed you our dear handsome boy, even O'Neill asks after you . . .

Please do you remember for me that written over a school –

Rugby, I think – are the words: Fame Is The Spur But Manners Mark The Gentle Man . . .'

(There was a lot of the news, that meant that all at Washashley was exactly the same: that the bells still chimed securely and sent the rooks flying, that tranquillity reigned . . . The letter ended as all letters from Aunt Lillie, he was to discover, ended)

I send you that kiss I suppose you don't want.

Fear God!

Aunt Lillie

217

Long before Saturday's cricket game – the first game against The Lion School's most respected (and feared) adversary: The Elms School (to which Teddy, his brother, had gone before its evacuation from the south coast) from over the hills in Herefordshire – James had a sort of emotional overcoming.

James knew only that Mr Montrose, awakened in the night by Matron's yelling – she herself had been awakened by his, James's, yelling – caned him, James, in his pajamas and bare feet, in the front hall, with his military swagger stick. It all happened so fast he didn't really quite know whether he was awake at school or asleep on the *Empire United*.

'Thank you, sir,' he said, stunned into reality. James felt, as well as the physical pain, an intense humiliation that put him into a secret and murderous fury.

'Go back to bed now, boy,' Montrose said – he sounded almost affectionate.

As James went by the Matron's room on the second floor, she said: 'And a jolly good thing too – I should hope so – waking up the whole school in the dead of night. You just do that again, Berkeley, and see what happens to you.'

'How many did he give you?' asked Hosefield.

'You heard,' said Joell Major – 'It was three – terribly hard ones, I thought. Bad luck, Berkeley. Jolly bad luck.'

'Sh-sh-sh-sh,' said Collins.

'*Cave* – Matron,' said Mogs Llewellyn.

Matron came in like a regimental sergeant major: 'No talking in here – and get back to sleep.'

Everyone but James was feigning sleep.

When Matron left, Joell said: 'Sorry, Berkeley – that was awful. Hitting you for a nightmare – I am awfully sorry.'

218

'Thank you. I'm all right.'

But the next day he couldn't eat or talk. (Teddy, his
brother, was teaching at a school in West Malvern –
waiting, of course, for his 'call-up' into the Fleet Air
Arm.) James wrote his name and address on a piece of
paper. Mrs Montrose phoned Teddy.

James expected Teddy would make things right –
would put things to rights, as Grandfather would say.

When Teddy came, James kept trying to catch his
eye but Teddy would not look at him.

Everyone agreed that they should go for a walk.

On the walk, James tried to hold Teddy's hand.

'Don't be a baby. Just jolly well pull yourself
together.'

After they had walked a long way James was
amazed that he was able to get out the simple truth:
'Teddy – I don't think I can cope yet – I think you
should consult with Christopher and if he agrees I
should go back to Washashley – even if only for a bit.'

'Wha?'

James said it again – adding: 'Do you think you
could do that for me?'

'Possible but not probable.'

'Ted, it's as if my wheels have been spoked with
sticks – will you help me get home?'

'Possible but not probable.'

'Could you contact Christopher?'

'Can't – he's on Active Duty.'

'You could telegraph him.'

'Possible but not probable.'

'The RAF would forward a telegram.'

Teddy gave the same answer – his face untouched
by emotion.

'Would you consult Mr Somers? Wouldn't he help?'

'Possible but not probable.'

219

'I can't sleep is the trouble, and all I keep feeling is the water.'

'You could pull yourself together.'

'Teddy, what happened to you the first day I arrived here – Christopher said you'd meet the train?'

'Meet the train? Meet the train . . ? Oh, yes. Your first day – sorry, I forgot.'

They walked back the long mile or so to the school. At the wooden gates, James asked: 'Will you help me please, Teddy?'

James wanted to throw himself into Teddy's arms – but some inner wisdom prevailed.

'Possible, old boy, possible. All you really need to do is pull yourself together.'

After being with Christopher, being with Teddy, James decided, was very like carrying around an empty thermos flask.

Teddy left the school, and James, hearing the crack and thump of cricket ball on bat and the shouts of boys, wandered out on to the field.

He was quite aware of where he was and who he was and why he was upset. He was also somehow outside, it felt, of his own body.

He had a strange yet rather certain conviction that he would die that afternoon. He didn't really know why. He thought he should somehow be out on the field.

The other boys invited him to play – but did not press him when he shook his head.

It was while he was out at the extreme edge of the playing-field – by the red-trunked fir trees – that a strange event occurred.

Suddenly, the whole area of the Malvern Hills seemed shattered by the roar of a low-flying and very high-speed aircraft. It was an Allison-powered P51

Mustang at almost full-throttle: it flew, below the level of the hills, straight across from the ancient Roman Camp to Great Malvern, to Malvern Link and to the Malvern Beacon – its altitude was about three hundred feet.

It flew straight across the school grounds – and then, reaching them, climbed straight up and did an Immelmann turn.

The school came as alive as a kicked bee's nest.

'It's Geoff Montrose.'

'It's Geoff!'

Many seemed to be shouting, but most stood in silent awe.

The plane had disappeared.

'It's Christopher Berkeley,' said James Berkeley to himself.

The whole event was mysterious – and then the plane came back from the opposite direction: now it seemed to be no higher than the trees and sedate Edwardian chimneypots.

Roaring across the school grounds it waggled its wings – it banked and curved at the great elephant-shaped Beacon and then came back yet again.

What was even more strange was that the plane did not have RAF markings, but USAAF Stars . . . James had never seen these.

Over The Lion School, the pilot slammed open his cockpit, and clearly and slowly saluted; gloved hand to forehead, where his goggles were raised at a rakish angle.

Then the Mustang climbed almost straight up in a vertical climb; as if to reach for the heavens themselves: it went straight up: it was impossible . . .

Then, just before its lost impetus would have resulted in a stall, it levelled out and disappeared high and heading south-south-west.

'It's Christopher Berkeley from Bermuda,' James said to himself. 'He came to tea, for my sake and just in time too.'

It was the combination of surprise and incredible closeness that was so impressive: the plane was so close that James had seen the very oil leaks on the under-cowling ... It felt as if he had smelled and touched as well as heard and seen the aircraft.

James went and joined the cricket.

'Was that your bro', Berkeley?'

He only shrugged.

He bowled – and when he bowled someone out, he batted.

'Do you think it was Montrose, Berkeley?'

James smiled in a friendly way, but he couldn't talk.

It was a Thursday and they played cricket all into the long English twilight.

The cricket match against The Elms, that bright, warm and dry Saturday, was another event that changed James's life – he learned a very simple but profound lesson: in life, ceremony is everything.

It was just a cricket match between two schools for small boys: but the grass was perfectly cut in green stripes, the white creases were perfectly laid out; the two teams were dressed to their last brushed hair of striving.

Then way out on the field, Captain Mogs Llewellyn said, at the exact moment when Mr Healey flipped his silver crown piece in the air: 'Your call, sir.'

'Heads,' said Baroda, the captain of The Elms – and they stood, arms on hips, nonchalantly waiting the turning falling coin.

'Heads it is,' said Mr Healey.
'We'll bat, sir,' said Baroda.

James had never worn his all-white flannels before,
never mind his bright yellow cricket cap with the
black lion on it; the cricket cap was more gold than
yellow, and he thought it very beautiful.

Mogs, the captain, opened the bowling.

(The Elms usually beat The Lion School handily –
though one year The Lion had beaten The Elms,
thanks to one boy, Griffin, who'd later gone on to
Fotheringham – and then played for England at
seventeen years old.)

In the first over Mogs took a wicket. No run was
scored.

Then Mogs nonchalantly threw the ball to
Berkeley.

'Right arm round,' Berkeley said to The Elms'
umpire's question. Berkeley took his paces: five
sounded good, and maybe one for good measure.

First ball, Baroda glided him for four.

It felt bad. But next ball, Baroda, The Elms' captain
and best bat, played James's ball on to his own
wicket – a lovely tinkling sound, out for four runs.
The applause from the little crowd was the first James
Berkeley had ever received for anything: he knew he
would never forget it.

Mogs Llewellyn took two wickets in the next
over – for no runs.

James caught and bowled an Elms boy his first ball.

The first innings turned out to be the lowest score
that The Lion School ever got another team out
for – an amazing, even for boy's cricket, nineteen.

Llewellyn took six wickets for seven runs, Berkeley
took four for nine – there were three byes.

The home school passed The Elms' score with eight wickets in hand... When his turn came, James Berkeley made a duck – 0.

But it didn't matter: he'd learned that he could bowl – and bowl with the best of his school against the best of their rivals.

Most rewarding of all, for James, was that, after the match, Mr Healey came by and touched first Llewellyn on the shoulder: 'Well played, you chaps,' and then him: 'Jolly good bowling – Berkeley – I am impressed. Llewellyn, good show.' And he went out muttering: 'Silly old wars come and go, but cricket endures.'

On the Monday after the victory over The Elms, James received an airmail letter from Bermuda. It had 6d worth of stamps on it: three 2d stamps – and they were, probably, the most beautiful stamps ever minted for and by that tiny colony. They had on them a blue sailing sloop on a broad reach with her spinnaker set: the sloop's name was *Sirius*. The sky was also blue and the word Bermuda written in blue – the edges of the stamp were red, with two small and delicate red seahorses in each upper corner.

'What are those things, Berkeley?'

'Do you know the size of a seahorse?' James asked his new mates.

Mr Healey, who had just come into the VI Form room, wanted to know also.

'That big, sir – about a half-inch most of them are.'

'And are they like that?'

'Almost, sir – but I think really more thin – more delicate.'

'How exquisite ... And the sailing boat – are there many like her?'

'No sir, only one.'

'And who does she belong to – the Bermuda Government?'

'She belongs to two people, sir – my grandfather and my godfather. And she sails like an eagle, sir.'

'Extraordinary. Lovely she is. I've heard Bermuda is paradise – is that right Berkeley?'

'Some of us think so, sir.'

'Did you ever read *The Tempest*, Berkeley?'

'No, sir.'

'Well, Mr Shakespeare, like Mr Marvell, also thought Bermuda was paradise. And now, if you don't mind, Berkeley, we will study what Mr Shakespeare had to say about a more important place than Bermuda – can you guess what that place is?'

'No, sir.'

'It's a place called *Love*, gent-ell-men – and that is what we are going to study this summer – a place called Love in Mr Shakespeare's *As You Like it*. I fear you chaps are a bit young to understand about love but I would like you to try – I can assure you, you will never regret it.'

'You must think we are really stupid, daft, Berkeley – to believe that bog about your grandfather owning that boat,' said Mogs Llewellyn.

'Yes,' said Collins '*and* that that plane was flown by your brother.'

The sea was washing over his eyes again – rocking the room and even the French doors through which one could see the green of the Malvern Beacon. . .

'You are full of bog, Berkeley – for a new-bug you are surely full of bog.' Collins had his new spectacles inches from James's nose.

'Leave him be,' said Joell Major. 'Leave him alone. I for one believe him anyway.'

Hosefield, his black eyes bright in contrast to his

225

slight frame, said: 'Let's wait and see – it all adds to the excitement, doesn't it?'

If he had been asked to bet, James would have cut his hand off and bet it, that his brother was flying that P51. But he hadn't been.

Matron seemed to take delight in relaying the information to the VI Form: she knocked, poked her head round the door and said in clipped Oxbridge: 'Sorry to trouble you, Mr Healey – but I felt sure the whole school would like to learn that Geoffrey Montrose just this moment phoned his mother to say that it was he who flew that plane over the school last Thursday.'

In his weakened state, this blow almost broke James.

Both Llewellyn and Joell Major were very considerate of him – but James was virtually unreachable.

This situation continued for several days.

Fortunately for James, he could hear his grandfather Eugenius Halcyon, saying: 'The gods that can deal horrid blows can sometimes deal reprieves as well.' I hope, I hope, Grandfather.

Mr Montrose, the headmaster, came into the VI Form room, as usual, without knocking.

'Berkeley. There's a trunk call for you. Usually they are not allowed – but you can take this one in our drawing-room.'

James rushed after him. Let it not be Teddy – and what was a trunk call anyway?

'Skeglee?'

'Who's that?'

'It's me – Christopher.'

'It isn't.'

'It is.'

'Where are you?'

226

'Look, I'm in Hereford – and I just had a word with your headmaster and he says I can take you out as a special treat.'

'Is it really you, Christopher?'

'As sure as sea puddings squirt water.'

'Are you really Christopher?'

'B'y, what do you do for a peeg with wind?' This was spoken in a very Bermudian accent.

'Didn't you fly over the school the other day in a Mustang?'

'No.'

'*You did.*'

'Look, I didn't. Can't hold up this line. It's two o'clock – I'll pick you up at three – before four anyway.'

'Christopher – are you in uniform?'

'Yes, of course I'm in bloody uniform. See you in a while, Skeglee.'

James's nose was pressed to a VI Form window – and, also, he knew, about six other noses were pressed against other windows.

Chris came up the drive, carrying his greatcoat, with his RAF cap on the back of his head.

'Wow – look at those wings.'

'And a flight lieutenant – none of your crumby pilot officer.'

'And what a roll and slouch,' said Mogs Llewellyn, imitating it.

'Bermuda shoulder flashes – wizard, eh? I've never seen those before.'

James runs to the front door. Mr Montrose is already there. (James looked for Mr Healey – but he was seldom around at this time.)

James hopes to hell Chris won't kiss him – especially on the mouth, the way the family always does.

Christopher shakes hands with Mr Montrose, and, by the time James gets to them, they are already talking about the war . . .

'Our Geoff escaped again – oh, how glad we are. The Yanks lent him a new plane.'

'Lucky, for him. Glad for you all, sir.'

Fortunately, Chris just shakes hands, but they are in the main hall with its tiled floor which echoes and Chris does utter the unforgivable: 'Well, how are you, m'dear? That's what I want to know – that's why I flew up, I mean.'

But it doesn't matter. Chris is delivered whole – to James's classmates, to the staff. . .

It's 4:15 already and they only have until 7:00.

'I thought I'd take him to a concert,' Chris says to Mrs Montrose.

'That would be good for both of you,' she says. 'I don't think I can stand much more of these Ranger Operations – never mind you fliers.'

'Well, it's much worse than it sounds – I mean, it sounds much worse than it is – and some of us do have amazing luck. All of us really.'

They left the school. James savoured the eyes that followed them not only down the drive, but through the gate and then up the hill where their heads and Christopher's shoulders were visible over the jagged Worcestershire stone wall.

Out of sight of school, James began to shake. Christopher took his arm. They walked and talked all the way up to Great Malvern.

'There's no doubt you are still suffering from the Atlantic crossing, m'dear. And the only way I know to beat it is to keep busy.'

'I thought I ought to go back to Washashley.'

228

'Well, it can be done. Trouble is – then you have to start over again. Let's talk it over – and you can make up your mind.'

'I kept asking Teddy and he – well, I couldn't get through to him.'

'Yeah. I've noticed that in the realms of sympathy – if you are looking for nothing, Ted's your man.'

'I just knew you waggled your wings and every-thing. And no one could fly that well but you – I thought.'

'Well, Geoffrey Montrose must be as good as me, that's all – pretty near impossible, but still.' Chris laughed his self-deprecating laugh.

'We haven't long. But I can give you a bang-up good tea – a good deal of my love – and this marvellous concert.'

'I don't want a concert – I want you.'

'You can have both. I promise you, Jamie – it's just what the doctor would order. I promise – and if you don't like it, we can leave.'

James was experiencing the agony of those who love a great deal and have a very limited time. It was, for him, twenty minutes of joy and then two hours and twenty-five minutes of painful counting of minutes.

'Can you fly over this evening?'

'Christ, I'm a passenger in an old Anson – but someday maybe I will.'

'When will you come again?'

'Soon as I can – but probably not this term.'

They had a 'bang-up' tea of bread and jam and buns and cake. Then they went to the Winter Garden and heard a part of the concert.

As a boy, in Bermuda, one of James's real joys was to climb under their grandmother's grand piano and lie quiet on the floor while she played . . . He'd never seen another instrument but his grandfather's nine-string banjo – which Grampy no longer played.

The little concert was, as Christopher suggested it would be, a soothing magic. James was thrilled with the violins, the violas, the woodwinds, the brass, the percussion, all of it. Then they played some Elgar – who was a local hero.

James was transfixed. 'It's better than flying, isn't it?' he whispered.

'The same – no – maybe it is better,' said Chris. 'It's flying and sailing together.'

Then they played Elgar's Concerto for Viola and Orchestra. James was moved to a state he had never before understood existed for humans . . .

'I'll go on with school. I'll be all right.'

After a long silence Christopher said: 'Thought you might.'

'What are those?'

Christopher had just swallowed a little white pill from a vial. 'Nothing serious – for hives.'

At The Lion School, Chris had a few words alone with Mr Montrose and then James was allowed to walk him to the wooden gates.

Please kiss me goodbye, Christopher. Please kiss me on the mouth, like Grampy always does. Please give me a hug as big as the Great Sound, Bermuda.

'I know you don't want me to kiss you, m'dear,' Chris said, holding out his hand. 'So I'll just say so long, and go, as usual, right?'

And then he was gone.

But James's stock at the school was high now; he was one of them.

'Don't forget to go out for the boxing team,' Chris had said.

230

James soon discovered that there was another colonial at the school – Old Bill.

'He was the only man in the First War who was shot right through the heart and lived,' said Mogs Llewellyn.

'You're kidding?'

James took the first chance to be close by where Old Bill was working. Bill had a hearing aid, appeared to be about sixty, and worked in the garden wearing a gentleman's herringbone tweed suit.

'Hello, who are you, boy?'

'I'm Berkeley – I'm from Bermuda.'

Bill adjusted his hearing aid.

'My father was born in Grimsby, Ontario,' James said.

'Oh, yes. I'm Bill and I'm from Hamilton, Ontario – I know Grimsby.'

'Oh, how great. How come you didn't go back to Canada?'

'I know Grimsby well.'

'Bill, how come you didn't go back to Hamilton – to Canada?'

'I didn't have the money.' James thought that Old Bill might be 'simple'. But Bill said, in an open way: 'You got another name besides Berkeley?'

'James.'

'Pleased to meet you, James.'

They shook hands.

'My dad was in World War I.'

'Oh yes.' Bill went on with his weeding. 'Where was he?'

'In the Dardanelles.'

'I was gassed on the Somme – and then shot through the heart at Vimy.'

'I heard that – how did you live being shot through the heart?'

231

'We Canadians are tough – I'm a testimony to modern science, aren't I?'

'Does it hurt, Bill – your heart, I mean?'

Bill looked at him long and hard – and said, straight into his eyes, 'Not now – not any more – it's dead, pal.'

'Well, so long, Bill. Nice to meet you.'

'So long, James.'

He must be simple: if his heart was dead, he'd be dead.

That night, or a few nights later, James began his *Love Story After Lights Out*, which became a popular nightly feature of life in the senior dorm at The Lion School –

'Well, I'll tell you a story. You see, once upon a time there was a school called The Lion School where all the masters and the matron had disappeared – you see.

'And all the junior boys had gone home – disappeared too – and there was no one left at all, don't you know, but six Sixth Form boys.

'And one day, this strange but handsome man – a father – delivers this absolutely beautiful young girl, his daughter, it turns out – she has blond hair and these small breasts blooming like rosebuds . . .

'Say, am I boring you fellows?'

'No.'

'No, Berkeley, go on.'

'Because if I am boring you or anyone is going to be damned telltale fink and twit, I won't go on.'

'No – no.'

'Go on, this, this beautiful young woman. . .'

'What's a fink?'

'A fink is someone who squeals – the lowest form of human – a rat – a telltale.'

'No. No. No.'

232

'This blond daughter – please go on.'

'Yes. Well, she's an extremely beautiful young woman. But our hero, Jack, is a wee bit concerned about this young woman – young girl – because, well, "Let's face it," he says to the father. "She's a wee bit too young."

' "That's just it," says the father. "She's a virgin and I've heard that you're the best bloke about and well. . ."

' "Well, what?"

' "Well, I was wondering if you'd do me the extreme favour of breaking her in – to the secrets of love?"

' "Well," says Jack, "to tell you the truth, sir. You don't know this but I've been watching your daughter from afar for a good many months.

' "Fact of the matter is, I'm sort of in love with her."

' "In that case, it's all the better and so I can leave my Marian here with you."

' "Well, you can if you are sure that's what you want – but what about her being so young?"

' "That's it entirely, isn't it, Jack. If she's young then she'll not be able to get pregnant – right?"

' "Right."

' "Well, then, I can leave her with you just this week. And you must promise me to teach her all the secrets of love – but you're not to take any non-sense from her. I expect her to be well and truly initiated – broken-in is the word for a young filly, isn't it? And if she gives you any trouble, Jack, don't hesitate to give her a good spanking – right on her bottom."

'And so, our hero, Jack, walks the father to the double wooden doors and bids him a fond farewell.

'And when Jack gets back to Marian he has a chance to look at her more clearly.

'And she has blue eyes that sparkle like water on

233

the winter grass. She has long arms and legs and her hair is straw blond and hangs right down to the middle of her back – it swings when she walks.

'Her body is just beginning to form – she has little breasts like the smallest waves of the sea. She has no other hair on her body at all – save a little brush of fuzz on her upper lip.

' "I've been watching you riding your pony by on the beach – and I've fallen in love with you long ago."

' "As a matter of fact, Jack," says Marian, "I've been watching you watching me and I've said to myself – if only that young man would fall in love with me – perhaps . . . Perhaps I'd let him . . ."

' "What?"

' "Well, maybe – I might just let him –"

' "What?"

' "Kiss my lips."

'So with the light behind her straw-coloured lovely hair, Jack kisses her very gently.

'Her lips are like strawberries but also as soft as cherries – and so they kiss and kiss. For the longest time.

'And then Jack says to Marian, "We've a beautiful swimming-pool here – so how would it be if you and I – were to go swimming?"

' "You mean, I assume, you very bad lad – without our clothes?"

' "Skinny-dipping, I do mean, indeed. Will you come to the swimming bath, now?"

' "I will," she says. "Indeed, I will."

'So, after dark, they go down to the swimming-pool holding hands.

' "It's lovely," says the fair Marian, looking at the water, and Jack, emboldened, says,

' "May I take your clothes off now?"

234

' "Yes," says Marian and blushes red as a tomato. "And may I take your clothes off?"'

' "Enchanted," says Jack, and they undress each other in the moonlight.'

'Naked, she is even more beautiful and her little breasts respond – actually change – when he touches them. The nipples become hard like a flower's stamen.'

'What are stamens?'

'Shut-up.'

'Jack says, stroking her arms as well as her breasts, and her lovely stomach – emboldened even more – "May I look at your flower?"'

'She nods. And so he looks at her little quim more closely. It's like a little behind – hence the term "ass" – she's a double-ender, he thinks.'

'What's a double-ender?'

'A boat, you fool – shut up.'

'So this little bottom, this quim, has a small white-pink hood, like a tiny nun's habit – And beneath this little nun's habit are two small lips, a tiny behind, and, between the lips, as Jack touches them, ever so gently, he finds the sweet little hole.

'He gasps, for he knows that is where the cock fits.'

'Is it, Berkeley? Is it really?'

'Indeed it is, it's the Holy Grail itself. The holy place all seek.'

'Go on, Berkeley.'

'No, that's all for tonight. It's all to be continued tomorrow.'

'Why you bastard.'

'You call me any more names and there'll be no more Marian and Jack – ever.'

'You sod.'

'Don't make him angry whatever you do.'

'It's called *The Soap Opera With The Fucking Left In.*'

235

'I thought you said it was a Love Story for Lights Out,' said Mogs.

'I changed it.'

'*Cave! Cave!* – Matron.' But when Matron entered the dormitory, it was to find them all sound asleep – two, even, snoring gently.

Before this, James had been glad to find out that the boys exchanged sexual secrets – openly and simply.

They'd compared sizes: most were all the same: small penises even when erect . . . Only Joell Major had a developed penis – and body hair.

Although they all played around and had happy sensations, none but Joell had any 'come'. All the other boys, except Joell, licking their hands, claimed that they had 'come'.

'At least, mine was sticky this time.'

'Yes, look.'

It was very like him and Llewellyn brushing their hair.

'Let me try your American brush.'

'OK – let me try yours.'

Mogs used James's New York brushes – brushing about fifty strokes a night.

James used Mogs's brush – which had its bristles set in rubber. 'It's good.'

They both tried to get their hair to lie down flat so that they looked more grown-up.

'Your prick is the same size as mine.'

'Exactly.'

'What does your dad do?'

'He's a parson – and he likes running over rabbits in his Riley. And that upsets me rather.'

'I guess I wouldn't like that – but my dad shoots

tomcats that get after his favourite females.'

'He does – in Bermuda?'

'Yes. I'm a bit worried – I haven't been to the bog today.'

'What on earth's there to worry about – if you don't go today you can go tomorrow.'

'Oh, is that right?'

'Certainly – sometimes I don't go for three or four days – it doesn't matter, Berkeley.'

'That's good to hear.'

'Have you ever screwed a girl?'

'No.'

'Ever felt one up?'

'Not really – only my sister when we were tiny.'

'I don't have a sister, you lucky sod. What I'd really like, James, is simply a girl who'd let me play with her.'

'Yes, you're right – me too. That would be perfect.'

'How do you know so much in the stories?'

'Ah-hah, that's my secret.'

'But I'm your friend.'

'So?'

'Say, Berkeley – I don't mean this as a prying question, but why do you have these nightmares?'

'It was the convoy I came over on, I think.'

'Is that why you cry as well?'

'Yes – you know something, Mogs – don't tell anyone, will you?'

'No. Not if you say so.'

'I don't have any control over my tears.'

Mogs went on brushing. 'Don't worry about it – it will probably go away.'

'In days of old when knights were bold and ladies weren't invented – they drilled great holes in telegraph poles and went away contented.'

'I'd screw any woman from five to fifty.'

'Any man or woman,' said Joell Major. 'Any tree, even.'

Hosefield said: 'I just want any man – or woman – to play with me – I think I'd rather have another bloke.'

'Like who?' said Morgan. 'Like Berkeley?'

'Certainly, like Berkeley – he's just my cup of Earl Grey.'

'I'd screw *anyone* – even Mr Healey.'

'Shut up,' said James.

'Yes – leave old man Healey out of it – he's special,' said Llewellyn.

'He's the most decent bloke I ever knew, I think.'

'You know that book about Mr Chips? – he's much better than that. I've had special classes with him now for three years. He's taught me Hebrew as well as Latin and Greek – and it's only because of him that I won the scholarship.'

It didn't worry James that, although they were friends, he and Llewellyn didn't pair up for sex.

He went with Hosefield: their game was that James could climb on top, while Hosefield was below with the covers between them. It had the added advantage of the speediest separation into innocence, should a member of staff come by.

Llewellyn and Collins took turns riding each other. It was pretty easy to hear approaching intruders on the loud linoleum outside.

'I hope we'll be friends forever, Mogs.'

'Certainly, why ever not? You can come and visit my family.'

'And you mine.'

'You live in a palace.'

'Like hell.'

'You said it has eight hundred oil paintings in it.'

'Well, they're mostly awful and valueless. But it's the flowers you should see, Mogs. The flowers at Washashley are the best. My Aunt Daisy does nearly all of it – she's not my favourite – Aunt Lillie is my favourite – but Daisy does the flowers.'

'And they are named for flowers.'

'Never thought of that.'

X

It was an incredibly dry, hot summer . . . They seemed to be continuously playing cricket. They played in the nets as soon as school was out. 'Bowls-Out-Goes-In.' They played it after tea and until call for bedtime – 9:15.

When they had matches – even 'away' ones – they practised in the nets afterwards.

About halfway through the season, it began to occur to everyone, even to Matron and Mrs Montrose, that the possibility of their attaining a 'Star Team' was in the offing.

Of course it was a very very long shot – after all, in the whole forty-year history of the school (every year's photo of every team was around the dining-hall wall) there had only been one Star Cricket Team . . . And that was when they had a captain who'd gone on to play for not only Clifton and later Cambridge, but for England as well . . . (The school had produced two England cricketers.)

After beating The Elms, they beat Malvern Link Preparatory – and then The Cedars, who were over past the Roman Camp. Then they beat Sleaford House in Hereford itself. Rain almost stopped them at Tewkesbury, against Standwell College, but Mogs Llewellyn caused another collapse for 59 runs and then he and Collins clouted 60 runs in less than sixty minutes – all achieved just before the game would have been called for rain.

It was in mid-July that Mogs came down with 'flu, and Joell Major was captain, and the heavy responsibility of opening the bowling fell on James – all against Strawberry Hill School, a very well regarded side.

The day before the match, running down the path from the school field, James collided with Old Bill, the Canadian gardener, in his herringbone suit.

'Oh, it's you – James Berkeley – from Grimsby, right?'

'Yes,' said James, embarrassed. 'I'm awfully sorry – did I hurt you?'

'No. No.' Bill looked off up the hills and then back to James and said, 'Well, we haven't done much yet, have we?'

'Done what, Bill?' James shouted against the man's deafness.

'We Canadians – we haven't done much in the War yet, but they'll find some bad mischief for us soon – they always do.'

'And you, Bill – do you want to be in the War?'

'Hell, no, fella – being killed once is enough isn't it?'

'Yes. So long, Bill.'

'So long, James.'

It was 20th July 1942. Strawberry Hill School batted first, and Joell Major, during their fielding, frequently conferred with James. James bowled far better than he ever had before – the lack of Mogs Llewellyn made

240

him strive hard, and with each wicket he took, his bowling seemed to improve.

For all that, Strawberry Hill made 72 runs – a considerable innings, especially since Llewellyn was The Lion School's best bat, as well as bowler, and he was in Matron's care with a temperature of 102.

James opened with Collins, and that day he found that he could do little wrong. Collins was out by 22, but Joell Major came in and stayed until 57 runs were on the board. Between this time and when he hit the winning run, James actually went to merely block a ball that would have taken out his middle stump –, and, to his amazement, saw the ball soar, not only over the bowler's head, but plop into the long grass of the boundary for six runs.

He was the hero of the day – and their team was a Star Team – all victories – and he had achieved more than that: he won his colours and, since Mogs Llewellyn was leaving for his public school – Shrewsbury – the next term, James had now proven himself his able successor as Captain of Cricket.

Mr Montrose confirmed it – on Mr Healey's recommendation.

Mogs said to James one evening between bouts of batting and bowling. 'Mr Healey is the very best, don't you agree?'

'Yes, of course.'

'Well, it's up to you other fellows to take care of him now.'

'How do you mean?'

'I mean just keep making sure that people really know who and what he is. Listen and I'll tell you a couple of secrets about him.'

'You know why he likes *As You Like It* so much?'

'Because his wife was named Rosalind, right?'

241

'Yes – and she's dead. Been dead a long time.
'But he also had a son.'
'Oh, yes?'
'Yes. Lost him in the First War.'
'How awful.'
'Doesn't stop there, Berkeley. Had a grandson.'
'No.'
'Bloody yes, I'm telling you. And he got leukaemia – and old man Healey sold his school that used to be there next door – to try and save his grandson from leukaemia. Took him to Switzerland.

'But he died anyway. So, you see, we have to take care of old man Healey. Joell and Hosefield know. Collins is no good for this stuff.

'But I figure you are worth it – all right, you New-Bug, bugger you. You just pass it on when you leave for Fotheringham. People have to take care of old man Healey – he's the top.'

'Of course, Mogs.'

'Not that he's helpless or anything. But he's sort of The Lion School's National Trust.'

'I agree.'

They broke-up on the 27th of July and James spent one of the happiest days of his entire life – alone on trains bound home to Washashley, from Malvern Link.

For the whole day (he had to change trains twice) he never once sat in a seat, but spent every minute staring out of his window watching the sights go by, waiting for the first familiar glimpses of Lincolnshire and home.

Every tree and field seemed vested with England's special majesty; even every ghastly factory-sooted city seemed beautiful – all because he was so happy.

242

He kept remembering Mr Healey as well – it was almost as if he took the old man along with him.

Mr Healey was a surprising man: suddenly, once, in a class he'd said: 'No person who hasn't experienced the agony of boarding school (except those who have done time in prison) can comprehend the euphoria of being set free ... You boys can understand this – right?

' "Please tell Her Majesty", Sir Walter Raleigh remarked when he was released from the Tower to go to the Indies to seek treasure for the last time, "that the pleasure was almost worth the pain." I think I've quoted it about right – though some things are difficult to recall when one is over eighty.'

Then he remembered Mr Healey stopping their appallingly bad reading of *As You Like It*

looking out at the gentle green Malvern Hills, saying, 'Boys, I wonder if it is at all possible to share something with you. I just wonder ...

'The truth is this, if you will bear with me long enough to take it in your heads – which I know would much rather be out in the sun – and perhaps they should be.

'But the truth is this: *I* am the same as you, and I know something that you don't – and I want to share it with you, because life is very very difficult – and you need, you must have this knowledge to help you.

'The truth is THIS: that wisdom is almost impossible to pass from one generation to another –

'But here is the truth that an old man like me told me when I was your age.

'ARE YOU READY? You might write it down – I did – and that was a wee bit before your time:

'It was in 1871 – Now this is the truth –

243

'There isn't anything in this life that is worth anything at all except Love.

'Now Queen Elizabeth put Sir Walter Raleigh in gaol because she didn't know what love was – and she had Sir Walter's head chopped off, but not before he'd written these words.

'Now understand: an old man is sitting laughing and a young couple ask him *why*, and he says, because he once loved a girl who didn't love him back – and so, they ask, why are you laughing?

'And Sir Walter says:

' "But love is a durable fire
In the mind ever burning;
Never sick, never old, never dead,
From itself never turning."

'Now if you will just remember that and write it down *and understand* – no real harm can ever come to you.

'Run along now, then, run along.'

James wanted to tell Mr Healey about the staircase at Washashley and how all Sir Walter Raleigh's adventures were carved there . . . and about the same words also being carved there. But he was afraid that he would sound like a braggart – that other boys or Healey, or both, might think he was bragging . . .

Also, who chopped Raleigh's head off – King James or Queen Elizabeth? But it didn't really matter, did it . . . ?

'Mogs – what are you doing with those effing flowers? Come and play Bowls-Out.'

'Shut up. I just swiped 'em. I'm going to leave them

244

outside old man Healey's door in this jam-jar.'
'Jolly good idea.'
'Sh-sh. *Cave.*'

'So how am I going to hear the rest of your *Soap Opera With The Fucking Left In*?' asked Mogs, who was, with Joell Major, the only person leaving The Lion School that term . . .
'Don't know. You'll have to come back.'
'Maybe I will.'
'I'll meet you at Piccadilly at noon on the fourth day of the fourth month of 1944, right?'
'Right.'
'Keep your pecker up.' James said.
'My trouble is getting the damn thing to keep down.'

Now he was whirling towards Lincoln. He had, as he had had for hours, his head half out in the train's slipstream, watching for the familiar.
About the last thing he'd said to Llewellyn was: 'My brother Christopher's hands shake terribly – and, you know what else?'
'No. How the hell could I – since you haven't told me?'
'He eats little white pills – and I reckon he drinks about a bottle of whisky.'
'A week?'
'A day.'
'Holy bog.'

When he saw Lincoln Cathedral, blue and faintly purple in the mist, he started to cry – with happiness. That's *our* Cathedral and our city – and Washashley is just three miles from there . . .

245

At the station Fenders had on his best serge suit and James thought it was in his honour.

But then, to his surprise, the car was the big Daimler that belonged to the undertakers. Aunt Lillie and Aunt Daisy were both there. The news was the last thing he would have imagined.

'We've not been able to warn you, dear boy,' said Aunt Lillie. 'Because it's only just happened.'

'And we can't get Christopher,' said Aunt Daisy.

'And even Mr Ted's disappeared into the Royal Navy – and been shipped, you couldn't guess where?'

'Where?'

'Back to 'Merica, Mr James.'

'No fooling?'

'Truth is, my lamb,' said Aunt Lillie, taking him aside and stroking his hand and arm, 'that poor O'Neill has taken his own life.'

'Good God, whatever for? I beg your pardon, Aunt Lillie – but how, why?'

'He left a note.'

'May I see it, Aunt Lillie?'

'Yes and no – your Aunt Daisy – indeed all of us are just shattered. Awful thing is, he can't be buried in consecrated ground.'

'Why ever not? What did he ever do wrong!'

'My dear boy – it's a terrible thing – and I feel that we should pretend he just died. But everyone knows now – and Christopher mustn't be disturbed any more.'

'Poor Aunt Lillie – you poor darling.'

Aunt Lillie, on hearing these few words of sympathy, put her head on his shoulder and sobbed.

'Poor O'Neill was the driver of the Rolls when it hit the little girl at Biggleswade.'

All that James had heard began to come back to

246

him.

'So, dear, dear Aunt Lillie – where are we now – I mean, where is O'Neill's body?'

'At the undertaker's, dear boy. He's to be buried tomorrow.'

James touched her cheek, stroked her tweeded shoulder and her arms. 'It's been too much for you to bear, Aunt Lillie.'

'He hung himself, James – in the stables – on a coat hanger – one of the awful new wire kind.'

He went on stroking her.

'Fenders has been a tower of strength,' she said. 'He got Dr Smith and then the police – Fenders did all the official things.'

James shepherded them all into the Daimler.

Fenders was on the jump seat, he with an aunt on each side.

The message on lined grey notepaper said:

Dear Madam,

Sorry. The Master said it weren't my fault – but I have not been able to hear him say it now these many

It were me who drove the car that killed the little girl and I carn't life with it any more. Please ask the Master ask them to forgive me for this and my other sins Bless Miss Lillie.

O'Neill

Another surprise for James was when he went to meet Dicky Dickens and Dicky said, right away in the Dickens' parlour: 'Everybody knows – it were your rotten old rich uncle did it – not O'Neill. He were to blame and he put blame on the innocent O'Neill.'

James drew his breath in, put his hand to his

mouth – and to his dismay, felt silent tears rolling down his face.

He turned and ran from the house.

His tears were still on his face when he ran in the south door of the Hall.

Aunt Lillie was there having a cup of tea – right under the ducks that were painted on the blue vaulted ceiling, the ducks and the fluffy white clouds.

'Dicky was horrid,' he blurted out. 'He attacked me – all of us really.'

'Oh, Jamie,' she said, her eyes twinkling with understanding. 'I expect Dicky is just hurt. Did you write to him at all?'

'No, I forgot.'

'Well, that's it, then, dearest boy – you'd better go back and say you are sorry – I mean about not writing.'

James must have looked puzzled.

'It's the hardest thing in life – but the best – to say one is sorry. Why don't you do it – and then come back and have cake?'

It took a lot of courage to knock on the Dickenses' forbidding front door.

After a long time, Dicky came and opened it.

'Can you spare a minute?' James said.

'Oh, aye.'

'I just wanted to say I was sorry about not writing to you.'

Dicky looked bewildered and then he started to cry too. He came out. He closed the door behind him.

'And I'm ashamed of what I said about Uncle – even if it were true. He's dead and I never knew him. So it's me who's sorry.'

'No, me. I did mean to write.'

A voice called: 'Dicky! Cum and do chores!'

'I have to go.'

'Me too – see you later.'

'Aye.'

'Did O'Neill have any family?' James asked.

'*We* were his family,' Aunt Daisy said. 'He really was a wonderful man, you know – he'd been in three livings with your uncle – It was just an accident that drove him a bit off.'

'Yes. Yes,' said Aunt Lillie. 'It can happen to the best of us. It was just the bad luck of life.'

James ate his cake. It was such a mixture of sadness and happiness. He loved the sound of the rooks and he loved being home – but he kept hearing O'Neill saying:

'The world were our Empire, wasn't it – and the Germans wanted it.'

Fenders did indeed take over.

'The vicar has agreed that Mr O'Neill can be buried in the little churchyard.'

'Good. Where is it?' James asked – they were alone in the hallway.

'Just beyond the main graveyard. It's damn silly,' he whispered. 'If you ask me, sir, damned silly. A separate graveyard for sinners – as if a bloke that finds life unbearable has done something wrong.'

'Well, I'll take care of my aunts. It's at two o'clock?'

'Yes, Mr James. At two.'

James took the Aunts through the little gates (he kept giving the stables a big wide miss wherever he went, he noticed). Aunt Daisy stopped at Uncle

Albert's grave, picked off two weeds, crossed herself.

The vicar said the whole service from the chancel steps.

The pallbearers were Fenders, Old Watkins (the walled gardener, bent like a willow tree), Tom Watkins (who looked like an unhappy forest animal in church) and several more men that James didn't even know.

James kept reading, over and over, the ancient memorial on the wall; erected by a grieved wife for her 31-year-old husband in 1745.

'. . . loved with unspeakable affection and mourned with a grief that would be despair if it were not for the hope of eternal life.'

He wondered what their 'unspeakable affection' had been and if they had reached eternal life together . . . He hoped so.

Into the Washashley summer, Christopher suddenly arrived and stayed a short but, for James, a very memorable time.

They talked and walked through the gardens and the parkland across the road, where the great beeches grew on the low green slope that silhouetted the pale Cathedral three long miles away.

Christopher said: 'Look – look – the deer.'

'Are they really from China?'

'Everything comes from China, you know, even china – but these are the deer of the New Forest bred with a strain from China.

'You can't catch 'em, you know – just try. The challenge is to sneak up to within fifty feet of one or more without their knowing it. I've been trying since I was ten – I believe it can't be done. . .'

'They are lovely.'

'As lovely as ghosts,' Christopher said. 'So, then, tell me about your school?'

'They were jealous and mad at me over the tuppenny stamp with the seahorses and the *Sirius* on it.'

'Well they might be – that was some six metre, that *Sirius*. She was the model for the new International One Designs, you know.'

'And Grampy owned half of her?'

'Oh, yes. Cousin Willie and Cousin Keith Sheringham, owned the other half of *Sirius*. She was designed in Norway – and built by Dad and they never lost a cup with her. I was bilge boy in one series.'

'Oh, I thought you were bilge boy on *Nea*.'

'No, on *Sirius*. *Nea* was long before my time. I always think of them as the reigns of *Nea* and *Sirius*. Anyway, *Nea* was built in 1897 – designed by James Halcyon, Grampy's brother. Built at Red Hole, Paget. She reigned until 1908. *Sirius* was built by Dad. *Sirius* reigned from 1928-1934 – when she was sold into slavery: to an American from Larchmont, New York.

'*Nea* was owned by Grampy and his brother James – "The Commodore" they called him, James Halcyon – he who died of the booze in New York. Well, never mind . . . *Nea* was *absolutely* the best Bermudian yacht ever.

'She wasn't grand – because she was all local built and designed and all made out of Bermuda cedar.

'She was named for the poet Tom Moore's lover, Nea. I guess you could say – she was the best Bermudian vessel ever built just for fun. But the name *Nea* is sort of a super-secret family joke –

'Anyway, she was only about thirty feet – a lot of

251

overhang in bow and stern, her half-model is the first half-model in the RBYC drawing-room. You can't miss it.'

'Wow. The *Nea* – the boat and the woman – the woman was Nea Tucker, right?'

'Yes, Skeglee. And Nea Tucker is believed to have had an illegitimate child by Tom Moore – that's why some of the Tuckers are so tiny –'

Christopher stopped and carefully took out one of his little white pills. James thought he'd best be quiet. Christopher's shaking hands were very disturbing.

He didn't know whether he should tell Christopher he should ask to be put in a hospital – or whether he should or could talk it over with Aunt Lillie.

If only Dad was here, was what he kept thinking. . .

'What are you flying now, Christopher?'

He thought it best to keep Christopher both walking and talking as long as he wanted to.

'P51. North American Mustang. Service No. 110422. Date of Issue – .'

He remembered how, in Bermuda, Christopher was always going down to the seashore to read the maximum and minimum thermometers. 'The water temperature this day, Grampy, is 72 – minimum 66.'

Grandfather sent the information to the Royal Meteorological Society.

'It's funny having two homes, Chris. It's confusing.'

'Yes. I guess it is for us all. But Home – with a capital H, is Bermuda, isn't it?'

'Oh, yes. I always dream of Bermuda – in colour.'

'I wish I always did.' Christopher kicked a stone. 'Yes. Confusing. But, when this effing War is over, Skeglee – all will be well.'

'I guess, Chris,' said James, 'we could say – about the yachts – who are we to have the right to own such

252

things . . . eh?'

'Yeh. Could say, who are we to have the luck to be born on Bermuda?'

'Yes.'

'Do you remember Soodi?'

'Sarah Hinson. No. I think I do – but I really think I don't. After all, she died in 1933 and I was born in 1929, you know.'

'Right. Well, Soodi was the top for me. If *Nea* was the best vessel – Soodi was the best human.'

'So how come she was the Top, the Boss, of this family and she was born a slave?'

'It was that she was so strong – strong and good both. She judged the whole Bermuda tribe of Halcyons and Hinsons. I tell you, James. I'll tell you what she said to me before I left – the first time I came to school in England.

'First, I'll tell you, Skeglee – that the best thing about Soodi was the way she smelled –'

'How was it?'

'I dunno – like Bermuda somehow. Soil and cedar. The inside of the cabin of an all-cedar boat with wet oilskins hanging, was the smell of Bermuda – old Bermuda. Sarah Hinson smelled of that and rain on grass in Bermuda on a fresh morning.'

'I like the way you smell too – and Dad – and Mother, of course,' said James.

'Smells are marvellous. You smell damn good yourself, Henry – or whatever your name is.

'Anyway, Soodi has me sent for, all the way from West Hill up to Beaumont. It's about 1931 or '32 – She's almost a *hundred* years old. Last Hinson born in slavery.

'She's there like the Queen of Sheba. Man – she has me – little me – up to Beaumont and she's sitting in this great big old rocker that belonged to King Joe

253

Halcyon himself. And she rocks and rocks in silence and then she says:

' "Aubrey Spencer" – now, no one had ever called me Aubrey but Sarah and God at my baptism – see?

' "Aubrey Spencer Hinson," she says.

' "Berkeley is the name, please ma'am," I say.

' "Don't interrupt," she says.

' "Aubrey Spencer, you just remember this: you are going among those unloving people – you may *not* be English. Fine, they are, but they have no hearts – Be proud of being a colonial, of being a Bermudian –

' "It Was Not By *Chance* That We Got Here, Us Coloured And White People.

' "You hear?"

' "Yes, ma'am."

' "You are to be proud and brave and remember who you are."

'She was something else, she was.

'Another time she said: "The Americans have no class and the English no hearts – but you are a Bermudian, and I want you always to remember it. You understand?"

'I kissed her and she knew I understood all right.'

'Wish I had known her.'

'Hope you do now. For example, you do realize that her colour was as black as anthracite – ?'

'And her hair white, right?'

'No – her hair was part black and part grey – she never did get white.'

A day later, inside in the rain, Christopher said: 'Of this place, Skeglee – I like just a few things.

'This statue – The Rape of the Sabine Maidens – the original is eighteen feet high – this copy is only two and a half feet – but look, the light shines through it so that you think you can see the sinews and the very

254

bones – and it's all a carving in Carrara marble.

'And this Adam fireplace – I know Uncle Albert bought it in London – but I don't care, it fits. It's the soul of Washashley.'

'I think the bells are?'

' 'Spect you are right. The bells and the deer.'

Christopher put his shaking hands in his pocket – after having a stiff drink of whisky just before lunch – 'I'll tell you one last thing about Grandfather Halcyon.

'He said, the last time he was over: "Gad, Fay, I'll tell you a funny thing about English people. Every time I find one that I really like – damn if they don't turn out to be Irish or Scottish or Welsh!" And Grampy laughed and laughed.'

'People envy us, you know – being British and Bermudian. We are like the new flying boats – transatlantic. But don't get smart, Skeglee. You know when the Dutch had flying boats?'

'No.'

'In the sixteen-hundreds.'

'But they were sailing boats.'

'And they called them Flying Boats and they were.'

'Say, Christopher, you know, as I said, when I see a Bermuda stamp even, my heart leaps. But, to see Dad's handwriting on the envelope – that's my biggest joy.'

'Why is that, dear boy?' said Aunt Lillie, going by in haste.

'Because he always writes such great news – of his shipyard and what he's building.'

She'd gone.

'It's Mamma's handwriting I look for. She's the biggest person in my world – my life.'

Christopher had had two whiskies now and he was quite rosy-cheeked.

'Whatever went wrong between you and Dad – did he hit you?'

'And I like the Marie Antoinette clock – she really did give it to an ancestor of ours.'

'Sorry. I didn't mean to pry. I just love Dad so much – and I wanted everything to be good between you.'

'Everything is, Skeglee. Mamma makes more of it than it was – she says he hit me with a chairleg. But the truth is, I can't remember.'

'Oh, he's spanked us – me and Widda-Widda – but he'd *never* hit anyone with a hard stick . . .'

'Perhaps not – anyway, m'dear, the more I see of this War, the more I understand Dad. Frankly, I can't wait for him to come over.'

'I could really use him right now,' said James, swilling his soda pop.

'Me too, Skeglee – me too.'

Silence.

'Why hasn't the gong gone for lunch?' Aunt Daisy said, breezing in with flowers filling her basket. 'Oh – it's O'Neill . . .'

'Dad's finished with Skids and now he's building the Fairmiles – 112 feet long and triple-planked mahogany,' James said.

'They look like yachts – motor yachts, he says. Ocean-going motor yachts. I don't like motorboats at all.' Chris smiled. 'I wish I'd been born when there were sailing boats only.'

XI

Christopher, Backwards Often,
Forwards Sometimes,
And Probably, Sideways Frequently

I

When This Fucking War Is Over, you and I will fall in love . . .

When this fucking war is over . . . a great tune – the music matches the lyrics – being an old hymn tune . . .

The act of flying is holy to me and always has been, and, in case you should have any doubts about it, I, Christopher Berkeley, baptized Aubrey Spencer, am now, I believe, partially mad . . .

To find oneself caught in a war is one of the major dilemmas of Man . . .

I would like, rather, to die to achieve this reality: That War Is Not Inevitable.

It all began, I might add, when I discovered, almost by chance, that the source of my Great-Uncle Albert Berkeley's, the Reverend Albert Berkeley, Squire of Washashley and Christ's Vicar of St Mark's Church . . . the main source of my great-uncle's income was a batch of houses in London.

(I loved the man: loved the man who tied his hunter to the gravestone outside his church's south door, preached his sermon after the first hymn – with his riding breeches underneath his surplice – and left the rest of his service to his curate and chased off after the hunt) – but this:

In Islington and Bethnal Green and Kentish Town – most of them in Kentish Town. Imagine. The Vicar of Christ owned not one house – and not one house in each borough – but a total of fifty houses.

257

And I, being on leave from the Royal Air Force –
'Bermuda flight', in number, one aircraft and one
man, me. I took leave and went to visit one of these
houses.

I did find several. But let us, for now, dwell for a
moment on No. 37 Victoria Road, Kentish Town,
NW5.

Exposure: west. View: good – into setting sun as at
West Hill, Paget East, Bermuda. View there: blue
harbour. Kentish Town: gasworks.

Number of rooms of No. 37, on ground floor: six,
excluding toilet. Toilet: dripping water but inoper-
able. Child crying nearby with running nose – self
withdrew hastily to avoid germs, from w/c and child.
Number of occupants of this floor, agent reported,
bailiff confirmed, about 25 or $4\frac{1}{4}$ per room.

Next floor: we say, second in Bermuda, Brits say,
first. Also six rooms – no toilet and one tap – leaking.
Occupants: 24.

Next floor ditto. Six floors, all ditto.

When I inquired to the agent about the w/c, he said,

'But a water closet is very rare in these parts,
sir – never mind one that is working. Most dwellings
have only outhouses. And no running water, sir.'

'I've never heard of any borough of London where
there was not running water and main sewers hooked
into.'

'If you will excuse me, sir. I would suggest that
there's several boroughs of London that you've never
lived in or even visited. These are not for gentlemen,
sir. These are investment properties.'

Flight Lieutenant Berkeley visited seven of these
dwellings of the fifty that his uncle owns – owned. All
he could manage in one day.

Conditions insufferable, unacceptable and unbearable. Income, incredibly good: percentage on invest-

ment only matched by properties owned by the Roman Catholic Church – and some Church of England institutions.

Total weekly income per room of each house measured in mere shillings – in annual income, netting the Rev. Mr Berkeley £1750 . . . The same pay as two air marshals in 1939 . . . And this, of course, being only part of his income . . .

Flying is holy to me. Even in this year of Grace 1942, after two years and three months of war

even the sight of my flying boots can cause great happiness . . .

The smell of an aeroplane (especially a Tiger Moth) gives me shivers of ecstasy . . . All biplanes have always given me shivers of ecstasy, I don't know why . . .

I have always been in love with flying . . . But I confess that the sight of a downed German Heinkel . . . more later . . .

I have always been in love with flying: I used to hitch-hike from my prep-school – age twelve – to Tangmere to watch the RAF fly there . . . Few people hitch-hiked in 1933 . . .

Do you know how the ground is all flat there at Tangmere – right on top of the South Downs? You do?

It seems to be the launching place of the Gods, the place to take off for the stars – for Mars, Saturn, and Jupiter . . .

Tangmere was always holy to me: the very smell of the dope they used on those kites – I thought was the smell of the rarified air they flew in . . .

Wasn't I silly? But I've never been able to rid myself of this mad, this crackers love of flight.

I was nine when I saw my first plane and I think it

259

was the first plane that ever came to Bermuda. It was
the Stinson Pilot-Radio and the year was 1930. It was
a strange day for Bermuda because there was this
heavy overcast – and we seldom have an overcast in
Bermuda. It looked like three silver cigars and it
glistened and sped across the sky and then glided
down (the fuselage and two great floats)
   to a silent landing on the harbour at Hamilton.
   Self was moved to tears – by the silence – later, self
discovered that, the reason for the silence was that
the Americans, a man and a woman, had run out of
gas . . .
   (Good joke . . . laugh here.)
This seems typical of self: tears of ecstasy precede
investigation by brain . . . An amusing failing in this
veil – veil of war
   But, as I was saying about this Heinkel, I really
had thought the Germans, the Jerries, were just a
bunch of shits until I saw – watched this Heinkel
being dug out of the soil.
   A sort of grotesque modern archaeological dig:
What emerges is this Kraut all-metal plane.
   '*It's an iron coffin*,' I said. 'Yes, old boy,' says
Colonial Aussie-Variety, my mate, 'that is exactly
what the German aviators call it.'
   One keeps looking back on life and seeing what a
fool one was and thanking God, you don't have to live
it all again.

It all started, perhaps, with my revered and beloved
mother telling me the story of Christ's Crucifixion . . .
At the time, I was four and I had a wooden sword
made out of two lathes and one nail.
   She told me the story and I remarked, 'I *wishst* I
had been there with my sword.'
   Mamma oft' repeated this story and my response

down to the last misplaced and extra 's' – so one must assume that she was pleased with my learning – by God and by Charity Halcyon Berkeley.

Other songs I like are: 'With A Song In My Heart, I Behold Your Adorable Face . . .'
Would you like me to sing it for you? and:
'There'll Be Blue Birds Over The White Cliffs Of Dover, tomorrow just you wait and see . . .'
Now, when Vera Lynn sings this, I do like to have my daily cry like some have their daily smoke or ale
But perhaps it helps to have seen the White Cliffs of Dover, Rye and the Cinque Ports, after many a Ranger raid – seen them at dawn
Seen them through the breaking clouds as one crossed from France to Blighty at approximately 350 mph – at dawn –
do you know that the White Cliffs of England (and of France for that matter) do look purple in the dawn?
Well, they do.

'Mrs Roosevelt" – she is my love and my plane right now. A P51 Alison-powered North American Mustang.
As good an aircraft as you could get for Ranger Operations and it would be a perfect match for its Jerry enemy, Focke-Wulf 190F – if it could do what its manufacturers claim/claimed for it.
Truth is, of course, it can't.
It's all a brilliant idea – but it's all executed too hurriedly: (there's a war on). The plane is cooled by a great device as big as a refrigerator and carries four machine guns in each wing . . .
Which means the P51 Mustang is under-powered, and if you meet a FW 190F – (if it's flown by any but a total friggin' idiot – which, fortunately, a great many

261

Krauts are)

The very best thing you should do is put your stick forward and get into a screaming dive and get the fuck out of there . . .

But I digress as I undress

Behold The Lamb of God, which taketh away the sins of the world . . .

Did I tell you I have, since the very beginning, been a Server in the Royal and Holy Catholic Church of England? – Oh, yes, and all of it on my mother's instruction:

Since I was eight years old: a Server of the Vicars of Christ Crucified; nearly always in Churches called St Paul's.

Now, St Paul, it seems to me, was and is about the cruellest and most anti-life sonuvabitch that ever lived . . .

But, to begin at the beginning, as I said: I flew in the little Bermuda Flying Corps School – indeed, I was No. 1 Student and my best chum, John Bewley of Devonshire, Bermuda, a distant cousin, No. 2 . . . (It is June 1939 and we are both Home, of course, on our holidays . . .)

Now when England/Britain starts a war you can always count on the colonies getting there to fight for Mother ahead of everyone else

Especially the so-called Upper Crust of the Colonies, who have everything to prove to Mum

So, in World War I, Bermudians were over and flying as soon as the kites were dry

My Dad, born in Canada, of an English father and a Bermudian mother, he got to England and into the air as soon as he was eighteen, and some of his older mates got to France before the British and French themselves

You think I jest?

All you have to do is say, *London Is Burning*, and every brave British subject, Black, Red, Pink and White, comes haul-assing across the Atlantic, the Pacific and even the Indian Oceans and up the Red Sea . . .

Enough.

I went from Bermuda to Canada where I trained at Prince Edward Island in the RCAF, the war having not broken out yet.

(John Bewley went immediately to England via the Azores and joined the Royal Air Force as an officer cadet – thus, as I've said, he was a couple of classes ahead of me)

And I gained my first wings after an amazing twenty hours flying time

I simply loved my chums in the Royal Canadian Air Force – after public school 'men', they were so free and open and friendly . . .

Unfortunately, I wasn't with them for long (August to September 1939 . . .)

Over to England I come with the first. Where I rejoin/transfer to the RAF and am at Cranwell, in dear Lincolnshire, a place, of course, that I know full well since 1930 when I came to school to prove me more British than Oolong tea

(me being nine in 1930 and prime time to go to prep school to prepare for public school to prepare for – you know what: either being an English gentleman, or to prepare for England's war – or wars)

What did I find at Cranwell? My father's name – he having been there in 1916 . . . of which, more later . . .

So I am in the RAF and at the Royal Flying School, the Holy of the Heavenly Host, Cranwell . . .

Does well, does Berkeley: he knows the Brits and at flying, they say, he's a natural . . .

263

It's love that makes it work . . .

Twenty-one hours in Bermuda and twenty and a half at Prince Edward Island

and then Tiger Moths – the little beauty, the butterfly herself. The Book: I learn the whole book of natural flight . . . from two of the best instructors who ever attempted flight and instruction

(here was where I was different from my father's generation: for them the instructors knew not what, and taught wrong. Though they knew it not – they taught Death . . . I've seen the flight manuals and they would have been much better named Death Manuals, or, How Best To Kill Yourself In A Totally Unairworthy Aircraft . . .)

To begin almost at the beginning, pretty soon what am I flying but an amazing aircraft called a Lysander . . .

Somewhere alongside this insanity, I do continue my love affair with words: the King James Version of the Bible, Mr Shakespeare, and all that lot of noble sound

as changes Man, as does flying

To which besides, let me mention that even Andrew Marvell would have been amazed had he beheld this British masterpiece

the Westlands Lysander

Now this flying craft is utterly amazing: as true a piece of English excellence as ever flew – to France

But I get a bit ahead of myself, don't I? As they say

The Lysander has long long tapered wings like the insect, the mosquito . . . She can take off on a cricket field, then on a ploughed field – finally on not much bigger than a rooftop, a pocket handkerchief field – almost anywhere . . .

this plane has windows all around so that you can

view everything

there's one thing about the P51 Mustang, it's a perfect piece of symmetry: the wings appear as wide as the fuselage is long ... The circumference of the beautiful propellers exactly the same as the tailpiece

Not so, the Lysander and – no speedster she. She's for general purpose observation – but also, having all this immense power (a Bristol Mercury engine) and lift for her size:

she's perfect for Secret Work at night into newly occupied places like France ...

And another thing a Lysander has (what a strange bird) lights: would you believe that she has landing lights as bright as day – in her, hold it, wheel-housings?

So that 'Bermuda' Berkeley, the Volunteer's Fool, soon makes up a little rhyme which he thinks might amuse his little brother James and his sister Victoria: Skeglee and Wida-Wida (The-Dove-With-The-Bite-Of-An-Adder) were they here to share it with:

'My lights, my lights are in my toes

Which is insane as anyone knows'

So thus do I do my first service really – flying these strange Lysanders

But it is Secret Service stuff and a bit frightening: I am the chauffeur to France for these daring young and middle-aged men and women

and it's many a time we land into a hail of bullets – once a hand grenade thrown on the seat – so I threw it back like a cricket-ball – and took off ... Bang!

and sometimes we take off into/with a hail of bullets sending us on our way – listening to little beeps on the wireless and watching for sheets on the French grass

(trouble is, you never know when a mission is going

to be betrayed to the Gestapo: it can happen any time)
after about ten or twenty or thirty-four of these
flights I complain and they haul me before the local
RAF psychiatrist (now you haven't really flown
until you've flown with a RAF psychiatrist)
to make it short: he took me for a flight and found
me wanting . . .

So, let me tell you about my first view of the P51
Mustang:
and how I got there:
First the RAF gave me another physical, where
they found only one thing physically wrong with me:
a slight tendency to Night Blindness
Which is why, I firmly believe, they put me on
Ranger Operations – which take place at night, so I'm
the perfect bloke . . .
(not that I don't like them and I'm sure I am very
well suited for them: because they leave you alone: it's
a loner's job and, Berkeley, Christopher, 'Bermuda',
is, essentially a Loner – a leader of men, like his
ancestors before him, but rather a Loner . . . Not the
best character for taking orders . . .)

So I first see my first Mustang and I start out by
thinking
'God she is so *big*, the propeller boss is entirely
above my head,' and I walk all around her and she's
enormous –
But *beautiful*, beautifully proportioned: the wings
and fuselage a perfect cross – of almost equal parts . . .
everything symmetrical . . .
And then I climb in and she is very roomy after a
Spitfire, very – feels enormous . . .
and that's how I started out: thinking how big she is
But, of course, after flying 'Mrs Roosevelt' for a good

266

long while – she becomes very very small. It's as if she becomes, in the end, the span of my hand . . .

This lovely craft becomes, by union with me, usage, an extension of my very body – so that if I do bump a wing I do feel it on my body as a sharp pain

But, of course, I am a very careful pilot and so I do not bump anything if I can avoid it.

What an extraordinarily marvellous craft the P51 is – and getting better all the time: as they increase her power – it's now a 1200 hp Alison . . .

Now they do have one, a P51 Mustang with a Rolls-Royce Merlin engine: half as much power, again – 1800 hp – but I do not have this Wizard. Only the wonky Alison: but having eight machine guns firing forward . . .

Now let me explain what a Ranger Operation is: You are free, to be a Ranger.

Britain being subjected to a good deal of tip-and-run raids by German fighter-bombers: these Bandits coming over one at a time and many at once, to confuse us

We, to confuse them, fly, when we get word from the Radar Control, Intruder Operations –

That is, we go and fly over particular aerodromes in France and Belgium, trying to guess which one they come from

The idea is: you get over their field and wait for them to come home.

(and during the waiting they can, of course, sometimes, get you)

If you see them, you shoot them up and go home.

If you don't see them, you get in the Enemy Flight Pattern and try to get them to turn on their lights

and then you shoot up the aerodrome all you can

or they shoot *up* you, whichever is quicker –

It all can get nerve-racking after many hours and many many nights stretched over weeks that run into months, that threaten years.

Secondary targets can be: trains and locomotives and things . . . That's why they called us Rangers: we are supposed to be free to roam and strike at our free-will

but I have to tell you this awful super family secret for No. 1 family member only:

I don't know why or from where it hath come, but, over these last many months of flying over enemy territory

Where they do shoot most incredibly accurately sometimes, and I mean, quite often . . . A hose of fire, tracer . . . worse, two hoses in the night or three or four

And I developed this screaming TERROR that one of these ack-ack is going to hit me in the arse

(I beg your pardon for the obscenity, madam or sir)

but there you are: that is my particular fear: TERROR. I hear ack-ack and my arse starts to twitch and

my veins stand out on my forehead: I can feel them and people *talk* about them when I get back and into the Officers' Mess – BAR for *whisky*

that is my terror – and all the time it gets worse and there's nothing I can do, it seems, to fight it

about which a deal more later . . .

It was an altogether spooky time was Dieppe – I mean, like ghost stories and dirty-tricks from Above . . . I did think that even God herself might have a hand in tricking us:

Why is God, feminine, you ask? A grandson of Faith Beltt Durrell Halcyon – about whom the joke (family secret again) is: She is *The Queen of Bermuda* and

268

approximately the same tonnage?

Why is God feminine, when a coal black woman named Sarah Hinson was our judge and jury and our inspiration? (And let us not forget our late Queen, of Happy Memory, Victoria R.I. . . .)

And, what else for the eldest son of Charity Halcyon Berkeley, the Commander-in-Chief of West Hill, Paget, Bermuda and all forces at War or at school overseas?

You noticed the way I crossed myself, did you? An agnostic like me. Well, that's early training for you.

And, inherited too – did you know that Christian mothers and fathers have been blessing their children as they go out the door for these one thousand, nine hundred and forty-two years?

Oh aye, as Fenders would say.

It was the 19th of August, it was.

And I, Aubrey Spencer Berkeley, have a sort of extra-sense that others don't: I, myself, am a spooky bastard . . . It was dawn . . .

Dieppe did feel and smell creepy. I think it began when I flew over this strange place Newhaven:

which is, was, no place really, Nowhere Regis on the coast: I mean nothing – not even a store or a post office.

Only, just as I first flew over it in 'Mrs Roosevelt', suddenly this great wharf – where there should be only a little dock for the one-time Newhaven – Dieppe ferry

The littlest, it used to be . . . now suddenly this mass of black, grey-black concrete – and it feels spooky as if the Devil did build it and it smells – literally – I open my cockpit and it smells of sulphur and then there is another smell

and I notice all these MEN in black-green uniforms,

269

insects and landing barges – these troops are so ready they send up this message in their smell: sharpened steel

and fast, and ready to run and kill giants with their bootlaces . . .

all amid the roar of my engine, tearing the night, the dawn . . .

The whole, the totality, feels funny

and I have the usual terror up my arse (but that isn't anything, ho-ho-ho) I mean: let me say, it all feels strange

Not that there isn't immense support for this operation but that something unmeasurable feels wrong

Why so many RCAF aircraft all concentrated at once? – that's just a little thing (and I'm keeping out of their way for I do not want to be bumped into by some inept kid . . .)

But why – why should I get suspicious?

Perhaps because of the radio silence and the non-use of Radar Control?

Now I'll tell you a secret that is no secret: and that is that the RAF has the best Flight Control by radar, by radio and by listening devices of any force.

It's all a MIRACLE – a marvel created by boffins . . . What the RAF has in electrical warning equipment and the likes is the talk and happy joke of every pilot's drinking fountain, Bar, Mess in Britain.

Not to mention in the secret places I have seen: Our radar is so super secret I don't think we even share the top secrets with the goddamn Yanks.

Why should I be suspicious?

Believe it or not: it is my little brother James, Skeglee, hisself, as we say in Bermuda . . .

270

A little child shall lead them . . .

Skeglee's tale of woe (not all true, as he told it – but true enough to make him have to lie). Why did Skeglee's convoy, which came over in January '42, and was some forty-eight ships, end up at Greenock with only nineteen? Why?

When, only a very little before, so many people I know came over without even an alarm going? It sets you to thinking . . . sets me . . .

So many. And why the simple fact that I heard in London at the Brasserie Universal that the *Queen Mary* and the *Queen Elizabeth* keep making it packed with Dominion and Empire and American Troops and never, hardly ever, even having an alarm?

I smell a decoy, a sacrifice . . .

Funny how Man thinks he can get away with dirty tricks – but they smell bad and eventually people like me talk and the world catches on . . . the truth will out . . . Like King Edward II's murder, at Berkeley Castle, oh foul deed . . .

So let me tell you then:

It is 67 miles exactly from Newhaven to Dieppe and I'm banking over these beaches and these White Cliffs and you've never seen so many effing soldiers

and why oh why is every one of them a Canook?

I know that Canooks are a very ferocious lot of blokes – mostly displaced Scots and Picts and Brits of several generations in Canada

They are all volunteers for this Raid – and, of course, for the entire War . . . All volunteers and they've been screaming and yelling for an effing flight since 1940 and before . . .

But it smells over the beaches of Newhaven: there's

271

thousands and thousands of black uniformed soldiers down there

Have you ever been looked up at by five thousand blackened faces? Has your plane been strafed by thousands of Canadian eyes and them mostly eighteen to twenty year olds and as innocent as children?

Not that the naval forces gathered was not enormous, and soon very very noisy

But it was that it was just slightly small – and a bit too noisy – and most, most of it, Canadian too – much of it. (There were plenty of Royal Navy ships – but there were, as well, too many RCN ships.)

I would to God that She prove me wrong this day and evening and night and new day . . .

But, I Christopher Berkeley can add, you know, too. Every time there's a disaster like Gallipoli, or some daring questionable endeavour: they send in the colonials, the Dominions . . . you've noticed?

Perhaps you have to have been a public school man to really know how the Old Boy system works . . .

And the Control silence until the last minute STINKS (we are all going in by dead reckoning) and this gathering in the skies of so many relatively green RCAF aviators . . . And I'm thinking, this is terrible, a day like today and we could lose twenty to twenty-five aircraft –

It is 67 miles exactly to Dieppe – down a straight line –

and do you know how long it takes me to fly that distance? about 11.48 minutes: without trying hard

And when I first traversed that distance, converging on Dieppe to do two things at once:

To give air support to our boys, and to fight off the
Luftwaffe
  me and 'Mrs Roosevelt' converging with at least a
hundred fighters and fighter-bombers in the first wing
  It was like a cowboy movie when they say, 'Yeah,
it's too quiet.'
  And then we were right over Dieppe at the exact
minute: my clock on my dashboard as accurate as the
BBC and Big Ben
  at exactly the minute: the seconds ticked off by the
sweeping white hand
  all hell broke loose

No matter what was said later – there had been no
softening up –
  there had been no bombing of Dieppe by bombers
  only us fighters were there to fight off the German
fighters.

Damn it, I'm no child but an old veteran
  I don't even have a urinal in 'Mrs Roosevelt' (I have
a very secret weapon strapped to my leg, under my
trousers, it's called a *Gentleman's Companion* – patent
1865, and I tell no one)
  When I went to pick up this new plane, this young
American is showing me the aircraft. 'Familiariza-
tion,' he called it. (Do you know a worse word?
Shakespeare is groaning in his grave and Ben
Jonson and Chaucer too . . .)
  I knew it really, but I said, 'What's this?'
  He says, 'Why, that sir, that's your urinal.'
  'And this is to be *my* aircraft?' I asked.
  'Yessir.'
  So I reaches down and pulls the rubber hose loose
and throws it out of the cockpit.
  'Why did you do that?'

'Because, when people come by my aircraft, son – they go – sniff, sniff – oh, a veteran. When I go in action, I don't need a urinal – I always piss myself anyway.'

Joke to hide my other fear; that is, fear up my rear –

But, anyway, when I get back to Ford Aerodrome, damn if the Yanks don't send it me in His Majesty's Mail – the urinal . . .

Anyway, here we are over Dieppe and all hell breaks loose

and I put 'Mrs Roosevelt' into a screaming slip and dive even before I figured out what height the ack-ack was and where the searchlights were.

Those RCAF kids were cut to shreds – the ones who didn't, as I did, in the naval term, hit-the-deck.

Searchlights? Searchlights in the half-dark of dawn and in the overcast skies. (It was one of those black pregnant August days.) You'd think that Jerry had brought every searchlight in France and Belgium and Holland to Dieppe and then sent to Norway for some more . . .

So that was one more thing. And the last is this: at exactly the moment when we are allowed to tune in to Control and have some direction: the ack-ack cuts off like an orchestra and then silence from Control too

SILENCE

too silent

(you wouldn't believe what I thought at that moment: The Silent Fart, known as the Butler's Revenge, the remark so loved by Dad, died with O'Neill, that's what I thought – as I tried to duck, even *inside* my cockpit . . .)

and then we are hit from two directions at once; or *they* are – for I am temporarily out of it: I feel like an observer,

and hit by FW 190Fs – I can see them: death scythes in the sky –

I have no time to think, because then somebody is opening me up like a zipper . . . a can-opener, always going for, up, my arse-hole

and I flip her over as I look in the mirror and bend on more power than full –

Oh Jesus God I do love to fly . . . But not with the Death of Children . . .

And before any of this, the naval bombardment had gone on and on – clappers of hell into utter silence (and that was peculiar: somehow it was as if the naval bombardment was too loud – a show). But into this silence –

as if twenty thousand weasels had gone to ground by an arranged signal from above . . .

the Germans never replied until exactly the moment, as if the whole battle of death had been rehearsed and rehearsed

And suddenly I know what I am: I see in one farcical flash of light: an historian is looking back on the story of the British in the year 2942.

In the year 1242 they had knights that rode off . . . Soon their knights had armour and even their horses had armour and they carried battleaxes. Then in 1942, the knights took to the air and the horses were airplanes: they looked almost identical, the old knights and the new: 'Sir Aubrey Spens Rides Out On "Mrs Roosevelt" – and carries not a battleaxe, but ye machine guns . . .'

But, it's when they go ashore – the moment – they
start from the ships in their boats to go ashore . . .
Below me this great panorama where fire breaks
loose by precise order . . .
It's a good thing I'm old and battle-scarred because
there are planes falling out of the sky all 'round me
like meteors from the Milky Way: the Milk of
Herras spread across the sky and
all of it our planes

Don't believe what you read in the papers or hear on
the BBC.
I'll tell you we lost so many planes that when I got
back (amazing, yes, amazing, 'Bermuda' survived) I
listened to the *German* news
and even little Goebbels, who is the biggest LIAR
since Judas, even Goebbels only had it half right
When I got home, Goebbels said that over fifty
planes of the RAF had been shot out of the skies . . .
Actually, we lost that many planes in the first sixty
minutes of the battle . . . There was no possible way
that we lost less than one hundred aircraft . . .

The scene below (jaysus this was supposed to be a
Commando raid) was the kind of carnage as one reads
about in the Battle of Waterloo . . .
and old grandfathers would say, pulling on their
pipes, mad, mad, mad, madness . . .
Everywhere this battle raged with the feeling that
determined young 'dastards' were attacking cement
abutments
where their brains were smashed in
or they were caught in the sea like fish in nets of
fire . . .

Then the sea sent up its message of silence from our
side . . . silence and
blood-foam and hopelessness . . .
The Luftwaffe, and Goering, those comical sods,
must have laughed, I thought, as they cut the ships
apart after they had done in and outnumbered us . . .

'Mrs Roosevelt' bid me, by clever warning devices,
return for fuel and bullets
But I could not recall firing any bullets
Then, as I flew home to the White Cliffs of
Newhaven in my 11.48 minutes, I did see my fight
reel before me like a boxing match
in slow motion: yet in boxing there is so much pain
and in fighting plane to plane only noise and the
flashing that continues on long after it is stopped
(Did I bag any enemy aircraft? – asks the prickless
padré later in the Mess)
No, it was not a day for counting downed planes –
but for just making a big noise on the left to relieve
pressure, and then on the right
Indeed, I refuelled and reloaded and grabbed two
soggy ham sandwiches and climbed in and tore back
across the Channel . . . nose down and tail high, haul-
assing to do what I could . . .
Which seemed, piteously little – what good are
aircraft out of formation . . . ? Not much good . . .
This veteran tried to throw a rope here, a lifeline
there – and withdraw to stay alive . . .
Twice I flew away to gain altitude and came
back – once at 7,500 feet, where I was immediately
jumped by three FW 190s and slipped into a cloud . . .
Once at 10,000, where the Jerries were even more
numerous: FW 190s and Me. 109s – I looked for a
stray and couldn't see any . . . Took on two and hit one
. . . ducked out of it again. . .

I tell you, there was something about everything that happened in this fight that STANK of betrayal and murder

Oh, yes, I'm a right HERETIC I am
a heretic to the backbone of my soul

Colonial Aussie-Variety and me went to visit Newhaven by RAF staff-car the next day, the 20th . . . (It is no distance . . .)

Some Commando raid . . .

'When we got to two thousand missing of which nine hundred must be assumed Dead, we stopped counting,' a young Canadian captain in Intelligence told us . . . 'This little lot is all that got back.'

We saw a young-looking colonel – a US Army colonel and Aussie asked him,

'Where have you been, sir?'

And the colonel answered in a Scottish accent: 'We've been to hell, Laddie.'

We moved away: 'Christ, they are *all* wounded,' said Aussie.

A young kid of a soldier said to us (these kids had yellow and green paint on their faces: they must have wanted to look fierce like Red Indians): 'We were dumped on this tiny little beach – hundreds and hundreds of us between the sea and the breakwater – cement breakwater where the Jerries were – it took them three hours to kill us all – to pick us all off. We tried to surrender – but they wouldn't let us. Just went on shooting . . .'

These remnants on the beach like flotsam at high tide on August Bank Holiday

The Grotesque August of Dieppe . . .

'Christ – they are *all* wounded,' said Aussie-Variety – as if he hadn't said it before and he smacked his hand up against the new black concrete of

Newhaven, Sussex, White Cliffs and lapping sea of blue . . .

I said, 'Could I have a smoke, Aussie-Variety?'

He said: 'If you'll give me a whisky.'

We swapped, you see, for I had never smoked and he had never drunk any strong drink – not even cider, until then.

So great was the pain to my soul, or psyche – as the Freudians would say – that I had this dream, that now recurs, but then for the first time:

I see this face of Adolf Hitler (who, let's face it, looks exactly like my father – truly – my father, with a moustache added – a dead RINGER)

and then the face of Winston Churchill

and the two faces merge into one and then they laugh and laugh and laugh

And the face speaks: just like Hitler, just like Churchill and says:

'We are going to get every colonial – every colonial with Negro blood and we are going to kill them

'The very same way as King Edward II was killed at Berkeley Castle – with an enema of red-hot iron.'

I can tell nobody of this dream.

Who could I tell? My father . . . an RAF psychiatrist? Try talking to one . . . I try to laugh: I call the face in the dream, Mr Adolf Churchill

As I told you, in the beginning,

I am, now, I believe, partially mad . . .

'Please ask the Master to ask them to forgive me for this and my other sins. Bless Miss Lillie . . .'

More later

Yours faithfully
Berkeley Bermuda

You know, when I was little fella (as Grandfather would say), when I was a boy and saw my first aircraft:

I had a vision: I saw a world where everyone would be happy, buzzing and soaring about in their own planes in the sun, with the blue sea below . . .

And so, then, after Dieppe, I am back on Ranger Operations, about which, more later . . .

XII

James always felt that all was well, when the bells of Washashley pealed: the last roll having its sweet preceding hesitation . . .

It made him think of the phrase, 'Where sheep may safely graze.'

Before he left for The Lion School and the Christmas term of 1942, in September, he went about inspecting things: touching things he loved . . .

Yet he thought that what he liked best at the Hall were the flowers – the gardens at front and back and the sides, roses and roses and roses. Daffodils and narcissus in the spring – but all manner of flowers almost all year round.

And Aunt Daisy seemed to do it all by herself – her and old Watkins (in the walled garden, through the crested gate) and a boy. It was amazing, what his aunt could do with flowers – and she never stopped . . .

He noticed an interesting phenomenon about the view of Lincoln: on a light and happy day, one's eye was drawn upward to and by the majestic Cathedral

(Could there be another like it: it not only stood on the highest hill, its foundations were actually found, he learned, to stand on the top of a Roman temple . . ?)

But on an unhappy day, on a dark day, one's eye was drawn – the whole city seemed to be ultimately drawn, magnetized and drawn down by the cemeteries along the road that lead out of the city to the south.

(There, too, was the sewage farm: 'Moonlight On The Sewage Farm,' Dad had said was his World War I theme song.)

This day, he touched the cigarette machine on the hall table: O'Neill always used to make cigarettes with this machine every morning – cigarettes for the whole family, and leave them in a little cedar box. The machine, absolutely the Delage of cigarette machines, was a piece of French mechanical perfection – it never missed.

A few days before he was to leave, Aunt Lillie asked him to come with her – she had something, she said, to show him.

He hoped it was a present.

He followed her bony squarish body into the billiard room where the red leather and brass bumper glistened in front of the fireplace.

She took a brown earthenware thing (that looked like something you'd find in a junk shop) out of a gold-edged glass cupboard.

'Dear boy – look at this. I wanted to share this with you. You see, it's nothing like anything else at Washashley – it's infinitely older than any of our things, or your uncle's. Look – look at the patina – there.'

She handed it to him.

It felt soft, even moist underneath.

'What is it, Aunt Lillie?'

'This, James, is the earliest eating vessel known to exist in all of Britain. It should be in the British

Museum. I want you to see it gets there – some time – don't worry about it.

'But, you see, James, this Washashley is a very, very old manor house – parts are tenth and eleventh century. Now the people who owned it before us, left this here, because it was found here about a hundred years ago.'

'It's incredibly moving, isn't it?'

'Yes, but it must go to the country – the whole nation, you know – you understand?'

'Of course, I'll take care of it – but you could do it now, Aunt Lillie.'

'And dear boy, dear Jamie; I wanted to say one other thing to you – you seem to think that you are not very bright – it says so in your Report Cards.'

She grabbed his wrist and made him look into her intense brown eyes: 'But I want you to know that *I* know you are *damned* intelligent. Do you know how I know?'

'No –' He smiled. 'You shouldn't swear, Aunt Lillie.'

'All real ladies swear like *troopers*. I know because I'm damned intelligent too. You hear?'

'Yes.'

'And your Mr Healey – he's clever too, isn't he?'

'Yes, Ma'am.'

'Well, he and I say you are bright. Now give me a small kiss to seal it.'

Her mouth was a bit dry and she smelled of silver polish.

'And just one other thing, young man. You hear, or you will hear, the story everywhere: the old maid aunt who lost her love in the War. But I am not just a silly old maid – and I *did* lose my love in the War. And I am a one man gal.'

'I am sorry, Aunt Lillie, and I do understand. Who was he – if I may ask?'

'Yes, you may. In the church there's a memorial to Lieutenant-Colonel J.H. Berkeley. That was him – he was your cousin and his name was James. Let it be a secret between us, all right?'

'Yes.'

A little while later she started to laugh. ' 'Course you could say, James, in addition to my being a one-man gal – it *could* be said, only one man would look at me twice – so of course I'm a one-man gal – but we'll keep that a secret too.'

He also went out to the garage which was next to the stables (he had not actually been in the stables since O'Neill's death) and unlocked the doors to the Rolls-Royce (he should ask Fenders but he didn't think Fenders was even anywhere about).

No sooner had he raised the white sheet and let in the grey light, and observed that the Rolls-Royce's angel had a wing broken, than he heard a step behind him.

Fenders in his bus uniform and white badge.

'I'm sorry, Fenders. I would have asked you . . .'

'So, Mr James – you wanted to see if there were any marks on her, is that it?'

James had never known Fenders be so narky – as they would say in the Merchant Navy.

'Perhaps I did.'

'Well, there aren't any, sir. I broke that angel – me and the Master did, not O'Neill.'

'I came to say goodbye to the car, actually, Fenders – isn't that crazy?'

'No, sir. Your aunt – Miss Lillie said you was going and I said I'd help. I've come to pack for you, Mr James.'

Back at The Lion School, James was amazed at the human's ability to close out other happier worlds and

283

embrace only this one.

There was a new boy – their age – that is twelve and thirteen – in the VI Form.

His name was Ian Aiken. He was a wizard at making paper planes and inventing all sorts of things. He had a hooked nose – like an owl – exactly like an owl.

There was a peculiar vagueness emanating from the headmaster, Mr Montrose.

Collins believed he was Captain of the School, yet Mr Montrose had definitely said to James: 'You will be Captain of the School.'

James went to ask, to get it settled.

The Montroses were having tea, with Matron, in the conservatory.

'Yes, James, what is it?' Mrs Montrose asked. He'd always liked her, she had a motherly look.

'I came to see Mr Montrose, please, Ma'am. I can come back later.'

'What's all this "Ma'am" nonsense, Berkeley?' Matron's eyes flashed – 'That is for servants.'

'Wait at my desk – I won't be a moment,' said Mr Montrose rather absently.

James, hurt, withdrew and had been standing by the desk for some while before he realized he was looking at familiar handwriting – his mother's.

A letter from his mother.

Appalled at himself (and her), he read only '. . . James is, I fear, a very difficult child . . .'

'Yes, Berkeley.'

It was the second time he'd been caught out in two days, counting Fenders and the Rolls's angel, he thought.

'I beg your pardon, sir – but there seems to be some misunderstanding. I was sure you told me that I was

Captain of the School –'

'– Yes . . .'

'But Collins says that he is, sir. Could you please straighten us out?'

Mr Montrose looked like a grouper at the Aquarium in Bermuda – and just as under water.

'I'll let you know in a week – for now, you both can be . . .'

'Sir. That's not going to work. If you will forgive me, sir – last term, you appointed me.'

'All right, Berkeley – you be it then.'

'Captain of the School, sir?'

'Yes.'

'Thank you, sir.'

James was amazed at himself. The double slaps of mother and Matron had made him behave with a decisiveness he hadn't known he had.

In the dormitory he still continued *The Soap Opera With The Fucking Left In* – as he had before – and Aiken loved it . . .

However, to James, it rang a bad note: he couldn't be both in charge, that is, Solomon, and Salome as well.

'Tonight is the last episode.'

'No – oh no,' said Hosefield.

'Berkeley, you rotten sod – I'll pay you. Sixpence a night – for the story.'

'It ends tonight. I'm sorry, but it has to end.'

Collins took the news like a sorehead.

Finally James said: 'I've told you. Mr Montrose has told me – if you don't believe me – go and see him.'

In that September Christopher dropped by – again totally unexpected.

James got permission to go out.

'Chris. It's a good thing I am Captain of the School – or they wouldn't have let me out.'

Chris didn't answer.

When they sat down to tea at The Winter Garden, James said: 'The Matron said my calling ladies "Ma'am" was like a servant.'

'You go on calling women Ma'am; it's the way you were brought up. You go on – no matter what the Limeys think.'

But, for most of the time, Christopher seemed almost as vague as Mr Montrose.

What could it be about Mr Montrose? Geoff wasn't killed or anything, they would have heard.

Chris said, in answer to a different question, 'My class at Cranwell is getting pretty thin, Skeglee – when we started out I thought we'd live for ever.'

'I'm sorry, Chris.'

'It's all right, mate.'

But James felt angry with him for being vague – just when he needed him.

After a silence, James said: 'Say, Chris – when we inherit the Hall, why not give the cottages away to the tenants?'

'What?'

James said it again.

'Yes,' Chris said, as if awakening. 'I agree – I've always thought that – Fenders especially.'

'Super. Let's shake on it?'

'Why are you so formal?'

'Dunno.'

Christopher smiled. 'Cheer up, Skeglee.'

'I sometimes pretend I go flying with you, Chris. You and me flying for England and Bermuda . . .' He stopped.

'Chris, why are you crying?'

286

'I dunno either, Skeglee. We weep for ourselves when we weep – it's identification, selfishness, really. I guess the worst kind of weeping is brass-band patriotism. I've done it myself and that is very bad.' He looked at James strangely and then said: 'Patriotism is all right, I suppose – but what if it were all wrong?'

'Aubrey Spencer, I don't know quite what you are saying.'

At one point Chris said: 'I feel as if the world has become a nasty boil – and this is it – and *we* have to see it well.'

'What are you flying, Christopher?'

'Still the Ranger Operations – over France.'

In the shelter (from the school's window, that is) of the dark trees by the gate, James said, 'Take good care of yourself, Chris, and come soon.'

Chris put out his mouth to be kissed, not even like a child – like a small bird, James thought.

But the touch of his lips and his rough chin and the family smell made James feel awfully happy.

Aunt Lillie kept writing her 'Fear God!' letters and Aunt Daisy wrote, when she did, in a scrawl that was almost entirely indecipherable – but it was good to get them, like hugs.

Collins accepted that Berkeley was Captain only when Mr Vegetable confirmed it. Baron Von Tobel had been anglicized to 'Mr Vegetable' – because of the War.

Mr Vegetable taught French. Invariably he'd arranged the class so that one boy sat with him, close, at the big desk, while the rest were set to learning vocabulary.

'Sit down, boy,' Mr Vegetable would say – indicating the book on the desk that they both would

287

share. 'Translate that.'

While one of them struggled with the translation, Mr Vegetable would run his hand through the boy's hair.

'No, not travelling – another word, think, boy?'

It was, of course, very hard to think when Mr Vegetable was caressing you.

He played no favourites: he heard them all, caressed them all. He seemed to like best to touch your cheek – his hand like a leaf.

He never caressed a boy below the neck. Although sometimes he'd sneak a little horse-bite of the knee after he'd said: 'All right now, boy – away you go.'

He was like a small fat bird – his face ruddy, his eyes quick and hunted.

'Is he a dirty old man?' they'd ask each other.

'Probably – but he never does anything more than that.'

'He's harmless.'

Baron Von Tobel was from Vienna. He didn't seem to have any friends – and he went for walks by himself, swinging his umbrella.

James was a little afraid of him.

Early in the term, it was reported to James that some stamps had been stolen. Not just any stamps, Hosefield's Queen Victoria 1d's – six of them.

'How much are they worth?' he asked Hosefield.

'I've looked them up in Stanley Gibbons – total is £2 17s 7d.'

'Good God,' James said. He was supposed to find them and bring the criminal to justice – namely to Mr Montrose. (Unlike the public schools, which loomed ominous and large over all their lives, at prep school prefects did not punish other boys.)

The question was how? It wasn't a very big problem

but it was very difficult to solve.

There were only seven people in the school who collected stamps. Four in the VI Form and three in the IV. Hosefield and Berkeley could be ruled out – though James did give a thought that Hosefield might have stolen his own stamps, to cause trouble. But James didn't think he would.

Then to confirm things, he found Hosefield, after two days, with his desk-top up – crying.

'What's the matter?'

'It's those stamps – my granny gave them to me just before she died – and it's all I've got that was hers.'

'Don't worry, Hosefield – I'll get the bastard.'

In the VI Form then, there was the new-bug, Aiken, and Collins. In the IV Form, Joell Minor, Lorenz and Barry Smith.

James had expected that, as a sleuth, he'd be pretty good. More days passed and he couldn't find any solution.

The truth was, he'd had his suspicions right from the start – Joell Minor just plain acted guilty. (He was just Joell now that his brother had gone on to St Paul's.)

He also suspected Collins. But Collins was somehow too solid to steal – too simple a boy.

And Collins said, right at the beginning, 'Why should I – only to get caught? That's damned silly, isn't it? Besides, I don't like Victorian stamps – Germany is my favourite.'

Anyone dumb enough to collect German stamps (the most glutted on the market) would not steal the special Victoria 1d's.

It wasn't Ian Aiken. He was much too smart, too smooth and too busy. 'Me? Since those stamps have been stolen I've designed four aircraft, two cars – and

I'm working on a game, Berkeley, that it is my intention to sell, for good honest money, to Parker Brothers.'

He even showed James the game – sanded little wooden stands and cards with different ships drawn on one side only.

A whole week went by and all James had were his suspicions, Hosefield heartbroken and Matron saying: 'Some people couldn't find something if they fell over it.'

It was a IV Form job. Barry Smith was an open kid with pink cheeks and yellow hair – very popular, who really only cared about soccer. 'My bro. gave me my stamps – and I've not added six this year, I don't think.'

Lorenz was a rough refugee from Hungary. 'Search me,' he said; 'I love to be tickled.'

'Well, Joell?'

Joell blushed as red as the Union Jack.

'I didn't take anything, Berkeley.'

By the end of the second week, James was very frustrated and angry.

He decided on a trick.

'I'm going to shake these stamps out of their tree, if I have to cut the tree down,' he said.

Mr Healey heard this remark, looked at him with questioning and displeasure, shaking his head and saying: 'Tut-tut-tut.'

A few days later, he hit on a trick.

He had the whole school assembled just before lunch and made a little speech.

'Quiet! Quiet!' He found, in just the few days he'd been Captain, that his loud voice commanded and got a good deal of respect.

'I now know who took the stamps. The mystery is solved. However, I'm going to give the guilty person one last chance.

'There's a silver cup in the front hall – on the table – and if the stamps are left there within the next twenty-four hours, they will be returned to their owner and the whole matter dropped.'

Mr Healey came in for his lunch. He sat down without a word – but he looked revolted by the whole affair.

James obstinately and determinedly sat up into the night – hidden in the 'Upper Bog', where he could hear anyone who approached the hall –

It was pretty easy because not one, but three stairs squeaked.

Just after midnight, he heard the stairs squeak – and, silent as the Gestapo, he slithered in from the Bog and grabbed Joell's arm over the silver cup –

'Gotcha.'

'Berkeley – don't twit on me, please.'

'Gotcha, Joell – you bastard. You thieving bastard.'

Joell started blubbering. 'I'm sorry. I don't know why I did it – it was stupid.'

Joell was standing there in his pajamas looking pathetic. 'You were friends with my brother.'

'That makes it worse, not better,' said the Gestapo.

Now Matron was out of bed.

Matron got the headmaster. The headmaster, looking like an unhappy shepherd dog who'd been dragged out of a river, said,

'What have you got to say, Joell?'

'Nothing. I did it. But Berkeley said no one would do anything. That it would all be dropped, sir.'

'What have you got to say, Berkeley?'

There was a pause. James could have said, 'It

should be dropped, sir.' But said, 'I caught him red-handed, sir . . .'

'All right, then. Everyone to bed. Joell, you bend over!'

Into the tiled hallway and up the wooden stairs, three flights and into the night, came the whistle of the swagger stick's cuts.

One

two – it would end at three.

Four.

At five, Joell started screeching: you could tell by the sound of him, that it was no pretence – it was total and public degradation as well as pain.

James knew he had taken on himself a pain he would not soon be rid of – he knew also that he had gone tough on Joell partially because he, Joell, was Jewish (his actions, secretly, appalled and puzzled himself – and he believed too, that Montrose had laid on six instead of three for the same wretched reason . . .)

Mr Healey did not speak to James, neither did he even look at him . . .

James was never to know how long it would have been before Mr Healey would have forgiven him, because two painful blows fell on him, themselves like shots in the night.

On 23rd September 1942, he was telephoned by Aunt Daisy. She lisped over the long-distance line like a girl.

'Is that you, dear boy? You'd better sit down.'

'All right, Aunt Daisy – it's Chris, isn't it?'

'Yes, dear boy – Missing – the Air Ministry say he's Missing. On the 21st.'

'Is there anything I can do?'

'No, dear boy. No.'

When he'd hung-up he realized he hadn't asked how Aunt Lillie was and why *she* hadn't called and was Aunt Daisy letting Bermuda know?

The Montroses were most sympathetic. James thought of Dicky Dickens – Dicky had been right. Having a brother Missing and hearing about someone else's were two entirely different things.

Mr Healey, at breakfast, not only patted his shoulder, but touched his cheek – in a rough friendly tap.

'Sorry,' he said. 'Sorry.'

James wanted to say *he* was sorry. Then it was too late.

Everyone in the school paid him a sort of God-like homage for all that day.

Joell said: 'Sorry about your bro', Berkeley.'

James smiled – he looked at Joell's yellow-brown eyes, seeing Joell Major's eyes.

Joell started to move away. There was no one but them in the Upper Changing Room.

'Hey, Joell. I'm sorry – about everything.'

'It was my fault. I didn't have to steal.' His total openness and decency was very moving and painful.

'*Please* forgive me and . . .'

'It's all right – certainly, Berkeley, of course.'

'Can we forget it?'

'Certainly.'

Even matron got into the act – which began to make Berkeley feel as if rotten meat were about.

'He's a terrific fighter, your brother and I'm sure he'll be back like Geoff,' she said.

'Thank you.' He hated himself for saying it.

In the next morning's mail came:

Washashley Hall
Lincs.

20th Sept. 1942

Dearest James,

The War Ministry have given us forty-eight hours to vacate the Hall with all our things.

Scorer has got them to agree to seventy-two hours. I said I would not let this happen, but it has. We can only grin and bear it. When you get home we will be in Watkins' Cottage. All our love.

Aunt Lillie

She had not even told him to fear God.

He had no one to talk to about this second pain.

To even mention it seemed so selfish, so smelling of affluence . . .

Poor Aunt Lillie, poor Aunt Daisy – what could he do? You had to do what the government told you in wartime, you just had to.

And the whole of Christopher's last visit, Chris hadn't called him 'M'dear' once . . .

XIII

Christopher, Backwards Often,
Forwards Sometimes,
And Probably, Sideways Frequently
II

'When This Fucking War Is Over,' I love to sing this

294

song, 'you and I will fall in love. . .'

I am incredibly shy of women. I haven't had much chance with them, young skirts – all I've ever known is public schools and War – least, that's what it feels like. . . Every time I get close, the family sends for me.

'What is this great bounty of flight that we should use it to kill?' That's the question I put in The Lord's Suggestion Box.

But, at the moment, there are other things on my mind: to-wit, to-woo: It is the 21st of September 1942 and I am back at Ford Aerodrome, near the coast.

It is sobering to realize how old I am (because I simply never expected to reach this age). In three months, less four days, that is 17 November, I will be twenty-one. They say that twenty-one is too old to be a fighter pilot.

I've just been to the Operations Room for briefing instructions from the RAF Intelligence Officer – who, it turns out, is now a master I used to have at Harrow. (I asked after the previous Intelligence Officer, Jones – and was told he'd been lost, shot down. . . Typical Op's joke.)

At midnight 21/22nd I eat the food they give us: I eat a good deal. It's bacon and eggs and only us air crew are allowed them – they taste good – or they used to. . .

I try to sleep, but cannot. At 2:00 a.m. I am alerted: me and 'Mrs Roosevelt' are expected to patrol an aerodrome over Amiens. . . I've been there five or fifty-five times before: Amiens is a hot-spot for ack-ack and other tricks. . .

Immediately my terror of the twitching arse-hole begins . . . *before* I'm even aboard.

When one thinks of the origins of this little rumble called World War II, it's good to remember Grand-father's remark: 'A difference of opinion makes yacht-racing possible.'

I recall another incident of my boyhood (for which I used to feel, aged about seven, intensely guilty). I would imagine a plane crashing in our garden so that I could see one up close, touch and smell it.

Well, I've sure got one in my garden now.

I get in 'Mrs Roosevelt'. Oh, marvel of mechanism: in a couple of minutes we are in the air and over Beachy Head (as I've said before: when we were children on the beach at Felpham and Bognor: when you could see Beachy Head, it meant it was going to rain. . .) where I immediately set course for the mouth of the Somme.

It is a clear moonlit night – oh how the weather mocks our war – the weather and flight. It is a night to set course for Mars and Sirius. . .

Some intellectual puzzles plague me: did the Depression cause the War or the War the Depression? I do not know if I asked this question of my brother Nasti or not.

That would get his juvenile Fascist canary out of its cage.

But I'll tell you a secret: not only do I have this terror of being hit – by flak – in the arse. *Up* the arse, to be precise. I also have a well-founded fear of Fascists – Nazis and the Gestapo.

It's not that we are secretly Jewish – oh, no – I've lots of chums – well, five or six, in the RAF – who are Jewish and are afraid of being shot down over German-Occupied France.

But I have recently come upon a fact that was – is – well-known in Bermuda, though no one in our family ever mentioned it. It is, to wit, that one of the old families in Bermuda who are known to have coloured blood – are the Hinsons.

Now our family, the Berkeleys, are descended from

296

the Hinsons and my mother's family, the Halcyons, are half Hinson. So, although it may give the whole family – and the whole of Bermuda – fifty screaming fits, nonetheless, it's pretty clear that we have coloured blood.

(Funny – you take a trip down to Nassau and all the people look part Negro... Then a pal of mine from St John's College, Cambridge – Uncle Albert's college too – came to Bermuda and he said – jaysus, I had to shut him up around Cedar Hill – he said: 'But my dear fella – I took it as obvious – you are all part native.' Seeing it through his eyes, thereafter, I knew that most old Bermudian families are...)

But my trouble as I climb to 1,000 feet – guess what for? to cross the French coast at a helluva clip – is that I am afraid of being captured and found out to be part darkie and then sent to a concentration camp for 'experimentation, etc.' – to quote the popular press.

(I was happy to note, at the Officers' Mess at Ford, that my urinal is still over the bar. I did not take a drink. I never do, of course, for twenty-four hours before a flight. And my peeing secret is, as I mentioned before, I carry a *Gentleman's Companion*...)

Now, at 1,000 feet, I open the throttle and make a long long dive – like a broad-reach. I am parallel to the French coast.

I am picking up speed now: 350 – the real, genuine top speed of 'Mrs Roosevelt', without the aid of the dive ... now 375 – now at 400 I am down close to the water – about fifty feet off it. She has 400 mph now and I turn smartly and cross the coast with fifty feet on the other clock.

Which is nothing, you know. I'm riding into the country like a steeple-chaser – doing 400 mph.

At this altitude, of course, I present a poor target

297

to any ground defences, enemy radar – and give little chance of being picked up by an enemy fighter either.

I am here and gone before you can fall out of your bed

I simply adore flying right on-the-deck – it gives one a total sense of speed and beauty and control.

One's dexterity is stretched to its uttermost – only a little bump on the controls and you'd be in the ground, or water. . .

It's marvellous.

I like to fly by moving the trim-tabs only – it's not for children. . .

Everything is so clear this lovely night: we roar into the moon which makes the silver river stand out as it twists and turns. I fly over the fields, hedgerows and farms. (Watching for telephone lines, I am so low.)

There is not a light to be seen anywhere: I wonder what Ma'moiselles I awaken and bring to the window . . . and then I'm gone, the thief in the night. . .

It is like flying in a giant painting – exquisite – hold, hold, hold moon and hedgerows. . . I am so low that, as I sweep up the river sections, I think that the prop will split reeds. . .

I have almost nineteen minutes, I know, before I have to watch out for ack-ack.

And it comes on schedule.

The flak over Amiens town is heavy – so I bank away – flying towards my designated Kraut aerodrome.

I pick this out easy – and they are quiet – too quiet as well –

I patrol for fifteen minutes, a very long time, you know, at 350 mph – but they are on to me and they won't light up the flare path.

I keep looking in my mirror, and over my shoulder. I am not as green as a banana shoot. . . There are tales of the Mustang having this blind spot for attacking FW 190s but I've never experienced it. . .

There is also this bad rumour about them: when you go to bail out, the tailplane is easy to hit – it chops you up or knocks you out so that you never pull the string.

A North American Mustang, P51, is known as a jump killer. . . Well, she is also one sweet aircraft from almost every other viewpoint – a joy to fly. . .

So I look around for secondary targets – lorries or locomotives pulling freight trains. We are not allowed to shoot up passenger trains, of course. . .

I follow the railway line north towards the town of Albert – an old friend of mine. (The town: I always think of Uncle Albert and his Peugeot Tourer roaring towards Paris to meet his brother, Cross-Channel Charlie. . . Bastard, he may have been, but their racing was surely as sensible – perhaps more sensible – than mine.)

But, oh, how I love to fly. France, thou lookest like a toy country. . .

and there's a locomotive

I swing the plane about to get the train silhouetted against the moon

I do a long slow run-in in order to get an accurate burst

And, as I get close, the engine-driver opens the fire doors and thus illuminates the engine and target for me, even more clearly.

I'm so close I see him dive for cover. I let the train have a long burst.

Looking back, in a few seconds, the target is all steam and smoke. . .

Moments later, Uncle Albert's town gives me a heavy flak message and I bank away sharply – and decide

299

most stupidly: to have another look at my aerodrome – that is, resume my flight according to orders,
but it's stupid of them to order and of me to follow. . .

Then I see a plane coming in: here's my man: A
Focke-Wulf 190 – could be F or D and he's throttled
back.

I decide to let him have it up his tail – because, no
doubt, my tail is twitching in its usual terrified
fashion

Five hundred feet away from him I'm about to let
him have my whole eight-violin medley

when I am rudely awakened from my moonlit
bucolic errors by all hell letting loose: not up my arse,
but up 'Mrs Roosevelt's'.

These clever Krauts have set me up for A Sandwich.

I see him in the mirror and hear him and bend on
full throttle, and peddle and joy stick sharp left and
then sharp right

But the Kraut behind me has got both above and in
control and I have to look about for the other half of
the Sandwich as well

In the second mêlée – I am unable to get them in
my sights because I have them both on my tail –
there's this little thing called *power*, guts in the
engine . . . and they have it, I don't. . .

I can read that I have only about 350 feet – and
then the German ground defences do a pretty unusual
thing: they throw on several searchlights

Which, by sheer animal luck, I believe, have got me
and hold me. It's totally blinding and what Aussie-
Variety would call 'demoralizing – to say the least.'

And then I hear exactly what I've been expecting
all these months:

bullets hit my radiator which is situated, hold it,
just behind and under my seat.

Right now, I just want to quit myself of all this

300

attention. . .

Although blinded I get control – I've got only about 500 feet at this moment, but I decide to bet it all on one wild card for freedom.

With wide throttle I now dive vertically towards the ground –

I can judge the ground level by the searchlights and there's no one on my tail – but I am screaming towards the ground like a circus diver

Now I am pulling out very close to the deck, but I've got a lot of speed in hand –

And my manoeuvres have shaken both the lights and Focke-Wulfs off my arse

But, as I am heading off in an easterly direction, I have the nagging reality enter my mind:

Berkeley, you are not getting home tonight.

The cockpit is now filling with fumes and the fine spray of the engine coolant from my damaged radiator.

(A moment's pause to reflect: at the risk of disloyalty to 'Mrs Roosevelt', that all this wouldn't have happened to me if I had a Spitfire. . .)

It's in my eyes – it's difficult to see – if I didn't have my oxygen mask on I'd be asphyxiated.

Putting the moon over my left shoulder I start a normal climb to see how high I can get before the engine cuts out

I am also trying, like one of Grannie's wound-up monkeys, to clear my instruments so that I can read how hot my engine is.

Using the emergency lever, I jettison the cockpit cover: it might clear the cockpit. I now have only the little windscreen, almost like a Tiger Moth

and right now I say that old prayer:

'Oh Lord, who art praised by the living, even as also by the dead . . . uphold and strengthen me now. . .'

301

Dear Nasti, or whoever might outlive me,
    This is the way it was
    this is the way it is
    this is the way
    this is
    this:

The two most oft-heard remarks of this War: 'What *me* – bring a child into *this world* – you must be mad?' and 'If I'm going to die just let me fly a few more times'

and the third one: 'He shouldn't have joined if he couldn't take a joke.' (This is always said when you are rolling up a dead mate's things to send home to his family. . .)

So, here am I at 2,000 feet over Enemy-Occupied France and I ponder the Eternal Questions of my Father's Generation, which ended with the dilly, 'Do Barmaids devour their young?' Too tough for me, Dad.

My jettisoning the cockpit cover has little effect, dear friend, of disbursing the fumes and coolant spray.

I have to wipe off each instrument before I can read it and then it's covered up again before I can really check it. . .

I am staying on course by the old sailing trick of keeping the moon over my left shoulder

Then, Nasti, I make my last, little touch with home: I turn on my two-way radio: at 3,000 feet I make contact with:

'Happy Wanderer this is Happy Wanderer.'

'Go ahead, Happy Wanderer.'

Blighty! They sound right next to me. The reception is like the moon.

I'm outlining my predicament – which they quietly acknowledge. I'm talking a long time, as we are supposed to – in order to give their listening stations in England enough time to plot my exact position.

'Engine temperatures are all right off the clock. Fuel: I have an amazing two-thirds capacity left in all my tanks: Perfect balance. Altitude, an amazing 4,900 feet and climbing. I am preparing to abandon aircraft.'

I am very reluctant to abandon 'Mrs Roosevelt'. Although I don't name her to them, of course. (She's a secret between me and she.)

Be damned if the operator doesn't give me not only, 'Good luck', but, to my mind, a very chilly and unnecessary English, 'Good hunting!'

When this fucking war is over, no more hunting with the Limeys for the Horrible Hun over France, I can tell you.

So this is the way it was

This is the way it is

Nasti, or Skeglee.

I don't expect the engine to keep running much longer and so

I am trying to gain as much altitude as possible and also am flying south to get away from the coast and the English Channel – when I have to bail out

And I want to make it as safe as possible when I leave this aircraft

I am probably overdoing this aspect – as, right now, I note, wiping my finger, in gloved hand, that I have 9,000 feet –

or, as you well know, approximately two miles, up. . . Two miles, anyone would concede is sufficient height to allow a parachute to open.

So what's gone on in my head, long long ago now – is, how long and how high would I have to be to glide back to Jolly Old. . . ? If I was a Tiger Moth, perhaps I could do it. . . But, as Henry my mechanic

303

says, 'If your aunt had balls she'd be your uncle –'

The engine is still giving an excellent performance – considering 'Mrs Roosevelt's' coolant system is
rapidly being drained over me and France...

Jesus Christ, she's been reading her highest indication – slam over, since 5,000 feet and now I've got
9,000... Has she started to run rough...?

The moment has come to jump.

The thing about War, Nasti, is that it gets more and
more like that drawing of Munch's, *The Scream* – as
you get into it.

Dear Skeglee, or whoever lives beyond me

I am a shit-hot pilot (a phrase I loathe, but I belong
in the group) who is about to lose his principle.

The engine is just beginning to run rough. I throttle
back – doing everything just right, like a cook over a
hot stove.

I release my cockpit safety straps; I hold the nose in
a gliding position – I am reducing speed...

I wait a few seconds as the stalling speed is coming
up – up – down begins the nose

I shove the stick forward, the nose drops fast, and
Berkeley Bermuda-Variety jumps both upward and
out to one side.

I've only one thought at this time: to clear that tail
section which has slammed, decapitated so many of
us – us fools jumping from Mustangs on September
days over Europe...

Jesus, I clear, float past, the tail with ten feet to
spare

'Mrs Roosevelt' falls right out of my sight before I
even think of anything else ... untimely ripped ...

Oh yes, the ripcord – the jolly old ripcord! What
else?

I am looking, I have it. The ring. I grip it and give a
yuk.

The yuk is immediately followed by a much greater
YUK
a St David's Island Yuk
and there it is up there above me: the chute, the
brolly
Bless you, William, I say, not to Shakespeare, but
our squadron's parachute man – he's never let us
down, but slowly...
I'm stunned
I'm in the midst of so big and so vast a silence
after listening for an hour and a half to a 1,200 hp
engine perform
This, surely, is the flying I've dreamed of...
The moonlight is as brilliant as Bermuda and below
me is this great country – this lovely countryside,
which I am observing now like some silently descending god (we hope not into a German bayonet or
bedstead)
Faintly, a way off, I can hear 'Mrs Roosevelt'
falling: I feel sorry for her, as if she were some horse
fallen in the traces which I should put out of her
misery...
Soon, in my silence, I see the fire where she has
landed – crashed into the ground...
What a waste of effort, hundreds and hundreds of
man-hours – and hundreds of thousands of pounds
sterling
I figure I've got about ten minutes descent-time.
Three have gone. It's so clear, there's not even a cloud
to judge my descent by.
It is so beautiful. One advantage to the height of
the jump – must be that there will be an enormous
distance between me and 'Mrs Roosevelt' – for she,
and her burning, will surely attract attention
Jumping in the dark, it concentrates the mind.
How long, Oh Lord, how long, am I to be thus kept

dangling? (I would sure prefer to be sailing in Bermuda, or kissing a young woman. . .)

The ground is coming up at me at a rate of knots – remembering to bend my knees, I nevertheless hit with one leg, and a sharp blow, and roll over and fall and get up and fall.

I've found my feet.

It appears to be a cut cornfield: 'Mrs Roosevelt' is burning only about a half-mile away.

I am unfastening the parachute harness, taking off my 'Mae West' (this would certainly suit Dad, in his answer to Mother's 'Oh, Angels, help women!', 'Oh, Mae West, help men!')

I am piling everything in as inconspicuous a pile as I can. . .

I run to the edge of the field. I can hear 'Mrs Roosevelt' burning and popping her ammunition now.

I take bearings by the moon.

I start off running south – my best direction, I figure. I want to put as much distance between me and that burning plane as I can.

It is now about 3:30, my watch says – wow, I was in England so short a time ago. . .

I am walking and running, running and walking – all the time keeping away from roads and farms – anything. . .

I walk and run and run and walk. I keep this up until 7:00 a.m. Breakfast-time.

Here I am at a small wood which seems to crown this large hill – from which I have a good view all around.

At this place, my back to the woods, I cut off all distinguishing marks from my uniform. I cut off the belovéd wings, rank circles, buttons, my best belovéd

306

'Bermuda' badges.

Then, as instructed, I cut off the tops of my flying boots – leaving as ordinary a pair of shoes as ever you did see.

Now I inspect my escape kit. Silk maps of Western Europe from the Baltic down to North Africa. French and Belgian money; concentrated food tablets, chocolate, little medicine chest, milk concentrate, water purifying tablets, Benzedrine tablets – and a compass.

I also have a compass made out of my collar stretchers – and another out of my tie clip. I have a rubber water-bottle and a small package of chewing gum.

Everywhere you look in Britain now there are Americans chewing gum. I will save these – I'm not of the chewing-gum generation.

I decide on one pull of water, one square of chocolate and another pull of water. All executed very slowly while I take a careful look all about.

Then I decide that this heavy grass here – with a depression at the edge of the wood – is as good as any a place to go to sleep.

I am so tired I could sleep standing.

I pull my coat over my face.

Next thing I know, I wake up. It's noon. The sun overhead. I see a boy near me – then his cow, nearer. It's a cowherd – the cow is breathing almost on me.

I am gesturing for the kid to come over: he's the first French person in France I see or speak to.

'Pardonnez-moi, jeune garçon. Je suis Anglais – aviator –'

I'll spare you the patter: in my broken bad French – with gestures of aeroplane – I tell him all I can.

I ask, are there any Germans about and will he help me?

He gestures that I should stay where I am – that he will help.

Trusting that he is not running to the nearest phone to contact the Nasties, I wait.

In a little while, he returns. He's small and about thirteen, I guess.

He leads me to a small one-room farmhouse.

Well, Nasti, this is how it is: these people are all smiles and friendliness. But they are obviously so poor I immediately decide it is useless to ask them for clothes. That is what I need: a set of civvies.

They give me my first French meal – the mother and father – it's a delicious heavy soup.

All that afternoon I sleep in their bedroom. In their bed. I sleep for several hours: the smell is like Portagee farmers in Bermuda.

I have decided that, as sunset comes, I will continue to the south.

I think Gibraltar is the place to walk to – a mere thousand miles or so . . . Bermuda to the Bahamas but it's somewhat easier to walk on the land. . .

That's what I think.

Let me tell you something about the French people: right off. . . There is a quality about them: you do not know it until you get here, but there is a quality about them, this is where our VALOUR comes from – yet they are all very down-to-earth.

It is IMPOSSIBLE to describe the pride and honour of the French people and their worldliness – until you've. . .

But I get ahead of myself again.

After sunset I leave the farm wearing an open-collared shirt and sleeves rolled up and carrying my tunic.

I walk until almost three the following morning –

308

when I come to a farming village.

There is no life anywhere about the place, so I wander about until I find a barn – which seems suitable to me – King of the World.

I go in, climb into the hayloft, make my bed like one of Grampy's dogs, and go to sleep.

Again I don't wake up until noon. I look through a hole in the floor, I see various animals, chickens, ducks and a farmer across the courtyard in the stables –

the chickens are the only ones who seem to know I am here.

It's obvious the chickens are going to give me away, so I climb down, and calmly go across the yard to the farmer.

'Bonjour – je suis Anglais,' I bid him – and with a lot of sign language and my lousy French, I identify myself further.

I show him parts of my uniform, identity tags – giving my name, number, rank, religion and service – also the maps and escape kit.

He starts nodding – these are adequate credentials for him.

He is friendly, but cautious: go back and hide, I understand him to say, I will bring you food.

I go and later he brings me food and wine.

When I've had a swill of the wine, I realize I've been so scared that I haven't thought about a drink for thirty-six hours now – that is amazing for me. I am that scared . . . I smile. I eat my fill – I am very very hungry after the walking. . .

He sits. In a while I tell him: 'What I really need is clothes – clothes, so that I can travel safely through France.' I don't know what 'civvies' would be in French.

Jesus, Skeglee, this is the way it is. I stay hidden all day in the barn. I am given supper – also in the barn, by lanternlight.

The cautious farmer then presents me (I had thought he hadn't asked me into his house out of fear and meanness) with his best Sunday outfit – a warm, black civilian suit.

It's very large for me across the chest, so I put my battle-dress tunic underneath my blue uniform shirt.

This gives me quite a bloated, elderly appearance, and, except for my hands, I look like any farmer.

I give my trousers to the farmer. 'Perhaps you'd better burn them.'

I offer to pay – he makes a very French expression of the lips.

'Pardonnez-moi, monsieur – merci beaucoup.'

I leave at sunset and proceed on my way to the Seine – intending, of course, to avoid large towns and any German concentrations – not to mention concentration camps.

(This sleeping in the day, and travelling at night, I have discovered, is excellent against the enemy of nightmares. . .)

How naïve I am. After I walk a couple of hours, I come to the Dieppe-Paris railway line, which I follow for about five minutes.

Suddenly I hear a rustling sound behind me and two policemen rush up to me – each pointing a gun at my head. (They are *Police Français*, a provincial constabulary – but I don't know it yet. . .)

I am unable to understand what they are saying – and, paralyzed with fear, I just stand there speechless.

One of them kicks a hand of mine – so I put both hands over my head.

'Je suis Anglais,' I am sputtering.

310

As soon as I speak these words, the pistols go back in their holsters and I am led away from the tracks and into the field.

In spite of my limited French, I identify myself – using the method I'd used with the farmer, showing my things. Gesturing: 'Pardonnez-moi. . . Enchanté. . . Je parle Français malade.'

I ask them, 'Is it safe to travel by train? I want to get to Paris.' (This is my quickest way of getting south, I'm sure.)

'Trains are seldom searched, monsieur – by either French police or by Occupying German police,' one tells me. I am very surprised.

The other says: 'Trains are a good way to go – safely – without detection.'

'There is a 2:30 train tomorrow afternoon from the village of Nestle St Saire – it is close by. Only a few kilometres distance. It is safe – a good bet, too – no police.'

These two kindly coppers are now making me rehearse what to ask for: 'Un Troisième Classe billet pour Paris.' I'm so bad at it, they write it down.

Then they are leading me to a haystack in a nearby field.

'Stay here until sunrise. Then stay here until the time just before the train goes tomorrow afternoon.'

Later, they too bring me food and wine.

Next morning, September 24th, I wake with a headache. But I wander about and locate the station.

Fascinated (ho-ho) to see several freight cars go by, each made up of two anti-aircraft 'flak' cars, manned by Krauts – standing as pretty as you please.

I find a stream and shave – with part of the kit. I also eat a bit of the food saved from that which the second farmer gave me.

A few minutes before the train time, I go right into the station – cautiously. I've already figured it empty – it is.

At the window: 'Un Troisième Classe billet pour Paris.'

I hand the ticket man a hundred-franc note – and he gives me the change, correct, and a ticket.

Out on the platform there are other passengers.

I find the public toilet and use it – gratefully.

Coming back out on the platform I am astounded to see, standing almost next to me – two German Wehrmacht – obviously to catch the same train.

Amazing, as I said, to see the enemy at such close quarters. It gives me the heebie-jeebies – but I manage to act in a very quiet and normal manner.

I figure I'd better get used to seeing Germans – to acting normal in their company.

Soon the train arrives and you climb up like Canada – not walk right in, like England. I enter this crowded carriage.

Opposite me is a couple eating strawberries – but what makes my mouth water is the incredible freshness of the young woman. Wow, the first French woman I've seen – with whom mating/loving is fanciable. . .

But all too soon I can hear a man coming round, asking for something. I don't know what he wants and I panic a bit, jump up and head for the toilet –

It's occupied.

I thought this man was a Controller – asking for identity cards.

Fortunately, no one notices my alarm. And I notice that he is a conductor – he only wants tickets.

We arrive at St Lazare Station, Paris, at 9:15 in the

312

evening. There is a Police Station Controller at the gate.

This is the way it was, Skeglee,

This is the way it is.

XIV

The Germans had bombed London and all the big industrial cities and even the small cities with industries, like ancient Lincoln.

But James felt, *they would not bomb Worcester*, just for jam and china, old Worcester where the vast billiard-green cricket field, almost, but not quite, reflected the slender spire of the Cathedral –

Worcester, where, even then in 1942, birds swooped amid the sound of bells and waddled on the High Street, only disturbed by the serious-capped boys of King's College walking crocodile or riding their bicycles past puddles reflecting the pillow clouds and soft blue sky – itself a benign canopy over the fruit fields, the ancient manor houses, farms and stables; over the Malvern Hills, themselves round, the fecund breasts of the Earth itself, upon which the feet of believing Man, one felt, has left no scars save mossy paths. . .

But they did: they bombed Worcester. Swooping out of the evening sky like black ravens, they roared and dived their guttural engines and whistling bombs. . .

They smashed the jam warehouses and the conservatories and the cricket field and King's College – and hit the little Cathedral too. . .

It wasn't a terrible thing, as twentieth-century things go, just stupid and cruel and enough to keep Malvern and Worcester sure that nowhere was safe – nor would be. . .

313

From late September until only a few days from Christmas, there was nothing James could do, he thought, for his brother (or his Aunts) but wait.

'My brother Chris always says to keep busy – but he didn't say that there are times when it doesn't help much.'

'Come on, Berkeley,' said his new friend Ian Aiken. 'Let's design a new paper plane each – and make it, each of us. I challenge you – for speed and flight endurance.'

It was a cold and mostly tiresome time. He liked being Captain of the School and, despite his mistakes, he liked authority. But he didn't like soccer, a game, he thought, quite without the grace and hidden inner meanings of cricket.

He got letters from Washashley – now some from Fenders and more from Aunt Daisy and only two from Aunt Lillie – and that puzzled and worried him.

'How are you, Aunt Lillie?' he wrote – but no one seemed to remember to answer.

He also heard from Bermuda. Soon, his father would be over – as soon as no more vessels were required by 'George' (meaning the King). That would be almost never, he figured.

Fenders said there were soldiers in the Hall. 'They are black men – but they seem to be all right – decent enough. But it's outrageous, Mr James, outrageous.'

'I reckon Hitler will win the War,' James confided in Ian Aiken.

'Why do you reckon that, Berkeley?'

'Because, to tell the truth – because he's such a bastard – and bastards always win. And he has the guys who make the cleverest inventions, doesn't he?'

'I'll grant you the inventions, man – but I don't necessarily agree that bastards always win. Besides, Berkeley, Britain didn't exactly lose the last war –

314

nor the last several.'

James liked Aiken. There was nothing small about him – especially not his mind.

'I give you this, Berkeley. The First War was damn near a draw – and the Boer War was wrong – our fault. But, the Yanks are in now, and that's the Big One.'

Aiken's attitudes were altogether above and beyond the normal English schoolboy. His father was a journalist, his grandfather a novelist and historian.

Only a few days before Christmas, James went all the way home to Lincoln, as usual, standing with his head half out of the train's window (in the corridor) – chilly but happy.

It was about three in the afternoon. Only Aunt Daisy met him – her hands in her big rabbit-fur gloves and her pink face a little more red around her twinkling blue Curfey eyes than before.

She had a taxi, she said. The driver, whom he didn't know, put his trunk on the roof. He held the door for his aunt and wrapped the blanket around her, as usual – as if it were her own car.

But as soon as he sat beside her he became 'not-himself' – as people then said.

'Something is wrong, Aunt Daisy, every time you meet me something terrible is wrong.'

'My dear boy – I'm not sure what you mean –'

'Well, what is wrong? What has happened?'

'My dear James – you see, we had to move out of the Hall –'

'I know all that, Aunt Daisy –'

'– and into Watkins' Cottage – and we had to pack and store everything from the Hall into Lincoln city, in two warehouses. Eight hundred and eighty oil paintings, ninety-two crates of books – And it all was

315

just too much for your Aunt Lillie. I'm afraid she's left us.'

'She's dead?!'

'She passed peacefully away.'

Silence.

James tried to clench his nails into his fists – but he still bit them and so they were no help.

'When?'

'Just about a week ago.'

'Why didn't you tell me, Aunt Daisy?'

'We didn't want to worry you. . .'

'Is . . . is . . . she buried?'

'About a week ago.'

Silence.

'What did she die of, Aunt Daisy?'

'Her heart, poor darling, it was a spasm of the heart.'

'Was she in pain?'

'Not very much pain – but it would have got worse, Dr Smith said. So it was a good thing – for her sake.'

Then James heard himself talking – as if it was someone else's voice. 'Why didn't you let me come and grieve over her body . . . like a human?'

His little aunt was quite angry. 'James, Lillie was my sister . . . she isn't even a blood relative of yours. How could you be so selfish? She was very sick for a long time.'

'I'm sorry – very sorry about her being sick, Aunt Daisy.'

The old Austin began to turn up the hill, the road past the Hall.

Aunt Daisy rapped her umbrella handle. 'Not that way, driver. The next turn – through the village.

'Yes, Past the Cross.'

The driver turned back.

'Where is Aunt Lillie buried?'

'Adjacent to Dearest's grave. Adjacent to *our* grave.'

'May I go there right now, please?'

'If you must.' Aunt Daisy pushed the window to the driver open. 'Please stop at the church – there, at the Cross.'

Half-blinded with emotion, making incoherent noises as if talking to himself, James got out and ran into the graveyard.

Up the path to the Chancel door was Uncle Albert's expensive Gaelic Cross –

There, beside it, was a grave of new soil and flowers, already bashed and soaked by the weather. It was part turf and part soil, the way new graves are.

On a wreath he recognized Aunt Daisy's zany handwriting. Another card, he could see, without bending, was from the Fenders.

He threw himself down, the whole length of his body on to the wet grass and tried to embrace it all – he tried to embrace her body.

'Aunt Lillie,' he said. 'Oh Aunt Lillie. Where are you?' He put his cheek against the ground, the soil. 'Aunt Lillie – where are you?'

He felt that he had, perhaps, gone out of his mind – as he had heard that other members of his family had.

Aunt Daisy took him to the strange cottage, which had familiar things in it – it must be home.

They started to give him some supper. It was almost dark now – and raining.

'I want to take my supper out to eat with Aunt Lillie.'

Aunt Daisy must have felt it better to humour him: 'Well, give him a tray and a lantern – a torch – Mrs Pickle. Yes, and he'd better have an umbrella.'

317

He walked back down the cottage path, into the road and down to the graveyard.

He ate his supper, under the umbrella, sitting on part of the stone of his aunt's grave.

'It can't get any worse than this.'

He seemed to hear her say: 'What can't, dearest boy?'

'The War – it can't get any worse than this, Aunt Lillie – I promise you.'

When he got back to the house, Aunt Daisy and Mrs Pickle clucked over him like two hens.

They showed him to his room. It was very small, but the walls were as thick as a fortress's – strange for a cottage, but calming.

He thought how clever it was of them to get together – the last remnants of the Hall: the one the former Lady, the other, the former Head Cook.

'Did you love your Aunt Lillie more than you love me?' Aunt Daisy asked him.

'No,' he said. I loved her more than I love anyone – more even than my own mother. (He felt fiercely disloyal, but it was true. . .) I loved her as much as I love Christopher – almost. No, but as much as Grampy Halcyon, the prince of sailing. . .

In the little drawing room – which Aunt Daisy had fixed up incredibly well and beautifully (considering the time and the cottage's smallness), he found her little desk.

And, on top of the desk were some bills. He read:

The Late Miss Curfey
Received the Sum of One Pound Nine Shillings for Church Fees.

Funeral. December 16th 1942
F. Dabb, Sexton.

and another from Dr James Smith 'For Attendance and Medicine October to December. 19s.6d.'

and another:

Mrs Berkeley, The Hall, Washashley
December 1942
Dr to: – R. Draper
Joiner and Undertaker, House Decorator and Paperhanger.
For one Oak Coffin and Shroud. Panelled; and Brass furniture and Plate lettering, and attendances, also bearers' fees.
For Miss Curfey   £14 0s 0d

In this little cottage, the Hall's furniture looked like real things shoved in a doll's house. In the drawing-room were somehow fitted, some stuffed chairs from the bedrooms of the Hall and a little sofa. Somehow, too, Aunt Daisy had rescued a Sheraton table – and had placed on it some of the finer pieces of Uncle Albert's enormous collection of porcelain and china.

On the mantelpiece was the Marie Antoinette clock, the face surrounded by leaves of pure gold. The hands gold – and even the delicate pendulum . . . a gold Sun God – all set on the whitest marble.

He explored some more. The front door of the cottage opened directly into a small dining-room in which Aunt Daisy had managed to cram the bow-fronted sideboard (groaning under the weight of silver urns and entrée dishes and a samovar), several of the

319

dining chairs –

On the floor she had one of the Turkish carpets – its red and blue and vermilion colours were lovely.

She had the little brass and copper ornaments, made in the trenches, on this rugged mantelpiece here; Chris, he hoped, still had the little boot – with the hole in its sole.

Upstairs there were three bedrooms. The largest must have been for both his aunts – now only Daisy. Here was another secretaire – which appeared to have innumerable secret compartments. It also had the black steel safe: which had always contained, he knew, the jewellery and special papers.

His bedroom ('You'll have to share with Christopher when he comes home,' Aunt Daisy said) had a lovely bow-front wardrobe; a window with leaded panels that looked out into the Dickenses' yard, the tall oaks at the back of the Hall and the church tower.

'It's good to be overlooking the rooks still, Aunt Daisy.'

'Yes, they are lively, aren't they, dear?'

It was very different from the Hall. James couldn't help but be impressed by the way his Aunt Daisy had adjusted.

First of all, there was no bathroom – only an outhouse – but here, already, his aunt had had erected a trellis fence, so that entrance and exit to the place were not visible to the nearby tenants of the other cottages.

'Come and 'ave a nice cup of tea, Mr James,' said Mrs Pickle, immaculate in her white apron, her finger pressed to her lower lip in a girlish way.

She was over seventy, he knew, but she was

physically, even sexually, attractive... She had her apple-pink cheeks and her twenty-inch waist. She was a busybody and a gossip, he knew, but she was also very funny.

The centre of the life of the cottage was the kitchen. It was a large room, dominated by the black open-grate stove – which Mrs Pickle kept alight day and night.

'It heats us, Mr James – as well as does all the cookin'.'

Mrs Pickle blacked the stove every day. It was not only their fireplace – it was the heart of the cottage.

In front of the hearth, was a black carpet – and a stuffed chair for his aunt – and a rocking chair for Mrs Pickle.

'We are all very democratic now,' whispered Aunt Daisy. Then, seeing that Mrs Pickle had heard, she added: 'I do the silver and the brass – and I lay the table.'

'And I do the cooking and the washing up,' said Mrs Pickle.

James soon discovered that it was not only a democracy – but that the two old ladies now had a continual running fight for captaincy.

'I've the keys to everything – dear boy,' said Aunt Daisy. As much as to say, and all the cash.

'All of which does her naught good at all – because she can't cook – not even boil an egg.' Mrs Pickle got a mischievous expression on her face. 'Begging your pardon, madam.'

'Mrs Fenders comes to clean once a week,' said Aunt Daisy.

'Tell me about the Hall, please Aunt Daisy?'

Aunt Daisy's girlish blue eyes began to cloud.

'They've torn the lawns with tanks and trucks – and turned my kitchen into a pigsty, Mr James.'

321

'James,' lisped Aunt Daisy. 'They have left us the walled gardens;– and Old Watkins still keeps on doing wonders.

'And we are allowed to keep the Rolls in the garage.

'It's awful what they've done. They've painted things white and bust things – lots of things. . . But I haven't seen any of it and I'm never going to see any of it. I absolutely don't want to talk about it. – Come out here, James – and I'll show you what I'm going to do in this garden.'

Outside Aunt Daisy said: 'We must just be careful *not* to tell Mrs Pickle everything.

'Look,' she said, making a sweeping gesture with her small arm. 'I'm not going to have any grass – except a little border. Just masses and masses of flowers. Row on row – at every height and of every colour and every season.

'You just see what I'm going to do, James. So that it will be lovely when your dear father comes.'

'It will be lovely. Who does the shopping, Aunt Daisy?'

'I do, of course. And I collect all the rents – and I pay all the accounts.'

Suddenly she took his arm and hugged it to her with both hands. He thought she was going to cry again, but she shook her head in determination. 'I'm a very strong person, you know. I can do things – and I'm learning a lot.'

He wanted to stroke her hair and call her endearing names – but he was too shy.

She put her mouth up and he kissed it.

'Bless you, dear boy.'

'Aunt Daisy, has there been any news of Christopher?'

'No – not since that squadron leader came by. What's-'is-name? You know, he said that although no one had actually seen it happen – that no less than four receiving stations had got Chris's message and that he had bailed out.'

'Leatham.'

'What?'

'Squadron Leader Leatham.'

'Yes.'

'Well, Aunt Daisy – it's been three months now. Does the RAF think that is good or bad?'

'I think they think it's good because they said that if he'd been killed we'd know through the Swedish Red Cross by now.'

'Yes – and even the Germans would have crowed about it, if they'd captured him.'

'Oh, would they?'

'Yes, ma'am. A boy I know says they always like to brag about catching any RAF pilot.'

'I do miss him most awfully, dear James – so I know you must even worse.'

'You know what I miss, Aunt Daisy? Seeing his silly old arms working in the garden – I love the shape of those arms.'

'Yes – me too.'

'And his beautiful hands.' James thought of his mother's hands – they were the same as Christopher's – incredibly beautiful. When he was very little, he used to hug and stroke his mother's hands; and tell her how beautiful they were. Once, he even told her that he'd like to carve them – in wood.

She only smiled and changed the subject.

When you told Chris he had lovely hands he'd say: 'Thanks, m'dear – pretty average fish haulers.'

'And Teddy?' he asked.

'He's in a place called Kokomo, Indiana – flying something called a Steerman. Now isn't that ridiculous. I looked it up on the map. It exists – and he's

323

with the US Navy and there's no sea there anywhere.'

He went by to have a look at the Hall. Even from the western road the building looked somehow lost and bereft – betrayed.

Some upper windows, on each side of the giant bays, were open at strange heights – like the eyes of a drunken man.

There was a sentry box at the front gate. James immediately noticed that one of the gate latch-locks had been broken.

There was a black soldier in the box with a rifle.

James went up: 'Excuse me, may I go and walk up to the front door?'

'Why – why should you?' The man's shoulder flashes said Nigeria.

'I used to live here.'

'What of it?'

'Please, call an officer.'

The soldier rang – and spoke, incoherently, into a phone.

It was the loss of it, the loss of home that James felt most acutely. This might only be his adopted home – but added to the loss of the Bermuda home, he felt more grief than he could understand.

'He says you can walk through the driveway – but you are not to go into any buildings.'

'All right.' James would have liked to chop the man to bits with a hatchet.

Even the drive was already overgrown with weeds, and chewed with truck markings and torn about. The front lawn was badly marked with tank tracks. Two urns broken out of twenty – one chain broken between the first set.

At the south door, the bell pull – which was several hundred years old – was hanging off the wall.

'Officers Only' was stencilled there.

He tried the gate to the walled garden. It was locked. But, looking through the gate he could see that everything inside was, amazingly, the same as it used to be: the paths even weeded. The moss in the centre of the paths, green and beautiful.

That was a relief, anyway. Later, perhaps, he'd go in. The painted crest was missing from the gate (this fact made him burn livid with rage. . .).

The rooks still cawed. He walked slowly around the gravel driveway.

Several Army vehicles were in the stableyard. The garages were all locked.

Approaching the garage door, he looked through the little window. He could see part of the sheet covering the Rolls. . . Turning back he walked a little towards the east garden.

Then he saw a very small black man in khaki, digging at a rose bush with a kitchen fork.

'She broke,' he said with a smile at James.

As James came closer he added, 'The poor rose, she broke. But I is fixing her.'

James saw that the rose bush had a splint made of sticks and cloth. 'I'm glad,' James said. 'Thank you.'

The black man smiled – as if to say, the white man crazy, I suppose, but I'll humour him.

In the park – the Great Park – he was amazed to find a soldier putting out hay from a handcart for the Grey-White Deer. 'They are not getting enough fodder this season,' the Nigerian said. He himself looked purple in the cold.

'The crest is missing from the garden gate,' he told Aunt Daisy.

She refused to answer.

325

But Fenders said: 'It's all right, sir – I packed them both. They are in storage.'

XV

Christopher, Backwards Often,
Forwards Sometimes,
And Probably, Sideways Frequently

III

'When this Fucking War Is Over, you and I will fall in love. . .' That is, Mr French Policeman, you and me, will fall in love.

Now I've got to figure some way of getting past you, Mr Police Station Controller, at the gate.

9:15 in the evening, Nasti, and this is the way it was, this is the way it is. . .

I loiter a bit and notice that they are only searching people carrying suitcases – interesting. I check, I double check. I do not want to be caught by the Krauts and experimented with – I want to get home.

Right now I'd even settle for a home for the night.

As calmly as I can, I, Aubrey Berkeley, of Paget East, Bermuda, keep in the centre of the group, and walk slowly past the officer – slowly, slowly

I walk on slowly through the station – noises and smells like London – but different: more about vegetables, sweeter somehow. I wander out into the city.

Me, Christopher, in Paris at last – isn't it the Eternal City? (Part of me feels like a small kid in St Georges for the first time.)

I am wandering about – there are many cafés where the customers are all sitting at small tables on the pavement – marvellous –

326

Except, Nasti, that most of these customers are 'ugly customers' – that is German officers – who I, A.S. Berkeley, pass *by* within striking distance.

Holy smoke: I experience a thrill and considerable satisfaction at not arousing the suspicions of the bastards . . . (and Christ they are arrogant: they have the beautiful women and shout a lot. . .)

I am looking for lodging for the night, right?

I try two third-rate boarding houses. Kind of places Grampy would never be seen in twice removed.

'Pardonnez-moi – un chambre pour nuit, s'il vous plait?'

No room. No luck.

I go into this restaurant: it's 10:30 and there are signs everywhere about the eleven o'clock curfew.

I feel hungry and pretty desperate but I see this woman who is too old for me by far – but something between us jangles a little bell. She's with a couple – a steady-looking couple – obviously man and wife.

'Je parle Français malade,' I say smiling at her – and at them.

The two women smile – the one I like laughs as well.

'Voulez-vous parle Anglais?' I ask.

'Yes, speak softly. Sit down,' she says.

I sit down next to her – and smile some more. 'I'm very hungry,' I say. 'I've some money, of course: I'd very much like some food –'

'That's easy,' she says, still smiling.

I notice she has a tooth missing – right in the front of her mouth. She orders for me – shouting, but not noticeable – very clever.

She has said, food of the house, for my friend.

'Worse – sorry to be a bother – but I need a place to stay – just tonight. Tomorrow I'll leave very early.

327

The end of curfew. Six o'clock?'
'Yes, at six the curfew ends.'
The food comes. I give her the money – she whips a bill from me and motions me to put away the rest.
'Eat quickly,' she says. 'I think I can get you a room at my boarding house – it's only round the corner. The owner is my cousin.'
Courtesy of Harrow, my French seems to be returning. . .

We bid them 'bon nuit' and I go with my friend Eloise.
By now I realize that she is not a very desirable woman – even if I did not have any convictions about staying pure. . .
But, being in a strange place and being scared makes me think of love – of arms.
But I couldn't hold Eloise. Her breath is very bad.
The woman of the house looks me over.
'It's a friend of mine, cousin – just for the night, all right?'
They show me to the room.
Madame will not accept money.
'Good luck, aviator – leave at six – not before – and very quietly by the back, if you please.'
Eloise and I are alone.
I am about to say, I am tired and feeling not very well, when she says: 'Forgive me, monsieur. But I am – how-you-say, a little under the weather just now? Another time. . .' She smiles.
'Thank you – awfully – Eloise. And the best of luck, then.'

The bed creaks. I don't care.
I turn in and sleep soundly – amazed at myself.
And I wake up at exactly 5:45.
I eat some cheese and bread, pee in the sink. Drink

328

some water from the carafe.

I leave by the back door.

There are maps all over Paris. Very handy. I discover that what I'm looking for is obviously the Gare Austerlitz – for the south.

I find my way without difficulty – as if I were finding the Underground out to Harrow. There are posters showing sunburned youths in Nazi helmets – asking me to join the Wehrmacht. Just what I need, clean honest work on the Russian Front. . .

And here at this big boomy station I am looking about – checking, checking. I want to know if there are any police and if they are checking for Identity Cards.

Now I'm looking for timetables *à Toulouse* and the south – where else?

While I am wandering about, I notice that at one of the gates gendarmes are making all passengers show papers.

No good. No embarking from this Gare Austerlitz.

I think I should try a station down the line, as the song says.

Well, Skeglee, after a quick jaunt of five hours – I come to the Paris suburb town of Choisy-le-Roi – and suddenly I am incredibly thirsty and tired.

It's also already 9:00 p.m. again.

I find a definitely third-rate café and go in.

It's very hot. One of those September days . . . in my black suit, I'm boiling hot. All I've got to say is, 'Biere, s'il vous plait' – but suddenly, confronted with the small proprietor, I say: 'Biere, *please.*'

He gazes at me and without change of expression, puts a bottle and a glass in front of me.

I ask him with my eyes, how much?

'Three francs,' he says in English.

Jesus, the jig is up before I've hardly started.

To hell with it, I'm thinking. 'Excuse me – I beg your pardon, I wonder if you can help me?' I ask.

'Perhaps,' he says.

'I'm a British aviator – I want to go south – to the border.'

Instantly, he smiles. 'You are very welcome,' he says. 'You have come to the right place. You have fallen among friends. Just drink your beer and keep quiet – and in a little while, I'll help.'

The café is almost empty now and the proprietor comes by. Again I am frightened as hell.

He swings his leg up on the aluminium counter and taps it with a spoon – hard.

'I'm a Belgian, the Krauts took my leg – 1916.' He spits. 'The bastards. I hate them – all of them, always and for ever.'

'How do you know you can trust me?'

'Your black tie is RAF issue, monsieur. Take it off – or put it away, at least.'

'Say, my new friend,' I say. 'Can you please buy me a ticket to Orleans – on the local line?'

'Oui – it can be arranged – but not tonight. Tomorrow. Tonight you stop at the inn – eat with me and my wife and son –

'Tomorrow, the whole family will put you on the train – that is the safe thing to do, all right, monsieur?'

'Chris,' I say.

'Jean-Baptiste,' he says. We shake. A grip like a wrench.

They feed me well. I sleep not so well.

But the whole family is taking me to the station. I give Jean-Baptiste the money and he gets me a ticket.

Then I notice that they all have tickets.

He whispers: 'We'll go with you just to Étampes – it's safer this way.'

These people are making me feel very grateful indeed.

Then, on the train, they give me enough food for several days – and a little leather bag. Nasti, these people are poor – really, the poorest innkeepers.

Madame puts a rough tie around my neck.

Everyone kisses me goodbye. I do not want to part with them. . .

It is very warming, comforting, to be kissed on both cheeks by a man with a rough beard – it is very civilized. Thus I discover another way the French are superior to us – the Belgians, in this case. . .

'Except for your blond hair, Chris – you are perfect bourgeoisie now.' Jean-Baptiste laughs. 'Blond hair makes you look like a Kraut – that's why I acted peculiar to you yesterday – at first.'

I've long been thinking that I had best slip off the train before she gets to Orleans.

Orleans is the boundary between Occupied and Unoccupied France – the Frontier. The dividing line, it says on the maps, is the River Cher – just beyond Orleans. . .

I jump off at Les Aubrais: it's the junction, just before Orleans.

I am walking into the city – not feeling in the least like St Jean d'Arc – I can tell you.

But I go right to the Cathedral and go inside

and have a look – and kneel and cross myself and say a prayer to the Lady. Who knows – she was kind to the armed forces, she herself was a soldier.

And, I trust, she will not think of me as a 'Goddamn'.

Then I cross the River Loire – I cross, Nasti, by a very familiar bridge. It is one I've seen from the air – during Ranger Operations – me, only about a month ago – no, two weeks.

I have used this bridge as a landmark.

My arse is tight – tighter.

I am walking and walking and walking south – I am following the vicinity of the railway lines.

After a long while, at sunset, I find a field and a haystack. Without any hesitation I burrow my way into the haystack like a large rabbit.

I sleep – again well – until sunrise.

Now I have to have a b.m. Very embarrassing to do this outside – brrr. Also smelly, and hay and grass are rough paper. I bury my refuse like a kitchen cat. I hate all this.

It's Sunday: man-oh-man, I suddenly remember: I'm not supposed to be here: I'm supposed to be in London.

I, Aubrey Spencer, have a date today – with a WAAF officer – and very nice too. In London. For once it's not my many-sided family who interferes.

This one time.

We were to meet at the Brasserie Universal. I wonder will Harry tell her I'm Missing – or maybe that I am dead. Perhaps she'll be picked up by another Bermudian. Florrie, her name is – and really nice too. Bright eyes and a quick smile and brown bangs. Full jib and a cute spanker.

332

I eat next to my haystack. Eggs, pork, and some bread and cheese – from my friends of Choisy-le-Roi.

Dear Nasti; This is the way it was
   this is the way it is
   this is the way
   this is
   this

I am walking for about an hour and come to a small town. I find the station – with a view to getting a lift a little closer to the Frontier.

My objective is still Spain ... but I am not going right up to the window – I loiter, and try to look inconspicuous.

Then I notice a young German soldier there behind the window – for the express purpose (of course) of examining Identity Cards.

I conclude this is a Frontier Control Zone. I make my exit immediately – and decide to walk to the River Cher. I walk the entire day – about fourteen hours, without rest. I walk my socks away.

I find a remote farmhouse.

I knock, and the farmer and his wife come to the door.

'I'm a British pilot – I am very hungry and thirsty – could you possibly be so generous and kind as to help me?'

I show them my wings – and maps and Bermuda flashes.

They smile. 'Welcome to our humble farm.'

They put me in their barn – hayloft – for the night ...

Next night – again I am walking all day – I come to a wealthy farmhouse.

A man answers. I repeat my message.

333

'I am Norwegian – you are more than welcome.'

The meal is plentiful and excellent. These people treat me as if I was royalty. . .

'Is the Frontier guarded – is it hard to cross?'

'The bridges are probably guarded. You will have to be exceedingly cautious, my friend.'

We exchange addresses – to use after the War – like travelling gentlemen. 'I put it in my book under Bermuda Yachts – you put it in yours under *fromage*, for safety.'

Late the next afternoon, I leave and soon I come – about eight o'clock – to the Cher.

On the far bank there is a sentry box – but no sentry.

I cross the Cher – and later I find another farmhouse – rough – but I am put up for the night in the barn.

Next morning I am in the farming village of Villafranche – here there is a narrow-gauge railway.

I buy a ticket, easily, for Montluçon.

I am on the railway all day. At Châteauroux – I have to change trains – oops.

Then I see several flat cars with damaged German aircraft resting on them.

The station is guarded both by Gestapo and Wehrmacht – the former in khaki uniforms with swastikas. Very tough-looking customers, let me tell you.

I continue to Montluçon and get off and find another haystack and sleep there – badly.

Next morning, I am talking to the stationmaster – and find I'm talking more than I intend

But he turns out to be a good Frenchman.

'I thought you were a German.'

'No, British. I'm a pilot trying to get to Spain – to escape. These are my things.'

'Come home with me – now!'

Again these people are very generous. The station-master's wife gives me five hundred francs for my Belgian money.

'It will help my brothers,' she says, and shrugs.

They give me a railway map, a timetable – for the entire system of France.

Things happen fast in France, Skeglee, my boy. I am just figuring that I will have only two hundred miles to go to the border, when I reach Montrejeau – I am riding into the junction of Eygurande-Merlines.

Here I am suddenly told to change trains. There isn't another train, though – until 4:30 the next morning.

So, at Eygurande-Merlines I find a hotel.

I go up to the desk. 'A room for the night, please.'

'Yes, monsieur,' the proprietor looks rather suspicious.

'And a meal please.'

'Yes, monsieur.' Now he looks so suspicious – my bad French, I guess – that I give my usual spiel.

'Eat well, monsieur. But be careful. There is a Luftwaffe officer who has the room next to yours.'

'It's all right, I'll leave on the 4:30 a.m. train.'

'Which is exactly what the German Luftwaffe officer intends to do.'

After I eat, the proprietor comes by and says: 'Do not catch that train. Stay in your room – we will help you.'

It is very alarming to the nerves, being in a strange

335

country... Next day the proprietor tells me, in my room: 'Look, I have a friend who is ideal to help you. He is a Scotsman who lives in the next town. For many years he has been a nurse in an asylum.'

Just what I need, I think, to get mixed up with a male-nurse from a booby hatch – but I wait all day.

The Scotsman proves to be very real.

And, this evening we chat for a very long time.

'I am so happy to speak English again.'

'And me also – very cheerful and much fun for me. Look, I have a friend – a Monsieur Dehn, an Alsatian, who has dealings with people who could help you. So I'll go and try to find him. Your case is very unusual.'

Dear Nasti; this is the way it was

this is the way it is:

M. Dehn, the Alsatian, is a very tricky-looking dark customer – like an Arab, not an Alsatian.

Again I tell my story and show my things.

M. Dehn jumps up: 'He's a German – I knew it. You ever hear a Britisher say "Jah"? No, he is a spy.'

'No – my "Yeah" is Bermudian – like American "Yeah" for yes. I am a Bermudian.'

'Boche – I can smell them.'

I-can-tell-you, it takes a while to calm M. Dehn. But I am soon to find out why.

A little later I am taken around the corner to M. Dehn's house – only about two hundred yards.

And here, Nasti, I meet Piquette – who is, hold it, seventeen years old – and M. Dehn's adopted daughter.

If it sounds like a spy-story by John Buchan – it's because it is. Piquette is like a boy – only very

336

slightly developed – but lovely. Shy. Blushes a lot.

Immediately she says to me: soldier to soldier, you know:

'I am very active carrying food and arms to the Maquis – who are hiding in the woods.'

'How do you know you can trust this man, Piquette – you blow your mouth off like a steam whistle.'

'The eyes – he has the eyes of an honest person – and the brows – his brows are like gull wings.'

'So do a lot of Luftwaffe officers –'

'They look hard as ice – he looks like honesty and valour in the eyes.'

'Thank you, m'selle.'

'Not-at-all.'

She is really very lovely. But I'm trying to look – in front of this father, at any rate – as if I am uninterested. It is impossible. Her femininity radiates like a candleflame. Her smell is unique, also.

I soon find out that M. Dehn is a very tough man – tough in this fight with the Germans. And tough with his daughter – stepdaughter – also. It is as if they are in competition with one another, perhaps.

Anyway, the Maquis, of course, consist mainly of young men avoiding forced labour in Germany.

'It's very courageous – what you are doing,' I say to her.

'It's not – they are doing more – you are doing more – I am just a small soldier.'

I do not dare laugh – her eyes are very strong – you can tell, it would be easy to make her angry... Her mouth is like a magnet... Again, her smell...

I stay with them for four days. First day, M. Dehn

337

took the two photographs I have and immediately
came up with a false Identity Card.

'How do you like that, Monsieur Aviator?'

As I say, things move and change fast.

After four days, M. Dehn suddenly says he has a
radio message that I can possibly get on a boat going
to England – from Quimper.

'But that's on the Channel.'

'Not exactly – well, it's south of Brest.'

'But I'm almost at the border.'

'Yes. Sometimes the border – sometimes we can
arrange a flight out. Sometimes a boat. This time it is
a boat.'

'But how will I get to Quimper?'

'You will go to Paris.'

'How?'

'I'll get you First Class passes – to Paris. Two. You
and Piquette. On the trip you must not talk.'

My Identity Card says I am a deaf-mute – born in
Alsace in 1919 – two years older than I am.

Sometimes I feel the part.

All this racing madness. I do not like it. I will but tell
you, Nasti, that we got to Paris in two days – and, as
impossible as it may seem, I never spoke.

First Class is very comfortable.

Piquette is very strict and even icy now.

Always at least two seats away. I never even got it
straight how the Maquis would make out without her.

(I'll tell you: I knew I would see her again – somehow, I knew this. Sort of, crazy, but, that's it. . .)

All the way to Paris, all I do is look at her – and
watch for the Boche.

She has these yellow-brown eyes – biggish – like no
one I have ever seen. A hooked nose, but very small.

338

She looks as French as the Loire ... water and blue-green grass.

And we also sleep (very apart) and eat our picnic – prepared from way back in Eygurande-Merlines.

Piquette takes/leads me to Montparnasse Station in Paris. It is a Monday night. We are to meet another woman who is to be my escort to Quimper.

The rendezvous is kept in the middle of the large station with Wehrmacht guards all about us.

The Frenchwoman turns out to be a Frenchman.

We nod and we are to travel again First Class to Quimper. I look around for Piquette – but she has disappeared.

This seems to hurt me more than I expected – a real wrenching.

My escort and I sit beside the window of the train – as if we don't know each other.

On the way, we pass Lorient. I have a good view of the U-boat base there – *absolutely untouched* by our bombing. (The RAF and USAAF have claimed to have wiped it out.) But the entire ancient town – across – on the wrong side of the river – absolutely razed and razed again. It looks like a cratered graveyard.

A terrible sight. Almost not a building left standing. This makes me shake with anger and pain.

We reach Quimper at 9:00 a.m. on a Tuesday.

There is a van waiting for us – and other vans for others.

I, who travel – truly only like to travel – in France, alone (except with Piquette, the small soldier, of course), do not like the fact that there is now quite a group.

Here I meet Fon-Fon, who is the Chief.

There are several others – to me, they look too

obviously allied pilots.

We are immediately driven well out of town – to a farm, a small cottage, where we stay for the rest of the day.

My companions and I are told: 'Keep quiet, do not even talk – it could attract attention.

'It might attract passing Germans. The farmer will bring a noon meal and another this evening.'

It is a very good steak the farmer gives us, and several bottles of wine.

I also feel that I want to get drunk – out of my mind drunk – to forget something – I can't think what.

But I don't allow myself to do that, of course. (I've had no phenobarbs in France and almost no booze. . .)

I am glad of an outhouse – which, by timing, I get to myself – together with some newspaper (much better than straw) for a long quiet one. . .

Afterwards, I listen to the sea and think of Piquette, and the smell of her, and home – Bermuda and Washashley.

How great it would be to have Piquette with me – and be taking her with me to meet the Aunts.

We have whispered all day: my companions are mostly Americans – crew of Flying Fortresses. We do a lot of very low-pitched laughing.

Just after dusk, we are driven to the coast. These operations seem to me slick in the extreme.

We are hidden in a cottage for two hours – waiting – obviously, for a German patrol to pass.

Then, to my amazement we are taken, single file, down to the beach, through a German minefield. One behind the other, like circus elephants – following the fisherman.

We do not have to be told to be quiet and walk

carefully. We are waiting ten or fifteen minutes for the boat.

The weather, I notice, is perfect for the job ahead – a complete overcast of clouds at two hundred feet – and thus very dark. The fishing boat arrives with three small rowing boats – which immediately come in shore to take us off.

There is a slight sea running, Skeglee, and as the boats are very crowded, we almost capsize. These people are not Bermudians. I am bailing frantically all the way out to the fishing boat. No one else seems to know what a bail-can is for.

But all thirty-five of us arrive safely.

The boat is wood. About sixty feet. She has sails as well as an auxiliary motor – Dad would call her badly designed, badly built and not now too seaworthy.

The plan is for us to meet one of the British high-speed launches. Like the Air Sea Rescue of the RAF – in which, I know, there are quite a few Bermudians serving. . .

At 9:20 p.m. we set course. . .

No sooner have we rounded a point of land, than it is becoming very rough. Heading right into the seas, the boat is pitching and pounding.

I go up on deck. They have hoisted a little sail which helps her considerably. I am about to offer further help but they seem to know what they are doing. Most of the boys are seasick. I almost am.

The boat has pounded all night – to make an alarming story short. Now she is beginning to leak.

On board are six allied fliers, and all the rest are Frenchmen from the Resistance Movement. The latter bound for Britain, for rest and a new assignment – to be parachuted back into France.

Nasti, this is the way it was
this is the way it is.

The water rises very fast and when it reaches the height of the carburettor – the engine quits. Leaving us only the sail.

Shortly after losing the use of the engine, Fon-Fon, who is also captain of the boat, announces: 'We are turning back. We will sink pretty soon – we have to make the French coast before. It is now impossible to make the rendezvous with the British boat – and because of the great danger, the boat will not wait or search for us.'

I am taking this very bad – and it is very frightening. But the effect of Fon-Fon's words on the Frenchmen is incredible. They act as if all is lost – and don't even want to help themselves.

They mumble, they fumble. There is no hope for them, if they get back to land. They will be killed.

I quite understand this: they are agents who are subject to torture and death. But I want to survive.

'Come on, let's bail,' is the universal cry of us fliers.

We only have one bucket and a bilge pump – which, like all bad bilge pumps, hardly works.

I am finding out: no tools to fix the pump. But we work the one we have – and, with our chain of guys on the bucket, we soon check the rise of the water.

The boat is half-sunk and consequently moving very slowly on the return journey.

But, before sunrise we come in sight of land. And it is long after sunrise, about 8:00, that we find an inlet to put into – along these very high cliffs.

Fon-Fon shouts: 'As I run the boat alongside – some of you jump.'

He rams the boat continually against the rocks – but there is a high sea running and a heavy surge and

342

it takes a half-hour for all of us to get off.

This delay, of course, causes disorganization and we are getting separated.

No sooner am I ashore – than I discover I've lost my valise – I had two bottles of perfume in it for Mummy. (I could have given one to Piquette too, perhaps. . .) Also, although I have my wallet, my fake French Identity Card has been so damaged by water that it is not presentable. . .

It could have been worse, Nasti.

We have been told: 'Hide in the bushes – near the coast and wait – wait for someone to come and get you.'

I, Christopher Berkeley, am waiting for some time and then I sneak out and back to the inlet where I hope to find Fon-Fon, the chief – as he had been the last to leave the boat.

However, as I look over the edge of the high cliffs overlooking the inlet, I see that the boat has sunk. And that there are several black ravens, German soldiers, standing about on the opposite shore looking at it.

Fortunately they do not see me. And I crawl on my stomach a short distance. And then beat it inland, as fast as I can.

I have two things on my mind: not to get captured: and Piquette. . .

XVI

In January 1943, at The Lion School, Ian Aiken and James became closer friends.

To begin with Berkeley and Aiken and Hosefield were given a separate senior table to eat at. Also they had a Senior Dorm – with just the three of them.

Aiken spoke with quiet authority: 'The Russians have turned the tide flow on the Germans at Stalingrad, Berkeley.'

'You mean that's as far as the German Army is going?'

'Certainly. Everything that has a beginning, must have a mid-point – and then an end. Just because we are in a war, we get to thinking that it will never end, but it will.'

James knew that Ian had heard all this: but he wasn't any parrot either.

'The tide of German conquest has reached its zenith – now the Russians, their winter and their people, will tear the guts out of the German Wehrmacht – just the way they beat Napoleon.'

'Sure hope you are right. But I don't suppose it will help my brother in France much. If he is in France. . .'

Ta-tum. Christopher.

'Sure it will,' said Aiken sagely. 'Just as the Americans have begun to turn back the Japanese – at Guadalcanal. Honestly. Both tides are turning.'

'How do you know all this, Ian?'

'Heavens, man – you should visit our flat in London. Reporters from all over the world gather there. I just listen – and accept the presents.

'I take it all in. Then I put it all to my grandfather. His club is one of Mr Churchill's. I ask a question: he tells me a whole newspaper. Then he asks me what I think.'

'What the hell do you say to a famous man like him?'

'Unless you really are smart and quick – he gets angry and bored. I said, I think it's awful living in a time when Britain and France and Germany have been at war with each other twenty-nine years.

'He liked that. He said, go up higher – elevate your view higher. How? I asked? A hundred years?

'Higher by ten times. We've been in a thousand-year war – This could be the end of the Dark Ages, my boy.'

'Do you think he's right?' asked James.

'He's right about almost everything – including cricket.'

'What's he say about cricket?'

'That rain invariably stops play.'

'Oh.'

'He says that's what life is like.'

Only a few nights after they'd been back Aiken said: 'Hosefield and the other blokes say you used to tell a hell of a story – something about, The Fucking Left In.'

'Yeah. But that was before I had to set an example.'

'Oh get off it, Berkeley. It's just the three of us – who cares?'

'Yes,' said Hosefield, in his whistly voice, through his bucked teeth. 'I would love a nice bedtime story, Berkeley – I really would.'

'Besides,' said Aiken, climbing into bed. 'My grandfather says keeping up appearances is rubbish. England, he says, is a society of six classes all saying, of the one beneath it, "*They* Don't Have To Keep Up Appearances." '

'I'll put out the light,' said Hosefield. 'Come on, Berkeley – I'll do anything you like later, in payment.'

'Once upon a time – yesterday, actually – there was a young man named Tony, who realized, having reached the age of sixteen that he'd never thought of

345

anything except sex since he was six.'

'Be serious.'

'I am serious.'

'Shut up, Aiken – you'll stop him – and it takes weeks, *months* to get him going.'

'Well, Tony was sixteen and very well developed – both in body and the size of his prick. Indeed his prick was so well developed, that he had to be careful to keep it tucked away – for fear he'd frighten people – Tony's trouble was that he was not very good-looking in the face. His body was okay, but he simply wasn't handsome.

'Now it so happened that Tony lived on a faraway island where there was an incredibly beautiful princess named Cynthia, who was only fourteen – not only developed – but lean and blonde and lovely.

'Tony was in love with Princess Cynthia.

'Only trouble was that when Cynthia looked at him – Tony – she could not see anything more good-looking than a left-handed cabbage head.

'Tony tried to please her with gifts.

'The Princess only gave the gifts to others and forgot him.

'Tony tried dancing for her. But she told him he was silly.

'So finally Tony built her a beautiful boat: a sailing vessel, with fine sails and a tall mast. It took him almost a year to build it.

'Tony had in mind that he and Princess Cynthia would sail off into the sunset and find another island where they could be totally alone and picnic on pomegranates and make love naked in the water.

'Now Tony wrote all this in a poem and put it in the boat and tied the boat, with all the sails shaking in the breeze, to the Princess's dock.

'Princess Cynthia found the boat and said to one of

346

her court (our hero, Tony, was hiding among the palmetto bushes, near the shore, within earshot): "Oh, it's one of those silly sailboats – what I'd like is a motor-racer. Now what is that note you've found, Elsie?"

' "It appears to be addressed to you, Madam."

' "Bring it here."

'Now Tony had worked at least a week on the poem alone – and he'd illustrated it with flowers he'd stuck on with perfume for her.

'Well, the Princess Cynthia, who had hair she could sit on and a behind twice as cute, took the poem and read it – to Tony's intense embarrassment – out loud.

'What was even more painful to him, she would read a couplet and then go into peals of laughter.

'She read the whole poem – of love for her – and then went into peals of laughter that became a fit.

'Soon the whole Court was laughing. They were roaring.

'Tony was mortified. He waited, patiently, until they had gone. And then he swore:

'Revenge. No one can be like that. No one can laugh at another's love.

'Tony took his beautiful sailboat and sailed her to the next-door island – a goodly way off. There he knew a man, an expert in disguises.

' "Brother Herman, I want you to disguise me – so that even my best friend wouldn't know me."

' "All right, brother Tony – and what else would you like? Many is the favour you have done me – so you have only to ask. Whatever you wish, I will grant it."

' "Brother Herman – I want the disguise and then I'd like a fifty-foot piece of white rope, a sack, also of white, and a sleeping draught to last a night.

' "If you can do and get me all these, all else I need is a motor – a simple outboard for my boat."

347

' "I can do it easily, brother. Just watch."

'Now brother Herman disguised Tony as a Red Indian and he also soon found him fifty feet of rope, a sack –

' "Now here's the sleeping draught – here in the vial."

' "Thanks, Brother Herman: I will return and repay you a thousandfold."

' "Don't mention it," said Herman. "You're welcome, I am sure."

'Tony sailed back to the Princess's island silently in the night.

'Now, when the Princess's guards saw the Red Indian coming ashore, they took off in terror. Our hero slipped into the Palace with his sleeping draught.

'(Now, before doing this, he'd placed outside the Princess's window, the sack.)

'He slipped right into Princess Cynthia's bedroom and slipped the sleeping draught into the glass of water on her bedside table.

'Now, while the Princess slept, Tony tickled her toes – which were outside the sheet – with a goose-feather.

' "What was that?" said the Princess Cynthia, waking up.

' "Nothing," Tony said in a falsetto voice – just like one of her ladies-in-waiting. "Have a sip of water and go back to sleep."

'The Princess scoffed the whole glass of water, and Tony waited exactly eleven and a half minutes and then, testing the Princess by tickling under her nose with the feather and getting no response, he hauled the sack in from the window – and tumbled the Princess into it –

'Not failing to notice, as he did so, the lovely rounds

348

and bumps of her breasts and bum and the cracks and slits of her private parts as they slipped by him.

'Later for that, he said to himself, and, gathering up his white sack, he headed for his sailboat.

'Now Tony sailed with the Princess Cynthia in the sack for half the night until he reached the island of Zeta, a small deserted coral island which had a house on it.

'Tony took the sack (first mooring his lovely boat most carefully) containing the Princess up to the house, unlocked it and then he took it to the big four-poster bed in the bedroom and there he dumped the Princess on the bed.

'Then, he tied the drugged and limp young woman, still clad in the white royal robes, to the four bedposts with the white fifty-foot rope.

'He tied one arm to one post and one to another – and then a leg to each of the lower posts.

'And then he stood back and looked at her, waiting for her to wake up.

' "What a pity," he said, "that beautiful young women are not as decent in their hearts and minds as they are in their looks, lips and behinds.

' "However, he who laughs last, laughs best."

'Of course, when she awoke, she didn't recognize him.

' "What am I doing here?" she said. "And what have you done to me?"

' "Nothing – yet," said Tony, and with that menace – kissed her on the lips.

'She didn't respond and so he kissed her again. He even stuck his tongue in her mouth.

'Of course, she bit him.

' "All right," said Tony. "That's the way you are, is it? No quarter then."

'Tony tied a gag in her mouth – just after she said

"What am I doing here with a fiendish Red Indian?"

'So while the beautiful and lovely Princess Cynthia watched with her exquisite eyes a-goggle, Tony tore her clothes off – very, very slowly, piece by piece.

'He tore off her blouse until he could see her cute underbodice and then he tore off her skirt until he could see her underpants.

'She struggled and squirmed – and squealed – all to no avail. Tony had tied her most securely.

'Then he tore off her bodice, strip by strip, until he could see her lovely breasts – like firm fruit on a tropical tree, but the colour of milk and honey, mixed.

'He stopped to kiss them. She squealed some more, but he only smiled.

'Then he stood at the bottom of the bed and above her, and tore off her pants.

'Beneath he saw her lovely parts – almost hairless, except for a fuzz such as one finds on a sago berry.

'The lovely lips of her parts were like rose petals – except when he touched them a little they opened and looked like strawberries in summer-time.

'She struggled and squirmed and squealed – all to no avail.

'But these squeals only excited Tony the more, and standing over her, he took out his fine, large prick and let her have a good look at it.

'She couldn't talk – but her eyes were screaming, no, and her belly was screaming, no, and even her breasts had risen and the nipples were screaming, no.

'With this, our hero slipped down beside her with his mighty prick in his hand.

'He kneeled between her legs and, touching his prick's soft head to her rose-petal parts, he rubbed gently up and down.

'She managed to scream and squeal beneath her gag – and now Tony, sweating, excited to shaking,

350

shoved his prick into her sweet body – While his hands now sought out her bare nipples – which he played with, as if they were the sea, while he was at his work with his prick. . .'

'Berkeley,' someone screeched. 'Ponsonby is having an asthma attack and he's almost dead.'

James jumped up, grabbed his dressing-gown and rushed into the next room, where poor young Ponsonby was gasping for breath.

He was the boy James had seen crying the first day on the platform at Paddington. Ponsonby crying while his mother looked as if she wanted to escape.

James remembered the mother clearly.

'Easy, lad,' he said. 'Let's open the window – and see if that helps.'

Ponsonby's usually pale and frail complexion was now flushed red and his body seemed to be also. Ponsonby was known as a whiner and a 'specimen'.

James opened the window, put Ponsonby on the chair near it, and stroked his forehead as he gasped.

'Easy, lad, easy. You'll soon get your breath if you relax.' James continued stroking him – while the cold air came through the window.

After about twenty minutes, Ponsonby was breathing better.

'Thanks, Be – B – Berkeley – that's decent of you.'

Then Matron burst into the room. 'What's going on?' she said.

'Ponsonby – he had an asthma attack. He's a bit better. I'm sure you know what to do, Matron,' said James, seeing her angry expression. 'I was just filling in here until you came.'

'Thank you, Berkeley,' Matron said.

She would have liked to have caught him, he knew – she would like to have something 'on' him.

But he was never going to let her, not if he could avoid it.

James knew (and all the senior boys agreed) that Matron was poison – a power-hungry poison.

And that night, as James walked back to their little senior dorm at the top of the house, he thought also of what Ian Aiken had speculated: 'Matron and Mrs Montrose are having an affair.'

'Get out of it.'

'No, I think so. Old Man Montrose doesn't like "it" any more.'

Now, as James passed Matron's door – which had been left partly open – he could definitely see that someone was in there. He couldn't see who.

Back in their dorm, Hosefield said: 'Go on, Berkeley.'

'Yes, what happens next to the Princess and Tony – he was just doing her.'

James got into bed, smiling:

' "Oh-oh-oh," she said when he unbound her, "I like it – do it again." '

Silence.

'Is that all?'

'That's all for tonight.'

'What was the motor for?' said Aiken.

'To rush her home if she didn't like it,' James said.

'Come over here and lie on top of me, please,' lisped Hosefield.

They had done it before. James and Hosefield (the latter still under his covers) would cuddle, and then Hosefield would turn over and arch his ass up, and James would ride him as if he were a woman. . .

Sometimes Hosefield would whisper out: 'Oh, yes, *do* me – *do* me.'

352

'Damn,' said Aiken, this particular night, 'I've got to get Collins and ride him, the dumb clod.'

'But be bloody careful,' James said.

'My father said I'd find a niche for myself at boarding school,' Hosefield said with a laugh and a satisfied moan.

'Gee,' said James. 'My father said the same thing. I think mine is definitely cricket.'

'You and your cricket,' said Hosefield. 'You aren't half a silly old thing.'

Aiken came back with Collins, and the other two, now in separate beds, left them alone.

Later, James said: 'Soon – but maybe not until next term – I'm going to invent a whole new series.'

'What about?' said Aiken.

'Who are the characters?' asked Hosefield.

'The bloke I'm not sure of, but the woman is going to be Sahara Bernhardt.'

'What?'

'Who – Sahara who?'

'Sarah Bernhardt, you mean?'

'No. Sahara Bernhardt – is going to be her name.'

The Malvern Hills were often half-covered with snow – which, with the hard dark-brown rocks, made the landscape look as if it belonged in the coal-mining area of Lancashire.

Mr Healey, shaking with age, but bright as polished brass, would say: 'The purpose of this school is to prepare you for your public school – and I'll do my share. But my purpose is to prepare you for life.

'Now, here's a little tip. Indeed, three quickies today, boys. We humans have bacteria on our skin. . . All very right and good as long as they don't get too aggressive.

'Aiken, are you listening to me, boy?'

353

'Yes, sir.'

'What did I say?'

'Bacteria, sir.'

'What else, Aiken?'

'—'

'Aiken, I didn't reach my age and garner all I know; I didn't become a headmaster to be insulted, you know. And I didn't come out of retirement to have you waste *your* time by not listening.'

'I'm sorry, sir. I'll pay attention. For a moment I forgot to, sir.'

'All right, then. Bacteria are natural on our skin – but to keep things under control, we must take two baths a week. And, here's the important thing: never put on soiled linen. Always put on newly washed underclothes. What did I say, Berkeley?'

James repeated it virtually verbatim.

'Very good, boy. If we can get you as good in Latin, we'll be all right.

'Second thing is: rubbing back of neck – like this.' Mr Healey stood with his legs astride like Atlas, put his hands linked behind his head – and moved his arms, thus rubbing the back of his neck.

'Now this back of neck stimulation – which was taught to me by a voluptuously beautiful woman – my dear wife's mother – is helpful to get rid of colds, arthritis and rheumatism. All right, you do it, boys.'

They did. Standing next to their desks.

'You see, you can do it even when old – even when sick – and it will help you get better. Stop, boys, and sit down.'

They did so.

'Third thing is this: this is a fundamental rule of human behaviour, which if forgotten or neglected, can bring you and your life down in tragedy. It has killed princes and kings, broken queens and brought

354

Conquistadores to their untimely deaths – ruined men in the services and even in business (should any of you be so unfortunate as to have to end up in it) and it's this:

'From whatever group you are part of, never carry a tale to another group – especially to a superior group. Don't be a snitch.

'Why, Collins?'

'Because someone will catch you out, sir.'

'No – why Aiken?'

'Because it's natural to us humans to be loyal to our kind, our group.'

'Excellent, Aiken. It's because it's *unnatural for us humans* – to snitch. Believe me, dear boys, although you may oftentimes be sorely tempted to think it is not so: honesty is also natural to our species, to us humans.

'That's all – I hope you'll remember – even a little bit – Now run along and play happily.'

Mr Healey hurried out with his elegant tottering walk. He had on his tweed suit today and James thought he looked quite smart. He'd also just come from the barber's and he always looked even more elegant when his hair and his wild eyebrows had been trimmed.

James floated in one of his rare flights of tranquillity – hoping, longing, not to be disturbed. . . These flights came seldom and did not last long. He lifted back his desk-top in order to be alone.

The flights seemed to be such sweet and gentle ecstasy – as if they might be the opposite, the reward for the pain of life. They sometimes lasted for five minutes, at other times only two – if he was lucky they would last ten or even twenty. . .

Sometimes it was the sound of a voice that

triggered it (could be either male or female)...

In these flights, as when listening to music (or sailing, as Christopher said) all the world tasted, smelled, sounded and looked majestic and totally unmolesting – the home of the gods... In comparison with these touches of ecstasy, even the moments of sexual ecstasy seemed short and pale – certainly less restful...

He wondered if he could tell Mr Healey of them..?

Ian Aiken was inventing another game. He had, indeed, sold one to Parker Brothers.

'It was called *Ship Warfare*, Berkeley, and they paid me ten quid for it. But my grandfather says, with this one, to come to him and he'll put his lawyer on them. And try to get "part of it." '

'What does that mean?'

'I'm not sure.'

James thought how Teddy would love *Ship Warfare* – Christopher!

Ta-tum.

Mr Montrose and the other masters were preparing them for their public schools. Which meant, preparing them for the Common Entrance examinations.

'These exams are probably the most important ones you will ever take in your life,' Mr Montrose said.

'Getting into your public school is the biggest step. But here's how we do it. Here are all the Common Entrance examinations for the last twenty-five years. We are simply going to do examinations until you can do them in your sleep.

'Passing exams is mostly common sense – *and* practice.'

Mr Montrose was in an awfully good mood. Geoff

Montrose, his eldest son, had escaped again from the Germans, making this his third escape.

'If they catch him now,' everyone said, 'they'd kill him *on sight*.'

'I'd change my name and have a face-lift,' said Ian Aiken.

James was still left, as was his whole widespread family, hanging: wondering about Christopher. Christopher had been Missing now for nearly six months.

James didn't need to be reminded of the fate of Dicky Dickens' brother, John. . .

He sought out Geoff Montrose, who was home on leave. It was difficult to corner him: flight lieutenants don't usually have much 'truck' with prep-school boys.

'I beg your pardon, sir,' James said. 'I'm Berkeley. My brother has been Missing for over five months.'

'Jolly bad luck. What did you say your name was?'

'Berkeley.'

'Oh yes. Where was your bro' flying?'

'Ranger Operations – in Mustangs. P51s.'

'Oh, was he? Never saw him. Strange. Your bro' is Regular RAF is he?'

'I don't know, sir. We are from Bermuda. He has "Bermuda" on his shoulder.'

'I mean, is he a Regular RAF officer – or is he a war volunteer?'

'Don't know, sir. He was flying over France.'

'Is that where he bought it?'

'Yes, sir. But he wouldn't talk much, of course.'

'Well, he'll have a good chance of escaping – if he gets to Vichy France, Unoccupied France.' Geoff Montrose was now moving his weight a lot. . .

'But I don't know about you Colonial Wallahs – there's a sort of separate set of rules for you lot.'

'How – what is that, sir?'

'I can't go into it now – good luck. Hope your bro' gets out.'

After Geoff had long been gone, James realized he should have said: 'My brother was at Cranwell – Royal Air Force College, Cranwell. He was first in his class.'

When he got back to Washashley in April, James told the whole story to Aunt Daisy.

'Yes,' she lisped through her little buck teeth – her pink cheeks red with anger. 'And you could have said: and my father was at the Royal Air College in 1915 and he was in the Royal Naval Air Service. And . . . and . . . and, you should have said, we Berkeleys don't know anybody named Montrose – we have never met anyone of that name before.'

James was hurt and puzzled by Geoff Montrose's behaviour, because he thought that he, having suffered so much, would be kind . . . decent the way Mr Healey was.

He was learning the ways of men and women, and a lot of them were cruel and unimaginative. As Chris had warned: 'You'd better go out for the boxing team.'

He thought that he certainly would when he got to Fotheringham – if the opposition didn't look too fierce.

But, before that, he still had one more term at The Lion School: the summer term of 1943: May to July, and he was really looking forward to being Captain of Cricket.

He felt sure they could have a Star Team again. Mogs would be sorely missed, but Ian Aiken said he was a pretty fair batsman.

It was awful to be thinking about cricket when his brother might be breathing his last gasp, but what else could one do?

Ta-tum.

358

XVII

Christopher, Backwards Often,
Forwards Sometimes, and
Probably, Sideways Frequently
IV

'When This Fucking War Is Over, you and I will fall in love. . .'
Dear Nasti and Skeglee and maybe Widda-Widda –
if you ever get old enough to understand.
This is the way it was
this is the way it is
this is the way
this is
this
is
The boat is sunk and I am beating it inland as fast as I can
A lot on my belly. . .
Soon I meet some fishermen: 'Pardonnez-moi,' I say. 'What place is this and where is the nearest town?'
'You are near Pont Croix, Finisterre, about 45 kilometres from Quimper. There is an American flier just in the next road – he is lost – too.'
I find this American. His name is Mac and he has freckles and looks about thirteen years old. He was on the boat.
'Come on,' I say and we run down the hill. The Frenchmen have gone ahead, already.
As we come around the corner, we see the French fishermen stopped by a German on bicycle patrol.
The German sees us and beckons us to come to him.
We backtrack and run up the hill. As I look back, from the top, the German comes in sight again, still beckoning us to come back.

359

He sees we aren't gonna and he unslings his rifle
– and he's about ready to fire
When Mac and I duck into another road – a lane.
We are going along like the clappers. . .
'I can't go no further.' Mac has lost his shoes.
'Sorry, Mac – I've got to go ahead – there's no point
in both of us getting caught.'
'Yeah. Go on.'
I'm thinking: yeah, I really like to be alone – and
you've got New Jersey written on your face.
I skirt the hill and find a wood on the opposite
slope – I hide in some thick undergrowth until late
afternoon.
I'm hungry as hell – but I am able to sleep –
because of bailing all night.
Late afternoon, I start out again. I keep seeing
German bicycle patrols pass.
I walk through the fields towards Quimper. I've
walked for at least an hour.
I hear whistling. I duck. I hear it again. Now I
realize it's to attract my attention.
It is Mac – with several French boys – and the
French are armed.
'We are Maquis,' they say. 'We will help you.'
'Yeah, old buddy. You should've stuck with me.'
Someone has given Mac some shoes – too small for
him.
I accept the Maquis's hospitality thankfully. We are
all hidden in dugouts among the thickets. The French
boys give us blankets and milk and cheese –
'Merci, merci beaucoup,' I keep saying. The food
tastes incredibly good – because, I believe I've never
been hungrier.
A little later we are all taken to a blacksmith's shop
that is not more than fifty yards from the coast – we
can hear the waves. . .

We post a guard for the night – so that the rest may sleep.

I stay here until early the next afternoon.

Then we are taken to a beautiful old château outside Pont Croix.

'The Germans are combing the countryside for your party,' the Maquis tell us. 'But they've already searched here.'

I look it over: it probably has twice as many rooms as Washashley. 'It must have taken them some time.'

'Oui.'

The lady of the château hides and feeds us for two days. Her daughter-in-law is here too – we never see her. Her son has been a prisoner in Germany since 1940.

I've still got my papers and among them my schedule. When the Maquis come back, I say: 'There's a 7:10 train to Paris from Quimper – how about one of you and me ride over on bicycles and you buy me a ticket and I catch the train?'

'Oui. I can get two bicycles – later I'll bring one back for you, Mac – the next train – tomorrow.'

Mac doesn't quite understand. 'I'd rather stay here a while anyway.'

'Fon-Fon has been caught – anyway,' one of the boys says. 'And most of the others. The big heat is off.'

'They catch the Chief, Fon-Fon – that's terrible.'

The Maquis says: 'He is not the Chief – his mother is.'

'Shut up,' says the other, firmly. 'Fon-Fon will not talk.'

These Maquis will not hesitate to use their revolvers. This I am certain of. They handle them rather desperately.

'The Germans regard us as traitors – and that gives

361

them the right to kill us on sight – or worse.'
'For not accepting slave labour in Germany?'
'Oui.'

My good luck continues to be uncanny.

(I begin to wonder if my good luck has to do with
the little brass and copper boot I still have that the
Aunts gave me at Washashley, the boot originally
made in France in the First War. . . ?)

That evening, without revolver, my French friend
comes back with two bikes and we ride to Quimper.
He is named Georges.

Our ride is uneventful. At the station, I give
Georges the money and he goes in alone and comes
back after ten minutes with a ticket. It's for Paris.

Very high on my list of priorities is to get back to
Piquette – and my original plan of escaping to Spain.
But, of course, the weather can turn cold any time
soon. . .

I am unobtrusively bidding my friend Georges 'Au
revoir', and then I go out on the platform. The train
soon comes.

I've a Second Class ticket. I get in a Second Class
compartment, I find a seat, and immediately feign
sleep so as not to become involved in conversation.

My fellow passengers, I am ascertaining through my
almost closed eyes, are three rather young men, one
about eighteen – travelling with his mother – and an
elderly gentleman.

Hardly have we left, when I am most unpleasantly
surprised by one of Darlan's Special Police (the
German-sponsored French Gestapo) and very bad
business, entering our car and asking for 'Cartes
Identités?'

This is very bad, Berkeley. He is asking the two
French boys – and he's questioning them and looking

362

at the cards very carefully. He is still questioning them. They've got this colonial bird half in the cage.

Mr Policeman is returning the cards to the boys – amazing. I am scared to hell. The jig is up. . .

I am reaching for my wallet but I know there is no chance he will accept that I am a deaf-mute from Alsace when he can hardly read the Identity Card, then suddenly, the policeman waves my wallet away – with a sweet smile. . .

And passes on to the fellow sitting next to me. He inspects this man's papers.

I look out the window, then close my eyes again. The policeman is leaving.

Why? Perhaps, with my hat off, I look so like a German he doesn't want to take a chance?

Whoa – man, I say to myself. Wait until we Hinson-Halcyons get older, then our Negro blood shows more. Scandinavian in childhood, German/British in youth, Negro in old age. . .

It is so shattering that I do not really get over it until we arrive at Montparnasse Station early next morning.

I'm a veteran of this now – I am getting through the barrier safely with no suitcase.

Now I have to get to the Gare Austerlitz to catch a train to the Toulouse area – to be close to Eygurande-Merlines.

When I arrive there by Metro it is packed with German soldiers, obviously in transit. I am figuring this is good, if I keep low.

The first train to Toulouse is packed with Germans and I let them go. In a lull, I approach a ticket counter: I write '2nd Toulouse' on a piece of paper and slip it to the ticket seller.

He looks at me, says an amount: I touch my mouth

like a mute and indicate that he write it down.

Whether he is believing me or not, he writes it down and I give him the money, nodding sagely. He gives me change.

Dear Nasti, around about here – moving from Paris to the south – I seem to lose a lot of time.

This is a wicked pun, Widda-Widda, when you seem to lose time on the way to Toulouse... In France I stay with many people and if I list everyone's name they may all be tortured and killed... Fon-Fon's mother's in Paris... I stay in three different and beautiful châteaux...

In one château Madame M informs me that my chills and fever are yellow jaundice... I am put to bed – for at least three weeks.

My new friends are extremely kind to me:

I remember, here, that my French is still bad and that Uncle Albert's definition of civilized man was: one who, first of all, can speak French...

And these French people: as I say, there are qualities about them that put us to shame: they seem to start out at a more realistic place in their thinking about human behaviour then come up with more honour, VALOUR and pride than we know about.

But, Nasti and Skeglee, here, in my escape and hiding, I seem to lose a lot of time... it gets concertina-ed.

Then, when I am stronger,

I cross the border as before, getting off, walking, getting on the train past the Cher. Finally, or penultimately it seems, I arrive at the station at Merlines.

I tell you, it's impossible, I am saying to myself – but there is Piquette to meet me. Piquette, the adopted daughter of M. Dehn. How come?

As I get off the train, she sees that we recognize each other and immediately walks away. . .

This I take as her signal for me to follow at a distance – and I do. I follow her to her house.

'How did you know to meet me?' I ask.

'I didn't, monsieur. I was to meet someone else – then you came.'

'If you were to meet someone else, why did you leave with me?'

Then I notice that she has tears in her eyes.

I touch her. She pulls away. 'Monsieur Chris, you want something to eat?'

'Yes. And how is your father?'

'Still with SNCF – he's well.'

'Will he be glad to see me?'

'No – he hoped you were away – a successful escape to England. It's been a long time. . .'

Soon M. Dehn comes in. He's friendly but austere – which is a French style really.

'I beg your pardon. I do not want to be any trouble. Can you put me up tonight?'

'No trouble – if no trouble comes – Piquette, it's up to her. You can manage him?'

'Yes. Easily.'

'Bon. So *La Mouette* returns, eh?' M. Dehn says, laughing.

'What's that?' I ask.

'Nothing,' says Piquette.

I tell a little of the boat disaster and how I still want to go over the Pyrenees.

'Oui. *La Mouette* can fly over the Pyrenees – is better.'

Later, Piquette and I are going for a walk. We talk.

'Have you missed me?'

'Of course. But I've been busy with the Maquis –
what you call, the Boys? Right?'

'Right. Maybe I can stay with them?'

'That might be safest – I do not know.'

This young woman, she is an enigma to me. Built
like a tomboy, with black-brown hair and her little
hook-nose, she's not even good-looking.

But her strange eyes – more yellow than brown. . .
And why am I shaking – is it because I am so moved
to see her?

On this little bridge she suddenly just brushes her
lips past mine – it wasn't even a kiss, was it, I ask
myself?

'While you are away I learn to speak English.'

I touch her hand. She bumps against me. Again, her
smell comes to my nostrils.

'Piquette,' I say. 'I am a very shy man – I have very
little experience with women.'

'Oh – so?'

'I go from boarding school – like Eton, you know –
Harrow – into the War. Only men in my life.'

'You are homosexual?' she smiles.

I laugh. 'Hardly.'

'*La Mouette* . . .' she says.

'What is *La Mouette*?'

'It is what we call you while you are away.'

She puts her lips against mine. Her little body and
her eyes make me almost cry . . . I am shaking worse.

Our lips touch. I kiss her gently. I am not so
experienced even at necking, and I fleetingly realize I
should have said so . . . (even my RCAF chums at
Prince Edward Island were more experienced with
women than me. . .).

But our lips touch like water – and gentle electricity. We touch our lips gently like this for a long

366

time.

'I think I am in love with you, Piquette,' I say.

She does not answer.

Me, smart-mouth Berkeley from West Hill, Paget, Bermuda, I tell her: 'I've always figured that someday I'm going to meet the girl I love – so, waiting for that day, I am still a virgin. I may be old-fashioned, but that's me.'

'*La Mouette* is from another century.'

'What is this *La Mouette*?'

'Do not be angry – it only means, the Gull – my father teases me.'

She sort of leads me home to her house. I am dizzy with the smell of her, so delicate, so all-pervading.

She gives me a glass of wine there.

She winds up her little Victrola and puts on a record . . . it is Chopin.

'I always thought Chopin's music has to do with flying – FLIGHT itself.'

She gives me another glass of wine.

'No, it's about love. You should go to sleep, Monsieur Chris.'

I have the feeling she is going to come into my bed.

My bedroom is their little library. A cot.

After I have got into bed – and am about to turn out the light, there's a tap on the glass of the door.

'Entrée,' I say.

She comes in. She is still fully clothed. I think she is the most beautiful woman I have ever seen.

'You are the most beautiful woman I have ever seen.'

'Yes. But I have something to tell you, Chris.'

She gives me a brush of her mouth across mine, just like our first kiss: lips going past lips like cashmere paintbrushes.

367

'Monsieur Chris, flying person, I have to tell you something. I hope you will understand – and not be hurt.' She goes near the door.

'I am not the girl for you. You see, I can't wait for you to grow up. Monsieur Chris – I may be dead tomorrow, you understand?'

Then she opens the glass door and slips out.

Dear Widda-Widda,
This is the way it was
this is the way it is
this is the way
this is
this
is
I

She leaves me alone with the cold glass of water down my trousers and on my soul. . .

I am a damn fool, I do not know this young woman and she does not know me. . .

In the morning Piquette is remote.

You do not have to throw ice in my face to get rid of me. . .

'How did you sleep?' she asks.

'Well, thank you – *et tu?*'

'*Nuit blanche.*'

I do not know what she means.

A part of me – the old-old Bermudian-American part, perhaps – keeps saying: let me out of this European madness, I want to be home.

'Piquette, would you please direct me to the Maquis – perhaps they will have an idea of how I can get out of France?'

'I can direct you. You can stay here if you like. Or

come back later, if you like.'

'I'd better get with the Maquis,' I say, meaning, ask me again to stay here. (The French do not talk our upper-class signals, I am pretty sure. I should have been more direct, perhaps. . .)

'Yes, that's what I thought. A man is coming at eleven – in a car, no less. Very rare.'

'Thanks.'

'It is the Chief of Resistance.'

'Oh, thank you.'

He drives me to Ussel.

'So, you are *La Mouette*?' he says, smiling.

'I guess so,' I say.

'Maquis will meet you with bicycles.' He smiles again. 'I can only wish you – again – luck. Here they are.'

The Maquis – two in number – have three bikes.

In silence we ride many miles. Then we go on foot.

We are between Neuvic and Ussel.

'It is the Forest of Correze,' one says – he has pimples.

'What is your name?'

'Georges.'

'Chris.'

I am here almost a week – or is it two? We live in dugouts in the side of a steep hill – with a stream at the bottom.

One day, Georges II comes with a parcel.

'For me?'

'Oui.'

I open it. It is the most beautiful overcoat I've ever seen. Black. Silk lining. Black lamb's-wool collar. It's magnificent.

'Cher *La Mouette*,

This is to keep you warm. The owner was liberated to Algiers and left it with us.

It is true I care about you, but I am not your One-in-a-lifetime.

A Kiss.

P.

The coat is warm – I have been needing it. A girl sends you such a coat – she must love you. But maybe she has known many others?

Maybe she is a camp follower?

I do not believe it.

At this camp, the boys do their own cooking. The afternoons are devoted to military training. Several of these boys have already been in the French Army – and they are excellent instructors.

They want me to take a course in silent killing with a knife – I decline. They do a lot of small-arms drill and practise with machine guns, hand grenades and explosives (all in silence, of course) – all supplied, dropped, by the RAF. . .

I am seeing a good deal of the crude Mark-2 Sten I've seen already in England.

The camp guard consists of one man posted in a secluded spot – close to the nearest country road. He has a telephone with the main camp.

Discipline here is severe. They have 'Orders of the Day'. Including Reveille and Retreat.

A big part of me is still hollering: let me out of this European madness. . .

I find I want Piquette very much. At night I want to hold her . . . I dream of her. . .

I also begin here my *nuits blanches*

It is very bad to have *nuits blanches*. I feel worse than an old man – I feel like a middle-aged man. . .

370

We, of course, listen a lot to the BBC News.

Everyone in the world is listening to the BBC News.

At this camp I even hear the programme, *Calling The West Indies*, in which I have sent messages home to Bermuda three times since 1940.

The entire camp is divided into three platoons, with platoon commanders, all of whom come under the camp Commandant and his adjutant. . .

One day I am told: 'The Chief of all the Maquis of France will come tomorrow.' It is Georges who tells me.

He is also interested in escaping to Spain with me. He has even greater hopes that we can get taken out by aeroplane.

Georges has said: 'The British have this great plane – the Lysander – it can take plenty of people.'

I do not tell Georges that the Lysander cannot fly this far – and only takes four people, at most.

At what point in a man's life, in his descent, does it come to him: the irrevocable truth that he is going to die – not tomorrow, but very soon? I do not know, but I know that that knowledge came to me *à Correze*, in the Forest of Correze. . .

Everyone in the camp is armed. They give me a choice. I do not tell them I do not know very much about small arms. I pick a little automatic with a pearl handle. It is .22 calibre. Made in Italy.

One of the Maquis smiles at my choice.

At the camp, of course, we are all sleeping in our clothes – I use my new little valise as a pillow.

It is a Saturday in December. I am rudely awakened by an alarm:

(I am dreaming that I have taken Piquette swimming in Bermuda and she is laughing at the fish and the colours and the clarity and cleanness of everything. I have, in the dream, already told her the joke statement I have about our family: It is that most people are made homeless in the twentieth century by war and concentration camps – but we Berkeleys were made homeless in the 1930s by being dragged on to luxury ocean liners that were called the *Lady Nelson*, the *Orduna* and the *Reina Del Pacifico* – and we were taken, by our mother, what was loosely called 'abroad'. . . All this I've told her. . .)

'The guard at the gate has reported: two truckloads of gendarmes to search the woods.'

I pull on my boots, grab up my valise (I am *in* my overcoat – in the pocket of which is my .22 automatic) and start running.

Obviously, the Maquis are losing all their possessions – armaments and blankets are everywhere. . .

Some boys have grabbed up small arms. We are all running and running and running through the woods.

I can run damned fast and I run for at least an hour. Somehow, I have a large loaf of bread.

There are three of us now. We rest at a schoolhouse. It is at the top of a hill commanding a good view of the countryside.

Then the three of us continue – concealing ourselves as much as possible by walking in the protection of hedges and through the woods – which are slimmer now.

In a little while, the two lads say: 'We will go and scout ahead.' They have their revolvers – at the ready.

I wait and wait.

Such is life, such is war – much waiting, a great deal of luck and accident. . .

The place is still and spooky; it is the dry dead of winter now, there are hedges, blue sky and, across the little road – a track really – a very small mossy pond.

Such is war. Such is life.

Suddenly into view comes a man on a bicycle. He is a typical Gestapo agent disguised as a French policeman. He has a rifle slung over his shoulder. The Boche, obviously. . .

This is the kind I've heard talk of. He has seen me, there is nowhere to hide.

Obviously too there is going to be a pitched battle – funny but I remember I first heard that phrase from my mother.

'Halt!' I shout and step out into the road.

The policeman just keeps coming.

'Halt!' I say again.

Now he stops, twenty feet from me.

He says something unintelligible to me – perhaps in French – puts his head down, does not look at me, and moves forward like a dumb animal.

'Halt, or I will shoot.' I realize I'm speaking in English.

He keeps coming. He is almost up to me now.

I repeat it in French. 'Halt – or I will shoot.'

He lets go his bicycle and I know he's going to unsling his rifle.

I shoot the .22 at him at point-blank range – maybe six or eight feet.

Zut!

He looks at me, startled, disturbed.

He has a moustache. He snorts. He makes no show of being hurt.

'Put up your hands!' I yell.

He stays, breathing like a dumb bull. His eyes look as dumb as Daisy the cow at Cedar Hill, Bermuda.

He does not move.

'Put up your hands and drop the rifle or I will shoot again.'

He does nothing.

Silence

Where are the others?

A little crazy with this standing dumb bull, I pull the trigger again.

Zut!

Again nothing seems to happen. It is a nightmare – no, the bullets are just absorbed into his heavy coat.

Nasti, this is the way it was
  this is the way it is
  this is the way
  this is
  this
  is
  I

Nothing happens. It is very hard, I discover, to kill a man.

I fire again.

Zut!

He absorbs the third shot.

Perhaps his eyes are glazed a little. He is Rasputin – he won't die.

Die, damn you, die.

I fire a fourth shot.

Zut!

Shortly he falls

First the rifle hits the ground almost silently – just two clicks as it hits stones and grass.

Then he falls, after it, falling forward.

I stand transfixed.

At last, I go to him.

I roll him over

To my horror, his mouth opens and he says what sounds like: 'Merci, monsieur – merci.' But I do not know exactly what he says.

After a long while he is silent.

'Someone! – anyone!' I call.

Personne

Silence

I move and force myself to check the policeman. His coat has fallen open – he has braces – what we call in Bermuda, suspenders.

His suit is darned in many places. His braces remind me of O'Neill.

Is he a Vichy policeman? Gestapo? He's a working-class bloke – like O'Neill.

And where are my *confrères*?

And what did he say?

I cross myself.

He is dead is Mr Policeman. And I have got to get rid of him

I feel this dull numb terror creep over me and the trees

All is vile in this world

Suddenly it is a world in which I have never been before

It is a world of black and silver leaves and death and silence.

But I am no patsy. I try to lift the policeman – impossible – he is bigger than I am. I drag him to the pond.

I can't carry him, I drag him. I can't get him in the pond – the only way to get him in the pond is to go in first myself.

Then the new shock is that he will not sink.

I am half wet and partially covered in green mossy weeds and mud.

I clean myself off – and he is lying there on top of the pond, like the peasant on top of the haystack in the Rembrandt etching at Washashley...

It is macabre.

I clean myself more.

Then I pile his bicycle on top of him.

Where are my friends? I can hear no other firing. This was supposed to be a battle.

I never before knew how hard it is to kill a man. They just seem to want to stay alive.

Then they want to stay around.

At last the bicycle and the man are going from sight into the ooze.

I throw the rifle on top.

Nasti, Teddy – you know what it is? I meant the rifle? It is an American Springfield. Jesus. The same name as the Halcyons' first house in Bermuda – Springfield... Widda-Widda's favourite family house because it is where great-great-grandmother, as a girl, had a free clinic for slaves...

I cross myself for the third time and start moving out – south – then south-west.

What do we men do when everything is bad, terrible? We repeat our behaviour as children. We run to the nearest woman. Piquette.

But first, I realize, I must hide.

Merde. Merde. The RAF was never like this.

The song goes through my head: Vera Lynn: 'There'll Be Blue Birds Over The White Cliffs Of Dover ... tomorrow, just you wait and see...'

I have this damn man's whistle in my hand.

I throw it away – into the bushes, into the trees.

376

I have been running and hiding for so long now I have the instincts of an animal. . . However, I do not know where I am or how long I've been there. . .

It is very nice at Monsieur Dehn's house: very warm: they are as kind to me as family. I tell them what torments me.

'M. Dehn, I do not know what he was saying. *"Merci"* it couldn't have been. So he was speaking in English, wasn't he? In answer to my English – yes – and he was saying, *"Mercy"* – for, have mercy.'

'It could be, Chris, it could.'

'Let me tell you something, police are not good people in any country, *La Mouette* – are they?'

'In Bermuda the police are good. In Britain the police are everyone's friends.'

'The police are always on the side of the powerful – and the rich – so, in Britain you are rich. It's all right.'

So I am looking at him. 'But who did I kill – was it a German?'

'I keep telling you – probably a French Gestapo, the same as German, bad bastards – have no fear of that. Frenchmen who work for the worst German murderers.'

'I cannot bear to have killed a Frenchman.'

'Secret Police are not good people anywhere at any time, *La Mouette*.'

We have nicknames for each other, we are that close now: he calls me *La Mouette*, I call him 'M. Dehn' – which sounds, in my pronunciation, like Mr God.

We call her Sainte Piquette, I think M. Dehn thought it up.

I say to him: 'It was a bad time – for too long I

377

thought, my last moment will be my next.'

'I like that: very good – I will remember it. *La Mouette*, if you get back to England, try to remember everything, eh?'

'Yeah.'

'You understand?'

'Yes, I understand,' I said. (But Nasti and Skeglee, and Widda-Widda, I did not.)

Piquette comes in. She kisses me in front of her father – it is very tender, very warming. Comforting is the word.

I touch her shoulder. She strokes my back.

'It's spring now, *La Mouette* – you and Piquette should get out more.'

'It's safe?'

'You are not stupid – you do not chew gum – as the young Americans, as you say, do, in Paris. Go out in the twilight. Go out and get plenty of air. Go out and love each other like butterflies.'

We are holding hands on the bridge over the river. The raindrops fall in, looking like .22 bullets that I do not want to remember.

'Piquette, I'm supposed to try to escape – to get back to my unit.'

'*Mon cher*, there is no possible chance over the mountains until late April.'

She is smiling at me – with love, but also a little like a keeper. 'A few days – we have a few days left, *mon cher*.' She brushes her cashmere lips against mine.

Suddenly, a Gestapo motorcycle comes out of the half-light from nowhere; it has two Germans, with black, white and red armbands.

We move slowly home.

378

'I don't care if you are saving yourself for some rich English or American, Chris, I don't care.'

'I'm sorry,' I say – stupidly.

'You only want Piquette as a mother – a nurse. You are a bastard – *bâtard*.'

I grab her and kiss her on her full wet mouth. I always kiss her with my eyes shut – now I open my eyes: her yellow eyes are burning at me.

Her little body burrows into mine: burns into my groin with her groin. 'You English know nothing of feelings – of love. You upper-class swine.'

She is weeping and rubbing her little body into mine.

Then she starts undressing: 'Come, Chris, I will do something to make it all better – and you can remain a virgin too.'

'Piquette,' I start protesting – but she is undressing me and I am undressing her, I cannot help myself.

Here in her father's study now – now, in the spring of 1943, we have no clothes on at all.

We are in my bed, like little animals – like muskrats, I am thinking.

Muskrats because of the feel of her brown-gold pubic hair. Her smell comes to me with total intensity now – it is like Angostura Bitters and salt water. Her young body is more heady than any wine.

Just being with her puts me where I have never been before – now this, these things, I've never known.

She is putting her head where I've never heard of – except in pornographic books and comics – and jokes in Officers' Messes. . .

She takes a large part of me in her mouth – then takes it out and says, 'A moi, aussi, bâtard.'

I bury my face between her legs, I lick her thighs, I

379

bury my face again – into all of her.

Somewhere in our revolving like a ferris wheel of wet loving – she cries out: '*La Mouette – La Mouette – La M –*'

I do what I am supposed to do for her (my instinct tells me) and do what I have never allowed myself to do for myself, let go. . .

It is one great wheel of love and then we lose reality. . .

We are exhausted and sweating and kissing.

'You see – you are still a virgin – and yet, well, you are not.'

I laugh. I know she is right and that I am a goddamn fool. All of my life is only a preparation for this – all my beliefs are just old burned paper in comparison with this. . .

'I am reborn,' I say hugging her head with both my arms.

'Me, also.'

There is a rapping at the back door. It is the Scotsman from the asylum.

I am in my trousers only. I let him in.

'Chris. You and Piquette – you must get away immediately. The Gestapo have taken Monsieur Dehn – same old shit, same bastard has squealed. Quick.'

XVIII

In the Easter Holidays at Washashley, the Hall had already begun to look unkempt – even from a distance. It was the ivy that did it: uncut and uncared for, it grew in the windows and over leaded roofs and raised slates.

James thought the house looked more than sad: it seemed to moan, like a great leviathan, as it sank into the damp ground. . .

'It is angry with us,' he said to Dicky, but Dicky did not understand.

'I'm right sorry about bruther – just like mine. He's Missing – Assumed Killed, is he?'

'Yes – aye – And what makes me so angry is that the family never seems to let me know anything. People die – they don't tell me. Chris is assumed dead, they let me be in ignorance.'

'Make them tell you, James – tell them you won't go back to school unless they promise never to leave you in bluddy ignorance again.'

'Good idea.'

'So what do you think of the Canadians?'

'What Canadians?'

'In t'Hall. The Nigerians have gone and you've got Canadians now – just like you. Your dad's a Canadian, isn't he?'

'Well – half – I guess. He was born in Canada: Bermudian mother and English father.'

'You're a right mess, you lot are.'

'I guess so. Have you spoken to the Canadians?' James thought it would be great having colonials in the Hall – his type of colonials.

'They're a rum lot, our dad says, a rum lot. What does Bob Fenders say?'

'I haven't seen him yet – he's away on a bus trip somewhere.'

'My Dad said about Nigerians: that they were lost black fellas, fighting to save one tyranny from another.'

'Perhaps – that's one way of looking at it.'

James thought of the Nigerians: what a confused

381

group they had been, purple in the British cold. . .
There was a part of him that identified with this
bewilderment of people from a hot climate – but a
bigger part of him hated them. They were trespassing
on Berkeley property and that pained him in a
primeval way. . .

Mrs Pickle saved their days with comedy: she introduced I.T.M.A. – 'It's That Man Again' – Tommy
Handley – to the family.

They would all move into the drawing-room to hear
it. It made fun of everyone: masters and servants, rich
and poor, the lazy, the arrogant, the War – drinkers –
everything.

James and Aunt Daisy and Mrs Pickle would laugh
until sometimes they fell over. . .

'There isn't nothing so bad that we can't have a
good laff, is it, Mr James?' Mrs Pickle said. 'It's good
for us.'

'That's enough now,' Aunt Daisy would say, but she
too was so weak after a broadcast that she could go off
into hoots again. . .

It came on once a week, on the Home Service, and
they never missed the show. . .

'Please, Aunt Daisy, no more not telling me things. I
am no child – I'm Captain of the School.'

'As you wish.' She looked hurt and lost. 'I thought I
was protecting you.'

She was not the only one.

A letter from his sister, Widda-Widda (Chris's short
for The-Dove-With-The-Bite-Of-An-Asp) gave him, as
if he'd already been told it, the news that his
grandmother, Faith (Durrell Beltt) Halcyon had
died – cancer was mentioned.

382

He got up and went out for a walk – like a person breaking out of a strait-jacket.

Granny at Cedar Hill. She was selfish and she was spoiled, but she was clever too and the Queen of Bermuda... The wittiest Halcyon ever, the head of the family...

And cancer: how had it been? Had she suffered and how long?

A world without his grandmother at Cedar Hill was something that he had never imagined. 'Gloomy Villa,' Uncle Joe Halcyon called Cedar Hill – but not if you climbed under the piano.

Granny would also tell all manner of tales about each person depicted in each portrait – devastating details of totally précis-ed lives:

'Commodore Jeremiah Beltt, RN. Came to Bermuda in distress – mate of the schooner *Molly*, October 13 1764. Saw Twins: The Pearls of Southampton: Elizabeth and Susanna Somers. Fell in love with both. Married first one and then the other.

'Fired a shot, out of anger, when he heard the Americans had won the Revolutionary War: shot hit tavern next to Trinity Church, New York, and is still there.

'Drowned on Jesus' Eve, 1811, in command of HMS *St George* – one hundred guns – seven hundred men – all perished save seven souls – in the Skagerrak. He was my great-grandfather.'

'What is the Skagerrak?'

'A terribly treacherous piece of water – the mouth of the Baltic Sea.'

And Granny's witticism to our pompous archdeacon would stand, James thought, in his memory, for ever.

'Come for tea on Sunday,' Granny had said.

'I'll come if God spares life,' he psalmed.

Granny said: 'Well, for goodness sake, don't come if

383

He doesn't.'

Granny said whatever she damned well liked – it was both enviable and very attractive.

An American multi-millionaire had announced in the newspaper: 'We'll have cars in Bermuda for everyone who wants them before the year is out.' That was in 1919. The man's name was Petroleum Nitrate Smith – his Christian names for his father's fortune. 'I would be very glad to hear that Mr Smith promises not to leave his property with any vehicle save a horse and carriage or a bicycle.'

'Yes, ma'am,' said Cousin David Hinson, who was in Government. 'It shall be done – or else we'll tell him he's *persona non grata.*'

'We want many things for Bermuda, but the *last* thing we want is motorcars.'

And poor Grampy, Granny was his reason for existing. . .

He asked Aunt Daisy, back at the cottage, what she thought.

'There are many letters from Bermuda for Christopher – I expect that the news of your grandmother is in one of them, dear boy.'

'Can we cable?'

'No, there's a war on – but you should write right away.'

'Oh, oh, oh Mr James – you are a sight for sore eyes indeed,' said Fenders. 'Come and have a nice cup of tea.'

It was good to see him again – and Mrs Fenders with her glasses as thick as the bottoms of jam-jars.

'Oh, welcome home, Mr James,' she said. 'We are worried sick about your dear brother – so we can only imagine how you are.'

They were so kind and hospitable.

'How are the Canadians, Fenders?'

'Awful – worse'n awful. They bang and bust everything. Oh, Mr James: they've tried to break into the wine cellar twice – with a sten gun once. Which the Nigerians never did. Dirty bunch of Niggers though they were.'

'Oh, Bob, don't.'

' 'Tis true. And Mr James, these Canadians – one of them has chipped – cut into our Adam fireplace. Right where it says, Adam – the signature of Adam of Edinburgh. This guttersnipe lout of a Canadian has carved his name: Robert McIntosh of Kitchener, Ontario. I can't wait until your father sees this – he'll make heads fall in Whitehall, I should imagine.'

'Fenders – has it ruined the fireplace? Has it?'

'Yes, sir – part might be saved, but I'd say it's quite ruined. If it keeps on this way, I can't see how we'll have anything left by the War's end.'

'Did you write my father?'

'I did sir. I did indeed. And oh, he's right proud of you being Captain of the School and Cricket. He can't wait to get over, he says.'

At The Lion School, James settled in looking forward to three things: a hot long summer, a Star Cricket Team and

Christopher streaking across the sky in a borrowed USAAF Mustang – one of the new ones built in Canada, with a Rolls-Royce engine – doing a slow Victory Roll. Christopher tearing across the sky above the Malvern Hills.

'You'll be bloody lucky,' said Ian Aiken, 'if we get a Star Team. And don't forget our weather.'

James had not told him about his hopes for Christopher. And anyway, nothing could dampen

James's ebullient spirit:

'If we practise hard, we'll be all right. Young Joell can wicket-keep better than his brother. And Collins is not a bad bowler either – and he's a good bat. And we've Hosefield and me from last year's team – and you as new talent. If we practise hard, we'll do well.'

They did practise hard.

'And we've to practise for Common Entrance,' said Aiken. 'I'd better turn in a good one. My family expect Westminster out of me.'

'Wow. Fotheringham is hard enough – but fortunately, I don't have to have Latin – they've agreed that we can substitute Geography for Latin – isn't that wizard?' James said. 'Never thought I'd live to get such a break.'

James's first match, against Malvern Link Prep, was an easy win in the cold. A bit of ice was still on the afternoon field – but James, with his Lion cricket hat set proud, kept encouraging and goading his side on – while he (and Collins) bowled the opponents out. Malvern Link only made forty-seven, The Lion School passed that with four wickets in hand.

Mr Healey's eyes sparkled from the boundary – and James kept looking over at him, and getting a little gentlemanly nod every time he made a decision.

'Jolly well played, Berkeley,' Mr Healey said, after the game. 'You were right to put them in – and right to go in yourself with Collins – you can almost beat them, just you two.

'However, if I was you and captain, I'd save myself for lower down in the order – to stop the rot in case it sets in.'

'Yes, sir. You are right and I absolutely will.'

Good luck next Saturday – and keep practising.' Mr Healey gave him a friendly shove in his ribs – and said, so no one else could hear, 'You make a good captain and you look the part. Don't let it turn your head.'

'Thank you, sir.'

But rain did stop play – indeed in the summer of 1943 it stopped more than half the games. Though Berkeley would keep looking at the sky all morning and saying: 'It's going to clear. Rain before seven clears up by eleven.' But very often, it didn't.

Towards the end of May, James started to get a strange pain on the skin of his stomach. It hurt when his cricket-bat handle bumped him there: it seemed to hurt *inside* his stomach. Which he thought peculiar.

But he wasn't going to Matron with it – that would mean missing cricket, and his playing cricket, and being Captain, was the best challenge he'd ever had. He revelled in it – it was as if it all came naturally to him. He felt that maybe he'd done it before, in another life – as Aiken suggested. . .

'*Sahara Bernhardt – Or, That Rarity: A Woman Who Loves "It*",' James began.

'Jolly good show,' said Hosefield.

'Excellent,' said Aiken. 'Just the three of us – but let me get Collins.'

(James was still torn apart, at times, about his fantasies about sex and violence: but he couldn't imagine there would ever be anyone he could tell about that. He suspected he was unique among men and uniquely evil. . . However, in the meantime, he'd tell a yarn for the others and for himself. What the hell, you had to keep on, didn't you, whatever happened?)

(Maybe one day he could ask his Dad – well, if not,

387

maybe Christopher. Christopher would be best, but however could you get up enough courage?)

'Sahara Bernhardt was that rarity in women – she knew exactly what she wanted in this life: she wanted to be fucked – again.' (He knew perfectly well that such a statement was preposterously absurd – no women, except loose women, liked it. Everyone knew that. . .)

'I've done it in the water
and I've done it on the lawn
and I've done it with the vicar –
me dressed in my yellow halter
me and the vicar we've done it on
the altar –
Sahara Bernhardt, the woman
Who loves It – To Fuck.
I've done it in the autumn and
I've done it in the spring
I've done it with Thomas Handley
and I've done it with the King
and I'm most glad, not sad
to say I've done it with
your lad and his dad
and if you think that's bad,
you'll never be near my navel,
Sahara, the woman with
the Burning Heart-On.'

There was a deathly silence.
'Steady on,' someone said.
'What's the matter?' said Berkeley. He couldn't discover the reason for the silence – he thought it must be the part about the altar.
'Aiken, what's the matter?'
'Nothing – I'm laughing my fool head off.'
'Hosefield – what is it?'

388

'I think you should leave the King out of it.'

'Yes – me too,' said Collins.

'All future rhymes will be about Mackenzie King, all right?'

'Fair enough.'

They agreed.

As to cricket, in the first four weeks of term they had four fixtures planned – and two of them were rained out. In one of the other two, they were severely beaten by The Elms.

'It was those Indian guys,' Berkeley said. 'I've never known anything like them, have you?'

'They were like The Elms' secret weapon, old man,' said Aiken. 'Sorry.'

That was the end of the Star Team.

Mr Healey smiled his bright-eyed best. 'It's all learning, lad, it's all learning. Cricket can teach us a very great deal.'

'Yes sir, I know. It's like life, isn't it?'

'How do you mean, boy?'

'I mean, sir – if you really love to bat, that's the only time you are truly alive – being out is death. You have to accept losing your life – at least once every game.'

'Very good, Berkeley. Very good indeed.'

'I'm sure that's all old stuff to you, sir – but still.'

'Well, I'll tell you – I have thought of it – but I never did at thirteen boy, I never did. You must keep on like that and I'll be proud of you – better still, you'll be proud of yourself.'

James didn't tell him that he'd been fourteen now since April 23rd. . .

He heard from his mother and his dad. 'Granny died of cancer – it was painful but not too long.'

389

His dad said: 'The poor old lady had it in her behind – they took her to New York and she had an operation but it didn't help much. They brought a nurse down and she was a big help.

'Your grandfather knew there was no hope – you know your grandmother had diabetes? Well, she did. Always craved sugar. Dr Somers was asked by Pop – she keeps asking for sugar. Dr Somers said, "Let her have all the sugar she wants, Eugenius!" They did and she died soon after.

'It certainly is the end of an era. There were more than fifty carriages at the funeral – even despite the oats rationing.' It was his mother's mother who had died, but his dad gave the best description. . .

James remembered a bad time in Bermuda, when his Aunt Helen, his grandfather's sister, had been dying of cancer of the stomach.

Her screams rolled down the hill from Beaumont – rolled across the lawns like mustard gas and filled all three houses of the far-flung estate. . .

Why was there nothing that could be done for a human in such pain? Why?

And they, the Halcyons, were supposed to be the richest – what happened to the poor? What, James wanted to ask, would happen to him if he got cancer?

It was now almost June: he wanted to captain every match ahead and how the hell was he going to keep quiet about this pain that kept getting worse and worse. . .

Now his stomach had a red patch – and it still hurt deep inside. . .

XIX

Christopher, Backwards Often,
Forwards Sometimes, and
Probably, Sideways Frequently
V

'When This Fucking War Is Over, you and I will fall in love. . .'

'*Mon cher*, we are in love – why do you keep singing that?'

'So that Mr Hitler won't get me – get us. It's a talisman. I am a colonial, you know. I have Negro blood. Mr Hitler would like me.'

'So what do you think I am – Swedish?'

Dear Nasti and Wuffless and Widda-Widda and Disgusting

(Christopher called James, me, Wuffless as well as Skeglee. 'Disgusting' was little George, who got the name at two – his most ingenuous time, when Christopher would also address him as 'You-Nasty-Looking-Bit-Of-Work.')

This is the way it was
this is the way it is
this is the way
this is
this
is
I

For me this running is now almost my life. For Piquette, the actual running is new – running *from* her home. I look at her face sometimes and I see all this pain – as if someone has torn part of her skin off.

We have literally run from Eygurande-Merlines to Toulouse. It's a good thing she knows so much, and so

391

many of the Resistance Party.

We are staying with her friends, the Cs. Here there is also a lieutenant of the French Army.

'I am going to lead a party into Spain – as soon as the snow melts.'

'Any chance you can take us?'

'Yes. You are British?'

'Yes. A British aviator – and this is my friend, Piquette.'

'You want to go too?'

'Yes. It's too hot for me here now – I'm French. I have an Identity Card. A real one.'

'No passport?'

'No, no passport.'

Madam C says: 'With *your* father – he never made you a passport?'

'I had to leave everything – even a change of underwear.'

'I have some – I will give you half of what I have, Piquette – that is what this war is about.' Madam C laughs: 'Three pairs of underpants.'

'What I need most badly,' I tell them, 'is a good pair of boots – heavy boots – with hobnails.'

They ask only for my size.

'We will also need four elastic bandages – no six,' says Piquette.

Monsieur C says: 'You two – we have to get out right away. The sooner the better.'

'It is too long,' I say, 'that I have felt that my last moment will be my next.'

They laugh. I wish instantly I hadn't said it. I think Piquette knows this was an exchange between her father and me.

That night we lie together in a sleeping bag, on the Cs' dining room floor.

'*Mon cher* – feel me. Stroke me,' Piquette says and snuggles against me like a woodland animal.

I stroke her head, her neck.

'Cher bâtard. . .'

I stroke her back. She is asleep. Her little body feels rigid – I shudder with the vision of a dead squirrel. . .

Next day, I am given boots. Piquette a passport. My boots are second-hand, and newly half-soled – and they have hobnails. They fit well.

'These also,' Monsieur C gives me two pairs of heavy socks.

'It's a Dutch organization that are going soonest. They will take you – Hollanders – see, that is how to call them. The Hollanders have a party going – and they will fit you in.'

'Me and Piquette?'

'Of course. You will be given food at the border. Eat well, you will need it. There are other Allied fliers in the party.'

'It is good?'

'The British Secret Service is behind the whole thing,' says Monsieur C.

'The best,' I say

'The best.'

It is a Saturday. I think it is 25th April.

The Cs take us to the Toulouse Station.

'Everyone has a ticket to a different place,' Monsieur C already told us. 'But it is this place – fifteen kilometres north of Bagnères where you will all get off.'

No sooner are we at Toulouse Station than I don't like it much. Our party is too conspicuous for an inquisitive German agent.

Piquette reads my mind. 'We have no choice. It looks worse to us because we know – they don't. Come on.'

We are saying goodbye to the Cs – they both kiss us both – the rough and the smooth. . . Good luck, goodbye – these are brave people – they could be caught at any moment, someone is talking and they know it. . .

'Au revoir.' 'Au revoir.' What a language.

The smiles.

At last we are moving.

To my joy, Piquette agrees to sit opposite me – so that (instead of a far corner, like the last time we travelled) one of my feet and one of hers, can touch in a way no one will notice. . .

It is to take several hours. Our destination is a very small country station.

It is then that I think we will be most noticeable. Thirty people alighting at once. I'd rather be just me, as usual –

or now, just me and Piquette.

Piquette has been given a new name: Jeanne Hubert.

'Piquette Dehn was never my name anyway.'

She is to say she is travelling to Algiers – the daughter of the former French Minister of Agriculture.

'He is already in Algiers –'

'Does he know?'

'No. Of course not.'

'Will it work?' I asked Monsieur C.

'A woman travelling with an Allied aviator can get through Spain.' 'A young woman alone can get many places,' this last was said by Madame C.

What views. What a day. I spend most of it looking at the bifurcation of Piquette's body – at her slacks – where her legs meet ... where my head has been buried. . .

Though the outside views are spectacular too and heighten my feelings towards her... I have never been in love like this before: it is as if one sees in focus for the first time, as if one feels with honed nerves. Being in love, I realize, is like flying or sailing – a great intensifier.

At the little station, dripping wet, I am very nervous about our party.

But fortunately, we are immediately loaded into a car and two trucks – and driven to a field – we are in the foothills of the Pyrenees, all right, it feels as if we are half up them.

'Everyone eat well – and be ready to move out at 8:00, after dark.'

'We can be together now, huh?' she says bumping against me.

'Yes. Why not. We've nothing to lose – attached to this lot.'

'Keep smiling,' she says and wrinkles her nose.

'Me – I am laughing, *mon cher* Piquette, laughing.'

We smile at each other as we eat.

Everything is going to plan. In the same trucks (with smelly exhausts) we are taken to the foot of the mountain.

Here a small wooden mill spans a stream – picture-book stuff.

'I am your guide. Georges.'

'Georges III,' I say.

'What?'

'Nothing.'

395

'It's good he is a Frenchman. I don't want a Dutchman to lead us.'

'The Hollanders are the best leaders in the world,' I say, putting my hand over Piquette's mouth, smiling at the Hollander nearest us.

At once we begin on our first leg.

'It is best not to talk,' Georges says. 'To save strength and against detection.'

Piquette and me, we go by squeeze signals of the hands.

The stream is a roaring rapids now.

We are tramping upwards for over four hours. . .

We come to a shepherd's hut – it is also a picture book: There is four feet of hay on the floor of the hayloft, making a comfortable bed for all thirty-six of us.

We are: the guide, two Maquis who are armed now with Sten guns, fifteen Americans, twelve Dutchmen, three Frenchmen – a Belgian – a Frenchwoman – and me.

Piquette and I are eating a little. Sipping a little water

'You are the most beautiful creature in the world,' I whisper.

We have the corner where it is very dark and the hay makes us very private – if we are quiet.

She says – into my ear, 'Make love to me, Chris – for pity's sake, for life's sake, make love to me. Heal me, *La Mouette.*'

Going on instinct – automatic pilot, I could say – I get out of as much clothes as I dare – and she dares. The cold is intense. The hay prickly.

It is peculiar, Widda-Widda, it seems as if I have known her body for many years.

396

I know where it wants to be stroked – Piquette is the woman with the cashmere lips that bring water and electricity... Again her tingling smell is all about me – Angostura Bitters and salt water and then I realize that she smells like St George, my father. Amazing and very moving – a union of families...

I think it is a very very long thirty minutes that we are loving when all others are sleeping.

I have heard much about a man's feelings when he first enters a woman – much good and much about slips and muffing: the feelings of me and my parts are so intense it is twice that of first hearing a violin, but similar. Similar to sailing with the rail under – but that would assume the vessel be as human and alive as you...

I know, instantly, that this is what life is for and about. That this is the best. That this is the truth about which all else is lies.

A long time later, the last electricity passes from my body into hers – where she had made our every move into her own electricity and given it back to me...

No wonder the ancients said to save this for true love; no wonder the Greeks believed it all the territory of gods where we mortals are but trespassers...

We do not speak: I am watching her eyes glistening in the night – they say love and light and then they close in sleep.

How can one so young, know so much?

Piquette, I love you – as another said, from the beginning which has no beginning, to the end which shall have no end.

Dear Nasti, and Wuffless and Widda-Widda,
    This is the way it was

397

This is the way it is

We wake up at 10:00 a.m. very refreshed. Wash in the stream. We eat a fine breakfast.

We are now climbing up all the time. At one o'clock, we are resting for a mite. (If I sound French, it is because I am French. . .)

We talk to the Belgian.

'I am thirty-five,' he is saying. 'Out of shape for this. Besides, I've been a prisoner-of-war for two and a half years. But I will do anything to get to the Free Belgian Air Corps – or any air corps to fight *them.*'

'Pretty old,' she whispers to me. 'But he'll make it. His morale is good.'

'And yours?'

'I am a tiger.'

'And me only a gull.'

'It is your wings on which we will fly.'

We fall silent as the guide moves on with great caution – through what is now heavy snow. The crust bears us well.

But sometimes it lets us through – we sink up to our hips. This all makes climbing very tiresome. At about 4:00 we are reaching the top of this mountain.

The day is indescribably beautiful and the sun is casting a strong glare on the snow.

'We'll get snow-blinded.'

'Close your eyes – half close them.'

Now we are walking due south, towards the mountain town of Bagnères.

And now we are going down into the valley – which is a helluva lot easier than climbing up.

Most of us slide on the snow.

I think of trying to make a sled of my greatcoat for us both – but we have to travel, even down, separately. . .

In the evening we are several thousand feet down – below where we were.

Here we are resting for two hours – waiting for it to get dark, because there is a village nearby.

I lie down on the ground and Piquette climbs in under my greatcoat. We sleep as one person, almost. I am very proud of her – that she is mine and I am hers – I am very happy. I have never before known what happiness is.

After sunset we are starting again. Skirting the village, ascending the other side of the mountain.

That is, we are not going over the top – but around the side – and, doing such I am very thankful for the elastic bandages that Piquette asked for and got for us.

In this going around, these bandages round our ankles and feet are a – I almost said, a Godsend, but they are a Piquettesend.

Now we are going down – descending steeply into a valley, moving very cautiously.

The grade is very steep now – we can't stand, we slide and slip.

At last, at the bottom we are crossing a river – it is the Garonne? We don't know.

And now we are starting up the other side. *Merde.*

We continue walking until 3:00 a.m. the next morning: I figure it is the 27th of April.

Now we come upon another mountain hut. Piquette smiles at this and I at her.

But we are not to have the luck or love we had before – how could we?

'We will all stay here until nightfall. We will cross the Spanish border – we trust – early tomorrow morning.'

Anticipate as we may have done, what we've got is this: a platform of bare boards on which to sleep – no bedding of any kind.

I gasp: 'We must make a ball of ourselves in my greatcoat – I think we will each keep the other warm.'

'Yes, man, yes. Totally proximity, if you please.' She laughs despite the altitude.

'Have we any food?'

'A little chocolate is all.'

I had not understood: we have only the daylight left to sleep in. At 8:30 we are rudely awakened – we ache, we pain.

Georges has gone.

The new guide says: 'I am your new guide. We have to proceed with the utmost caution. German patrols are everywhere. Talk little, do not clank any metal against metal.'

We are just starting. It is 9.00 p.m. We are walking around the mountain for two hours and more. Now we have a view of Bagnères, far, far below us.

'Look,' she says: 'It looks beneath us – like stars in the trees.'

It is one of the most enthralling views I have ever seen – even counting from an aircraft.

We now descend again.

Down, down, down. We are being extra careful as we cross the railway and the road – very bad business.

The guide is sharp. He gets us through – across. On the other side, we are resting for a few minutes before starting another upward climb.

This is the way it is.

It is midnight when we begin and Piquette clings to me like exhausted glue.

But *after* this, we are climbing for six and a half hours. . .

This is the most gruelling feat of endurance that I have ever attempted – and I am very glad that I am only twenty-one. So Hannibal took elephants over the Pyrenees – poor effing elephants.

The atmosphere gets rarer and rarer. It is impossible to speak now – I only smile at Piquette and she at me.

One boy cannot go any further. Others are helping him. I have no strength to help even Piquette.

I keep taking Benzedrine tablets which I still have from the time I was shot down. I share them with Piquette.

I do not think we could have made it without them.

The label says, one every four to six hours – and one additional only in extreme exhaustion.

We have had four each. I do not feel any effect from them at all.

Several are in better shape than we are – they help the boy – and another, the Belgian.

I begin to fall down many times.

Piquette gets down on her hands and knees and indicates that I do the same.

It *is* easier to crawl on hands and knees rather than walk upright.

We are now nearing the top, I believe, and must believe. We rest every five minutes. . .

But it soon becomes so monstrously cold that we have to go on – no choice – to keep warm.

It is about 6:30 in the morning. It is April 28th and the sun is rising.

The guide stops and sways and gasps: 'We are at the Spanish border.'

'Over it?' asks Piquette.

401

'*Oui*. Over it.'

With this news, Piquette and I sit down and have a good cry.

We rest for several minutes on top of this mountain and watch the sun rise. The colouring is exquisite – totally unique – brown and black mountains and rocks, largely snow-covered, and, through the mist and wet and the drops, every colour of the rainbow – All as the sun rises a little higher.

'Magic,' she says and I squeeze her small body against mine.

There is another mountain higher than us: 'Is it Super Bagnères?' I ask.

'Mount Perdido,' says the guide.

I know we are at about 12,000 feet – because we are all having effects from lack of oxygen.

Our relief is enormous: Piquette and I laugh and maul at each other like drugged bears.

'I have to leave you now,' the guide says.

'We will give you our French money,' I say, moving forward. Piquette grabs my arm.

'We have 600 francs – they will be no use to us.'

'*Sacré bleu*,' she says. 'Money is money.'

This descent now is very relaxing, funny. It is also extremely easy.

'Like this,' I shout, laughing at Piquette.

I pull my greatcoat tails between my legs: I use my stick as a rudder.

'Look – like a boat,' I shout and she shouts and laughs and we descend the whole mountain with much speed.

It is incredible – lovely and funny.

She has her own smaller coat and she is riding on a little canvas bag – that I didn't know she had.

402

We stop. 'This is a helluva lot of fun, eh?'

She hugs me. I kiss her nose – her eyes, my mouth wet with snow.

We go on sliding down and down to the edge of the snowline, the snowcap.

Here Piquette and I find a field (the others have spaced out from us – as if everyone wanted space for themselves) by a little river, and we drink and then lie down in the warm sun.

We have no trouble in getting several hours' sleep –

(I forgot to say, that morning, just before we crossed the Frontier, as we were walking along what appeared to be a snowcap between two ridges, we suddenly heard a rumbling sound and felt the snow under our feet, sink several inches. It made a terrific noise, not unlike thunder.)

We wake up. Now we can hear these thunderings of snow-slides intermittently. We decide to go on on our own – just the two of us. There is only one route anyway: a valley road which runs beside this tributary of the Garonne river.

Piquette and I are standing looking down the valley, and we can see several groups of our party, standing out along the road.

'It is very conspicuous. We will all be picked up by Spanish police,' I say.

'Maybe that's all right,' she says. 'They are not French or German.'

We walk, happily, bumping into each other down from the mountain to the valley.

I check my map. We turn towards a town called Viella.

Piquette and I have walked several miles and then we come upon a happy party of our people – our 'boys', I call them – at a roadside inn.

They are eating eggs and toast and drinking wine.

Piquette goes to the woman's room – and I go to the earth-closet for men. It is a big relief.

We eat slowly and well – in the sun. We get to feel better and better. The two of us, eating and touching in the sun.

Dear Widda-Widda and Wuffless,
This is the way it is
this is the way
this is
this
is
I

What would I have done differently had I known what lay ahead for Piquette, for me, for us. . ?

It is right what I said before: the world has become a nasty boil – but I no longer believe it is possible for us to see it well –

We are eating and drinking wine – grapey and blurry-purple taste on the tongue. (I haven't thought about whisky or pills for months and months . . . isn't it peculiar, I must have been severely bonked on my head. . .)

We get up (I think we even have a silly little argument here before we go on).

We go on down the road – we do not even go very far, before the Spanish police arrive – in a car.

I listen to what they are saying: in Spanish and French. 'Walk on to Viella – while we escort you.'

Immediately I am aware that these police are eyeing Piquette with a special interest – this, in my Bermudian vernacular, gets my deck pig out of his cage.

404

I have no idea what they are thinking.

At Viella we are taken to the police station.

I am about to kiss Piquette – in fear that we will be separated for a while – but she is grabbed and taken across the tiled floor, to a tall door.

'See you soon, Piquette,' I shout.

'Moi aussi,' she shouts, referring to our first love-making.

She is gone through the tall official door.

All our other 'boys' are here.

It is the Belgian who speaks: 'It is very bad for the girl.'

He is menaced by a policeman.

'Silence!'

'Name?'

'Berkeley. Aubrey Spencer.' I can see it will take a long time for this man (who appears to be the senior) to get even my name straight.

'Rank: Flight Lieutenant, Royal Air Force. A407697.'

Now I realize I am to be simultaneously searched. I have ten letters to be mailed for friends.

'The letters, sir. Please will they be returned to me – they are personal – for friends – to be mailed?'

'Be quiet. They will be returned.'

This search is rude and unattractive. I think of Piquette – how are they treating her? Sons-of-bitches.

They take also my maps – my lovely silk RAF maps of all of Europe – Germany, France, Spain and other parts of North Africa (I thought to save them for my children, maybe even my grandchildren somehow. . .).

'When were you shot down?'

'21st September 1942.'

He looks incredulous.

'You have been free in France eight months?'

'No. Captured in Paris. Escaped.' This is what I've been told to say: uncaptured members of the armed forces of one country can be treated as invading hostiles of a Neutral country – unless they have escaped captivity. . .

'I beg your pardon, señor – but I have under my protection my French friend –'

'The young lady?'

'Yes.'

'She's French?'

'Yes. She is bound for Algiers – her father is a French Minister.'

'So. So. You'll see her later.'

We are taken to a dilapidated hotel adjacent – on the square. We are given a meal.

It tastes good. I am surprised I can eat.

'What should I do about my friend?' I ask the senior Hollander.

'I don't know. The American – Johnson – he has already got through to the United States Consulate in Barcelona. Has let them know we are here.'

Another American says: 'And the Consul has already contacted the Police Chief here at Viella – telling him to take good care of us.'

I go and try to use the phone – the manager says, no.

'I want to phone the British Embassy in Madrid.'

At this, a policeman appears from nowhere. 'No more phone – orders, Chief of Police.'

The Belgian makes the most sense.

'Where is your girlfriend?'

'At the police station.'

'Go and demand that she be released.'

'Would you come with me?'

406

'Yes. I would.'

We go to the police station. I ask to see the Chief.

They keep us waiting a half-hour. It is very late afternoon.

I get up and go to the desk. 'Be so kind as to tell the Chief that Flight Lieutenant Berkeley wishes to see him.'

'And Lieutenant de Lisle also,' says the Belgian, standing by me.

I feel bad now. But the Chief comes out.

'You,' he's pointing to me. 'You only – come.'

In his room: 'What is it you want, Lieutenant?'

In my tenseness I have forgotten Piquette's name on her Identity Card.

'My friend – you have my friend the French woman. When will she be joining us?'

His eyes snap with a policeman's automatic thinking. 'Are you related to this young woman?'

'No.'

'Are you married to this young woman?'

'No – but I have got a message through to the Air Attaché at the British Embassy in Madrid. He knows we are here at Viella.'

'And tell me, Lieutenant. Of what interest can this British Air Attaché have in a young French woman?'

'She and I are friends,' I say most sharply. 'And anything that happens to her, I will regard as happening to me.'

I can see that this hits home. The Chief looks a little stunned.

'Tomorrow morning, we will release her – most likely. Go and have some wine and forget her, young sir.'

'I will *not* forget her – not for one instant.'

'Good night, Lieutenant.'

'Good night, Señor Chief of Police.'

407

The next morning 'the boys' are all buying oranges and bananas and figs – which I have not seen for years – and laughing and pranking about.

I go to the police station again. I bang and yell now – it is past eleven and Piquette has not been seen.

The Chief has me in again.

'The British Embassy and the American Embassy are aware of our presence here. Where is my young French friend, M'selle Jeanne Hubert?'

His eyes are like black beads. I begin to hate every smell of Spain – bitter like Brasso polish, somehow.

'Young Mr Lieutenant, let me tell you something. You officers of the Armed Forces are one thing. People wanted for criminal offences by a neighbouring country are something else. Also, of course – this country does not permit entrance to criminals or prodstituents.'

'When will M'selle Hubert be released?'

'Soon. In God's time.'

Stupid and young I did not quite get his meaning.
Nasti, Skeglee and Widda-Widda,
This is the way it was
This is the way it is
This is the way
This is
This
is
I
watch, with several others of the boys, standing around the central square,

I watch, incredulous:

a German car drives up. An open Mercedes-Benz. A German driver and a Wehrmacht officer – the fact that this man is Wehrmacht and not Gestapo fooled me at first.

The German officer, in full uniform and wearing his side arms – a Luger – goes into the police station.

Now the whole square is full of our boys – every one – to have a look.

The Spanish and the Germans are shameless.

After about thirty-five or forty minutes: the Spanish Chief of Police emerges, with two assistants – all armed, of course – and the Wehrmacht officer, who has a person handcuffed to him.

It is Piquette. I can tell by her shoulder alone, even though it is now slumped over, somehow.

I rush forward, am restrained by my friends. I break loose, I rush again:

'Piquette!' I shout. 'Piquette!'

By now, the Germans have moved her – like chained cargo, into the back seat, the officer is beside her.

He gives a Nazi salute.

The Spanish police, on the steps, return this salute.

'Piquette!' I shout and run towards the Mercedes – which is now moving with horrible precision.

At this moment, Piquette breaks loose somehow – stands somehow, and shouts: loud in the square

'*La Mouette*, you are my mother and my father. . .'

It is hard to imagine how she can get all this out: her eyes are blackened.

'. . . and my child – you are everything. . .'

At this place in her speaking, the Wehrmacht officer hits her with a black stick.

She falls. I run. I run. I run. . .

I cannot catch them. When I get back, even the entrance to the police station is barred me.

'You should have married her in France,' one Hollander says.

409

'I'm going after her,' I shout like a madman. 'I will steal a car or a motorcycle and get her back.'

My Belgian friend is restraining me: 'You can't go back to France – they would kill you.'

One Hollander says: 'It must have been a tip-off. The two police are in cahoots – obviously.'

'Obviously'.

'Besides,' says the Belgian aviator. 'You are not allowed to go back – are you? You are under orders to escape back to the Royal Air Force.' He roughs my hair. 'My dear friend, you are a brave good man – but you are no free agent – but a member of a group – with rules, eh?'

At a place called Sort, where we stop (as we are being marched out on the snowbound country roads), I fly into a rage at the Mayor – who will not let me use the telephone, to phone the British Consul in Barcelona.

The Mayor is threatening to put me in jail.

'Chris,' says my Belgian friend. 'Don't lose your temper with Fascists – that's how they win. Besides, don't you fuck it up for the rest of us.'

We are kept in Lerida for three weeks. But the British Consul does come – with money and cigarettes.

I am able, while here, to send cables home. It is May 20th.

Then a Spanish Air Force officer escorts us to Madrid.

While in Madrid I go to two concerts: real cute: the Madrid Symphony conducted by the German, Karl Shuricht. It is useless to try to fault them. It is perfection. Mozart and Beethoven. Starved for music these many months, I weep long and silently . . . for Man's folly and wickedness, for myself and in pain

410

and longing for Piquette... But Piquette is like a whole apple, unchewed at all, stuck fast in my throat...

At the border, leaving Spain for Gibraltar, I turn: silently, in the few feet of space, I make a curse on Spain and all her police: a curse I learned in Spain. (They can curse even better than Bermudians.) 'Fascist Swine: I piss in the milk of your mothers, may you die sucking the rectums of your ancient priests.'

At Gibraltar, May 30th 1943, I am given RAF battledress uniform again – and turn in my civvies...

There follows interrogation after interrogation by our side – All this time I ask for help and advice about Piquette...

While in Gibraltar, this RAF Intelligence Officer says: 'Never give up hope. It's amazing what happens in these escape routes and stories.'

'I cabled my family in Bermuda and England – from Lerida, I did. The cables would get through, wouldn't they?'

'Liable to be very held up by censors. Cable your family from here. You are a very interesting case to *us* – never mind the Spaniards and their German friends.'

'How do you mean?'

'I, for one, thought you were a German agent, at first: you were simply loose too long in France to be believable.'

After three days I am flown back to England by BOAC, landing at Bristol. The aircraft is like the old Cavalier – the old Empire flying boat, powered-up, of course.

Orders: Report to the War Office for immediate interrogation.

411

There I discover I am written off as Dead. However, in their quiet British way they write me back on to what is called 'The Active List'.

It's good that I have a lot of back pay.

'I am absolutely certain that I can *not* fly a kite any more, I've lost it. I've forgotten how.'

They only smile.

'What do you need now, Flight Lieutenant – what do you want?'

I open my mouth. No sounds will come. I want a French woman named Piquette, I want this fucking war to be over.

I start to cry, silently.

This is the way it was, Nasti, Skeglee and Widda-Widda,

This is the way it is

This

Is

I

Now I go to Malvern to see James, Skeglee. . .

XX

'It doesn't matter what you want, Berkeley – you are going to damned well stay in bed until the doctor gets here,' Matron said.

James had said to her: 'But my brother Chris has escaped and he could get here any time and there's the cricket.'

He showed her the telegram that he kept with him all the time.

'YOU MAY CHANGE LISTING TO FOUND ASSUMED ALIVE LOVE BERMUDA.'

The doctor came and looked him over and took his temperature and checked his stomach.

'Shingles,' James heard him tell the Matron in the dispensary next door. 'A complaint brought on by worry – which occurs in middle-aged and old people.'

'Good heavens,' she said. 'Are you sure?'

'Positive. It's of the chickenpox family – so you'll have to keep him isolated from everyone except those who've already had shingles or chickenpox.'

Matron and the doctor came back in. 'His brother – one of our heroes in the RAF – is coming this afternoon. Can he see him?'

'Certainly. If the brother has had chickenpox.'

James raked his memory back: Yes, all the family except himself and little George had had chickenpox.

'Yes, sir. My brother has had chickenpox: 1937: on the *Reina Del Pacifico*.'

'How can you remember that?'

'Because, sir, Ramsay MacDonald died on the ship – and all the family had chickenpox except me and my father. How long do I have to be in bed, sir?'

'At least three weeks.'

James was so happy over the news about Christopher that he was almost levitating, himself and his bed.

Chris came in. He did look different – it might be the new-type uniform.

'Skeglee!'

James, not hearing Matron's protests, was up and out of bed and hugged his brother – blinded by tears.

Somewhere he heard a motormower – it was a sound like a symphony.

'Chris. Oh, Christopher. Oh, Chris.'

Backbreaking hugs and Halcyon-Bermudian-pats – as if administered by vibrations from a woman's spring shoe-stretcher.

'I knew you would come back. I knew it. Everyone else knew you were dead.'

I am dead, actually, James.

'What's this that you got?'

'Shingles.'

'You'll soon be over them.'

'Tell me about France.'

'It's beautiful – James – like England only the sun shines and people LIVE.'

These people are dead, boy. You should have seen my woman's parts – her red and purple parts – If she is dead, James, I don't want to be alive. . .

'Matron – could you please ask someone to bring us some tea.'

'I'll be thrilled,' she said and disappeared.

If pushed, James – if cornered in an argument, Uncle Albert was rather amusing. He was capable of stamping his foot and saying: 'I am not only the Squire – who, until recently, had the sole vote for every man, woman and child – I am also the representative of God on Earth in this hamlet.'

'And Christopher,' James was giving him the Halcyon pats again. 'When are you going to fly again?'

'Soon – maybe.' Let us not forget, Skeglee, who the real criminals are. They are US. That is the only important thing to learn about war.

'It was awful about Granny – I'm sorry, Chris.'

'Sorrier for Grampy – he'll be absolutely lost. Mummy says *he*, Grampy – asked her – he said: "I can't remember all Fay said to me, Charity. In the next life do you think I will be able to remember?" Mummy said, "Yes." And she cried.

'But, Skeglee – guess what?'

'What?'

'Grampy is making a joke. He does not believe in another life – only in this one.'

414

'*No.*'

'Well, perhaps he does. . . What's this shingles?'

And do you know, Skeglee, the joke: It is said that the King, Bertie, said, on learning that his brother would abdicate to marry a twice divorced woman: 'Into every reign a little life must fall.'

But, James, I'll tell you the secret: Cousin Toby Isherwood was at Court at the time

And, Toby says to me: 'He's an absolutely decent and brave man – but he isn't capable of making jokes on that level, my dear fella.'

Toby also told me to read *War and Peace* – 'That's the end of Tsars – when Pierre comes upon the Tsar on the battlefield.' But I, Chris Berkeley, happen to cherish this deep affection for K.G. VI – because of his courage over the stutter and his caring for the common people in the bombing. . .

'Christopher – I'm sorry too about Aunt Lillie.'

'She was marvellous. I can't bear it, James – so I know you must feel worst still.'

Since I've seen you Jamie, m'dear, I've killed a man, face to face. A man much like O'Neill.

'*All that* happened while you were away – so much happened, I'm sorry you got it all at once.'

'Nada. Let's have tea – Matron, shall you join us?'

'Aunt Lillie said some special things last holidays –'

'Yes. Tell me.'

And Cousin Toby – sometimes I think he's the only sane one in the family. He, our only inherited title: renounced his baronetcy as soon as he inherited it.

Marvellous – put us all in our slot; we all wanted that baronetcy. With it, you are 'moored' – you are 'in' – and without it, you are irrevocably 'out'. Out of the society, we, the whole family want: that is, that rung above us unattainable except by the luck of birth –

Toby quietly kicked it all aside – like useless baggage:

'My dear fella – it would cost me two hundred a year just in tips. And Alison – can you see her as Lady Isherwood? I'm a painter, thank you, that's difficult enough.'

'Did you know when you were in France that the Hall was taken by the army?'

When Widda-Widda frowns, James, her eyes, her face – look exactly like those of a spaniel puppy.

'No. I spent the whole time running.'

As to Bermuda Negroes, I do not think that they are – that we are any better than them. I simply don't think that you could teach one of them to fly. I'd *like* to think it's possible, but my mind tells me it's impossible.

But I thought you said *you* were part Negro?

Quite – and that's why I know I can't fly any more.

Well, I think you are irrational – crazy!

You'll get no argument with me on that score.

'Did you meet any beautiful women?'

'Yes.' They talked about putting me up for the DFC. What do you bastards want, are you that short of pilots?

What, a DFC for saving my own skin? For falling in love, perhaps. . ? Piquette, I cannot live without you; there is no question. Without you I would, simply, and without any fuss, rather be dead.

'Geoff Montrose said to me: were you Regular RAF? And, he didn't know much about us Colonial Wallahs –'

'He said, what?'

James told him again.

'What unmitigated gall – and balls too. There's only about twenty Regular RAF types *alive* – and most of

416

them, Air Marshals. Ignore it, who cares?'

'What do you want to do now, Chris – go back to Spitfires?'

'Done my time on Spitfires. Loved it. Loved them. But they've got me sort of channelled into US planes now, I think.' And I can't fly anything. I couldn't fly a public toilet around Hampstead Heath. . .

'Why didn't you answer me, Chris?'

'What about – I did?'

'Dad.'

'What about Dad?'

As to the Halcyons (never mind Dad and the Berkeleys) the Halcyons are just too too damned arrogant. Too blown-up with their own importance. A Halcyon is supposed to be a Kingfisher, fabled by the ancients. . .

And a lot of the Halcyons of Bermuda have never done anything. Take Uncle Joe for instance, charming and beautiful, and good at two art forms and all games. Possessed of Bermuda's greatest gift: a helmsman.

And he's never even held a job.

And Grandfather's brother designed, built and steered the *Nea* and then did nothing but be Commodore of the Royal Bermuda Yacht Club – and slowly drink his years away in storytelling. . .

Who do they think they are?

'When will he come over?'

I'm struggling to think what it is that James wants from me? What?

'I don't know when I'll be back. Going to go to Lincoln. Then to Scotland for a rest, they say.' He needs to hear something from me?

The birds were singing in the silence between them.

'How long can you stay?'

'I have to go rather soon.'

Matron said: 'Yes, he's got a temperature and he's supposed to rest. I know Mr and Mrs Montrose are looking forward to seeing you.'

'Yes,' said Christopher, fiddling with a button, throwing his blond hair back off his forehead with his usual shake of head. 'I've got it, Skeglee, Dad will be over soon – hold on, Old Man – isn't that what he says?'

'Yes, he calls me, Old Man ... funny, isn't it?'

'You be careful, m'dear – and get lots of rest. And get well soon.'

Going down the stairs, I meet this old Montrose fella, to whom I say: 'Are you Geoffrey Montrose –? Well, you listen to me for a moment. This "Colonial Wallah", as you call us, went to Harrow and is going to St John's – our family college – after the War. I also went to Cranwell. I've flown in numbers 118 and 303 Squadrons, RAF – and some others I forgot. I've been in Hurricanes, Spitfires, Mustangs, Lysanders, Ansons and damned Tiger Moths. Goodbye.'

When I get down to the bottom of the stairs, I turn and call:

'So stick that in your pipe and smoke it.'

'Would you like me to phone for a taxi for you, young man?' this Montrose man says: 'You just sit here quietly and I'll phone a taxi.'

Three weeks later James was back in Mr Healey's class.

Mr Healey was talking about Shakespeare, his favourite subject –

'You lads will be gone soon into all the hurly-burly of public school and life – and that's all very good. I'd like to share with you a couple of secrets that might

418

just turn out to be keys – golden keys, for you.'

Outside, the Malvern Hills sat, green and gentle and unperturbed. Far overhead you could hear an aircraft. (It was impossible now not to hear at least one aircraft anywhere you were in Britain. . .)

Sometimes, Mr Healey's mind would wander:

'You see, the thing about *As You Like It* is Rosalind. I'd speculate that Shakespeare loved a woman named Rosalind.

'We don't know much, of course – except from the Sonnets. Poor chap had bad teeth and bad breath – though he was a mere lad of fifty-two when he died.

'Look, boys – what I wanted to share with you is this that he said:

' "The friends thou hast and their adoption tried, grapple them to thy heart with hoops of steel." That's one thing.'

'Rosalind, sir,' said Aiken.

'Yes. A little bit before your time – back in '79 – was that before your time? Oh yes, of course.'

'1879, sir? That was when my grandfather was born.'

'Oh, yes. Well – Berkeley, pay attention. Back in 1879 – was the coldest winter in living memory. . .'

James was listening very carefully – because when Mr Healey got into a mood of reminiscing, one got that rarity from adults: the truth.

'That year – I was in London – and the whole Thames froze over. 1879. It was frozen past Tower Bridge. There was a great fair on the Thames, on the ice, by the Houses of Parliament.

'And do you know what, boys? They had fires on the ice – and they were roasting entire oxen on spits on the fires on the ice.

'I went down and took this lovely young lady. I was nineteen or thereabouts – and she the same age. And,

419

I took her to the fair on the ice.

'Can you see it – the fires and the sun setting west into the Thames and all lit up red and orange?

'And I took Rosalind – this lovely young lady, who two other chaps wanted – but, fortunately, she wanted me – and, on this afternoon and evening in 1879, we were skating arm in arm on the Thames, Rosalind and me – skating. . .

'She became my wife in 1881. . .'

Mr Healey, overwhelmed with his memories, now fell silent and merely looked with seemingly unseeing eyes into the garden and the great hills beyond.

No person in that class moved. . .

Ten or eleven whole minutes passed.

'What are we talking about?'

'*Julius Caesar*, sir,' said James.

'A deadly dull play – no love in it – no matter. Come along then. Here's another secret – and a *hot* one:

'When you are writing an exam: put all you know in the first sentence. *All of it*, concisely – and write slowly and legibly.

'That way you'll pass any exam. All examiners have fifty papers to read and they are *all* tired. So imagine you are them.'

James knew darned well that was good advice.

'Sahara Bernhardt was the lady who loved "It" – but, one day, a strange thing happened to her.'

'What was that, Berkeley?' Aiken said.

'Shut up, Aiken – or he won't go on – you know how he is,' said Hosefield.

'Sahara had taken a fancy to this handsome young man – with yellow hair that hung across his forehead.

' "He's not very beautiful," she found herself saying. "But I seem to care an awful lot about him."

' "Mind you," she said. "He's a terrific lover – and

no mistake. Got a way with his dick, I can tell you."

'But however hard Sahara tried she couldn't get the image of this guy out of her mind.

' "I just simply don't care about anyone else – and this has never happened to me before. I can imagine all the best cocks in the world – but all I can think about is Harry."

'One day, Sahara Bernhardt and her Harry – went down by the river.

'Now Sahara had on all her very best clothes. And she didn't like anything to happen to her good clothes. But, no sooner had Harry touched her left breast – nipple – which was underneath her clothes, two layers deep – than she went quietly crazy.

'About three hours later she found herself sitting happily on the grass by the river.

' "Harry," she said, "how did we get my best clothes in such a mess?"

' "I don't know," he said. "I guess love is like that – it makes us forget things. It's amazing how messy one gets when one's in love."

' "Do you mean to say that you are in love with me?"

' "Yes. I am."

' "You are in love with me, Sahara Bernhardt, The Woman Who Loves 'It'?"

' "Certainly, Sahara – been looking for you all me life, as-a-matter-of-fact."

' "Funny, Harry. And I've been looking for you." '

'Is that the end?' said John Hosefield. 'Why, you old gyper – I liked it better when everybody was giving everyone else the big dick. Never can trust you Berkeley, that's your trouble.'

'I thought it was charming,' said Aiken. 'Simply charming.'

421

The Common Entrance exams were much less formidable than they expected.

'We've just done so many, haven't we?' said Aiken.

'If it wasn't for Old Man Healey, I wouldn't have done a sausage,' said Hosefield.

'Me too,' said James.

But Aiken said: 'It's public school that frightens me: a strange place and eight hundred boys –'

'And a hundred rules one doesn't know,' said James. If there was anything more frightening than a public school – he didn't know about it.

The cricket was not an anticlimax – because being captain was, he realized, what he'd longed for without knowing it. Like cricket itself: a game, he reckoned, he'd always longed for. . .

'Berkeley, I wish you all the best of luck in the world,' Mr Healey said, heating some toast on his gas-fire.

James had never been in Mr Healey's room before, the old man kept his retreat sacred – silver frames and gold clocks and spectacles and some old cricket- and rowing-caps almost rotted away. . .

'It's Hebrew, you know, that is the basis – the plinth of our civilization. Our first written stuff – you know, Hebrew.'

'I didn't take Hebrew, sir.'

'I know perfectly well you didn't, boy. You weren't even any good at Latin. What I'm telling you is: Hebrew is the plinth of our civilization.

'Hence the reason for anti-Semitism. We get jealous of the Jewish people because they had The Word first.'

'Yes, sir. I understand.'

'It's true, boy. Few people do understand. It's "In the beginning was The Word. . ." That's the very first

422

thing – and it's Jewish.'

Silence.

'Sir. I don't mean to embarrass you, sir – but I did want to say...'

'What is it, then, spit it out.'

'Just that I've learned a lot from you, sir.' James found that he couldn't talk.

'That's very good to hear – good of you to say so and thank you. I say, I had an original thought in the night and perhaps you'd like it – it's this – you know all this talk of St Francis of Assisi preaching to the birds?'

James nodded.

'Well, I suddenly realized that St Francis was much too clever to do that – he was letting the birds preach to him.'

James smiled. He knew the time had come and he didn't want to say goodbye.

So he just waved to Mr Healey, from Mr Healey's door, and ran out into the passage, and down the steps and out into the garden.

Where an English twilight was turning the distant blues into purple and pink...

XXI

*Christopher, Backwards Often,
Forwards Sometimes and
Probably, Sideways Frequently*

VI

When this fucking war is over, you and I will fall...

In my blue hospital uniform, I hand the letter to the RAF psychiatrist:

The place I'm living in is very like Cedar Hill – that is Victorian and draughty – 'airish', as they say in Bermuda.

Only thing wrong is that the Sister here who reads our mail and censors it, is called 'Tits' by us because she doesn't have any

I think she was, in another incarnation, a jailer in the Tower for Queen Elizabeth

It occurs to me that I, Berkeley, A.S., Flight Lieutenant, now in my twenty-third year, probably outrank her

But, since she can cut off my food and happy pills, it cuts no cubes of ice or Oxo

A previous doctor has examined me, a couple of years back, and found me wanting, so I don't expect this doctor will be out of fashion.

I thought I'd better come to the point: I can no longer fly aeroplanes because I am terrified of flak hitting me in, up, my posterior.

Yours faithfully,
A.S. Berkeley

'Excuse me, Flight Lieutenant,' the doctor says. 'I've read your interesting and helpful letter and let me explain my position immediately.'

'Yes sir.'

'I'm a doctor in civvy street, and I'm doing my bit here in the War, as you are. However, what you say to me is entirely confidential and will go no further than these walls.'

'But you have to make out a report, sir?'

'No need for any "sirs", just "Doctor" is all right – whatever you like. Yes, I put in a report – but only generalities – no details.'

'Really?'

'Truly. In the First War – I broke my leg in a rugby

424

match – subconsciously I did it to get out of going to the Front. I felt awful about it for years. Tortured me with guilt.'

'Really?'

'Yes. Tortured – but the leg break was a good friend to me.'

'How?'

'Well, if I hadn't done it, I wouldn't be here now trying to help you a bit. I'd be dead in France, I expect.'

Silence.

'If I made out a report on myself then in the First War, I'd put: "Suffers from intense fear of death." '

'But we are all afraid of death.'

'Exactly. So with you, I'll say the same. "Suffers from intense fear of death." The details are your business – and mine – not the Raf's.'

'You're unusual.'

'I hope so, lad. Now let's look at your letter together.' I find this doctor's tender Scottish accent very soothing after the harsh Oxbridge accents. . .

'This is what I *may* be able to help you with right away.'

'How could you?'

'I'm an old bloke who's been about a bit and seen a bit. That's my trade – untangling fishing-lines in the head, if you like.'

'And my fear of . . . up – here.' I tap the last paragraph of my letter.

'Yes. This fear of being hit in the *derrière* – posterior – do you want to tell me anything else about it?'

'It's very intense.'

'Oh, it can be – can't it – and very painful and worrisome. Makes life hell, I imagine. But you don't have it all the time?'

'No, just over enemy territory.'

425

'And the fear is of being hit *up* your bottom.'

'How do you know?'

'You said so here.'

'Oh, I do, do I? I guess I do.'

'It's not uncommon, Aubrey – may I call you Aubrey?'

'It's Christopher – Chris. I've had this fear since I can remember.'

'Chris – it's not uncommon to have fears about one's private parts. That's our tender and secret places, isn't it?

'I myself had a good bit of fear about my prick being too small – but I've got over it. It's about average and that's fine by me.

'I always joke to any male patient – I say, in sixteen years of my practice, many men have told me they are afraid their prick is too small – and not a one of them has said, Doctor, I'm afraid my prick is too big.'

I find the doctor looking at me.

After a while even I begin to smile.

'Of course, with my women patients, not one of them brings it up.'

Silence.

I laugh – I sound gruff, like Grampy.

'I'm afraid of being hit up my arse – terrified – so terrified, I freeze and can't fly.'

'You see, Chris, it's usually connected with something that happened when we were very small – tender.'

'Oh.'

'Yes – the younger we are, the more tender we are, like young shoots of trees or plants. Tell me, Chris, did anyone ever give you enemas or something like that – as a laxative when you were a wee kid?'

'Yes. Mother was nuts about us being regular.'

'Ah – that could be it. And she gave you laxatives?'

'Yes – and enemas too.'

'Well, she probably meant well – but the trouble

426

with an enema is that it's an invasion and we don't like invasions – us humans. Indeed – it makes us lose control.

'We don't like to lose control. Especially when we are little and we've just learned to control our bowels – it's the first thing we learn to do for ourselves, isn't it?'

'I guess so.'

'And then along comes this great super-person and takes away our control – invading our private parts.'

'Yes – that's Mother – she gave all of us enemas.'

'And you are the eldest.'

'Yes. I'm Number One.'

'The eldest would get the best care – in this case, the worst care.'

'Yes. I remember those enemas now – I was always terrified. Tell you what, Doctor.'

'Yes. What is it?'

'I'm so terrified of enemas that my arse starts twitching – and my guts too – even if I see a hot-water bottle.'

'Ah, yes. I quite understand. And when we are little we are so powerless. An enema can leave a very bad scar on us. Do you think you had more than one?'

'Oh yes, Doctor – she gave us one whenever we weren't regular. Often once a week.'

'Well, then, that's where your fear of flak hitting you *up* the posterior comes from.'

'But I'm still afraid – now.'

'Yes, lad – but, since you know what caused it – you are fifty per cent cured of the fear.'

'Really?'

'And truly. Every time you get it – now you can say, oh yes, that's my silly old fear from the enemas. I know about that.'

'By God, Doctor. You are bloody amazing. I do

427

believe that you are right.'

'I hope I can help, Christopher. That's my job – what I'm paid for.'

'Good Christ – I'm sorry doctor –'.

'That's all right, I'm not superstitious, Chris.'

'Well, I thought I was some kind of a monster – over my behind fear – a monster as well as a madman.'

'Many of us can do that.'

'I've just been loose in France for nine months and I was also terrified of something else.'

'Oh,' the doctor says, gently, as if everything is all right by him.

'I was terrified that the Gestapo would get me. I'm from Bermuda, you know, and we are all part Negro – us colonials.'

'Go far enough back, Chris, and we are all descended from amoebas, never mind Negroes. But yours is a bit of a peculiar fear.'

'Why's that?'

'Well, I don't know you well yet – but you look like a total Angle to me. "Not Angles but angels", didn't the man say? You know the story?'

'Yes.'

'Well. Hitler would like you – he'd like all of us. It's the Jews and the blacks and the Red Indians he has a phobia about.'

'Oh, yes. They did think I was German – in France they did.'

'I don't doubt it. I mean no disrespect – but you do look like a German – or a Norwegian. You're more likely to be mistaken in Lincoln for being a Kraut, aren't you?'

'How did you know I'm from Lincoln?'

'It gives your address here – you wrote it, Chris.'

'So where's the fear come from?'

'Not sure yet. These things can take time. At any

rate – I'm sure I've got French blood, Irish, Viking, Jewish and probably Negro too.'

'You are, really?'

'Yes. That's all of us, that is.'

'Doctor, do you know what's the matter with me?'

'Not sure, old chap – I should think it's what used to be called Shell-shock.'

'That's maybe it, Doctor – because I just feel – all the time that I'm falling to pieces. . .'

'Yes.'

'Can you help me?'

'It'll take time – but I'll do what I can, yes.'

'There was this young French girl, seventeen. I fell in love with her – and she with me. And the Germans have her and she's Jewish and they've killed her – probably killed her.'

'Oh, that's bloody awful. Horrible.'

'And, Doctor, if she's dead – to tell the truth, I'd rather be dead too.'

'I quite understand that. I've been in love like that. I know what you're talking about.'

'Who have you been in love with then – ? You are lying to me.'

'No, I'm not. It's my wife. I loved her when she was not seventeen but eighteen – and I felt then that I'd die if I lost her. And I still feel that way. It's not only you young fellas who love passionately, you know.'

'Can you help me then, Doctor?'

'I'll do what I can. It'll take time, though, Chris.'

Right here I start crying.

'What is it – I'm afraid our time is almost up – but what is it?'

'You're a damned decent doctor – I haven't known any like you before.'

'Thank you – I'll take that as a recommendation.

And I'll see you later in the week. Is three times a week all right with you, Chris?'

'Yes. I'd rather have every day, Doctor.'

'Can't do that. Rules. But three times a week is fine. Same time, Monday, Wednesday and Friday.'

'Doctor, would you answer me a question?'

'More than likely.'

'Do you think I'm crazy – that I'm out of my mind?'

'No. You are talking to me very intelligently and openly. That's a very strong sign of sane-ness. All right?'

'Yes.'

'So I'll look forward to seeing you the day after tomorrow.'

'Right, sir – sorry, I mean, Doctor.'

The Doctor shakes hands. He has a strong shake and I am very glad for the physical warmth. He has a great smile – like Grampy in Bermuda.

Dear Grampy

I have a pal here who keeps going around saying, 'It buggers description. . .' He means the war, but I mean this castle. . .

XXII

Fotheringham, I

'There are three things you can get beaten for,' said the Captain of School House, Evens, to the lined-up new boys ('Frogs'). 'Buggery, not getting enough "Boys", and not knowing the school rules – all of them – within three weeks.'

His name was Knightly – and he looked tough and mean. (Obviously, he shaved, for one thing. . .)

'There will be a Chivvy twice a week – just like

430

now,' said Cock, the Captain of the School: 'And you will be expected to have learned a good deal each Chivvy. Also, you must have your Boy Card – here – signed by a praeposter twelve times twice a week.

'At each Chivvy, you must show the card – with twelve initials on it,' said another praeposter in the seated crescent.

James had heard, from a boy only a term their senior: 'Boying here is just like fagging at other schools. Cock is as fair and decent as they come. Knightly is a bit of a sod. All the other praeposters are a mixed bunch – mostly bad.'

After this first Chivvy, James and his bunch of Frogs held an impromptu meeting.

'I reckon this is damned tough – these first weeks – I say we all stick together and help each other,' James said.

'What's your name?'

'Berkeley – and yours?'

'Richmond.'

'I was captain at my prep school – now here I am trash again,' James smiled. 'I guess that's life.'

'Me too. I was captain of my school,' said Richmond.

'Me too. I'm Fenwick – Pip Fenwick. I was captain of my school – and captain of cricket and soccer.' Pip was small, dark-complexioned, brown-eyed, and looked quite like a pretty girl.

'Me too.'

'Yes – me also.'

There were six of them. All had been heads of their previous schools. Fotheringham took the top only. It was, James thought, an indication of how tough this new life would be – you had been a big shot, but now, so had everybody, and it counted for nothing anyway.

'And now we are all in Evens?'

'Yes. School House is Odds and Evens and we are

all Evens. I'm Herman.'

James immediately thought Herman looked like a Gestapo – a German. It would make remembering his name easier.

'I'm Block – my school was in Hemel Hempstead.' Block was very tall and very pale – with a quick shy smile.

There was a handsome boy with blue eyes, pink cheeks and yellow hair. 'I'm Larry Rhodes,' he said. 'Rhodes lead everywhere. You can't forget me.'

'Well, if we all stick together and share our knowledge – we will be stronger. Do we agree?'

'Certainly. Makes good sense,' said Richmond. Richmond also had yellow hair – but tight curls. He also had bright blue eyes, and James could see he was as quick as varnish. He liked Richmond.

As a matter of fact, he liked them all – they all seemed very capable. It was Fotheringham he hated: it was big and cold and hostile – but it was something to beat, to master. He had the thought that, when they left Fotheringham, it would seem small and the outside world big – that was what it was all about. . .

'All for one and one for all,' he laughed.

'Agreed,' said 'Rich' Richmond: 'The six musketeers – is that it?'

'Agreed,' said Pip Fenwick, flashing his brown eyes.

James had an instinctive feeling that these handsome young-looking boys, like Fenwick and Rhodes, would be naturally popular, especially with the older boys.

Before he'd left Washashley, in that summer of 1943, James had had two experiences; first, coming upon Old Watkins, as he was going into the walled garden.

'Oh, say, Watkins, can I come in with you?'

'Oh, it's you sir. Yes, of course. Come quickly. I

thought you were one of those horrible Canadians.'

'Are they giving you trouble then?'

'Not too bad, sir. I won't let them. How do you like it?' Watkins gave a swing about – of his stiff and bent body – moving like a creature with steel in its back. 'The gardens, I mean?'

'They're lovely, Watkins, lovely. It's truly incredible.' James looked all about – everything was the same. The paths even more kept up than before. The flowers, the fruits and even the greenhouses were immaculate.

'How do you do it, Watkins?'

'Have to do it, sir.'

It was the only thing that had stayed as it had been at Washashley.

James looked at him and Watkins looked as old as the walls themselves. His eyes set in his prune-like wrinkles – but he also looked determined.

'Here, Mr James – have a damson.' He held out a beautiful plum. 'It's the ones on the sunny wall – the south wall – that are sweet – the ones that don't get enough sun are sour. It's good, eh, Mr James?'

'Marvellous.'

'I just keep on with my work. Those Army can't stop me. Not army from all over the world – not the Germans can stop me, if they come.'

'Marvellous.'

'I don't know nought else. Been in this garden all me life. Was here long before your uncle cum in '97, you know.

'Your auntie, she's a good one with plants – they like her.'

'Yes. And you are the best, eh, Watkins?'

'I'll keep on – that's all I know and all I can do, sir.'

It was extraordinary, the Hall (though James was not

allowed entry) seemed sadder and more broken each holiday – but not the walled garden. It seemed as if, as the War raged all around, Watkins kept the garden safe within.

James's second experience was outside the wall.

In the long twilights of the summer evenings, he got into the habit of lying in the grass of the Great Park and watching the bombers take off.

It had long been common knowledge that there were thirteen aerodromes in the fifty-square-mile area.

Now the planes' activity seemed much increased. It was truly amazing: James felt like a lump of honey on a picnic for bees.

At every altitude, there were bombers – all British – circling for height. Lancasters, Sterlings and Halifaxes. . .

It would begin around seven, and then, just before dark, around ten – the whole sky would be black with planes

and, then, in the half-darkness, you would see them only by the incredible flashes of their exhausts – like machine guns in the night, sixteen to each engine, four engines to each plane – groaning with their great loads

One night, just as light was fading, and he was riding Fenders's bike towards Heighington, there was suddenly a great crack in the sky

He was knocked right off his bike – like being at sea again

purple and red and white flashes

and he was just congratulating himself that, fortunately, the explosion was a long way off when he put his hand up to his head. . .

Something sticky and warm and wet had slapped

his forehead and left ear

His hand looked reddish – it was blood and then he saw a piece of leather, fur-lined leather on his handlebars. . .

A helmet, just like Dad's from the First War – only this was a piece of one and covered in blood. . .

He saw a bike coming the other way – Bully Dickens, Dicky's brother. Embarrassed, James shook the bike, and let the piece of helmet fall to the grass verge.

He started back towards Washashley.

'Are ye all right?'

'Yes, thank you.'

'Did y'smash your face when bombers collided?'

'No, I think it was something from them.'

'Oh, ye'd better wash it off at pump – come on.'

Bully rode with him to the pump.

He washed his face off with his hands and cleaned off Fenders's bike with his handkerchief.

'Ye'd better not tell anyone – they'll only ask a lot of daft questions.'

James didn't want to tell anyone.

James had heard his father say: 'I missed out on public school – and that made me miss out on everything.'

His mother said: 'We've scrimp't and saved to put you boys through – it's the best opportunity known to Man.'

But when he saw Fotheringham: with its stone corridors and iron railings and nettings across the gaps of every stairwell (he quickly put that together: nothing but a suicide by diving over and on to the paving-stones below would have made the authorities do that) and its smells of wax and disinfectant; with its swagger sticks hanging handy for beatings on

435

study walls –

He regárded it as a war: and the message that went through his brain to his nervous system was: survive, survive this hell and this prison sentence for four years. . .

'There's the school song in Latin we have to learn,' said Pip Fenwick – 'I've got it half down cold now.'

'As far as I can make out,' said Herman – 'Shad', his nickname was, 'the most important portrait is in the School House dining-room. It's of Pilot Officer Peter Robinson-Kittish RAF VC. He has yellow hair and blue eyes, and he's the school's only VC. He was twenty when he got it – and it was posthumously awarded.'

'And then there's *two* graces in Latin,' said Rich, smiling and showing the pronounced but not unattractive gap between his bright front teeth.

'Why bloody two graces? Wouldn't one be enough?' said Larry Rhodes.

'One is before the meal and one after,' said Richmond.

'And I'll bet after four years we are heartily sick of them,' said James.

'Yes,' said Rich, who was clearly a considerable organizer. 'It says here grace is said before and after every meal, three times a day.'

'God.'

'Blimey,' said Block, the pale fellow with a very slight hint of a Cockney accent.

'And don't make a mistake with Cock – he's Captain of School House Odds and Captain of the School,' said Herman. 'And the balls on the school gates are called Cockey's Balls. A new boy last term called them Cock's Balls.'

'Jaysus,' said James, 'an easy enough mistake.'

'The weirdest bloke in School House is P.J. Broadlipp,' said Pip Fenwick. 'He doesn't believe in anything we believe in. He's Irish – and mad.'

'He's second-in-command of my dorm,' said James, who'd already decided that he rather liked Broadlipp. 'Tell me what you know?'

'He's a year our senior. He's a poet and he's crackers, that's all. And he's been beaten about five times and he doesn't care a damn.'

A few evenings later, in their dorm, Berkeley got a deep and amazing taste of Broadlipp's mind. His black eyes flashed as he talked:

'Yes. Well, the secret to understanding the British Empire is to know that it was deliberately fashioned on the Roman Empire – as, of course, is Mussolini's Empire in Italy and Abyssinia. And nowhere is this imitation more obvious than in the public schools.'

Broadlipp now took delight in playing the role of the man interviewing him.

'And Mr Broadlipp – I'd be glad if you would make that point about the age of public schools in Britain?'

'Certainly, yes. It was and is a fancy piece of humbug. Of course, they all want you to believe that the public school system is terrifically old – 1066, and all that. And there *are* some old English schools – like Winchester and Sherborne –

'But there are no old public schools. The whole system is Victorian – and late Victorian at that. All thought up by one Dr Arnold of Rugby who was a sort of Do-gooder Church of England Bully.'

'But I think we should – briefly and quickly, Mr Broadlipp – get down to details. What is the centre of the public schools, what do they worship?'

'The public schools worship what Mr G.B. Shaw, the great Irishman, called the seven deadly virtues – that is:

'Honour, Duty, Chastity, Industry, Discipline (of which Cleanliness is a part), Willpower and Patriotism – of which, of course, Religion is a part.'

'*Religion* is a part of patriotism – really, I think that's a bit extreme, Mr Broadlipp.'

'Do you? Well, you will notice that every day at Fotheringham, we go to Protestant chapel – twice – three times on Sundays.'

'Whether you are Catholic or Jewish?'

'Yes – and, at the end of the service, they pray not only for the King Emperor, but to him as head of their religion. Then we all stand up and sing to the Godhead, God Save the King.'

'I say, I think that's a bit steep, Mr Broadlipp.'

'And I think you'd better be careful, Broadlipp – or you'll get us all in trouble,' said James.

'Don't worry, Mr Berkeley. Mr Broadlipp has the ears of a Daemon.'

The other boys were looking absolutely bewildered.

'Strangely, Mr Berkeley, let me enlighten you to this fact: the greatest Roman Empire worshipper at Fotheringham is also one of the most intelligent and tender people here: Mr Scabby Stick who runs the library – and he designed it – and it's the best school library in Britain.

'And most boys tease him half to tears – because he has scabs on his scalp, from being gassed in the First War, which itch him. So don't you be a part of it, Mr Berkeley.'

'I won't, Mr Broadlipp.'

'Mr Broadlipp – will you please say something about public schools in comparison to prisons in Britain?'

'One can compare public schools with borstal institutions – prisons for juvenile offenders – and the borstal institutions come out milder on every level, except that public schools have holidays, three times a year.'

James was now smiling rather nervously.

'Have you anything further to say about Fotheringham now – Mr Broadlipp? I mean, something that you learned there? Some piece of the Classics – or even the Moderns you'd like to recite for us?'

Broadlipp danced about with his arms hanging long and loose like a gorilla's: 'Oompah, oompah – stick it up your jumpah.'

'Is that all you've learned, Mr Broadlipp, is that absolutely all you learned at public school?'

'Yes.'

'The school song,' said Rich Richmond, 'ends up: ". . . hunc scholam diligentibus, hunc Fotheringham, hanc Fotheringham, hanc Fotheringhamensibus. Sic Felicitat." '

'Oh golly, I'll never get it,' said Block.

'Somehow I will,' said Berkeley. 'Somehow.'

'Get it or get beaten?' said Rhodes. 'I'll get it – tonight.'

XXIII

*Christopher, Backwards Often,
Forwards Sometimes and
Probably, Sideways Frequently*
VII

'What I wanted to tell you, Dr Macdonald, is that one of the reasons that I am afraid I may have lost my mind, is because my father sort of – went around-the-bend. . .'

'How do you mean, around-the-bend?'

'In World War I – he went out of his head.'

'Oh. Did he tell you?'

'He and Mother – of course, Mother says he is just *weak*.'

'And how do you feel about that?'

'I guess he is weak – she wouldn't tell any lies. I mean – my father and I have not been close. I love him but. . . There's been some bad stuff.'

'Perhaps you should tell me about the "bad stuff".'

'Doctor, I wanted to ask you first – I mean – I beg your pardon, I wanted to get it straight. I'm afraid to fly right now. I don't want to fly right now. I don't want to fight any more.'

'Christopher, I would say that as long as I have anything to do with it, that any question of your flying any more would only be when *you* want to. There's no question of you being a shirker of your duty.

'As to fighting any more, I would say that that is absolutely not to be recommended by any competent person, as to be in your future.'

'Why, sir –? Sorry, I mean, Doctor?'

'Well, you have shell-shock – and it takes a very long time to get over it. And, a part of your cure must essentially be the knowledge that you will not be required to be in action any more.'

'I don't want to kill any more – anyone.'

'*I* understand – and I will do my utmost. However, although I don't believe anyone here would go above my decision – I must warn you, Chris, that I'm not a marshal of the RAF. Only one of them could give an order that couldn't be countermanded.'

'I guess I understand.'

'Perhaps you could give me an example of your father being weak – I don't mean to pry, of course. My father, I can't remember him at all – only a shaking hand on a teacup.'

440

'I'm sorry.'

'It's all right. He died when I was five.'

'My mother says he is weak – example – our little cousin fell down these very steep stairs at West Hill in Bermuda. Mother is at the top, yelling at Father to catch the boy – who is pitching headlong.

'Mother yells at Father. Father stands stock-still and watches as if frozen, then steps aside. Lets our cousin hit his head on the wall at the bottom.

'Mother yells at Father, how could you be so stupid – as to just let him hit the wall? You were there, why didn't you catch him?'

'And your father said, what?'

'Never heard him say anything about it – that's what makes me think she's probably right.'

'Maybe, at the time, he protested. Does she go on about this incident?'

'She goes on about every incident. She is always making him out to be worthless – a coward – just a businessman – everything bad.'

'I don't think,' Dr Macdonald says quietly, 'it's recommended that we catch a falling child without professional apparatus – I think the danger is that if we touch them we can do them worse harm. It's best to let them hit – and then pick up from there. Least, that's my training.

'But there's been this unhappiness between you and your father before?'

'Yes. I think I partly hate him and he maybe doesn't like me too much – except that now he's sent. . .'

'Love and hate are two sides of one coin. Fathers and sons, Chris, are notorious for both hating as well as loving each other – especially first sons.'

'Oedipus,' says I.

'Indeed. So you're your mother's favourite, is that it?'

441

'Well, I am and I am not. I'm her first-born and she makes a lot of fuss over that. But Teddy, my closest brother, is her favourite – the one she favours.'

'Do you know why?'

'His looks, I think. He's got this Grecian profile and a dark complexion – olive. She says he looks like a Greek god.'

'And you? What do you look like?'

'I'm supposed to be the Good Knight.'

'An uncomfortable person to be.'

'Why?'

'Good Knights are on pedestals – jolly hard to go to the bathroom on a pedestal. Or to make love?'

'I've only made love twice...' These stupid tears start down my face.

Silence.

A long silence.

'Well, some things are too too painful.'

'Yes.'

Then the doctor says with his gentle cheerfulness: 'What is that that you have there?'

'Oh this – I didn't know if I should bring it. If it would be allowed? It's my Father's *Journal* of the First War...'

'So you borrowed it to have a look at his war?'

'No, he sent it to me – from Bermuda. You see it says – very childish – STRICTELY PRIVATE – so young, he couldn't even spell.

'He sent it to me. Because, he says, he feels terrible that he can't get here – but he's building these ships – wooden ships – Fairmiles. Sub-chasers, for the Royal Navy. He feels he should be here to help me. He knows I've lost my mind as he did.

'So, he apologizes for the *Journal* – because he says it doesn't show him in good light – but bad. Shows

442

him, he says, he guesses, as, if not a coward, certainly something close to it. Someone who cracked up.

'But he says – here in his letter – "I send it to you just in case something I went through can in some way help you. Fathers are supposed to help their sons – and I haven't helped you. I've marked the most powerful places: four – but, although it's an awful confessional thing, you can read any of it that will help. Your everloving, Dad. P.S. I will get over the moment I can – and I've some fancy ropes I can pull!" '

'Do you want to read part of it to me then, Chris? Is that it?'

'Yes. All right. If I can – here's a part he marked. He's at Chingford in Essex, near Epping Forest, February 1916 when he was just a kid of nineteen, learning to fly.

'It says – a little back here it says: ". . . This habit I have of falling in love over and over has got to be stopped."

'It says: "Sunday February 20th 1916. Got in a rolling flip of five minutes at 1:30." A flip is a flight, Doctor. Goes on, "Saw Tom crash and burn to death at three. His fuel tank exploded and he appeared to have his strap jammed and could not get out.

' "He fell across the River Lee which is about twenty feet across or more.

' "We couldn't get across at first. I had to run from the sheds and when I got there several had swum the river and were doing their best to get him out. The heat was terrible and they could not reach him.

' "When one person did – before I got near – they found that the strap would have to be cut.

' "When I got there the flames were all around him. I couldn't figure what to do. The heat was incredible. An old engineer petty officer knew to pull the rear part of the machine around – like a weathercock –

443

rear to the wind.

' "And Tom rolled out on the ground with both feet burnt completely off, arms also. His face burnt off and his eyes burnt out – a most terrible sight to look at.

' "For a long time we heard his pitiful cries – he was quite conscious. He said, 'Doctor, where are my legs?' and, 'I play centre-forward –' He's screaming it. 'For Upper Canada College.' And 'Why can't I see?'

' "Once he held up his arms to show that he was helpless and I could see the flesh slowly burning off.

' "The sight of that poor fellow, my friend, sitting hunched up, crunched up, watching the flames creep up upon him and slowly burn him up, made a sight that I will always be able to see.

' "Out of the black mess that was his face came one last word when all believed life had long left him. 'Mother!'

' "The worst death imaginable. We did so try to get him out. Murray nearly did reach him and then dashed back crying 'My God, I can't reach him it's too hot.'

' "They poured oil on him and it was awful to look. If it is my lot to be killed pray God not to be burnt as poor Tom" '

Silence.

'That is very very touching. So your Dad went from boyhood to manhood in one afternoon. His baptism to fire was indeed that, wasn't it?'

'Yes. Awful.'

'He got a very great deal of war in one ghastly lesson. More than the average person experiences in a whole war, I mean.'

'Yes, Doctor – and here, a little later, 2nd March 1916. . . ' "Rob and I picked up a couple of girls and took them to the forest – no luck." Rob was his best friend from his hometown, Grimsby, Canada.

444

'A little later, Doctor, Rob is killed, but here he is: "Sad to relate Rob went into the hotel and came out a little tight and I had a bad time getting him home to bed and keeping it quiet." '

'Terrible. I suppose Rob was drinking on account of the burning.'

'Yes. I would guess so. Anyway, here's Monday, March 6th 1916. "Spent afternoon in cleaning the parts of poor Tom's machine. Rotten and ghastly job as it brought back memories." '

'Very, very rough experience. The authorities cleaning the man off the machine – saving the machine and hurting the man – several men. Very bad, Christopher.'

'And here, Doctor, on the 24th March, he goes to Lincoln to go and see his uncle whom he has only met once – but he must have wanted some family sympathy. But Uncle Albert sent his man to the station – and guess what means of transport they had to get home to the Hall in?'

'Don't know.'

'They walked. It's three miles, past the cemeteries and the sewage farm. Father wrote his own song of that war, it was called, "Moonlight On The Sewage Farm". Anyway, so Dad left the next day for London and Chingford again.'

'Here, Doctor. "March 27 1916. Rob took his first solo and in consequence got horribly drunk as did about a dozen others." My father seems very upset at his friend's behaviour.'

'Well, it's very understandable, isn't it? I mean, after their solo – comes the possibility of burning up. To their minds after solo comes burning up. The man who burned was a solo pilot, wasn't he?'

'Yes. And there are countless references to how terribly hard the planes are to fly – of course, being my Dad, he blamed himself and not the aircraft.'

'And the aircraft were very bad, obviously.'

'Yes – they tended to ground-loop – and to pull over with torque – not to mention being the worst craft to fly. And the fuel tank was over your lap.'

'Very convenient for catching fire, eh, Chris?'

I really like the Doctor's face – he looks like your most concerned best chum, only older.

'Says here: "March 31. Very dejected as made a bollocks of my flip. Up and down, up and down. I was rotten. This may mean I may never be able to fly." Truth was, Doctor, they were impossible planes – they didn't know enough to teach people to fly properly anyway. They taught them all wrong. But here, even the old-fashioned authorities soon had to scrap this aircraft.

'However, here is his worst time, Doctor: "Sunday April 30th 1916. Rob killed at 10:30 and I had to go up to London to cable. . . His death is a terrible blow and I would rather not make any further mention of it. The only friend I ever had gone from out of my life."

' "Tues. May 9th 1916. . . Stayed up 65 minutes – and had a crash."

' "Thursday May 11th 1916. . . Had a good flip and was greatly pleased to hear that I had been given my ticket without really flying for it. . ."

' "Sat. May 20. Cranwell. Got settled and ready for the new station which is a hell of a nice place." '

'So hold up a bit, Chris,' says Dr Macdonald. 'I take it this settles the matter of your father being weak or a coward?'

'Oh. I guess he was just sensitive.'

'But certainly no coward. Seems certainly very hard on himself.'

'And they were getting nightly Zeppelin raids down there – also.'

446

'But, Christopher, I was thinking that it takes an incredible amount of courage – even cold nerve – to fly an unstable plane that both, you have crashed, and you've lost two friends to, into the bargain. Yet your Dad managed it, didn't he? And you said the planes were very bad.

'So we could say he was a rather special young man, couldn't we?'

'Do you really think so, Doctor?'

'I do indeed. And there's the big act of courage.'

'What's that?'

'To send the *Journal* over at all – he took the chance of you hating him. I take it he still doesn't have a very great opinion of himself?'

'I guess not.'

'Well, I would say, that this, then, is his big act of courage in this War. That your Dad will – in fact – draw fire – or run the risk of drawing fire on himself – to help you.'

'Yes. I did think it was awful about his friend Rob. You see, Doctor, he has told me that Rob was killed crashing on the railway tracks at Chingford.

'Then he was sweeping mines in 1917 and 1918. But he also crashed at Cranwell – where they assumed he had been killed. He further said they sent out the garbage truck – but he sent them back for the ambulance.

'Actually, you see, Doctor – he hasn't sent me the *other* diary – and that is when he went out of his mind.'

'So there were the three crashes at Chingford – counting the burning – and then one at Cranwell. I think that would be enough to put anyone out of their mind, wouldn't it? To give him shell-shock.'

'Yes. I guess so.'

'Then there's still another piece of brave conduct

447

your father seems to have –'

'What's that?'

'Takes a bit of nerve to write it down. To keep a *Journal* like that.'

'Do you think so, Doctor?'

'Indeed I do. Is he a writer?'

'He tried to be – but he had to give it up. I'm a writer – but I've had to give it up too.'

'Well, only temporarily. You can begin again any time you like.'

'No, I can't, Doctor. That is perhaps the most awful thing the War has done to me – I can't write. I've dried up.'

'Well, if you could find a way to beginning again – it would help you, just as, I imagine, it helped your Dad in 1916.'

'I hadn't thought of that.'

'It would be very helpful to your recovery now.'

'Doctor, there's two questions I wanted to ask you. One is about this premonition I had of death in France. In the Forest of Correze. I had this premonition. I knew I was going to die.'

'Oh.'

'I have this extra sense – sometimes I know when things are going to happen.'

'Oh.'

'Yes. I knew I was going to die. Not exactly when, but that it was going to be soon. But I think that what I had was a premonition of the death of Piquette.'

'Your lover?'

'Yes.'

'But you don't know she is dead.'

'No.'

'Well. Let's hope she's not. You can, after all, make inquiries. And, Christopher – although it may not feel like it now, this war *is* going to *end*.

448

'It *is*. This war is going to end.'

'You really think it is?'

'Yes, all the other wars have come to an end – and this one will too.'

'Good. You see, Doctor, when I flew over Dieppe – I had this strange experience. I began to realize that it was all a trick – it was betrayal.'

'How?'

'I mean – like a big diversion – for something else. A raid must be a surprise. No one must know of it. Dieppe was put off for a month. The Germans were waiting. It was an all-Canadian affair. Everytime it's an all-colonial anything – it's like Gallipoli.'

Dr Macdonald writes something in his notebook – what the hell is he doing, he said he didn't keep notes.

'Was your father at Gallipoli?'

'No.'

'Any of your family?'

'No.'

'But you were flying at Dieppe and you are in the RAF – not the RCAF? Right?'

'Yes.'

'And you are from Bermuda?'

'From Bermuda and Lincoln – both places.'

'But your dad is Canadian?'

'Canadian and Bermudian and British.'

'Oh.'

'Doctor. Another question is: how soon will they make me go back to flying?'

'I don't think they will.'

'Forgive me, Doctor – but I do. I wanted to ask you one more thing please?'

'Yes. Then our time, just for today, is up.'

'It's about this man – this French policeman I killed in the Forest of Correze. I killed him with a .22 calibre automatic. He would not die. He was like a

449

dumb bull who wouldn't die.

'I shot at him and shot at him. And he wouldn't die – but then he did and I put him in the pond – but he wouldn't sink. So I put his bicycle on top – and his rifle and then he sank.

'He had braces on his trousers just like our man – our man O'Neill who was a very decent working bloke – And I thought the policeman was a German disguised as French. But he was a French working man – really.'

Silence.

'Yes. I can see this would be very very distressing.'

'And please don't write down what I've said.'

'I won't.'

'The last reference before his death, about Rob Liddle, in my Dad's *Journal* is a funny one – at Washashley Hall – it says, "Rob – The-Mechanical-Wizard, got the entire French lighting system, which has never been used since Uncle Albert bought the house in 1897. Rob got this strange electric-gas system going. Lit up whole of Washashley Hall – all in one night. Then Rob played billiards with the butler!" So Uncle Albert must have been thrilled with Rob, to let that happen. It would have taken a great event to break down that barrier even for one game. To understand the scene, one must realize that Rob Liddle from Grimsby, Canada, probably had never seen a butler before.'

'Well, you start writing *your* Journal again, all right? What kind of an aircraft was it your dad flew?'

'The engine was a Le Rhone. I think the aircraft was a Blériot.'

XXIV

Fotheringham II

'Boy!' screamed any praeposter, and ten to twenty new boys bust and scrambled over each other to get the job.

'Clean these shoes.' 'Make our tea.' 'Make toast.' 'Get my football boots from the changing rooms and scrape them and dubbin them – and get back.'

There never was such an efficient and fast-learning group as Richmond, Fenwick, Rhodes, Herman, Block and Berkeley – at least, that was what they figured.

They soon discovered that the most sacred moments at Fotheringham came during chapel, just before the last hymn, when the headmaster, Mr Walking, got up, in his robes, to make 'The Announcement'.

There would be an expectant stillness among all gathered. . .

'Notice has come to me that the following old boys have been killed in action: Second Lieutenant John Smythe RA, nineteen. Lieutenant-Commander Hugh Keane Burch RNVR, thirty-two. . .'

The headmaster made 'The Announcement' about once a week. Mr Walking's voice would shake with emotion, and James would feel the skin tighten at the nape of his neck. . .

(Every week new deaths, more names to chip in the chapel memorial. 'But they'll never catch up to the last war – just look at the size,' said Rich. There were indeed, hundreds for that war, only scores for this one.)

'The Announcement' would end with: 'Let us stand and observe two minutes silence and prayerfully honour these men who have given their lives for us.'

Larry Rhodes said: 'Certainly makes it difficult, not being able to talk to anyone except those a year or less one's senior – but where there's a will, there's a way. Besides, my Dad's a fair operator.'

'Really,' said Berkeley. 'I bet he knows a lot.'

'You needn't spread it around – but that's what my Dad does – he has a part of Brighton Pier. When he comes, you must come out with us. We have a Chrysler.'

'Damned decent of you. So look – those guys, Callum and Broadlipp, they can help us. Right?'

'Yes. I do believe so,' said Larry Rhodes knowingly. 'And Broadlipp seems to like you – and Callum definitely likes Lord Pip Fenwick.'

'Is he a Lord?'

'No. But his Dad is. And Broadlipp – the funny Irishman – he fancies you.'

'Oh, stop it. I've no time for that. I've got my "Boys" to get.'

'But that's what makes the world go round,' smiled Larry.

'You'd better be *damned* careful who you say it to,' said James.

'And don't I know it, Berkeley – but I figured you were one who knew it too.'

'What?'

'That – in this place, as in the world, it's who likes who that matters.'

And James knew Larry was right: 'But it's just some people are attractive, some less so. Some are attracted to some, others to others.'

452

'And here, Jim – they call it a "pash". Right now, Knightly has a pash on Richmond – loves his curly head. Callum has a pash on Fenwick.'

'It may be, Larry. But no one owns up to it. It's like the lies people tell outside – in the world. You know, how it isn't what people say – but what they say underneath.'

'You've got it, mate. I knew you and I would be pals.'

'Thanks. Good. Glad to be pals with you. But, this kind of talk is not for anyone else.'

'I agree. But I think Richmond is a real straight-shooter.'

'Well, Larry, be careful how you go.'

'I wouldn't tell anyone else about my Dad running an amusement park – I can tell you, Berkeley.'

'Well, I'm a colonial – so we are, sort of, two of a kind.'

'God, you know what I hate most about this place – the lavatories?'

' "Lats" they are called. Me too – no doors – it's horrible.'

'Inhuman. Are you really going out for boxing?'

'Yes. I used to do it in Bermuda. And my older brother was a boxer at Harrow.'

'Not me, mate. I'm an actor. I'd rather not get my mug smashed.'

Larry's 'mug' looked very like a pretty girl's – and he, James noted, like himself and Fenwick and Richmond, had not even begun puberty.

Block and Herman already had dark upper-lips – and the gaunt paleness that seemed to accompany this change in life. . .

'Obviously,' said Rich, 'we've got to do something to quietly impress the House.'

'Agreed – we're the bottom. Let's make a good mark,' said James.

'Fives,' said Pip Fenwick, 'is the place for us. We could be Even's Junior Fives Team.'

'But none of us has played Fives,' said Herman.

'No one has. So, if we start off quickly, we'll be ahead.' Fenwick had a quick smile to go with his very dark complexion and his small attractive body.

('It's Callum he wants to be with,' said Rhodes when they were alone.)

'Could be a good idea – the six of us going out for fives – hard as we can. Bet we'd make it. We were all games captains at our prep schools.'

They all agreed.

Block said, rather sourly: 'Someone's not going to make it.'

'Why?'

'Well, look there.'

They followed his pointing hand. They had all changed and got ready for Fives and when they got to the courts, Fenwick was already there, getting what seemed to be a lesson from Guy Callum – a boy two terms their senior.

'He's really quick – and good,' said Berkeley.

'You mean cute and fast.'

'I'll box and you act – and we'll both play Fives.'

Rich said: 'I'm for old soccer and Fives.'

So it was with Block and Herman.

'Fenwick will fence, I'll bet.'

'Why, Rhodes?'

'Bloody Callum fences.'

'Boy!'

You had to know when to be where and when not. You had to know which praeposters gave more than one 'Boy' on your card for a good shoeshine.

'You have to move – Berkeley – move.'

'I'm moving. I've got nine "Boys".'

Larry showed a full card of twelve. Then he smiled and pulled another out of his blazer pocket – it had another twelve.

'You clever bastard.'

'When was the school founded?'

'1597.'

'Who by?'

'Richard Platt.'

'Right.'

'When is the Chivvy?'

'Tomorrow night.'

'All right – let's all six of us rehearse.'

The very first day, James had found it incredibly hard to tie a stiff collar – to get the tie and the collar and shirt all together and tie the knot all at once.

He had practised at Washashley with Fenders – but he hadn't got it right.

They had fifteen minutes to dress and make their beds and get down to 'Call' at 7:30. He tried everything and it wouldn't work – so he made his bed, got dressed in every other way including his black jacket and black shoes and then he tried again.

A bit better – but then his fingers slipped and he seemed to have bent the collar. He checked his watch. Six minutes left.

Broadlipp said: 'Fasten the shirt, then the collar – holding the tie ends up. Then tie the knot.' Then Broadlipp flew out of the door and down the steps.

Four minutes... With two minutes left, James did it. He had amazed even himself. It was so with everything in the early days...

'You box before?' asked a very tough-looking boy

455

named Tyder.

'Yeah,' said James, feigning nonchalance.

Tyder appeared to be Oriental and he was tough and he was also very quiet.

They paired off and started sparring. The gym – the converted chapel – was full of boys in pairs, sparring. At the opposite end, the fencers were fencing. They swapped a few blows.

James threw a couple of combinations – pulling his punches. Tyder did the same.

Without saying a word they communicated: I know a good bit about boxing.

Yeah, and I do too – do you know this?

No – and how about this?

Tyder was not only tough and quick, he was inscrutable. James knew a bit about that asset. He knew that, in a contest, you needed to add the act: I can never even be hurt: All your blows make me laugh.

James had learned the hard way: boxing with his elder brothers – and, Ted was a teasing bully who liked best to hold you with his superior reach.

James had also had a few street fights and Tyder had too. . .

James figured: his streets were Hong Kong or Singapore; mine Bermuda – but Bermudian Portuguese and Bermudian Negroes too. . .

Their efforts soon brought the sergeant major.

'You, boy,' he grabbed Berkeley. 'Do what you was doing – to him – to me.'

James did – still pulling his punches. 'Go on. Bloody well 'it me, boy.'

James threw feints and combinations and hit the sergeant – a bit harder, but still pulling his punches.

'You see what he does – there – do it again. I want you all to see.

'What's your name?'

456

'Berkeley.'

'Well, you're all right, Berkeley. We can use you. Do it again. But hit me. Go on, hit me.'

James knew perfectly well he could hit the sergeant-major – and hit him hard. But that was not smart. . .

So he hit him a halfway punch.

'That's more like it,' the sergeant-major sputtered. 'But now I can hit you back.'

James let the sergeant do it. There was a counter-cross here he could have, but didn't, throw.

'And what's your name?'

'Tyder, sir.'

'You don't have to sir me, Tyder. I'm Sergeant Bucking. You are both damn good – keep it up.'

Tyder and Berkeley were to spar with each other for three years – to fight each other in two terrible bouts in which neither sparring partner gave an ounce of quarter.

In the sparring, they never hurt each other – no more than lambs. In the contests they tore each other apart. They had an immense respect one for the other: all their exchanges were of the eyes.

Tyder was Odds and Berkeley was Evens – yet in three years, strangely, they never spoke a single sentence to each other. . .

James Berkeley's reputation for and as a boxer spread – but he wasn't really aware of it.

He knew he was a good boxer: so was Tyder: Tyder was the toughest opponent he'd ever known – perhaps. Perhaps even as tough as 'Ears' Hayward, of Bermuda, who'd died of leukaemia. . . Ears had had a crouch into which he could disappear and from which he could clean your clock. . .

'Look what it says:

' "This Free Grammar School was founded through the Charity of Richard Platt Esq Brewer of the City of London For The Poor of This And Adjoining Parishes Anno Domini 1597",' Larry Rhodes read the plaque that was over the School House side door.

'Free! My old man says it's costing him a king's ransom.'

'The food should be free.'

'And there's no heating,' said Larry.

'And they cane us,' said Richmond, giving James a friendly shove.

James said, hoping to make Rich laugh, for he really liked Richmond the most and hoped they would become best friends. . . 'The school where they charge half a prince's ransom to have us half-frozen, half-starved and half-beaten to death.'

'I heard that.' It was Knightly, appearing out of nowhere. 'Berkeley, I'll see you in my study at six – just before supper. You hear?'

'Yes, Knightly.'

When Knightly had gone, Rich Richmond said: 'He can't actually beat you – I don't think – until we've been here six weeks.'

'We've been here six weeks,' said Pip Fenwick – with a touch of a smile. 'As a matter of fact – seven.'

'You'd better put blotting paper in your trousers,' said Block. 'That'll help.'

'Then you'll get six instead of three.'

James was terrified: he felt he was still smarting from his beating at The Lion School. That was the only time he'd ever been beaten with a swagger stick.

'I'm awful sorry, Jim,' said Larry Rhodes. 'I'll give you a piece of my cake later.'

'Thanks.'

458

'Maybe Cock will step in and help you,' said Rich.

James had been hoping that himself. But, as the hour of six approached, a suspenseful hush fell over School House, much like a jail, he thought, at the time of an execution...

People were smiling with excitement – and it made Berkeley angry and even more afraid.

What was Chris's advice? They can't kill you. But they sure can hurt you.

The worst news was: Cock was away at Westminster playing Eton Fives for the school ... Cock was Captain of Soccer, Fives, Hockey, Cricket – and the School

'Maybe I should go and see Mr Parrot,' James said. 'He's our Housemaster, isn't he?'

'Wouldn't help. Sneaky-Doyly-Pee never interferes between praeposters and boys,' a second-year boy said.

'Is that what he is called?'

'Yes – sneaks about in his rubber shoes. Likes to catch people. Has his teddy-bears on top of his wardrobe.'

At exactly the moment the clock struck the first note of six in the Great Tower, Berkeley rapped on the head praeposter's study door.

'Come in.'

Knightly was there – alone in the half-light of evening.

'What is it?' said Knightly, facing his fireplace.

'Berkeley, Knightly – you sent for me.'

'Yes, Berkeley. I really ought to send you to the Headmaster. The least I should do is send you to our Housemaster – what is his name, Berkeley?'

'Parrot – Mr D. Parrot.'

'Well, that's what I should do – but, instead, I'll

459

keep your betrayal of the school between us. Go to the next-door study and ask a praeposter for witness – go.'

James's stomach was like Bermudian jellyfish pumping against the tide – but he betrayed not a flick of emotion as he stared at Knightly and then moved as directed.

Some inner or inherited cunning helped him.

He went out. Knocked on the next door.

'Excuse me. Knightly would like a praeposter for witness.'

'I'd love to,' said one.

'Stop that,' said another.

'Whose turn?'

'Mine,' said the first.

Back in Knightly's study, Knightly was swinging his swagger stick through the air in preparation.

'Bend over.'

He bent over the small oak chair, touching the seat of it.

'Touch the bloody floor, Berkeley.'

'Easy,' said the praeposter witness – whose name was Burns. 'Is this really necessary?'

'You can get out if you don't like it.' Knightly cut the air with his swagger stick like a fencing sword.

Berkeley was half over the chair.

'Touch the floor I said.'

Berkeley touched his fingers to the floor.

Knightly swung: ONE

James saw stars of pain.

Knightly swung again: TWO

James was knocked half off balance.

'Are you flinching, Berkeley?'

'No,' said Berkeley without any inflection but clarity.

THREE.

'Now you can get out, Berkeley.'

In the latrines, James tried to check his behind – there was no way to see it, because there were no mirrors as well as no doors. But, after he'd touched his hand over his buttocks, it came away with the stain of blood.

'Blimey,' said Block, the first of their gang to arrive. 'Did he do that? He must have put chalk on the stick and hit you in the same place – once or twice.'

'Yeah,' said Herman – who seemed to like these facts – 'Look – there's the chalk.'

James stared at his two friends, then he pulled his flannel trousers back up.

'Let's see,' said Pip Fenwick, rushing in.

'Leave me be,' said James.

'Don't be like that – did it hurt much?' said Herman.

'You'll have to wait until you get yours,' James heard himself say – both voice and statement, he thought, quite unlike himself. . .

'Here's the cake,' said Rhodes. 'Fresh from my tuck box. Put it in your pocket for later – for after supper, we've to rush now.'

'Sorry, Berkeley,' said Rich – 'But now you've had the worst – and you are our star in a way, aren't you?'

James smiled – it was now hurting more and he was wondering about the bench he'd have to sit on for tea – supper.

In the middle of some nights, for several weeks, James would wake himself up hollering – or just afraid he'd hollered out. . .

'You're all right, mate,' said Broadlipp, the night of James's caning. 'Nothing worse can happen to you, you know. You can have that sense – they can't do

461

anything worse to you.'

'They could give me six.'

'But even six wouldn't be so bad, would they – now that you know?'

'Maybe you are right. My older brother – Chris – says, always remember they can't kill you.'

'That's a good one. The English bastards – all they understand is beating, beef, battleships, bayonets, and buggery.'

'I beg your pardon, but don't you consider yourself British?'

Broadlipp frequently amazed James – he went to the ancient latticed window, opened it with a loud creak – and spat outside.

'That's to the part of me that's British, Berkeley.'

'Good God – but what are you if you aren't British?'

'Irish – you prick.'

'But you are at a British public school?'

'I'm an Irish aristocrat – that's why. I'm descended from Irish kings. But I wish I wasn't here.'

'What could be better than here?'

'Anywhere, you idiot. Once you are in a public school – it's like the old joke – nothing-further-can-happen-to-you.'

'What's the joke?'

'I'll tell you later.'

'Jesus Christ, you'd better be careful.'

'I am. Don't worry.'

'Why did Knightly do it?'

'He's stupid – that's why. You can't make jokes about the system with Knightly. If Cock had been there – he would have stopped it.'

'Oh.'

'Knightly is afraid of me.'

'Why?'

'Because of my mind and my tongue. I think he's a

bit afraid of you too – otherwise he'd not have done it.'

Broadlipp gave James some salve. 'Put this on your bum. It won't hurt and it will heal. It's what Grimsby fishermen use – for cut hands. Take it and shut up – the others are coming and I'm not supposed to be friendly with you.'

'Thank you very much, Broadlipp.'

'So, who's made the Junior Fives Team Finals?' said Larry Rhodes.

It was incredibly well done: under the school's dignified coat-of-arms were the words, in Cock's handsome handwriting:

The Following Will Represent School House Evens in The School Finals:

Callum G. *Captain*
Fenwick R.
Richmond R.F.
Rhodes L.
Berkeley J.B.
Herman H.G.

'It's out of order,' said Berkeley.

'Right, you should be with me,' said Richmond.

'And,' whispered Larry Rhodes: 'Block should be playing and not Shad Herman – because Block is better.'

Block had not heard this but soon he came by. His face registered intense hurt.

'You can't win, can you?'

'Better luck next time, Mac,' said James.

'Yes, Block – that's bad luck,' said Rich.

'I'll live.'

463

XXV

Christopher Backwards Often,
Forwards Sometimes and
Probably, Sideways Frequently
VIII

'So, Christopher Berkeley – how are you today?'

'All right, thank you. I'm writing.'

'What, your *Journal*?'

'Yes. I started by putting down the date – Tuesday 16th December 1943 – and I go from there.'

'Just as your Dad did?'

'Yes.'

'Well, that's very good. If nothing else, it helps you get better. It helps the shell-shock. But, with you, it can be a way back to your career.'

'What do you know about my career? I'm an aviator.'

'But you told me two days ago you are a writer.'

'Sorry. I'd forgotten.'

Silence.

'What am I supposed to do, Doctor?'

'Nothing – if you don't want. But if I can help – the way to the greatest amount of help is for you to say the first thing that comes in your head.'

'Oh, that's how it works – Freudian analysis.'

'Yes.'

'Oh. Well, right now I'm thinking of a Bermudian sloop my grandfather used to steer – a sloop called the *Nea*.'

'Nice name.'

'It was a beauty of a cedar sloop – the first really

truly Bermudian yacht. Our ancestors have sailed these sloops all over the world – for a living. Only in my grandfather's time did we really get to sailing just for the sheer beauty of it.'

'And that's why you like flying?'

'Yes. They are very alike. My other grandfather – Berkeley. I just discovered from Dad's *Journal* – *he* was in love with flying too.

'You see, Doctor. Flying is sacred to me. . .'

'Probably was to your Dad and to his Dad.'

'Right. Sometimes, when flying, Doctor – you won't laugh, will you?'

'Not likely, Chris. We've pretty serious business here – I'll not laugh – *at* you – but I will with you.'

'Sometimes when flying, I have felt the presence of all the young men who have dreamed of levitation. I've felt them all around me like invisible fluttering wings.'

Silence.

'I went back after our last session, Doctor, and I suddenly started crying – like a bloomin' baby.'

'Over the friends you've lost.'

'How did you know?'

'Well, your Dad was mentioning his losses – your pain was bound to emerge.'

'I've lost two close chums – and most of my class at Cranwell now. You get numb – and then along comes Dad's *Journal*.'

'Yes.'

'Only friend I lost to fire was a little dog – Patience I called her. The ground crew at Plymouth did it. It was an accident at first – but they were bored and they set her a-fire – when anyone gets sentimental about the RAF, I like to remember that they also set my little dog on fire while I was up and away – oh, to hell with it.

465

'Next I lost a friend who got his canopy stuck from heat. It happens a lot. Actually, he was the only Canadian in our squadron. His chute burned – he was hollering out. He went into the drink on fire – singing, oh God – he was singing "O Canada" all off-key – the silly sod. He said he didn't want to sing "God Save The King" – because it was "My Country 'Tis Of Thee" and American. All this on our two-way radio. I'd never heard "O Canada" before –'

I start weeping like a leaky punt and so it takes several minutes for the session to get airborne again.

'Hence your upset over Dieppe.'

'You mean I shouldn't have been upset?'

'Oh, no, you've every reason. But I think *some* of your upset was irrational. After all – you can't say it was a totally Canadian show if you were there – and you are RAF and not RCAF.'

Another silence.

'Doctor. About my drinking. I had no need to drink while I was in France. Now I want to drink all the time.'

'Were you a lot with your girl?'

'Some. When I wasn't with her I was running – Come to think of it, when I *was* with her I was running too.'

'Did you fall in love with her right away?'

'Yes. Almost as soon as we had met.'

'So she filled the gap that you drank to fill – before – and want to now.'

'I was thinking of my losses in relation to Dad's – and that all my losses are nothing in relation to Piquette.'

'And what's the news of her?'

'Silence. I've got the British Red Cross and the American Red Cross. And my chum, Colonial Aussi-Variety, he's got the Australian and Canadian Red

Cross. And we've an Agency in Switzerland.

'But there is just this horrible silence – as soon as one mentions that she was Jewish and that she and her father were involved in the French Resistance Party – as soon as people hear this – there is this immediate silence like the throwing up of hands.

'Despair. That's what it adds up to. And Doctor, I am my Grandfather Halcyon's grandson – that is, I'm a one girl man.'

'I understand.'

'I am – was, and am, very shy of women. So she was the first woman I touched.'

Silence.

'What did she call you?'

'La Mouette. She called me La Mouette – it was partially a joke. But Doctor, it was the smell of that woman. . . It *is* the smell of her.

'She smells like Angostura Bitters and salt sea – but she also smells like mushrooms. I haven't told anyone, Doctor, but her parts smell of mushrooms.'

'That's a lovely thing, isn't it, Chris?'

'I'm glad you think so. I thought it would shock you.'

'Not at all. That's love. Smells and tastes as well as the rest, of course.'

'Yes. And tastes – and the look of her. Her eyes are very bright like a little animal's – yellow. And she's this yellow-brown hair and a small hooked nose – like a Greek – and an owl too. And she's as French as the Loire – she moves as if she's French.

'There's a quality to the French people, Doctor – earthy. They should have taken half the people in Britain and made them marry half the people in France – then we'd have a decent happy island.'

'We've done that, you know. That is, they did it to us.'

467

'Oh, yes?'

'It was called the Norman Conquest.'

'Too long ago. Look Doctor, I've this friend here, Harold. Harold has been on Bomber Command. And Harold keeps saying – and I understand. He keeps saying, his kids are going to ask him, what did you do in the War, Dad? And he's going to say: "At a conservative estimate, I killed 17,250 old men and women and children." '

'Oh, it's Harold M.'

'Yes. Himself. I quite understand him, Doctor. And he's not mad. He just doesn't want to kill any more.'

'And you?'

'Me too. But I wanted also to tell you of this dream I have: it's a dream in which Hitler starts off looking like my father and then looks like Churchill. I call him, Adolph Churchill. And he just orders – killing killing killing until everyone surrenders unconditionally. So what do you make of that?'

'The Hitler being like your dad could be – *could* be, I'm not saying it is, it could be that you think that there is something of Hitler in you.'

'You're damn right. I think the evil of this War is US – all of us. Me, in particular.

'And as to Jews. There's no more anti-semitic places than the public schools. I know. I was at Harrow.'

'Well, I agree with you. The evil that created and creates war is everywhere. Chris, I didn't understand before quite how deep your mind is – for your years, that is. It's pretty unusual.'

'Chrissake – on my next birthday I'll be twenty-three, Doctor.'

Silence.

'I wanted to tell you – yesterday – last time – whenever – The *Journal* didn't say that Dad hid his glasses under his goggles. He was not allowed to fly and wear

468

glasses – so he hid them.'

'Your Dad emerges as quite a scrapper – a scrapper with life.'

'I hadn't realized. I'm learning such a lot. You see, I was so *dumb*, Doctor. I was seeing us in the RAF as the Knights of the Sky.'

'But, in a way, you are.'

'What, and kill seventeen thousand two hundred and fifty old men, women and children? Impossible. We drop blockbusters that systematically destroy whole cities.'

'Well, that's the bad. The good is the Battle of Britain and you aviators saving us from Hitler.'

'I wasn't in the Battle of Britain and my dream is really about, Doctor, about seeing Churchill and Hitler as two captains of a sort of deformed soccer match. . .'

'But Mr Churchill, for all his faults, is a far more noble bloke than Hitler.'

'Why?'

'To start with, Churchill is like you and me – good and bad. A good and bad bloke. He rabble-rouses, he yells and shouts and leads us into the bloody fray – but he also paints and he writes. . . And, I'd guess, laddie, he knows a lot about black times.'

'And Hitler is mad, eh, Doctor?'

'Yes. Hitler is quite clearly a madman. Mind you, Chris, I have my doubts about the sanity of Stalin – and Pétain. But Roosevelt and Churchill, I'd have to certify them as sane as you and me.'

'Well, then, Doctor, you don't know what I know and have seen of the cloak-and-dagger work of our side. Of the swap-offs – the trade-offs. The agents we've put down – and later we hear they were a diversion. You can't be dealing in tens of thousands of human lives and be what I call *decent*.

'I tell you, Churchill is a killer – a King of Killers – and I have been one of his hired killers.

'It's as simple as this, Doctor. What I've done is wrong – and I don't want to do it any more.'

'I am in total sympathy with that – and I don't believe you should *have* to, for other reasons than your convictions. I'm here to help you get home happily and safely.'

'All I want is to get Piquette and go back home to Bermuda and never leave.

'All I'm going to do is *fish* – if I have to – I'm simply not going to be involved in killing any more.

'Up here in Scotland – in this place – I've discovered several poets I never knew of before. Perhaps you know them?'

'Who then?'

'Sassoon and Wilfred Owen and Isaac Rosenberg.'

'Yes, I know Sassoon and Owen.'

'Well, my family and my school never got me past Rupert Brooke – and the corner of a foreign field that is forever England.

'But Sassoon and Owen and Rosenberg are talking of *deeper truths*: that the whole concept of war is terrible, awful, hopeless and must be stopped by you and me – who are the people who started it.'

Silence.

'Well, I can't say I don't agree with you – because I do. Therefore you are a pacifist by conviction.'

'I guess I am. I'm simply against humans killing humans.'

XXVI

Fotheringham III

It was the Exeat of March 1944, when they saw the wounded Hurricane fighter wobbling about in the sky. . . And all the boys of School House – indeed all the boys from Fotheringham School – had gone home for three days holiday.

Rich, Richmond had not gone home because his sister had just had a baby in Leicester and his parents had gone there and he couldn't go to Leicester. . .

James Berkeley had not gone home because he never did go all the way to Lincoln – last term Larry's parents asked him, but, this time, no one had. Besides, he was glad to be with Rich, because he still wanted Rich to be his best friend (Rich's best friend was Pip Fenwick even though Pip Fenwick, as everyone knew, had a 'pash' on Guy Callum – but friendship had little to do with pashes. . .). He, James, still palled about with Larry Rhodes – but he didn't like Larry as much as he liked Rich.

(Just before the other boys had left, there had been the usual Chapel Service, which had ended up with the chaplain's blessing: 'And, now, may the blessing of God the Father, God the Son and God the Holy Spirit be amongst you and remain with you always.'

James was always very much soothed by the blessing: it seemed an ancient and familial embrace. . .

The organ struck up an anthem, and, as the senior boys – most of whom were soon to join the armed forces – filed past them, Rich whispered:

'Lucky buggers – by the time we're old enough, the

war'll be over.')

Rich was an amazing person: just in the last week, for instance, Rich had 'made' two cameras – to go with the 35mm film (RAF film) his brother-in-law had given him.

James was just musing on the scientific wizardry of Rich (who'd made a sender and receiver radio when he was eleven – they were now fourteen – and it had taken the authorities two years to track him down: sender radios were illegal in wartime – as, of course, were cameras of any kind for civilians) when they both saw the Hawker Hurricane overhead.

The Hurricane's engine was misfiring and the plane appeared, also, to be flying erratically.

'He's in trouble and he must be heading for the old aerodrome,' said Rich.

'He looks as if he's been hit,' James said. 'Let's go.'

Taking their cameras, they rushed across the field and over the fences.

Fotheringham Aerodrome was almost right next to the school – but it had been closed by the RAF early in the War because the runway was too short. Then, during the invasion scare, cement blocks had been put on the existing runway to stop enemy gliders from landing there.

In their run, sometimes they could see the fighter, at other times, the trees and hedges hid it.

'He can't possibly land –'

'He could crash-land alongside the runway.' James jumped over a stile.

At last they were on the field. The Hurricane was still wobbling about – making a sort of erratic circle.

'He's been hit,' James said again. He even thought it could be his brother, Christopher.

Yet he knew it couldn't: Chris was in Scotland and he flew Mustangs. . . But when he saw an RAF plane,

472

of course, it was impossible not to think of his brother.

'He's certainly in trouble – let's get a photo – in case he goes away.'

Rich put his home-made camera up to his eye – and flipped the shutter.

He had said to James, earlier: 'Our shutter speed is one hundredth of a second – but the Air Force film is very fast. The aperture is F11.'

'I think those are bullet holes.'

It was thrilling to see an RAF fighter up this close: you could distinguish the break in the pilot's Mark VIII goggles that were pushed up on his forehead. It was even closer than the USAAF Mustang he saw in Malvern.

You could distinguish the paint lines on the aircraft's markings.

'Is he going to land?' said James.

'Don't think there's much doubt about it – what time have you got?'

'Three-twenty – why?'

'Let's get a bit more clear.'

The Hurricane had now made a longer sweep to the east and seemed to be lining up to come in.

'It's a helluva place to land.'

'He'll be okay if he doesn't use his wheels.'

'How do you know?'

'Just what my bro' tells me. Short runway, on grass – best to use no wheels.'

'You mean,' Rich said, looking only at the plane, 'that on wheels you roll too far.'

'Yes – and on rough ground you nose over – that's the worst, I think.'

The Hurricane was coming in: it seemed to be pushing its largish nose cone towards them. The nose cone was a reddish orange.

'What can we do?'

473

'Just wait,' said Rich.

'He's put his wheels down!' shouted James.

The plane came on and on, lower and lower, wobbling and sputtering as it came.

Rich and James watched – now in trepidation – as the plane bounced on the grass, went up, then mushed in tail low and nose high –

Then hit its wheels again on the soft grass – touched its tail at about the same time – that did seem to slow it –

But then it struck: nose down – somehow like a shot animal hitting a lake of grass.

The crash echoed against the rusty hangar.

Rich and James ran forward as fast as they could and didn't stop until they were about forty feet away.

There the Hurricane was, tail up, nose in – the ground and grass in front of it pushed up like a frozen wave of the sea, James thought.

Silence.

Before James left Washashley in the Christmas holidays of 1943, he'd been over to the Fenderses' cottage for his usual tea.

But Bob Fenders had something to report that was unusual.

'Those damned Canadians have really done it now, Mr James. I don't know where to begin, sir.'

'What is it, Fenders?'

'Well, you know the Nigerians had a go at getting into the wine cellar?'

'Yes.'

'They even tried shooting at the lock with a .303. But our old door held out against those black bastards. But these Canadians didn't mess around with a mere rifle, sir. When that didn't work – they machine-gunned our old lock.

'I do believe, Mr James, that our dungeon door withstood that onslaught too – but then these Canadian bastards – excuse me, Mother, but there's no other word for them. They put a grenade down our wine cellar, in the well-like – and that did it.'

Fenders's face was red and his eyes flashed with fury.

'But it isn't even that, Mr James, that makes me so hurt – it's that these gaolbirds – and that's what they are. Dock-sweepings and gaolbirds. When they got into the Master's wine cellar – got in with wines that were, some of them, one hundred and thirty-five years old – what did they do? They bust the necks off of the bottles and tasted them, and then poured them out on the ground.

'Old Man Watkins heard the explosion and he went there uninvited from his little cottage. And he heard one say "It's mare's piss" and spit.

'When I think of the wines the Master bought and cared for. And poor O'Neill turning bottles a half a turn a year – and a quarter – and all that. Hundreds and hundreds of pounds wasted. And the Master's pride and joy. And these swine don't even drink it – but smash it all up.

'And, I can't even get a civil reply from their commanding officer – he's a lieutenant colonel – and Mr Chris should be on him. But we can't trouble Mr Chris and him sick in Scotland. . .'

Fenders's anger got the better of him and he sat down and cried.

'It's all right, Fenders,' James said, awkwardly. 'You've done the best you can do.'

Fenders continued to cry: and it was a shocking sight, particularly because Fenders was, James knew, a proud Scot.

'We can only tell Dad and let him take it up with the War Ministry. You've done all you can and more,

Fenders – so don't worry.'

'That's exactly what I keep telling him, Mr James. Do you hear Mr James, Bob Fenders? Well, you'd better.

'And how about we all have a nice cuppa now – there's nought else we can do, save thank God we've our health and strength – and bless our friends.'

Mrs Fenders poured everyone a cup. Put a cup in her husband's hands, put her arm around him and said: 'Here's a good cup to Mr Chris – and all absent friends. God bless 'em.'

She nudged Fenders.

'God bless 'em,' he said through his tear-streaked mouth, still hiding his eyes. And then he started laughing.

The laughter spread to Mrs Fenders and to James. Soon they were all laughing.

James and Rich, on the aerodrome at Fotheringham, stopped stock-still and listened and sniffed the air like hunting dogs.

Rich put his camera up to his eye – but he never took a picture.

'What should we do?' said James.

'It could blow up,' said Rich.

'I reckon we gotta get him out,' said James.

They went forward gingerly.

A slight but cold wind blew from the east – the pilot had landed downwind. James felt even more sure that the aircraft must have been in action and been damaged.

The plane was utterly still. The wind whistled in the aerial mast behind the cockpit. In the cockpit, the pilot's head was slumped forward.

The aircraft's hatch, which had been open when the Hurricane flew around, had been shut – either by the

476

pilot or by the crash.

They went closer and closer.

'It could blow up, I tell you,' Rich said.

'Not if he turned the ignition off – least, I believe that's so,' said James.

They sniffed the air. They couldn't smell anything.

The silence was appalling –

'That great hot thing is a Rolls-Royce Merlin,' said James.

'What of it?'

'Nothing.'

They went closer. Now only about twenty-five feet from the plane.

'We are to windward,' said James, 'and that's sensible. I reckon we should try to get him out.'

'If only someone would come.'

'No one's been here for years.'

They moved closer and closer.

Now James could see the actual leather of the airman's helmet.

'He's dead,' said Rich. But the head moved – and they heard a distinct moan.

James ran forward and climbed up on a wing. He hesitated, then, seeing the canopy slightly open, he went towards it.

Taking it in both hands, he tried to move it back.

It wouldn't budge.

'Here. Try on the other side – both of us together.'

Rich ran around and climbed on the other wing. He said: 'Jim: a crashed aircraft is a mass of fuel near the spark – many sparks – of the engine.'

'Maybe he turned it off,' said James. 'I believe he's supposed to have done so.' He was thinking that if he was in the aircraft, he'd sure like someone to get him out.

Together they couldn't move the many-paned

canopy.

But then Rich took off a shoe and started hitting with it. James did the same.

The canopy was going slowly back.

Many smells seemed to assault James's nose: but the strongest now was high-octane fuel.

However, the canopy was now quite back.

James touched the pilot. No response. He took both hands and moved the head a little –

The man moaned.

'Jesus, Rich. *We have to get him out.*'

'It's the straps – we have to undo his straps,' said Rich and reached in from his side to do so.

His hands came out bloody.

'He's wounded,' he said. 'Perhaps he's got the joy stick stuck in him. It was a helluva wallop.'

'The straps should undo in the centre.' James reached in. The pilot moaned a little again. James withdrew.

He thought: It could be Christopher, it could even be bloody Teddy. Then he tried again.

'You hit the brass centre,' said Rich. 'I think.'

James's now bloody hands got a click out of the harness –

'Free. Now – how do we haul him?'

'We haul him damn fast, that's how,' said Rich, already climbing astride the aircraft, on the pushed-back canopy. 'Berkeley, if you get me burned to death – I'll come back and haunt you.'

'Pull together.'

Together they got the pilot about a quarter out. He groaned.

Then they slipped. He went back in like some ghastly automaton.

'Again together,' said James.

They were puffing and gasping.

478

'*Quick!*'

'Quick-as-we-can.'

This time they got his body half out and turned it – he fell, bent over, half out of the aircraft. (During this manoeuvre, his helmet had come off his head as if pulled by some ghostly hand.)

'Gently now.'

'Get his boots free.'

'Get 'em off.'

'Don't stop.'

'Let's go.'

In all this, James had a chance to register that the pilot had a young face and a pug nose.

Hauling with all their strength, they got the now totally silent – and incredibly malleable, and thus exceeding awkward, load – they got it twenty feet from the Hawker Hurricane.

Here they rested, wheezing in the March air.

They looked around. Still no one came. They were utterly alone.

'It's not enough. . . It's not far enough,' said Rich.

Again, hauling together, one to each arm and shoulder, they hauled the pilot further away.

At about forty yards, they lay him down, face up.

They saw an RAF Hillman Minx bouncing across the rough grass.

James and Rich went a little way off as the RAF car got closer. . .

They slumped down in the tall yellow grass, gasping. . .

James was thinking: I've never been that scared – then he laughed – he had: on the *Empire United* when the ship nearest them blew up.

He was thinking: wow, we did it. We saved him. Vaguely he thought they might get a medal – not a VC, of course, but a George Cross, perhaps.

Rich thought the same, he later said; he thought they'd get a medal. Anyway, their pictures in the papers. He thought his mother and dad would be very proud.

Then, he said, he thought he should hide the camera – but he couldn't remember where he'd dropped it.

Snippets of an old hymn came to James: 'Who would true valour see, let him come hither . . . one here will constant be, come wind, come weather. No lion can him fright, he'll with a giant fight. . .'

An RAF officer, obviously a doctor, jumped out of the Hillman with his bag and rushed to the pilot.

Two other men followed him close by. They had various pieces of apparatus –

Then a large ambulance started waddling across the aerodrome like some prehistoric creature.

Silence.

Clearly they heard the doctor say: 'He's dead.'

The two orderlies looked embarrassed and awkward.

'Must have got the stick stuck in him.' The doctor went on: 'Bled to death – would have been all right if those meddling little bastards had left him alone. All those damned Biggles books they read.'

Later they heard – trying all the while to look invisible: 'It was a training flight. It was the bloke's first solo.'

James went forward.

'Is there anything we can do?'

'No.'

'Come on, Jim.'

'You don't want our names?'

'Why did you have to give them our bloody names?'

'They would have found us later anyway.' James walked on slowly. 'Never realized it. . .'

'What?'

'A Hurricane still has a fabric fuselage at the back – I thought that went out with the Gloster Gladiator.'

'You get our cameras?'

'No. Let's get them later,' said James.

Chris, James said to himself. I'm sorry. I really fucked that up – every time I try to help you in your war, I fuck it up.

XXVII

Christopher, Backwards Often.
Forwards Sometimes, and
Probably Sideways Frequently
IX

Dear Nasti, Widda-Widda, Skeglee – and even Stinker (if you get this far)

This is the way it was
this is the way it is
this is the way
this is
this
is
I

I am rudely awakened at Abbotsford, Scotland, by a nurse with squeaky sneakers (it's 6:30 in the morning and this is supposed to be a Rest Centre)

who hands me this note that is unbelievable unless

481

you are a true believer in the Holy Royal Air Ministry

(Squeaky sneakers disappears after giving a little shake of her ass at the door – which would be all right, except she's the one who steals half our sweets from home and her ass is exactly the same girth as HMS *Barham*)

I open it, in my usual careful way. I know who it's from – it's Dr Macdonald – the brightest person, and one of the most decent, I've known, I think, in my whole life.

Dear Chris Berkeley,

I hope you will read between the lines and pass this message to all the lads on your floor who were my patients. That is, Harold, Michael, Francis, Thomas, Jules and Sebastian. . .

I have been summarily relieved of my position at the hospital and I very much regret that there has been and will continue to be a complete change of direction in treatment and thinking.

I am far more than sorry but one cannot kick against them.

Professionally and personally I wish you *all* health and long life.

All the best,
R.A. Macdonald

P.S. Perhaps we'll meet again. I'll be in London. This war will not last a great deal longer. I will be in the phone book. (Christopher, it's your mother we haven't looked at yet. . .)

I don't think you guys can quite comprehend my feelings: I say to Harold, 'Dr Mac was a father to me.' 'He was both mother and father to me, Bermuda.'

The feeling is the same throughout the floor.

After three days of rumours, I am finally interviewed (I want to say interrogated) by a new doctor here.

He is RAF issue: he starts off by saying (a refained gent: pronounces the 'h's in 'white'):

'Berkeley – isn't it?'

'No, Doctor, it's Berkeley – like A Nightingale Sang In.'

No laugh. No smile.

'Well, Barklay – you look perfectly fit to me. What is your trouble?'

'Dr Macdonald said I had shell-shock, Doctor.'

'Never mind what Dr Macdonald said. I have here two cards for you Flight Lieutenant Barklay. One is a white card and one is a pink.'

'Is Dr Macdonald's work to be entirely abandoned?' I ask incredulously.

'That might be a fair word. The feeling at Head Office, MOA, is that there are altogether too many layabouts at this hospital.'

'Are you, sir, calling me a layabout? I think my record speaks for itself.'

'I am not calling you anything, Flight Lieutenant – and I do have your record here. *And* I have Dr Macdonald's notes – here – a white card and a pink.'

'Dr Macdonald didn't keep any notes. He said it was private between doctor and patient.'

'Here are his notes.'

'Dr Macdonald was working towards a recovery for me and for several others, from extreme shell-shock. He was – *is* a brilliant man. He cared about people.'

'Flight Lieutenant, I am not only a psychiatrist – I am an ordained minister. If you have any worries I'd be glad if you would confide in me.'

'May I have your name please, Doctor?'

483

He gives it to me.

'Dr John W. Woolsey.'

I've got it written down. Much good did it do me – I don't think.

'I have here a clean bill of health for you,' Dr Woolsey holds up a new and very large white card.

'I have here these notes of Dr Macdonald.' He holds up a small pink card.

'What do they say, Doctor?'

'It says that you are a neurasthenic.'

'What's that mean, please, Doctor?'

'It means you suffer from vague complaints of a physical nature that appear to be mental in origin.'

I start laughing – that was typical and clever of Dr Macdonald, I think, but then he says:

'Then there's this mention of the rectum.' Dr Woolsey cleared his throat. 'This is the kind of thing, isn't it, lad – that is better kept to oneself. And wouldn't you rather I tore it up right now?'

(Obviously he doesn't listen to Tommy Handley.)

He's waving the white card and the pink card.

'This stuff about rectums –'

That's where he gets to me.

I nod.

He tears it up.

'Berkeley, I think it's fair to tell you how valuable you are to the Royal Air Force.'

'Thank you, I know.'

'I don't think you quite do. I want to point out to you that the Royal Air Force had invested in you thirty thousand pounds sterling – the first time you went Operational.

'That's the lowest it could be. Now it would be over a hundred thousand, wouldn't it?'

I do not answer this.

I begin fidgeting with some papers.

'What is it you have there?'

'Nothing.'

'It isn't nothing, Flight Lieutenant – I can *see* it's something.'

'It's a secret message – from the Gestapo.'

'You can't fool me – give it here.'

'I won't do that, Doctor. Because it's my property.'

'Oh yes you will.' He grabs it out of my grasp.

It is a page – a paragraph really, from a letter from Grampy, which I've kept in my wallet for years, because its Bermudian-ness has always touched me. It says:

'Granny says to be sure and *not* wear your woolly underwear – it'll only itch you to death.'

Dr Woolsey reads it. 'It isn't a secret message. You are playing tricks on me. I will record that on your record.'

There follows a long time of his wretched pen scratching on paper.

Then he looks up at me and says:

'Flight Lieutenant Berkeley, you look fit to me. Are you ready to go back to your squadron?'

'Doctor, I would like a complete physical checkup.'

At this point, Dr Woolsey looks pained.

'Yes. That can most certainly be arranged – you'll be passing through Glasgow. I'll tell them to be particularly attentive to the rectal area.'

The last two questions Dr Woolsey asks me are:

'Do you believe in God, Berkeley?'

'Yes, I do, Doctor – if you are referring to the source of all inspiration.'

'What on earth are you saying, Flight Lieutenant?'

'I believe in William Shakespeare.'

'That's enough. The next question is, are you willing to fly again?'

'I don't know if I can.'
'But you'll try, Berkeley?'
Silence.
'Will you try to fly, Berkeley?'
'Yes.'

April 1944

Dear Dad: Did this happen in your war? We had a
Communion Service for us Church of England blokes
      I didn't go
But my friend Harold went and then he snaps-his-
cookies on the parquet floor. 'God Berkeley,' he said
between heaves, 'I was eating the body and blood –
blood – all those bodies in Hamburg and Stuttgart.
We blow them up and it drives us batty so they
restore us with the body and blood of Jesus Christ. So
that we can do it again.'
      Please take care of yourself

Your everloving son,
Christopher

Dear Nasti and Skeglee and Widda-Widda
      This is the way it was
      this is the way it is
      They are definitely cleaning us all out of here.
      There seems to be a Big Show coming up.

I am back at my aerodrome. There are a lot of
changes.
      We have the new Mustangs and they are very
beautiful-looking and they have the Rolls-Royce 1800
hp engines and the four blade props which should
mean we are a match for the FW 190F and even the

FW 190D.

Everyone has confidence in my ability to fly but not I.

(I'm to take some hops, what Dad used to call a flip, in smaller planes – a Magister probably. . .)

The news is not good.

John Bewley is dead. He was a good friend – going back to the *Reina Del Pacifico* long before the War, and the SS *Orduna* with her raked yellow funnel.

Some might call her the Banana Boat, but she was a piece of British excellence and

John Bewley and I used to go swimming in the canvas swimming pool they slung on deck

Bewley had an English Dad who always met the boat – and then he disappeared. I think he was lost in an Empire flying boat disaster

In any case, Bewley had that bewildered stance of heart: part old Bermudian and part upper-middle-class Brit.

He was not my best friend, like Aussie (and guess where he is?) but he was the first Bermudian in the RAF and he flew in the

Battle of Britain.

Which leaves me: Colonial Aussie-Variety, whose mother's cake has just arrived from Brisbane and it's exactly six weeks now since Aussie was blown up over, guess where?

Lorient. . . Hitting the sub pens on the wrong side of the river.

Colonial Aussie-Variety and I, had we flown today, would have flown together, one thousand five hundred and fifty days. . .

SHIT PISS FUCK – FUCK ENGLAND FUCK KING FUCK GOD

'When This Fucking War Is Over, you and I will.'

XVIII

Fotheringham IV

'Gee, Rich. How were your hols?'

'Marvellous, thanks, Jim – you crazy Yank. I've perfected the cameras now and I've got an even faster film.'

'Great. It's damned nice being in our third term, rather than Frogs, isn't it?'

'Yes – indeed. Have you ever seen such traffic?'

'No. There's a giant American Negro on every road.'

'Several of them, you mean. The invasion must be going to happen soon.'

'Yes.'

'But the weather,' said Larry. 'it's like winter still.'

'How's your Dad?'

'Furious at being moved inland. Furious at the Pier being used to embark the Army – He's so furious he has ulcers.'

'What are ulcers?' asked James.

James wanted to play cricket at Fotheringham more than any other sport.

He tried out for the Under 16 Eleven. When he got to the pitch there were about twenty-five players.

'Everyone was captain of his prep school,' said Pip Fenwick.

James said to the master: 'I'd like to try out as a bowler and a bat, please sir.'

'So would everyone.'

They played a game. James did get a chance to bowl: he was just getting into his stride – having bowled two overs and taken one wicket – when the master replaced him.

When it came time to bat, James had a 'lacklustre' day. He made seven runs, none of them boundaries, and then got run-out by a bad call.

He put a smile on it – but, the next game day, when he showed up, the master said: 'I've picked my fifteen – were you on it?'

'No, sir. But I'd like another chance.'

'Name?'

'Berkeley.'

'Oh yes – you're the West Indian. They want you for swimming.'

'But I don't want to swim.'

'Look, Berkeley. I've twenty cricketers like you and the school has no swimmers. Don't you want to help the school?'

'Of course I do, sir.'

'Then go out for swimming.'

As the summer term wore on, the roads everywhere were almost jammed with the military vehicles. It seemed that every army truck in the world was running around southern Britain.

British and American mostly . . . there wasn't room for civilians, one felt.

The papers in the School House Library, *The Times* the *Telegraph* and the *Daily Mail*, were full of talk of 'Invasion' and 'The Second Front.'

What Rich kept saying (and also Guy Callum – who was, after all, a year older than they were) was: 'You can tell we've almost won the war because there's no air raids.'

'Yes,' said Callum. 'If one was horse-racing, one would say there's no hoofbeats – no one is making a challenge.'

'Of course,' Rich smiled, showing the gap in his

white incisors, 'it could be a trick. Hitler could be playing a trick.'

'But it just feels as if it's over, thank God.' Guy Callum was a very smooth character: he didn't brag and he seemed to quietly believe in just getting by. Everyone liked him.

His affair with Pip Fenwick was quiescent more than over, James thought.

James sure hoped the War was almost over: but the 'powers that be' had not amassed, he reckoned, all these men to attack a dead dog. Anyway, Hitler and his mates were the cornered desperadoes now.

Larry and he were not the close friends they were before – he was closer to Rich. But Larry was sometimes the best to talk to.

'Hitler's going to pull a trick – that's what I'm afraid of.'

'What kind of a trick?'

'My bro' is always saying the German aircraft are one step ahead of us – every time we get a new Spitfire or Mustang, they've got a better Focke-Wulf or a Messerschmidt.'

'So what do you think Hitler's trick will be?'

'I don't know – he's going to take Sweden or Turkey.'

'What good would that do him?'

'Hit the Russians from a different direction. Hook up with Japan.'

'Tripe, Jim, tripe. He's on the ropes, hollering for mercy.'

'Maybe he's got six pocket battleships to slip out of the Skagerrak and smash up the invasion – smash all the Atlantic convoys.'

'Don't you worry about it.'

'I'm not worried. I think we'll win.'

'Blimey. Of course we'll win. Are you crackers?'

'No. I've thought it was very very close for a long

time. I was in a convoy, remember?'

'You've got a biased opinion. Hitler's got no more chance than Max Schmelling had against Joe Louis.'

Larry was, for all his youthful and even feminine looks, a great authority of heavyweight boxing.

On the 6th of June 1944 everyone was glued to the wireless.

Masters would say – as boys came into the form-room: 'What's the news?'

'They reckon that we've landed at two to six different places in France, sir.'

'Heard that – what else?'

'Heavy naval bombardments – four thousand ships.'

'Very little sign of the Luftwaffe, sir, the RAF and the Americans rule the skies.'

'Scotty' Scott, the Geography master, even had a wireless right in his special form-room. It ran all day long.

('The school wouldn't give me the right equipment – so I bought it myself,' he told them.

Everyone knew he was one of the best Geography masters in Britain and 'he set the Oxford and Cambridge exams for years'.

'The future belongs to America and Russia and China,' he'd say. 'But the biggest in production is America by a common mile. You know why? Because the flow of weather and the mountains are in the right place in America, and the wrong place in Russia – look here –

'A Kansas farmer can make such a good crop he can close up the farm and go to Florida for the winter.

'Also, in America – and Canada – the rivers are in the right place in relation to the iron and the coal – look here.'

He could pull down all sorts of maps, spin all sorts of globes. You could learn more from him than a

491

hundred others. . .

Scotty had a rather high-pitched voice and no children. 'I said to me wife after we were married: what would you like first, a car or a baby? She said, a car, you damn fool.')

The next day, the papers were full of news of what appeared to have been a virtually undisputed series of landings.

James was anxious about Christopher, who he knew was Operational again, but one headline said:

'*Not One British or American Aircraft Lost To The Luftwaffe*' and so he tried to forget that worry.

On the 13th of June 1944, at about four o'clock in the morning, the whole school was harshly awakened by the air-raid sirens.

It had been so long since an air raid that, at first, few believed it. But Rich Richmond, in the Lower Passage bed next to James, whispered:

'Come on. It's a raid – and a new one at that.'

'What do you mean?'

'I just woke up to this strange sound – no fooling – strange sound in the air – like a motorbike. I'm going to take my camera. Come on, let's get to the shelters.'

It was voluntary as to whether you went to the shelters or not. Most people, this late in the War, didn't pay any attention.

But the shelters were there for anyone who wanted them. The School House shelters were down by the Home Farm.

No sooner were Rich and James outside in the Quadrangle, than they seemed to be assaulted by a loud noise. They looked up. Rich leapt out with his camera.

It did sound like a motorcycle. And then they saw

it: streaking across the sky – low and fast – a red exhaust. Rich put his camera to his eye, swung his head and body as if he were shooting a bird, and clicked his home-made shutter.

'It sounds like an old Norton,' said James.

'Yes – if you ever saw a Norton do five hundred mph.'

'Even if you get a result – what can you do with the picture?'

'Nothing – but it'll satisfy my curiosity. OK, Jim,' said Rich lightly. 'Don't tell anyone, all right?'

'Probably won't be any more of those, anyway,' said James.

'Probably it was ours – you mean.'

But on the 14th of June, the *Daily Mail* had a photo of bomb damage in Bethnal Green.

'New Bomb. Very High Powered Explosion Kills Nine.' It further said that the Air Ministry was mystified and seeking all and any help.

Rich said: 'I developed my film – and I've got a damned good photo – if I had an enlarger – I could really tell – really see a lot.'

'You'd better tell the Head.'

'What? And get beaten?'

'I think they'd make you a hero.'

'Well, mate, we've had enough of that, haven't we?'

'Yes.'

But Rich did go to see Cock, the Captain of the School, with his photo.

Cock said: 'Come with me to Mr Walking.'

Mr Walking, the headmaster, took one look at Richmond's photo and said: 'What is it – can you make it out?'

Cock said: 'The photo is very clear, sir.'

Richmond said: 'Sir, I believe it's a bomb with a drip-fuel jet engine.'

Mr Walking said: 'What are you doing with a camera?'

Cock said: 'Sir, that's how he got the photo – and I think the Air Ministry would like it, sir.'

Mr Walking phoned the Air Ministry and within two hours an RAF car drove into the Quadrangle and parked under the giant poplar tree.

Richmond was sent for.

The group captain looked at his photo – under a hand magnifying-glass – and said:

'What do you make of it?' He was talking to his assistant, a pilot officer, but Richmond (unable to contain his enthusiasm) answered:

'It's a bomb powered by a drip-fuelled ram-jet, sir. That's what I believe.'

'I wasn't asking you, young man.'

'Well, sir. I could make a model of it if you would like –'

'A lot of bloody good that would do us.'

'– a flying model, actually, sir, if you would like?'

'No, I would not. But we are confiscating these photos.'

'There's only one, sir.'

'No more?'

'Sorry, sir, no. But I could make a working model, sir.'

'Oh shut up, boy.'

On the 15th, at Fotheringham, these 'flying bombs', as everyone called them, were going by, all day and all night.

'I've figured it out – one goes by exactly every twenty-one minutes,' said Rich.

'Well, Richmond,' said Mr Scott, 'my count is one

494

every seven minutes.'

The next day, 16th June 1944, a vice marshal of the RAF arrived at Fotheringham at 8:45 in the morning.

'Did you say that you could make a working model of this thing, Richmond?' the vice marshal asked him.

'Sir, if I'm given a spark-plug for a model aircraft – such as were common pre-war, and a clockwork magneto, I believe I could make one on the school metal lathe.'

'Oh could you, by God – well, you just do it, young man. I'll get the parts for you. And what did you say it was?'

'A drip-fuel ram-jet, sir.'

'Oh. Very well. If I get you the parts – how long would it take you?'

'Depends, sir.'

'Depends on what Richmond?'

'Can you get me off schoolwork, sir?'

'Of course.'

'Then I could probably do it in a few hours.'

XXIX

Christopher, Backwards Often,
Forwards Sometimes and
Probably, Sideways Frequently
X

When This Fucking War Is Over, you and I will fall in love ... a great song – the music matches the lyrics – being an old hymn tune.

Dear Nasti, Widda-Widda and Skeglee (or whoever lives beyond me)

This is the way it was
This is the way it is
This is the way
this is
this
is
I

I am to take off today, for the Big Invasion – there
are to be four thousand nine hundred fighters like me
in the air: and a great many more bombers. Imagine
that – we who used to sweat hell to come up with
fifty. . ?

It is the 6th of June 1944

The act of flying is holy to me and always has been,
and, in case you should have any doubts about it, I,
Christopher Berkeley, baptized Aubrey Spencer, of
Paget, Bermuda, am now, I believe, partially mad. . .

It helps. . .

To find oneself caught in a war is one of the major
dilemmas of Man. . .

I would like, rather, to die to achieve this reality:

THAT WAR IS NOT INEVITABLE

As I take off now, in my new Mustang – equipped
with an 1800 hp engine – a Rolls-Royce

I have my little boot with me – from Washashley
Hall, Lincoln – this little boot was made of brass and
copper in the trenches of World War I and given to my
uncle by one of his tenants – who was the creator in
the trenches, who made this little creative gesture
against annihilation:

a boot, complete with copper threads for laces and a
hole in its sole

that's me. . .

I had news, yesterday, the 5th of June, that my
love, Piquette Dehn – unknown to any authorities by
that name – has been traced by the Swiss Society of

Refugees, as Jeanne Hubert.

Jeanne Hubert is known, they said, by two different 'parties' to have been executed at Toulouse by the Gestapo in May 1943.

So, here am I off again into the blue sky

sorry that it is so grey and windy and wet this sixth day of June – you'd think this whole Mission would be scrubbed, but it won't

because General Eisenhower has shaken hands with the King and we are all off ... and General Eisenhower has had his orders from General Marshall and the King has had his orders, presumably from God...

And many will die, I don't doubt – because of the very bad weather here in the Channel – the English Channel...

So off we go: have you ever seen so many planes? They've been going over for hours and hours and hours ... the noise must have wakened everyone in Britain.

Now this Mustang is a beauty – with the right power and design at last. It's taken four years. My suggestion is, that, in the future, British and American designers get together at the start

for one thing is sure in this War – those things designed by one country alone, have not been too successful ... British *and* American, now there's the way to success...

Note my mad wide white stripes: three in number, across my wing and down my arse. Everyone knows, these big wide white stripes are Allied aircraft – all others are enemies... None of these stripes are enemies...

I have figured out much – since I last saw my good doctor in Scotland, at Abbotsford. . .

I've got an easy one today: flying screen over US Navy Escort Vessels, themselves escorting troop carriers to France.

An easy one. It's said that the RAF and the USAAF have pulverized and ploughed up every airfield in France, Belgium, Holland and Denmark.

So here's my place: 1,500 feet, the Isle of Wight below, where my great-grandfather was vicar of St Saviour's-on-the-Cliff; he never missed a Sunday sermon for forty years, including the Sunday after his death, because he made a record of his sermon before he died and it was played from the pulpit – year was 1898

How about that?! St Saviour's, no less, and Queen Victoria used to come to the little church. . .

and Grandfather and Uncle Albert and Uncle Charlie and the two princes had their portraits painted in watercolours – by the princes' tutor: The five pictures are at Washashley and all five boys are gone now . . . no matter. . .

Rolling hill and dale, precious patchwork with white cliffs – is there a more beautiful place than the Isle of Wight?

No. . . No. . . No. . .

The memorial to my great-grandfather says: 'To the dear and honoured memory of Edmond Portman Berkeley MA. . .', which means simply that he was much loved by those who put up the memorial. . .

Away just off to the starboard there, are the magic and sacred places of England – Arundel and Felpham and Tangmere. . .

I'll just take one gentle little sweep across the sea to have a look – I've several minutes to spare.

She sweeps at 375-378 mph/ball-in-the-middle/no trouble... Now we zoom out towards France.

Everywhere in the sky there are aircraft – squadrons and squadrons at every height, coming and going. They move from the south-west to the east – come and go from every direction.

The ships below are as numerous. Now I see what I have heard about: the massed fleets of America and Britain that are bombarding the shores of Fortress Europe.

There go those that have done, and here come those that will. The bombers continue night and day and have continued, ceaselessly for weeks.

Only a little of this softening would have saved us at Dieppe.

I watch like a hawk, newly unhooded, for Goering's boys in grey. (Think what a deathly colour grey is and we are Blue like the sky...)

There's France – and her white cliffs – and now, sweeping the skies with my face and the mirror – I turn back for Britain

The map on my knee.

Here we are, Sector KBI – now, all I have to do is settle in next to this convoy and screen them

Here are both my wing men –

And at 500 feet. Please God, be no damn fools on these ships, for, at 500 feet and throttled back, you could hit this aircraft and this mortal man – with a seagull's egg and bring him down, never mind a rock.

So here am I on station: 500 feet over the mighty Armada – for thus they are calling it, already, an Armada

But fortunately for me and for England, this Armada is travelling away, not towards England...

'Oh, England, England, *mother*, save me!'

But mother is become a murdering woman who is reaping a wilder vengeance than even that sown...

'Any evening, any day ... any time you want to play ... you'll find us all, doing the Lambeth Walk...' These songs have I loved

These words I am sending you now, Skeglee and Widda-Widda –

(dear Widda-Widda, always will I remember how you said, in reply to the soppy slogan of *Boy's Town*, All Boys Are Good Boys – 'All Boys *Is* Bad Boys'...)

These words are really *Words From The Depths Of The Sea* by The Bermudian – that is the title of my unfinished book (a few poems you will find) and the pseudonym is mine too...

Words From The Depths Of The Sea by The Bermudian – you got it?

Tracer coming up over there – who for, who at? I see no enemy.

I look all around and *up*

I've always liked only this from Nasti and Skeglee's school, Fotheringham: Richard Platt's prayer:

'Oh Lord, who art praised by the living, even as also by the dead...'

I see that tracer again – a bit too close for my taste. Who's he after?

I have a little piss in my Gentleman's Companion, which my other grandfather (Halcyon) always took sailing in the *Nea* in the 1890s... 'Get aboard, Grampy, if you don't get aboard get a plank...' 'A difference of opinion, Grampy, makes boat racing possible.'

Now the blue sky is coming out a little and that

500

makes me think of the Royal Blue of France

'I can't wait for you to grow up, Monsieur Chris –
tomorrow I may be dead, you see.'

I do indeed Piquette, your La Mouette sees...

That Yankee bastard is shooting at me.

Procedure One. It says here: Waggle wings

I am waggling wings. But I don't trust him. That
tracer stream is coming up

and streams do tend to build streams and a river
make

this is no time to be shooting at a brother, brother

Now that tracer is opening my kite up like a
zipper – again, and this is all wrong...

Doctor, I begin to see with blinding sight, just as
that fluid is beginning to hit my instruments again...

I'd better gain altitude FAST

Full power

the fluid is, I quietly realize, very quietly, not fluid,
but my blood

I see with blinding sight: look to your mother, you
said, well I do:

I, Christopher, was part of Charity's Plan: I went
from Server at St Paul's into public school and into
the RAF – and here am I, Charity Berkeley's Sacrifice
to Her Empire (which wouldn't really have her as a
first-class Pukka-Sahib Brit', but must surely accept
her now.)

Here I go, Charity gives her First Begotten Son

Aubrey Spencer Berkeley, your only function was
always, simply, to make Her Mightier Yet...

... But I (losing consciousness now as well as my
little bit of altitude) have one thought of my own: it is
that

no Frenchman or Frenchwoman (except two very
skegly boarding houses) ever turned me away from

501

his or her door . . . for which I say. . .
merci

XXX

Fotheringham V

At noon on the 16th of June 1944 another RAF car screeched to a stop in the Quadrangle next to the poplar.

'Mr Richmond,' a warrant officer said, when Rich had been fetched from the IV Form. 'Here's your spark plugs – I didn't know which – so I brought several. And here's several clockwork magnetos.'

Rich looked them over. 'This little fellow will do splendidly and this little fellow here. Thank you very much.'

'May I assist you, Mr Richmond?'

'No. Not now. Might need you later.'

'I was told to wait. When you're ready we'll rush up to the Ministry.'

There were two other RAF personnel in the car and an escort of two motorcycles.

As they talked, a flying bomb went by overhead. Richmond ducked his head to one side, so did the warrant officer.

Suddenly the motorcycle-like engine stopped.

There was the whining whistle of a falling bomb.

Everyone threw themselves to the ground.

Then, amazingly, the bomb started up again – and continued on its way. Beh-beh-beh-beh. . .

'You see,' said Rich to the warrant officer. 'A drip-feed – he's going on the last bit left in the tank. If it wasn't a drip-feed, he couldn't behave like that.'

At two o'clock, Richmond emerged from the Physics Lab, where he was building his model.

'I need a brass cylinder – a bit bigger than a .303 casing.'

Sergeant Major Bucking said: 'Would a spent signal shell do?'

'Yes, Sarge, the very thing.'

'I've one in my office.'

'Has anyone got a pint of petrol?'

'Here, Mr Richmond. Here's some high-octane fuel from the Air Ministry – sorry, I forgot about it.'

'Great. I thought I was going to have to refine some ordinary petrol. That's the very thing. Just the job,' said Rich and went back into the Physics Lab.

At a few minutes after three, a banging roar like a very small Norton motorcycle was heard from the Lab.

A little later Rich Richmond, aged fifteen, emerged carrying a brass and copper and aluminium model in his hand.

'Does it work, Mr Richmond?' asked the warrant officer.

'Yes.'

'Are you ready to drive to Whitehall, sir?'

'I'll just get my mac,' said Rich, and walked into School House.

When Richmond got back to School House it was past twelve – and by the time he got something to eat and up to the Lower Passage, it was past 1:00 a.m.

'What happened?' said James, among others.

'Well, at first they wouldn't believe me. Several air marshals and group captains and people. So then I flew it for them in the Park.

'Mind you, it was a bit of a ropey flight – but it did give them the idea.' Rich gave his characteristic little laugh, and shook his curly white-yellow-haired head.

'Had to borrow some gum off a Yank – to make it work. Also, a lot of rubber bands. But I flew it for them.'

'Great Scott!'

'Heavens.'

'They have about a dozen really good photos now. These showed clearly what I was trying to tell them. Showed a helluva lot I never dreamed of too.

'Then me and two other chaps drew some plans.'

'Gosh, at the risk of sounding silly, you must be a national hero,' said James.

'And I'll bet you don't get a sausage,' said Larry. 'Not a sausage for your trouble.'

'I don't want anything – I just wanted them to accept what I told them, because I knew I was right – and they did.'

'They'll phone you again,' said James. 'I'll bet they write you a splendid thank you – a Commendation.'

'I'll bet they don't – but they did give me tea and biscuits and stuff.'

'Rich?' said James, just as they were about to go to sleep.

'Yes, Jim.'

'How the hell did you know all that about drip-jets?'

'The principle has been known for some while.'

'You're a clever bastard, Rich. You really are.'

'Thanks, Jim. But those Jerries that put it together – they are a cute lot! Do you know that thing carries nearly a half-ton of explosives?'

'No.'

'Yes. And it goes four hundred mph – and we've hardly got a fighter that can catch it. So there's another problem. And then – they think, but they don't know, that maybe the bomb explodes *before* penetration.'

The siren went again.

'Let's just get under our beds,' said Rich.

'Good idea.'

A lot of people were going to the shelters now.

Mr Parrot, the housemaster, came by. The light was on, all the blackout curtains up.

'You chaps better go to the shelter.'

'Richmond says we're pretty safe under our beds,' said Berkeley.

'Perhaps,' said a hesitant Mr Parrot.

'I'm so tired sir.'

'Very well. Good night.' But Mr Parrot didn't leave – he sort of lingered about. He was always lingering about him and Rich – James couldn't imagine why... Yet his nickname wasn't Sneaky-Doyly-Pee for nothing... What did he want and what made him tick anyway?

The next day, the 17th of June 1944, James got a telegram.

He read it and then he saw a sort of vision.

And this is what he saw:

A headline.

The Royal Gazette and Colonist Daily
BERMUDA'S HERO
WELCOMED HOME

Thousands cheer and bands play as Aubrey 'Christopher' Berkeley, Bermuda's Ace of Aces in the RAF, is welcomed home.

The Governor's Barge Landed from Durrell's Island bringing Chris Berkeley home to a tumultuous greeting by rich and poor, black and white.

The Bermudian, who shot down eighty-two enemy planes, including Herman Goering, said, modestly:

'It was just a job of work and we did it.'

Then James saw Bermuda, in all its colours: Front Street, the Governor with plumed rooster-feathered helmet.

Christopher stepping ashore and the sparkling clear, transparent green and blue water.

'I brought my brother along too – just for the ride.'

James waved – the crowd roared. . .

Then he had another vision: It was six months later, Christopher Berkeley was working in the Bank of Bermuda.

He didn't care what he did, he said, as long as he could stay home.

One bright day, around noon, a masked young man came into the bank.

He went right up to Berkeley's teller window. Stuck an automatic on the grille – pointed right at Berkeley.

Chris Berkeley just looked at the man. Looked and looked at him and then said softly: 'Look, you had better just put down that gun. Because, young man,' Chris was mumbling along in his usual gentle – even soothing way –

'Just quietly put that gun down. Because I want to tell you a little secret. I've just finished five years of very very long war – and I was flying see, for Bermuda in the Royal Air Force. And the whole fucking Luftwaffe couldn't scare me, so you needn't think you can.'

The man looked first bewildered, and then hesitant.

'So, if you'd just hand me the gun – very quietly and gently, then everything will be all right – all right?'

Chris held out his hand and the masked man put the gun in it.

Headline:

WAR HERO BERKELEY STOPS BERMUDA'S FIRST ARMED

The telegram said: James Berkeley, School House, Fotheringham School, Hertfordshire. Most terribly regret Christopher now Missing Assumed Killed D-Day stop fear we must expect worst best love Aunt Daisy and Mrs Pickle.

After his Bermuda visions, James went into one of his tranquil trances; it was Rich and Larry's voices that began it.

'Sorry, Jim – really sorry.'

'Worst possible luck, Berkeley, old boy.'

'Wish there was something we could do.'

'Maybe your brother'll be all right.'

James just shook his head most positively, at that. He knew what he knew. . .

Why can't I feel anything? Why can't I feel? James thought, and then: perhaps it's like being back on the ship?

Ta-tum.

Christopher.

If I allow myself to feel, to understand, I will drown – and I have to go on. . .

Christopher.

Christopher has been/is my everything. . .

You cannot open up that well, Berkeley, or you will fall for ever.

They were in the Lower Passage (the oldest dormitory in the school, built in the 1500s), Knightly, the Captain of School House Evens (who only came to bed long after lights out): Guy Callum as second in command of the Passage; Fenwick, next to Callum, then Rhodes, Herman, Block, Berkeley and Richmond.

Berkeley and Richmond had the beds closest to the

clock tower (from where the water was drawn) and where there was one of the two doors that made the dorm a passage.

Rich was a sort of Explainer of the Bombs.

At first, as soon as they heard one: the beh-beh-beh-beh of the airborne motorcycle, they all climbed under their beds.

'Just wait,' said Rich – 'if he keeps going – we don't have to move.'

Beh-beh-beh-beh.

It went on and on until it flew away.

'How come they fly *over* us on their way to London – and we are north of London?' said Callum.

'Because they are coming from north of us,' said Rich.

'It's the Hook of Holland – or Denmark. Or Norway,' said James. Chris will shoot them down.

'You don't have to move until he starts down,' said Rich.

Beh-beh-beh – SILENCE

Then the whine of a falling aircraft – a falling bomb

'You still don't have to move,' said Rich. 'Listen.'

Beh-beh-beh-beh.

'On he goes, the little monkey,' Rich's laugh was very infectious – and it came out in tight situations. His blue eyes always looked at you as if to say, and-what-do-you-think-of-that?

'If we get it right, we don't have to move until he's done his descending for a slow count of four – you watch and listen and count.'

It was not long before a bomb would come by to illustrate his point.

There was, first, the harsh banging motor – sometimes it went on – In the night, it was a flashing red flame of exhaust as well. . .

Sometimes it cut out:

508

Wha – aa – ahahah

Sometimes it cut in again:

Beh-beh-beh-beh and on to London and others

The bombs always woke them up

After the engine cut, if you counted, one-a, two-a, three-a four-a

Then it was time to roll over and get under your bed because the next thing you heard was

Kah-boom

The biggest explosion that the War had so far brought.

After a few days, Rich said: 'It isn't a half-ton, it's a ton. How could I be so stupid?'

In the nights they learned to sleep and roll under.

It was a good thing it was summer.

'The windows will be blown in soon,' said Block – and he was right.

'Keep blankets over your heads, I think,' said Callum. They did.

Soon the windows on the west were blown in. It was a sort of shame – because they were very old glass. . .

'The Wound-Up Death Monkey,' was the title Rich Richmond gave to it. 'Don't let him get us down – he's just a scare tactic.'

In the day-time, they came over about four an hour – sometimes the master would go on with a class. Sometimes they'd tell everyone:

'Get under your desks!'

Sometimes they'd say,

'To the shelters!'

Sometimes they'd say,

'Class dismissed.'

Sometimes now, masters began to show exaggerated character traits. Most of the boys were always hungry, they all didn't have enough to eat, and it was usual for their stomachs to rumble.

'If you don't stop your belly rumbling, boy,' the Maths master, Mr Fox, yelled, 'I'll cut your behind.' (Mr Fox was usually gruff – but also usually amused and kindly.)

James and Rich and others took to stealing crusts of bread from the kitchen to carry in their pockets to stop any stomach noises.

(James, who had written his mother and father once a week, now took to writing even more often – asking his father to come as soon as he could. . .)

Of course the bombs came over four an hour all night as well.

This passing of bombs, some cutting out, some falling, some going on, went on and on and on. . .

It started on 15th June – and it continued into July and then through all of July. . .

'A hundred flying bombs a day, for five weeks,' said Larry. 'That must be a total of over three thousand bombs.'

'It's like being in a convoy,' James said. 'It has the same effect – you are scared nearly all the time.'

Ta-tum.

'It's getting me – it's getting me crazy, Jim.'

'Well, at sea,' James told them – Rich had just come by – 'the other frightening thing was – well, if you got hit you were in the water. The water was freezing – or almost – so you'd drown or freeze to death.'

'Christmas.'

Christopher.

'Well, perhaps it makes it a bit easier for me – at least I know that the school can't sink in the sea.'

'Some bloody consolation,' said Larry, strangely chewing on his own tongue.

'We've *got* to keep laughing,' said Rich.

'Yes,' said Callum. 'That's the order, the ticket – everything – We've got to keep laughing.'

Matron, who was a very sassy woman – 'considering she's thirty years old if she's a day –' said:
  'We should call it: The Maiden's Disaster.'
  'Why?' someone asked.
  'Because it explodes before penetration.'
  They all roared with laughter.
  'I should say,' said Matron, another night, laughing, 'that it's a typical German *or* British bomb – explodes *before* penetration.'
  'What does she mean?' said Pip.
  'Well, a bloke who explodes before penetration wouldn't be much good, would he?' said Callum smiling. 'To the woman.'
  'Oh,' said Pip. 'I'm not up on *everything*.'
  'Not much, you aren't,' said Larry, in a low voice.
  But for all the talk of pashes and note-passing – there was no overt sex going on. . . (Neither had there been before the bombs came.)

At Fotheringham, most boys said their prayers. Now, in School House, every boy got out and said them kneeling on the floor.

'The trouble with the flying bomb is,' said Rich, 'that, unlike the Blitz, dawn doesn't bring us any respite.'
  'Even with the fire-bombings – at least there was daylight to look forward to,' said Block.
  'Neither does bad weather stop them,' said Herman. 'Not even clouds.'
  'You've got to hand it to the Germans,' said Rich: 'The Wound-Up Death Monkey is better than anything we ever thought up.'

Some boys were rumoured to be going to be sent home. After all, there were no bombs in the north or west.

'You could go home to Lincoln,' said Block. 'Hemel Hempstead's as bad as here.'

'As bad as anywhere,' said Pip, but no one else was interested, at this time, in snobbery. . .

'Southall too,' said Rich.

'I'm in Hertfordshire,' said Herman.

'Surrey – no help,' said Pip – trying to change his act. . .

So it was just Callum, who lived in Leicester, and Berkeley in Lincolnshire, for whom going home made sense.

But while they thought about it, the weeks passed.

Even by the end of June, it was quite a common sight to see a boy sitting in class quietly crying.

'It's been my problem, for some years,' James told Rich.

'Get off it – you aren't a cry-baby.'

James only smiled. . .

A lot of windows were blown in now. The main cricket pitch was blown to smithereens – its drainage system, a marvel of old-fashioned engineering, was entirely smashed.

'They just keep on and on and on – it's horrible,' said Guy Callum. . . 'It's like being tied to the middle of the road.'

'It's more like a clockwork bomb,' said Mac Block, his face like a pale full moon.

'Nar,' said Rich – 'The Wound-Up Death Monkey is the right name – I said it.'

It was about the first week in July, that the boys began to notice that sometimes a master would start crying – silently.

'It's all right, sir,' some boys got to saying: 'Why don't we have a singsong?'

James noticed that the boys' sympathy for the masters seemed, for the most part, to be greater than the other way round. Perhaps it was that they were more resilient.

The big exception was Scabby Stick – the school's most wounded veteran of the First War, and the Classics scholar and librarian.

'Anyone who wants to, can come to tea at my house.' Many did go – but James was too shy.

'Mrs Stick gave us hot tea – jolly good – it was. Scabby can't hear much.'

'Scabby cries a lot – but seems to get stronger.'

Mr Scott organized walks and runs. 'No one can sleep without a damned good run. Come on.'

But it wasn't long before no one ran but Mr and Mrs Scott.

The boys in Mr French's House had the best morale. Fred French was a tartar, and he made his boys dig outdoor shelters and he himself supplied tents.

And he and Mrs French stayed with the boys outdoors.

'England is not going to fall to inanimate objects,' he said over and over, smiling.

By the second week in July, the mail stopped coming. . .

Overhead, new marks and makes of RAF planes (every plane made James look skyward – with a surrealistic hope – and then look down at the ground . . .) chased the buzz bombs, as they were now called:

Hawker Tempests and Typhoons, the de Havilland Mosquito.

James vaguely remembered that somewhere, some time, his grandfather had had a sailboat – a racing dingy – called the *Mosquito*: because she was so light on the water, and had so many sails that she flew. . .

This Mosquito aircraft could surely fly too. . . It was rumoured to do five hundred miles an hour.

'I'll ask my bro' . . .' James began . . . *Christopher!*

'It's good to see them get chased,' said Matron – 'The horrid things.'

The papers said: 'Britons Laugh at the New Threat' and, 'Buzz Bombs Make London and the Home Counties Feel Tougher' and, 'Britain Fights On Undeterred'.

But, everybody noticed, by mid-July, that everything, and everyone, in London and the Home Counties, was falling apart. . .

P.J. Broadlipp said to James: 'I saw an article that said that the buzz bombs haven't hurt England a bit.

'But Berkeley, I'll tell you – it's my belief that if Adolph Hitler landed on top of Big Ben *tonight* with a penny firecracker in his hand, the whole of Britain would surrender to him.'

James didn't laugh.

'You're not laughing because you know it's true.'

'What are you doing here – if you hate them so?'

'Laughing at them – laughing at *us all* – don't you worry, lad, you want to ask yourself the same question: what are you doing here? Don't be upset now.'

Ta-tum.

'They say we are going to be evacuated,' Rich said.

James kept silent a lot of the time. . .

'You and I should go home,' said Callum.

'I'll stay,' said James.

Even the heavy bangs of the buzz bombs reverberated in James's awareness with but one word – Christopher.

By mid-July, James got a letter from Mr Somers. It said that he had only to ask, and he, Mr Somers, would put James on the train to Lincoln.

On the 17th, Guy Callum's parents arrived in a beautiful Humber Hawk.

'Why, those *nouveaux riche* bastards,' said Pip Fenwick, before he realized whose parents they were. 'How do they get the petrol?'

'My dad's in War work, as a matter of fact,' said Guy, who almost never took offence.

'Mr Walking's pride is that the school has never evacuated,' said Cock, at roll call. 'And we'll all back him up.'

But James himself – returning a loaned book – heard Cock say: 'Mr Walking says we should trust in God – that that is the school motto: In God Is All Our Trust. But his God is going to get us in trouble.

'I didn't see you, Berkeley – you are *not* to repeat that – gentleman's honour, right?'

'Agreed.'

On the 18th of July a buzz bomb hit the Radlett Gasworks – the explosion seemed to point a direction. . .

The term was supposed to run until July 27th – but the relentless bombs had won. . . (James even said to himself: 'Hitler has won – but he doesn't seem to know it.')

Fotheringham was relatively deep in the country: a

515

mile's walk to the nearest bus, five miles from the Underground: but, on the 19th, students just started wandering off down the road, caught the buses and then the Underground and went home. . .

On the 20th of July, Mr Walking officially closed the school. . .

Only that day did James head north himself.

The train stopped at Ely. James got out on the platform. A stationmaster was happily looking at his pocket-watch – he had a relaxed expression such as no one in the London area had. James had forgotten that such a human expression existed.

'Excuse me.'

'Yes, sir.'

'Have you had any buzz bombs?'

'Oh no – not a one – thank heaven. And you – are you from London?'

'Yes – glad to get out.'

'Glad to have you, lad, would you like a cup of tea? Train will be seven or more minutes.'

James thought it was the best cup of tea he'd ever tasted – dark brown. . . Then he started the silent crying. . .

Christopher.

Water was pouring over everything – just like at sea again.

'You all right, mate?'

James nodded, as best he could, and got back on the train.

As the train moved, he waved his thanks. The stationmaster gave him a big and knowing wink.

James reckoned he must be a veteran of the First War, an Old Comrade as they called themselves.

XXXI

What If The V-3's Come?

It was late September 1944

'My aunt wasn't going to let me come back,' James said.

'My parents weren't going to let me either – we've all been in Hereford,' said Larry. 'Very peaceful. I say, it *is* wonderful not to have to "Boy" any more.'

'Certainly is,' said Rich. 'Look at those poor sod new boys –'

'Wretched Frogs,' said Herman.

'Poor blighters – let's give 'em all the help we can,' said Rich.

There was a Frog aeroplane once . . . *Christopher.*

'All the hell, you mean,' said Pip Fenwick.

'Rich. Tell me all you know about these new bombs?' asked James.

'Yeah. You know everything,' said Pip. 'What are they and why?'

Matron went on by, smiling and rosy-cheeked.

'Did you have a good holiday, Matron?' Rich asked.

'I certainly did, Richmond – and you?'

'Great thanks, Matron.'

'Do you think we've had an end to the doodlebugs? – Those fellows that explode before penetration, eh, Berkeley?' She looked James in the eyes and chuckled.

'Have to ask, Rich – he's our expert.'

'I should think we've definitely had an end to the V-1s – truth is, this V-2 – well, you can multiply the V-1 by everything. The V-2 is a rocket – and it travels at about 2,500 miles an hour – they say. But I'll tell you it's more like 4,000.'

'Also, it's a straight up, straight down journey. Think of forty to fifty *miles*. Just like a rocket in fireworks – but, again, it has an enormous bomb load.'

'And this one explodes after penetration?' said Matron laughing.

'You'll get us all in trouble, Matron,' said Block.

'Are we not allowed to laugh now?' she said. 'Is that a new rule?'

'Oh, no.'

'Well, what about the buzz bombs?'

'Finished, I should imagine. This V-2 is better by a thousand per cent.'

'So they started this month – we all know that – but how long will they go on?' asked Matron.

'Well, it's really a question of who will overrun whom? I think,' said Rich. 'It's a helluva weapon and it's doing a lot of harm. But, it's very expensive to build and very difficult to build.' Rich had everyone listening – all six Musketeers, Matron and others.

'It's just a matter of when will the Allies overrun their launching pads and their factories.'

Silence.

Block's gaunt face moved into a clown-like smile. He shoved his hands deep in his pockets – and, with his legs wide apart he rocked back and forward. 'Say Rich, what if the V-3s come?'

Rich only smiled.

Everyone looked stunned.

'Anyway,' said Rich. 'I say the Wound-Up Monkeys of Death are finished.'

When Matron had gone and James and Rich were alone, James said: 'I could really go for that Matron – if she was a bit younger.'

'We've come to that, have we?'

518

'She's got a lovely way about her – so sympathetic.'
Christopher.
'Steady, lad.'

James got a cable from Bermuda. 'The Reverend R. Souls, and Lady Osborne will arrive shortly by royal courier. Berkeley.' He hoped it meant his father was coming but he didn't let himself believe it for fear belief would make it not happen . . . Besides, a courier was a special postman . . . Rich said, 'It's probably a book.'

In the previous holiday, at Washashley, James had had the closest time with his Aunt Daisy he'd ever known.

'Oh you poor darling,' she said, the moment he arrived at the cottage – having taken the bus from Lincoln. 'You do look so like your dear dad now. Tell me all about it?'

Mostly he was numb, but sometimes he could talk. She was a good listener and a good questioner – and she had, literally, a magic touch.

As he'd noticed when he first arrived at the Hall from Bermuda, Aunt Daisy's touch had a sort of electric soothing mechanism built in. . . . He wondered if it was not, perhaps, the fabled gift of healing.

She would stroke the backs of his hands as they sat in the garden; the top of his head, as they waited in the kitchen for lunch or dinner.

Sometimes, she'd stand behind his low chair and massage his neck and shoulders

'Don't do anything, Jamie,' she'd say. 'Just sleep and eat – and we'll take care of you.'

One day when they were alone in deck-chairs – beside the enormous sea of flowers she had turned the little garden into – he said,

'Is this how you soothed Dad after his crash?' He hoped to learn a secret of that faraway time.

'Oh, no,' she said, with her little buck-toothed lisp. 'He was older than you are – and I was much younger than I am. . .'

'You are so very kind, Aunt Daisy. I did want to tell you that.'

'It's a treat to have a man to spoil,' she said. He wondered how old she was.

'When will Dad come?'

'Soon, I should think,' she said.

There was a little letter from Christopher. (He tried to sneak up on it sideways.)

'They are very short – because there was one for every member of the family.

'And, then, dear boy, there's this from Squadron Leader John Leatham.'

Dear Skeglee,
Got nothing to say but keep-on and make us all proud of you and maybe you can take up poetry where I leave off.

Keep laughing.

Remember there's a helluva lot of luck in this life.

Give my love to Mum, Dad, Widda-Widda – and to Wavy, I mean Toffee

   Alway your everloving brother
    Christopher

James folded it and put it in his wallet, carefully.

He picked up the squadron leader's letter. The squadron leader must have thought Aunt Lillie still alive:

Dear Miss Curfey and All at Washashley Hall

It's my awful duty to tell you straight out and at once, that, although 'Chris' Berkeley is listed as Missing, I was flying with him on the 6th and I saw what happened.

His plane was hit twice very hard and went into the sea. The impact of the aircraft was severe. At no time did I see him endeavour to get out – either during the plane's descent – or in the water. The plane both broke up and sank immediately.

I flew over the spot and there were no signs. Also an RAF Rescue launch was on the scene in fifteen minutes. They found nothing. I ordered them back twice.

I most regretfully must assume that your nephew (and my revered friend) perished. I do not believe he suffered. I believe he was killed in the first burst of fire.

I can only send you my deepest sympathies and hope that his beautiful personality and loving character will endure with you as it does with all of us here at his squadron.

He was The Best and everyone knew it.

Yours faithfully
John Leatham

P.S. You probably know that Chris was unhappy and he was suffering a great deal of grief for other friends. He told me recently that he couldn't ever seem to sleep. 'I just have *nuits blanches*,' he told me just last week. I don't know if these facts are helpful, I hope so.
P.P.S. I've written his parents in Bermuda also.

Still numb, James had hugged Aunt Daisy. He kissed Mrs Pickle.

He went out that evening into the strong sweet smells of the Washashley cottage garden. The moon was bright and full.

He looked up and said,

'Speak. Christopher. Speak. You will never know another *nuit blanche*, but I have to keep on. Speak to me. If I cut my wrist, will you hear me?'

Fenders cried and Mrs Fenders cried – she holding her white handkerchief in a little ball, the knuckles of her fingers red and swollen like her eyes.

She hugged him: 'Begging your pardon, Mr James – but God bless you.'

Fenders broke into sobs – which, of course, his Scottish upbringing made him try to strangle. 'It's . . . always . . . the best . . . that get . . . killed. . . He was the best. . . Nicest man . . . I know . . . right credit to his uncle . . . the Master

'And your Dad, of course.'

They had a 'cuppa' and then several more and Fenders said,

'There's several others around here we could do without – so they got Mr Chris – it's rotten, Mr James, rotten. Somehow we'll build a memorial to him – you and I, shall we?'

'Yes, Fenders – indeed – I would like that.'

Mrs Fenders suddenly said, 'They are not going to kill us all, those *bloody* Germans – they are not. They may think they are, but they are not. We are a very ferocious people and we will never forget.'

'Yes,' said James. 'I agree.'

Several weeks later, Fenders said: 'Those horrible Canadians have gone now, sir. Went earlier this week. And I know you couldn't guess in a thousand years who's got the Hall now.'

'You mean, what troops? Poles?'

'No. British – English – but bloody paratroopers. And they've got two soldiers from Bermuda with them.'

'*No!*'

'Yes. They're white – but not like us, sir. Not like The Family.'

James met one the day before he went back to Fotheringham.

The man was a Portuguese Bermudian from Devonshire.

'U'm right pleased-to-meetcha, Mr Berkeley. Tony is my name – Tony Pimental.'

'Tony Pimental – sure sounds like home.'

They shook hands.

Tony Pimental said: 'So this is your place too?'

'Was.'

'Nice place – pretty beeg. All Bermuda would go in the land – huh?'

'Just about – Tony – are you going to be about for a while? I have to go away to school. But I'll be back at Christmas – maybe we could get together?'

'Um-mum – Christmas. Fact-of-the-matter-truth, we're on "Stand-by" – we could go anywhere anytime. But I sure *hope* to see you again, Mr Berkeley – Truth is, I used to know your cousin – George Berkeley.'

'Sure.'

'Him and me was in the BVRCs together. He's a real *nice* fella.'

'Yes. Thanks. Isn't he nice? Yes. Well, forgive me Tony – I've got to run – great to see a Bermudian. Good luck and I hope to see you again.'

Tony Pimental's handshake was so strong it startled you:

'I miss home so bad I could lay my head down and

523

cry.'

'I absolutely agree.'

'If I don't see you anywhere – I'll see you back in Bermuda – right?'

'Yes – you bet. It's a very small world, isn't it?'

'You are saying nothing but the fact-of-the-matter-truth, James.'

'OK, Tony.'

'OK.'

George Berkeley was his first cousin, and he was, indeed, a very nice person. . .

'Anyway,' said Rich, 'we're not afraid of the V-2 bombs, are we?'

James was not sure about that; he needed time to think and time to experience them.

'I guess we don't get a chance to be afraid – you get the explosion – blam – and then, after that you hear the bomb coming down,' said Larry Rhodes. 'The world is getting to be a very mad place.'

'The V-2s seem to have stopped the buzz bombs –' said Mac Block – 'So, my granny and I – we figure we are all for them.'

James said: 'They are an august weapon.'

'It's September, Jim,' said Guy Callum, kicking a pebble with an immaculate black shoe.

'Oh, shut up.'

James was not prepared for what happened on 23rd September 1944.

Mac Block came into the old Schoolroom of School House (their recreation and living-room) and said in a very bad but admiring imitation of an American accent:

'There's some American man wandering around the school asking to see Berkeley. I've no idea who he is – might be a film person, that's my guess.'

When James saw his father and his sister, saw the sparkle of their eyes, in the purple light of that particular September, he experienced a constriction of the arteries and blood vessels that felt like a heart attack.

'Hello.'

'Hello.'

'Hello.'

They stood and touched hands to the outer clothes of each other. They all seemed to cry in the same shy way. They began to move, rotate, slowly, to the left. . .

'Been a long while, Old Man.' His father started to hug them both and then they wheeled about to the right now – like drunken fools. . .

James had forgotten even what they were like and now experienced it all over again. His father's compactness and sort of magic presence: he looked just like the Duke of Windsor – only stronger. . .

And Vicky's sensual and gymnastic littleness: like the Isherwood side of the family, she was constructed so delicately that when she held her hand up to the sun, you could see light through it, see the bones like an x-ray.

'Skeglee,' Vicky squeaked. 'Skeglee.'

Christopher.

'Oh Widda-Widda – this is awful. I'm supposed to be a brave bloke.' James felt tears running all the way down and inside his stiff collar.

He still barely dared look at the sparks of light from his father's eyes. . .

'Look – son – can you get permission to come to London?'

'Dad. . .' followed by what Widda-Widda would call

525

a water-closet. '*You* could get me off – by seeing the Head.'

'Steer me to him, Old Man.'

They walked to the School House Library door (over which was written 'This FVEE GRAMER SCOOLE. . .').

'It's right through there, sir. Only *you* could get me off by permission of Mr Walking.'

'I'll give it my best throw.'

As James took Victoria's arm and walked with her to the circular wooden seat around the poplar, he became aware of what had changed in his sister since he'd last seen her:

at every window of School House was at least one set of very intent male eyes.

'Tell me everything.'

'Easy, you Skeglee-Rat you – you first,' she went into peals of laughter. He was amazed at her Ariel-like beauty – and it seemed impossible that she had any flaws at all, either mental or physical, but, he knew, she did – her feet had little bumps on the top where a bone, one on each foot, seemed a bit misshapen.

The Dragon, their mother, had convinced Vicky (over these feet) that she looked like a crippled toad.

'So Vicky can take your head off,' Chris had said, 'like James Thurber's cartoon, "Touché" – without you knowing it sometimes.

'But treat her right,' Chris added, 'and just being with Vicky is like a brisk sail on a sunny winter's day.'

'You are a man,' she said.

'And you are some tomato.'

'Keep it up – I love it. All Boys Is Bad Boys, thank God.'

'Christopher –'

'Not now, Skeglee. Later.'

'OK.'

There was a large but very distant explosion.

'What's that?'

'Just a V-2 – not very scary.'

'You can say – scares me.'

'After the V-1s, these V-2s are a piece of cake.'

'Why?'

'If you hear them, you are OK – if you don't, you are dead. And the chances of death are one hundred and twenty-two million, seven hundred and fifty thousand to one.'

'Who says?'

'My best friend, Rich Richmond – he's quite a genius and you should meet him.'

'I'd like to, dear Skeglee.'

His father came quietly rushing out: 'All fixed: you've got until ten tonight,' he said.

'No kidding –? A Tenner – that's the hardest to get. Praeposters only. How did you do it?'

'I said we'd just arrived at Portsmouth – personal guests of the Admiralty and Admiral Sir Michael Jenkins and that I hadn't seen you for two years.'

'Two years eight months and twenty-one days.'

'*Really*? How awful. Tell you what then. We'll take a taxi to Town.'

'St George – stop that – it's twenty miles.'

'Who cares – we'll take a taxi to Simpson's and have roast beef. The best in London.'

'For such extravagance,' she said, gurgling with laughter, 'that's two hairs.'

'Two what?'

'He knows his punishments,' she said. 'He knows.'

In no time his father had found a taxi.

James had got his mac – but he couldn't find

527

Rich – and he had to hurry.

His father pushed across the little slide window.

'Driver, is Simpson's still the best place to eat?'

'Not on a Sunday, sir.'

'The Savoy?'

'Savoy or Claridge's sir.'

'The best – not the gaudiest, please, driver.'

They agreed on Claridge's.

It was lovely – but there was no room for anyone without a reservation. Father said: 'Wait here,' and went in.

In a moment, he came back with the head waiter.

'This way,' the head waiter said so that everyone could hear: 'I'd quite forgotten Your Honour's reservation – a standing order, of course.'

They were seated at the table closest to the grand piano.

'You bad boy – stick out your hand,' said Vicky, when they were seated.

She pulled a hair out of his hirsute wrist.

'Ouch,' he feigned great pain.

'Another, Frankenstein.'

'Ouch!' he cried again.

James was very shocked that his father had obviously 'tipped' their way through. Yet he was proud of him, and exceedingly happy to have his protection and guidance.

The head waiter came back immediately with a menu and wine list.

'What do you recommend?' his father said very gently. 'We've been out of the country for six years.'

'Easier to say what's on, than what's off, sir – these days. I've some good wines – no whisky – and all food is officially five shillings.'

'Well – Jennings, is it?'

528

'Johnson, sir.'

'Of course – Johnson – I would say,' his father smiled with his usual genuine consideration. 'Send us your wine waiter and scramble up whatever you can for us.'

'I'm the wine waiter too, sir – we manage with just three of us – and five gals.'

Widda-Widda started her frown that looked like a spaniel puppy's.

'You're a regular in here, Dad?'

'Never been here before in my life.'

James marvelled at the knowing ways of men...

'It's like this,' she said: 'He didn't die, you see. He came home to Bermuda and the weather was just beautiful that spring.

'And he wouldn't work – he just sailed a boat about all the time – to rest. To rest from the War, cradled on the deep turquoise sea of Bermuda – being rocked in the cradle of the deep, if you like.'

Their father had gone to the men's room. James realized that it was, partially, to give them a chance to talk.

'I'll tell you mine in a minute –'

'OK. In a minute. But this is what happened to Christopher: he came home and met this young woman who was so beautiful, radiantly beautiful – that, at her home, in Toronto, she was known as The Face and The Body and The Brain. That's how beautiful – and she just stepped on Christopher's sailing boat and she fell for him like a sack of sugar off the Banana Boat.

'The Face and The Body and The Brain. And they are married in Toronto and it's the biggest wedding of the year –'

St George came back and sat down quietly –

529

without interrupting.

'And I'm the Maid of Honour and you are Best Man, you and Nasti both, and they live on Jarvis Street – the parents – and it's a very big society wedding

'And Chris hates it – and so, they hurry back to Bermuda and build a house out on our island – and live happily ever after. That's what happened to Chris.'

She just sat there looking like a china figure that was about to shatter. 'I left out a bit,' she said, 'they spent their honeymoon at a place called Lake Nipissing in Ontario – there is a place called that – and with Chris's awful male vulgar humour, he has to go out immediately and pee in the lake. That's all.'

Silence.

'Funny. I figured a Hero's Big Welcome Home to Bermuda. . .'

'Strange,' said St George. 'But you know, I always imagined he'd be married in Toronto too. Why did you imagine that?'

'Don't know. Just did.'

'Why Jarvis Street?'

'Don't know.'

'My mother lived on Jarvis Street all her childhood. Her father – a doctor from Bermuda – had a practice there.'

She smiled.

'Tell you something funny – there's always something funny,' said St George.

'What?'

'Jarvis Street used to be very posh – but it's the red-light district now.'

She didn't laugh. James thought everyone looked like china – and he hoped someone would change the subject.

530

St George said, 'You know how your mother is always tearing down the Berkeleys?

'Well, your Uncle Edmond – my brother – just gave her a birthday present. It was a full-size white pisspot – with what he said was the Berkeley coat o'arms on it. He had it hand-painted. It was a skunk, holding its nose and raising its leg.'

'She laughed?' asked James.

'Yes, she sure did.'

'I think the punishment for that is one hair, but I'm not sure.'

St George patted the back of her hand. 'Dear Blossom.'

She drew her hand away – not unkindly.

'I wanted to say, Skeglee – that he had a unique strength, Christopher did. Strength like a smooth stone.'

'Yes. That's right,' James said.

Christopher.

Silence.

'I can't go to the b-r again. But I'll save a joke Chris told me – to tell you later as we go home in the taxi.'

'We have to find your sister a school,' St George said, just before they left Claridge's.

'St George, Binky and I went to the Den School – as boarders, in case you've forgotten – when I was seven and he was five. And that shouldn't have been allowed, St George, and I won't go any more.'

'Tell me about the boats, Dad?'

'Finished all the Skids and all the Scottish fishing vessels and all the Fairmiles. All for the Admiralty. And all finished. Some of the men are let go. If we don't get something soon – I'll have to close the whole operation.'

'Who's running it – is it all right?'

'I've a good man running everything – I just couldn't be away from you all any longer. I had to come over here to help you.'

'Wish I'd seen the Fairmiles.'

'I do think we did the Royal Navy proud with them, Jamie. All teak and mahogany, you know. Appointed better than yachts. Beautiful of line, they are too. And much better sea-boats than the old motor launches I was on in 1916 and 1917.

'A Fairmile can cross the Atlantic, you know.'

'I thought they could only go one-third.'

'Well, in favourable conditions they can cross.'

Vicky got up. They did too.

In the taxi, James said: 'It's just been the happiest . . . the best. . .'

'So we'll go up to Lincoln. Find a place – that cottage is much too small – for your holidays – for all of us. And soon it will be your holidays – and, anyway, your mother will be over soon.'

'Can't wait.'

'How do you like Fotheringham?'

'St George,' said Vicky, 'you promised a funny story. . .'

'Well – you know one thing Christopher and I always did share and that was a good joke over the word "balls" –'

'Careful, Monster – or you'll be for it.'

James thought: the biggest thing that you and Chris shared was really a painfully evident, so-called secret, dislike. . .

'Anyway, puns on the word, and the word – we always liked. One day – it was the day I had to go back to Bermuda and I took him out and I said: "You can have or do anything you want today – what would you like?"

532

'He said, without hesitation, to fly in a real aeroplane. So he must have been ten. So I hired a plane and they flew us around the Isle of Wight. I took some moving pictures – remember?'

'The joke now please, love.'

'Yes. Of course. Sorry. We walked around Arundel – after the flight – we went from Tangmere, of course – and there was this sign – no word made up, Vicky. The sign said: "Balls and Balls, Solicitors" and I said to Chris, they should have a child, a son, and be "Balls Balls and Balls, Solicitors". And Christopher said very quietly: "They should have a son and christen him, Stillmore." Never forgotten that.'

They laughed.

Christopher.

'What do you know about these V-2s, son?' his father said, away from the taxi.

'Well, apparently – we are about to overrun their factories. And they aren't up in Lincoln.'

'Please let me know – immediately – the minute you are safe from them here.'

'I'm going to do Christopher's turn and run, Dad.'

XXXII

'Your sister is wizard-looking, old chap,' said Larry Rhodes.

'Thank you.'

'Sorry I missed her, Berkeley.'

'Sorry you did too, Rich.'

James then got a letter that had been written just two days before his father and Vicky's visit.

Leaview Washashley
21st September 1944

Dear Mr James

I have the most horrible news to tell of as ever I had to tell any Berkeley. Mr Watkins and me was wakened by Millie screetching through the cottages that the Germans had landed. Well, they had not, but it was as if they had.

The soldiers in the Hall, paratroopers (who have been held in reserve since D-Day and never seen any action so there is no excuse) cornered the White Deer in Park with their truck lights and a searchlight. Even a Bermuda soldier was in on it, but not your friend Pvte. Pimental. They shot (I should say slaughtered) the poor defenceless things with Sten guns. All of them they killed, the bucks and the does.

Tom Watkins went in to stop the suffering but it were hours and hours too long. He killed eleven crying deer, he said, seven does, two bucks and two yearlings.

All of us Berkeleys are trying to keep it from The Madam but I can't promise because everyone knows including Mrs busy-body Pickle.

Ashamed to bring you this turn of events, sir, I remain, with best from my Mrs,

Your humble and obedient servant.

R. Fenders

Again, it was something James had to keep entirely to himself.

You couldn't tell about deer in your park being slaughtered and expect sympathy from boys who were afraid for their lives, now could you?

James had to carefully put the pain of it away – in the same place, really, with Christopher. . .

All through that term until Christmas 1944, what haunted them – with the wide-spaced but unremitting

534

explosions of the V-2s – was Block's phrase:

'What if the V-3s come?'

This haunting fear went on right up until March 1945. Very similar fears, they knew, plagued everyone in southern Britain where the V-2s kept landing.

Despite all this, James went up to Lincoln full of expectation. His father and Vicky met him.

His father had a virtually new black Hillman Minx.

'It was the Demonstrator of 1938 – it's perfect,' said St George, with his magnetic and theatrical animation. 'It does thirty miles to the gallon.'

'It's a beauty! But how do you get petrol?'

'We've a little ration. I do, after all, still work for the Admiralty.' St George gave him a big wink.

'We've a place to live, Binky – but we have to share this woman's house. And she's a grump and her name is Mrs Leech.'

'She's very nice,' said Dad, 'and it's impossible to get housing. And the Hall's full, as you know. And your Aunt –'

'How is Aunt Daisy?'

'Well, very well – and she's coming to have supper with us tonight.'

'Oh, I am glad.'

'James, she knows about the deer. And now there's been some damage done to the carved stairs – and she knows just that fact.'

'The stairs, Dad – the Raleigh stairs?'

'There's been some damage done – and we are to see it tomorrow.'

'*I'm not* going to see it,' Aunt Daisy said.

'No. I don't think, for a moment, you should.'

'May I come, please, Dad?'

'Yes. I think three of us will be acceptable to the

wretched Army.'

James told his father and Vicky when they were
alone:

'Fenders wrote to me about the deer. It was the
paratroopers. But Fenders said that the Bermudian
that I met – Tony Pimental – was not in on it. He was
in the BVRC in Bermuda and he knew George.'

'Really?' said Vicky. 'Amazing.'

'Most of the soldiers are away right now – the Hall's
apparently almost empty. There's to be a separate
enquiry about the deer. At any rate, we'll see
tomorrow.'

Inside, the Hall was light but desolate – as if no one
was living there at all.

It echoed their footsteps and their voices.

James's eyes kept saying to his father – Do you
remember? But his father seemed too moved to even
look him in the eye.

'I don't know what's been done and what hasn't,'
said a major – who lit one cigarette from another
with orange-stained fingers. 'It wasn't my lot, anyway.'

What had been done was that the entire front-
stairs railing, that went all the way across the upper
landing, the whole carving of the life, adventures,
travels and ships of Raleigh – and the main characters, and Sir Walter Raleigh himself – the whole
carving in oak and ebony, complete with the words of
Sir Walter's poem. . .

the whole thing was gone. Nothing was left but
little iron stakes sticking up.

'Where is it?' said James, rushing forward. 'Where
is it?'

'It's been burned,' his father said.

'It was Christopher's most favourite thing – that and the Grey-White deer –'

'And mine also,' said his father. 'And Uncle Albert's and Daisy's. . .'

In the grates of the great reception rooms – ashes lay grey and cold and lost

'*Who* did it?' St George said.

'I don't know anything – they were not my lot.'

'Well, what is your name and your number – and we'll begin with you – until we can get somebody better.'

James had never seen his father so icy.

He himself felt as if he were looking over the side of the *Empire United* again, feeling the pull of the pitiless ocean – the vertigo. . .

Christopher. Christopher.

'Come on, you Skeglee bastard. Thou unnoticing ne'er-do-well – say it with me. Love is a durable fire, In the mind ever burning; Never sick, never old, never dead, From itself never turning.'

There were three griefs here at Washashley that seemed to merge. . .

There were the deer, which he kept seeing, in his imagination, lying all bloodied and broken – their little mouths still. . . There were the Raleigh stairs, broken and gone for ever (for a work of art, like a person, was unique and as easily annihilated. . .). And then there were Christopher's arms that he kept seeing and the way they moved – and the smell of Christopher.

The griefs let a chill into his awareness: a shaft like a stalactite –

He seemed to stand over Christopher's grave and realize there was nothing there and that whatever had been Christopher was never going to be again. . .

He rushed away down the wide pine stairs and out the south door, and considered himself damned lucky to find the gate to the walled garden open.

He moved to the warmest part of the south-facing brick wall, and, looking around and seeing no one there, he let out a very Bermudian utterance:

'Gone, oh, gone. . .'

He wept. . .

'Lost. . .'

It was even warm here and then the sun came out.

They could talk all they liked about heaven and hell, he knew that there was, within him, a dispassionate observer, who knew that death was annihilation.

What was deeply bad about Christopher's death, was that Christopher was so rare and that he would never be again. . .

And when he had figured all this out, he'd stopped crying.

What would Chris say, he asked himself? He'd say: 'Thou Skeglee bastard – you don't believe in what the poem says and me only gone ten minutes. I'll never leave you – you'll never be free of the grief, but you'll never be without the warmth, the love, either.

'And, as to people, there's good and great people born every year. . .'

James smiled.

In a little while he went and found Vicky and his father.

She patted him with Christopher's vibrator pats.

'There should have been a copy,' his father said, meaning of the stairs.

'Yes. There should have been.' James.

'I'd kill them, sir – if I could. We have to find out who

538

did it and make them pay.'

This time, James accepted Mrs Fenders's embrace – she had tears running down under her glasses. He kissed her.

'Bless you, Mr James.'

'It must have been terrible, Mrs Fenders.'

'Well, you've got your Dad and Miss Vicky so all's right with the world, isn't it?'

'Yes.' James smiled, tears in his eyes too.

'And what do you think of the Hillman, Mr James? Smashing isn't it? I've a bit more work to do on the engine – then she'll be as good as new.'

'Yes. She's super – and so smooth for a little car.'

'I should say – ' Fenders's eyes now rolled with happiness – the return of the Master...

'And soon as Hitler's beaten – we can pull the sheet off our lady, XV 2350.'

Which meant, of course, the Rolls.

Later, in Aunt Daisy's cottage, St George said:

'I think the shooting and bludgeoning of the deer in the park is the worst thing of all. How can an entire herd of forty head of deer be murdered – and we've been nurturing them since the turn of the century?'

'A lot of them were stock from Arreton and Steyning,' said Aunt Daisy – but then she added: 'I'm not *going to think of it*, I simply cannot, dear boy. I cannot.'

George comforted her and James did too – and Vicky. Daisy did so like Vicky – their shy smiles seemed to match...

Victoria had been going through Christopher's papers, which the RAF had so carefully sent back. The papers were in his tuck box which dated back to his entry

539

into the Lion School, at Littlehampton, in September 1930, when he was not quite nine. Very hesitantly, she showed these clippings to James.

'This is what upset Christopher so much – and his friend Harold, the bomber pilot. Look:'

'*23 November 1943*

'FOURTH GREAT ATTACK ON BERLIN IN NINE NIGHTS – LANCASTER BOMBERS RAIN DOWN 1000 TONS OF EXPLOSIVES AND INCENDIARIES IN 20 MINUTES ... A THIRD OF GERMANY'S CAPITAL CITY LAID IN RUINS.

'Swedish Newspaper *Allehanda* said that 40,000 had been killed and 500,000 made homeless. . .

'A Swedish woman said: 'Hundreds of people are camping day and night in front of the Zoo – Tiergarden. I have seen several groups of people kneeling in the streets praying and singing psalms.'

'Another eyewitness said: 'Berliners were in a daze. What has happened exceeds anything you have read and everything you can imagine. People talk of the stoic calm but no one speaks of those Berliners who stand at street corners and wring their hands with dumb despair. . .'

'And this,' Vicky said, 'Chris marked The Greatest Obscenity:

'Air Marshal Sir Arthur Harris, C-in-C Bomber Command, has sent the following message to all workers in Royal Ordinance Factories:

'In eight days Berlin has used up more than 6000 tons of high explosives and incendiary bombs. No bombs dropped anywhere could have had more effect. No weapons used elsewhere or in any other way could do more to shorten the war.

540

'Bomber Command has been working for more than four years to achieve the ability to do what has been done in the last week. It has been a hard long struggle.

'Now, when we are right on top of the enemy and have shown what we can do to his capital city, I ask you to put as much effort into this last lap of the race as the crews themselves.

'As you make and fill the bombs remember that you and the crews of Bomber Command have started a New Reichstag fire which this time will put the Nazis out of office!'

'Chris thought it all mass murder,' she said.

'I hadn't quite understood,' James said. 'And don't quite yet.'

She also showed him a large ledger which was in the tuck box. It was labelled:

'History, family-type, of Aubrey Spencer Berkeley. Backwards often, forwards sometimes and probably sideways frequently.'

Inside the entire volume was empty except for the first paragraph which James read:

'First of all, I was born, I proudly state (go to hell you Limey bastards who I love) in the colonies, particularly in the colony of Bermuda, which is an island unto itself in whose soil my conscience is.'

'That's all?'

'Yes – that and a few random notes. But there are the poems – and the Journal, but it's pretty sparse too. . .'

Ever since his Atlantic crossing in 1942, James had had a 'contracting colon' – which no one knew the cause of. He would about once every three weeks, get a heavy ache in the lower abdomen – which gradually

541

increased and increased, until, sometimes, the pain was so great he passed out.

His father took him to a specialist – who prescribed a medicine that contained a little opium... This doctor knew the cause of his contracting colon, and he told his father but they never told James...

When he felt this ache coming on, he was to go to the Sick Room. Matron had been forewarned about it. After the Matron at The Lion School, this kindly and humanitarian one was a deep and lovely shock.

'Oh, you've got a pain, have you?' she'd say. 'Hurry along into bed and I'll bring the medicine.'

It's you I'd like for medicine, James thought.

The pain came on relentlessly: but the opiate took it on, fought it, and won. After knowing the pain without the drug – it seemed miraculous.

When the pain was almost gone, James would lie in the bed and float in a flight of fantasy – that usually involved Rita Hayworth... (Sometimes it included tying up young women and spanking them – and that still tormented him with guilt...) But a lot of it was Rita Hayworth and what he'd do with her naked ... on a desert island, for about a year and two days...

On the 12th of April 1945, James was just recovering from a colon attack, when the radio in the Sick Room, where he was quite alone, said:

'This is Alvar Liddell, we interrupt this programme to bring you the following message. It has just been reported that the President of the United States, Mr Franklin Delano Roosevelt, died today at his retreat in Warm Springs, Georgia ...'

James felt a very personal grief – as if he had lost another member of his family... When he was a boy in Bermuda, he would often listen to the President's Fireside Chats

He also felt that President Roosevelt was a great

and good and honourable man. . .
Christopher.
(Perhaps it was from that day on that he knew he was more of the New World than the Old. . .)
He also thought it was lousy luck that Roosevelt should die, when victory was obviously so close. . .

1945 was when he began to keep his *Journal* (perhaps in imitation of Christopher) to try to catch the 'Big Events' that took place:
Adolf Hitler was reported dead, 30th of April 1945, and then came VE Day on the
8th of May. He wrote, 'Most of us went a little wild and most of us cried.'
The Atomic Bomb was exploded at Los Alamos, New Mexico, on the 16th of July,
an atomic bomb was dropped on Hiroshima on the 6th of August,
another atomic bomb was dropped on Nagasaki on the 9th of August;
on the 14th of August was VJ Day.

James tried to catch every event he could, but, for the Berkeleys, and everyone whose life and heart touched theirs, the Main Event of 1945 was the Coming (Back) to England of Charity Berkeley
(here insert: flourish of colonial cornets)
No woman exists or existed to measure Charity Halcyon Berkeley against:
before Her Coming, the Fenders loved old Mrs Berkeley (The Madame) and every Berkeley and all the Berkeleys loved the Fenders
and Mrs Pickle loved old Mrs Berkeley (especially when she would do what she was told and not be a naughty girl. . .)
and George Berkeley was loved by everyone and

James too and Victoria too – and they all loved in return

and all were happy

Then, like some gunslinger, but wearing her three strands of real pearls – in a blue velvet choker around her handsome neck –

she came to town

Her children rushed to her ample maternal bosom with their griefs, but they were not to be listened to. . .

This is what she said about Aubrey Spencer Berkeley, born 17th November 1921, died 6th June 1944:

'No one suffers in comparison to a Mother – *He was MINE – and I have given him to My Country and My God!*'

Beneath the umbrella of this statement were swept away all the feelings of all others as always and for ever.

James was suffering from a frightening case of mumps (puberty, of course, being a bad time to get this disease) when his mother arrived. He was sure she'd rush to take care of the sickest of her brood first – she stood in the door and waved at him.

'Pip, pip,' she said. 'Get well soon. Can't come any closer or Little George might catch it.'

When James realized there were tears on his face, she had already gone.

Victoria, who had previously won her Cambridge School Certificate in Bermuda at fourteen years old with seven Distinctions, was booked into a boarding school. 'Her mind must have the benefit of English tuition' – all despite Vicky's protests.

Charity now faced the problem of what to do about

the beloved Washashley, beloved Aunt and beloved servants.

She managed it with one masterstroke:

Her sister had purchased, for a retirement home for her husband (the Dean of Norwich) and herself, a timbered house in a remote part of Hertfordshire. But they did not need it yet.

She rented it.

'It will be near James's school.'

As to Aunt Daisy; she had 'her place and her friend and housekeeper' – and, 'anyway – Daisy's not totally honest – at least not *our* kind of honesty'.

Little George was booked into The Lion School – of course, nowhere near Hertfordshire (Victoria's school was even further away, in western Dorset).

Everyone was to move to Hertfordshire – except, of course, Fenders. Fenders wanted to bring his whole family and live in a farmer's cottage nearby. She would not allow that. He'd come, for the Master's sake, and no one else's, by himself, he said. Leaving his wife and child behind. Not-a-bit-of-it.

It was at about this point that James noticed that Grandfather Halcyon had not been mentioned.

'Where's Grampy?'

'In Bermuda, of course. He wouldn't like this climate,' his mother said.

'But he'd want to be with us – to be with his family. Why can't we send for him?'

'He's with his sisters – the Beaumont Aunts – and he's had a stroke, you know.'

'But he'd rather be with his own family – especially if he's been sick. He loves us and needs us.'

'His sisters are his family – a lot you know, James.'

'But we are his – we are descended from him. He's ours. Besides, I, for one, want him.'

'He would never leave his friends.'

'*His* remark was: "I don't have enough time for my friends – I have too many family – but that's the way I want it." Besides, he must be utterly lost without Granny.'

'Shut up, James. You are just an upstart boy. You are not to mention it again. Don't you know the pain of being without my father is almost more than I can bear?'

James knew that something was wrong about these remarks but a child, of course, cannot soon understand that a parent is an egotist.

Why did George Berkeley allow all this? Because he'd been brought up in a family where a strong and frustrated mother had ruled over a charming and loving and weak father (who'd been nurtured himself in a very similar home. . .)

And, also, because St George felt deeply guilty about his 'affair' with his aunt in World War I. . . Charity was moving on the open wound of his guilt. . .

No sooner did she have them all in Hertfordshire, than she began to tear down the reputation of the dead.

'Your Uncle Albert was a horrible old man' – who never paid his bills – 'would rather ride to hounds than be a vicar.' To get all the things he had, he'd obviously stolen – and a man of God was supposed to have nothing but 'sackcloth and ashes'.

His education was dubious (he was, of course, a Fellow of St John's, Cambridge) and the source of his wealth even more dubious. . .

(Here she was on better ground, of course, than she knew. . .)

'Christopher adored the ground I walked on – and would have thrown himself in front of a train for me.'

It was questionable as to what would have been achieved by this action.

And, in Christopher's History there was a line that she would surely have destroyed had she known of its existence.

'My childhood was a torment by tongue more terrible than Lady Macbeth's.'

She had good things to report about Teddy. 'The brave boy got his wings at Kokomo, Indiana, and went on to win his Commission in the Royal Navy at Corpus Christi, Texas –'

But, then Lend-Lease ended, as did everything else the 'treacherous' Americans did, prematurely with the end of the War in Europe, and so Teddy neither got into the fighting, nor got a real commission. . .

He came back to Britain late in 1945, a petty-officer, RNVR.

St George nicknamed him: 'The Corpus Christi, Hero of Kokomo, Indiana'

and added with delight: 'The first Berkeley ever to enter a service an officer and exit a petty officer.'

Epilogue

I'll put together the few remaining pieces – mostly from my *Journal*, and from letters, the last of which is from Christopher to my father, and was shown to me two summers after it was written, that was 1946...

My father, 'St George', wrote to me at Fotheringham while the War was still going: 'Sometimes I have a purely instinctual feeling that this is England's last great effort – after this, like an exhausted leviathan she will lay down and die – And, oh, there is much good in her and they will cut her up and eat her and use her oil for lamps...'

Journal Dec 13th 1945. The atmosphere at school has turned mean with the Peace – as has the weather. There is no possible way of getting warm in this depressing dump with no heat – and the report is 'Worst Winter in Recorded History Expected...'

Journal Dec 15th 1945. The very stones of the school – especially School House, weep with homesickness and unhappiness...

(Fortunately, two things seemed to have helped me through my last year at Fotheringham – where grief for Christopher permeated everything. One was Eric Broadlipp's humour and two, was that I fell in love, with a Greek girl...)

Journal Dec 17th 1945 ... into all the gung-ho God-Save-The-Kings, Rule Britannias and Land of Hope and Glories, Broadlipp's one-man Irish rebellion rings out. Today he says, 'All right then, Berkeley: up the stairs and pull on your rope, Goddamn England and God bless the Pope.'

I tell him he's going to get us both executed, he

says, 'No, castrated.'

Journal Dec 18th 1945. Today Broadlipp gave me a Christmas concert, just the two of us.

'Would you like to hear my new words to Land of Hope and Glory?' he says.

Of course, I says.

So he stands up on the edge of the cricket field in the cold wind and sings:

'Land of Smoke and Boring
  Mother of the Fog,
How shall we escape Thee,
Who were born quite free?

'Wider still and whiter,
Shall thy loins be set,
God who fucked you, Blighty,
Fuck you mightier yet?'

'Eric,' I says, 'you'll get us hanged.'

'I bloody hope so.'

January of 1946 came in with a storm off the Polar Cap – and it clung to us.

Seagulls came inland that winter – all the way to the cricket pitch – and waddled about in confusion

I thought of my shipmates on the *Empire United*, all that while ago, back in early 1942.

I wondered what had happened to them: seagulls, I'd often heard at sea, were the souls of drowned sailors. . .

All I wanted to do, I think, was to get my Oxford and Cambridge School Certificate and get home to Bermuda. . .

I managed it.

On the way I won a few laurels and survived the psychic torment, the cold and the sermons. . .

A letter from my mother of March '46, draws an accurate picture.

'... You were a sorry-looking lot. I watched them file past at your Confirmation. And I thought, where do these creatures come from? They are all spots and lumps and pale as thieves – and every one green at the gills.'

Dad wrote me the same month:

'You know, I read the other day ... a man suggested that if we had just let Hitler overrun the United States. Just let them walk in. That an Occupying Army of Germans over America would never work – because, the Germans would be too far from home and, anyway, their ideology was too trashy. For example, he said, forty young Germans occupying Wabash, Indiana. Come the first spring, when these German lads see those Wabash girls. . . By Christmas, those Germans would be American-boys.

'What do you think?'

Having tried to please my mother with my confirm-ation, I was also busy trying to please Christopher with my boxing.

Before term was over, I'd won the Welterweight Public School Title – and two weeks after that, the Light-Heavyweight Title. ('You can fight one weight above your weight, Berkeley – and you're the one lad who can do it: I never had a boxer quicker than you, that's a fact.' 'I'll get slaughtered, Sarge.' 'No you won't, I wouldn't put you in if I thought you could get hurt.' 'All right.' 'That's the boy.')

The bouts took place at the Lansdowne Club in the West End of London. The audience, for the evening, were dressed in long gowns and dinner jackets. (I was thirty-six before I realized that 'the meal' they were dressed up for, was us battling boys. . .)

Now the school gave me my Colours; School House Evens gave me my Square, and I was named to be Captain of Boxing, Shooting and Swimming the following September – three captaincies. (This made me smile: I had a few hopes for that September myself and none of them included Fotheringham School. . .)

Journal 10th April 1946. Dad said while we were driving home,

'I really wanted to live in the Hall, you know.'

'We still could,' I said.

'No. It's slipped beyond reach of repair now, I fear. Anyway, one has to be realistic – there couldn't be two mistresses of Washashley.'

'Three – counting Mrs Pickle,' I added.

We are planning another visit to Washashley this summer.

Journal 13th April 1946. I met, through Vicky, this terrific girl. She has big brown eyes and blushes a lot and is exceeding shy and gentle – and has the most beautiful smile I ever saw.

(I wrote and asked if she could meet me for lunch, although I'd only met her once. I suggested a restaurant on Oxford Street, not far from Bond Street Station – the only restaurant I knew, except the Brasserie Universal. . . To my amazement she accepted. We met, I can remember everything she wore and everything she said.

She liked the ballet and theatre and opera – through the whole meal I tried not to look at her lovely round breasts. . .

Of course I fell in love with her

and she with me

And although we barely touched each other then or ever

yet I will never love anyone the same as I loved her – Mr Raleigh was right

it is 'a durable fire' and it is 'never sick, never old, never dead, from itself never turning. . .'

The mention of her name, like the word Bermuda, still stops my heart. . .)

I told her all about Christopher.

Journal Fotheringham 8th May 1946. Got my first letter – second, really, from Cecile M. Her handwriting is the roundest I've ever seen. Each letter is shaped like a breast, a nipple. . . She signs it 'with affection' so I live in hope.

Journal 6th June 1946. . . Being able to write a girl is The Big Bounty of this gaol – and getting letters back, best of all. . .

Journal 8th Aug 1946. Dad came back from Bermuda. He keeps saying, life is very short. He has bought a Rolls-Royce. It is 1935 20-25 with a Barker body. You can't hear the engine, it has a red light to warn you. It will do a genuine ninety-miles an hour. You can start it without touching the starter, three times out of four, just by flipping the Advance and Retard lever on the steering wheel. The world viewed from within a Rolls-Royce, down the bonnet of a Rolls-Royce, to the angel, is a world of magic.

Journal Sunday 15th Aug 1946. Went to Washashley. Raining. Part of the lead roof of the Hall has fallen in. Dad put some flowers on Uncle Albert's grave. . . The bells pealed out. The rooks cawed and flew away from the high trees behind the Hall. I put flowers on Aunt Lillie. 'With the exception of Christopher – Aunt Lillie was about the best person

I've ever known, Dad.'

'Yes. Funny. I was just thinking the same thing.' Dad smiled in his shy way.

'She did get her reward,' he said, 'because everyone simply loved her – everyone. I guess that's the best we can get. Look, here we are putting flowers on her grave.'

Aunt Daisy smelled of lavender and we managed the walk from cottage to church, without looking at the Hall – a considerable feat.

She has a poignancy, a delicacy that seems to emanate somehow from the bottom edge of her bucked-teeth; they, the teeth, seem to scent the air, like a race horse, and find it a bit too menacing today.

Dad said he'd begun proceedings with the War Reparations Commission, but told Aunt Daisy not to expect much – maybe sixpence in the pound for the damage done the Hall.

He said there's simply no hope to the claim that the Army did irreparable damage.

(The Hall was so damaged it was never to be lived in again . . . but only to fall, slowly, into a thistle-ridden ruin. . .)

I asked after Old Man Watkins.

'He was a miracle –' she said. 'He just kept on and on and on – but he died you know – and ever since, Tom Watkins is a reformed man: he's taken over the gardens. We are a sort of partnership now – but go and look at the gardens – as good as ever.'

Last thing Aunt Daisy said was,

'*You* are always in my thoughts – dear George,' then she lisped, 'you and Charity.' She must be the most polite person in the world.

*   *   *

We went to the Fenderses' cottage. I would have promised Fenders if I had been my father, I thought, that he could have a trip to Bermuda.

Fenders stood at his gate in his serge suit. We got out – Fenders saluted my father and my father saluted Fenders – kissed Mrs Fenders (which made her blush so that I thought her glasses might fall off).

Then my father opened the door of the Rolls and held it open for Fenders. Dad let Fenders drive the car all around and around Washashley until every one of Fenderses' friends had seen him and his Mrs.

I sat on the jump seat. Dad beside Fenders.

Fenders seemed to purr – silently, like the Rolls.

After tea, Father said, 'Fenders, I've spoken to the Madame, Miss Daisy, and she agrees that you are to have this cottage after her death.'

(I told Dad that this was what Christopher hoped – he said he thought as much.)

Then Dad said: 'If all comes fairly, I promise you at least a year in Bermuda – a sort of working holiday, I hope. To make up for all you've done.' Fenders was fairly bursting his buttons.

(And where is the earliest known eating and drinking vessel in Britain? It was lost among the humdrum and hurly-burly of a family's life . . . lost and gone . . . I could never find it, after Washashley. . .)

Journal 16th Aug 1946. Dad's birthday. We came home in the Rolls.

'Biggleswade', a sign said.

'This is where O'Neill killed the girl,' I said. I think I can quote exactly what was said thereafter.

'Yes. It was awful. She ran out – all that long

distance – but the common is lower than the road – you see? – so O'Neill couldn't see her. Terrible.'

'Poor O'Neill. He said, Dad, he said, about the War – "The World was our Empire, wasn't it? – and the Germans wanted it."'

'Wish it were that simple. I had a letter from Christopher after he died, Jamie,' Dad said.

'Me too – would you like to read mine?' I took the letter out of my wallet.

We had stopped at an old inn, for lunch. It was called, appropriately, the White Hart.

'And this is mine – I guess you can see it, Old Man,' he said.

(And so, later, I made this absolute exact copy, realizing that the date is Charity's and his wedding anniversary. . .)

In Your Reply Always Use No. A407697
Ford Aerodrome, West Sussex
30th April 1944

My dear Dad,

Forgive my brevity. If you get this, I'll have taken my last 'flip' – to use your slang.

I don't know if you'd even like me now, Dad – I'm a complete and total pacifist.

I wanted to say, sorry about the long misunderstanding between us. I think you are the Best – and best man I ever knew and the best Father.

And I wanted to say thanks for sending your *Journal* – (it's here safe for you) – it was a tremendous help. Our wars were very similar – it's all the same, death breeds death. . . You put your hand on Death and it's got you – that's the true deep evil of war, isn't it?

I think the funniest things I've heard in life are from you – especially a Butler's Revenge.

555

Take care of 'em all, Dad.

Your everloving son

Aubie

P.S. Brightest man I've known – a doctor – said you were a very brave and plucky fellow. Who the hell else would get in a plane that had burned up one friend, killed another – and that you had already crashed twice? Well, you did.

Did you know that that aircraft, because of the Le Rhone engine, is reckoned the least air-worthy craft that ever flew? *La Pierre*, the French called it, the stone.

P.P.S. Dad, I fell in love and I made love – so don't think I missed anything, because I didn't.

Before I left Fotheringham, my brother George (who is always sending me little things of great value) sent me from The Lion School, a card which had been pinned up on Mr Healey's wall ('Old Man Healey died and this was being swept out'). It said, in his beautiful but tremulous hand: 'I weep tears for human things. . . Ovid.'

In September of 1947 I said my goodbyes at Fotheringham and then Eric Broadlipp and I, as an antidote to school, went up to Piccadilly Circus and just watched the women go by for two solid hours: five to eighty-five, they looked delectable to us.

'I'm going to be a poet, Berkeley – what about you?'

'An aviator.'

'So where are you going, Jamie?'

'West.'

'Why west?'

'Because west is the way Man has been going since the beginning.'

556

Winged Victory

Britannia's system was:
all over the Empire
from New Zealand to Bermuda
and Ceylon to Burma
and Cyprus to Canada
and Newfoundland, and,
the British West Indies –
to Australia and South Africa,
and Kenya,
Uganda and
Tanganyika
and Hong Kong to Guyana
and the Seychelles
and Zanzibar
to India –

she trained the boys, from nine,
ten and eleven to drill and
fight with Boer War carbines,
to go to World War I; she
trained the boys for World War II
with the rifles of World War I. . .

'It costs almost nothing.'

But I have stood and looked up Lincoln
Cathedral's face
in bright sun with a chill
and roaring north wind
and heard the bells at eleven
and amid the bells' cacophony
I heard the rustle of wings – not
only my brother's, but of all
young men and women
who have dreamed of
levitation –

And I have stood at the Acropolis at
Athens and faced west and
felt their winged
victory. . .

For while you rooted
in mud and medals,
they sailed away
to the Moon
and the Planets bright. . .